All best wishes to

Marianne Want

from

Alan Sillitoe

4·5·93.

THE ❧ OPEN DOOR

Fiction
Saturday Night and Sunday Morning
The Loneliness of the Long Distance Runner
The General
Key to the Door
The Ragman's Daughter
The Death of William Posters
A Tree on Fire
Guzman, Go Home
A Start in Life
Travels in Nihilon
Raw Material
Men, Women and Children
The Flame of Life
The Widower's Son
The Storyteller
The Second Chance and Other Stories
Her Victory
The Lost Flying Boat
Down From the Hill
Life Goes On
Out of the Whirlpool

Poetry
The Rats and Other Poems
A Falling Out of Love and Other Poems
Love in the Environs of Voronezh
Storm and Other Poems
Snow on the North Side of Lucifer
Sun Before Departure
Tides and Stone Walls

Plays
All Citizens are Soldiers (with Ruth Fainlight)
Three Plays

Essays
Mountains and Caverns

For Children
The City Adventures of Marmalade Jim
Big John and the Stars
The Incredible Fencing Fleas
Marmalade Jim on the Farm
Marmalade Jim and the Fox

Alan Sillitoe

THE
❧ OPEN
DOOR

GRAFTON BOOKS

A Division of the Collins Publishing Group

LONDON GLASGOW
TORONTO SYDNEY AUCKLAND

Grafton Books
A Division of the Collins Publishing Group
8 Grafton Street, London WIX 3LA

Published by Grafton Books 1989

A CIP catalogue record for this book
is available from the British Library

ISBN 0-246-13422-4

Photoset in Linotron Bembo by
Rowland Phototypesetting Ltd
Bury St Edmunds, Suffolk
Printed and bound in Great Britain by
William Collins Sons & Co. Ltd, Glasgow

THE
❧ OPEN
DOOR

Chapter
❧ ONE

You left England one person and came back another. The
customs people were looking for the difference, and if they
found it they'd tax you to the eyeballs, because you weren't
supposed to smuggle anything in. But he was already on dry
land, and whether or not that invisible self was by his side
(maybe everybody else had one as well), he was unwilling to
put up with any cheek from snotnoses walking around with
clipboards as if they owned the ground they trod on and were
treating it carefully in case one day they had to get on their
knees and eat off it. The idea that other ranks might have
anything valuable to declare brought so many laughs you'd
have thought Bob Hope was doing a turn, because most had
little except that invisible self which hadn't gone out with them
and wasn't – yet – on the forbidden list.

The leaden sky of summer blocked each doorway of the
enormous shed. Brian Seaton had wanted to stay in Malaya,
but had come back to England as if God's hand under the water
had pushed the troopship along like a toy boat in a bath. He'd
come back, he supposed, because his time was up. He could
have signed on for seven years. He could have wangled a demob
ticket to Australia. He could have got work on a rubber estate,
or at a tin mine. But he hadn't, and didn't know why. He had
always wanted an adventurous life in the tropics, but when the
time came he hadn't done anything to get one.

By his feet was a kitbag, a big pack and a rifle, and a bulging pigskin suitcase which, not wanted on voyage, had been stowed in the hold. Some had trunks with number, rank and name stencilled in white along the lid, put into crates knocked together by native chippies in the outstations of the East. England was on rations, so maybe they had tins of sugar and meat, or other things to trade. His grandmother wanted rice, because she hadn't seen any for eight years, but he'd heard she had died, so was saved from bothering.

An inventory of his belongings would list little more than a sports jacket and pair of flannels, two sets of white drill, blouses for Pauline, a fort and soldiers for Gary, as well as tobacco, cheroots, and tins of cheese, none of it bought on points because all places beyond Blighty were lands of plenty as long as you had the cash.

In Malaya he'd felt the luxury of new clothes on his back, and the European assistant, who looked as seedy as if he had been in a prison camp through the war, addressed him as 'sir', the first time anybody had done so. His bearer called him 'sahib' and, remembering both occasions, he inwardly laughed, because now he was back in England he would hear no more of that.

Tantalising whiffs of dinner drifted from wagons outside, and squads were dismissed to stand in the drizzle and get stuck in, the same old hot mince and powdered spuds he had hoped never to taste again. The ship had docked at five, and by eight they were filing down gangplanks, laden with kit like a scene from Movietone News. It was August, but those of thin blood donned greatcoats, waiting as if at a parade and kit inspection combined, the mood lax after thirty days on the boat.

A goods train shook the ground. Forehead hot as if he was getting a cold (he had brought that in, too) he recalled how more than two years ago he'd gone out of Radio School for a walk one Sunday, neither guard duty nor classes to keep him in, and climbed to the White Horse cut from the chalk Downs, walking over legs and head and on to hind quarters with no sense of trampling the skill of whoever had shaped the horse. Thirsty and winded after the rapid ascent, he buttoned his uniform as if even up there fearing to meet some martinet of a warrant officer on the prowl for such derelictions of proper dress. From the crest of the hill, an embarrassing pressure of tears forced him to sit on dry grass and enjoy the translucent green comb that shut out everything else and pierced him with a view of paradise, a talismanic picture taken to Malaya and now brought back, of no monetary value but not to be sold over the counter for ration tickets out of a book.

The customs man with his clipboard turned icy-grey eyes on to Kirkby. 'How much tobacco do you have in your kit?'

He must have spotted us lighting up half an hour ago, Brian supposed.

'One ton,' Kirkby said.

'What does that mean?'

'One *tin*.'

He looked as bilious as if last week's butter ration had gone reesty. 'Any drink, drugs, firearms or playing cards?'

Kirkby clutched his small pack like a loony. 'I ain't got anything, honest!'

The customs officer had met his like before. Or thought he had. In the Bay of Biscay, closer to home waters, the sea had been fiercer than in a monsoon. Even a ship made with prime materials and the best British engineering could hardly stand such a battering. While Brian slept in the hammock between decks, doom-laden words leapt into his ear from the white of a real world that surrounded the yoke of his dreams. 'Gerrup! The ship's sinkin'!' Bulwarks were giving way, nothing to do but relax and die, all ties snapping sooner than he'd wanted, a radiance easing him down through the cold in the hope that sudden warmth would black him out. But his fist drove horizontally at Kirkby: 'Next time, I'll chuck your fucking glasses overboard.'

'What about perfume?'

Kirkby cringed. 'I ain't gorrany o' *that*,' he said in his heaviest Nottingham accent.

'Open it.' The Orderly Officer, eyes like gimlet-holes after a farewell swine-and-dine session on the boat, disliked his duty, but sparks' chevrons didn't give them the right to take the micky out of all and sundry. Baker would have turned the shed into mayhem, but he had stopped a terrorist bullet in the jungle.

'Pack it in,' the Orderly Officer said sharply. 'The sooner we get this over, the better.'

Kirkby must have thought honour was satisfied, though it never was with someone so cunning. He took so long to open everything that the customs officer passed the next half dozen without question.

'What was all that about?' Brian wanted to know. 'What were you trying to smuggle?'

Kirkby looked at him, though not into his eyes. 'Shut up, or they'll get you as well.'

'His pack's stuffed with opium,' Selby joked. 'You can tell that customs bloke never got his knees brown, or he'd have sniffed it out like a shot.'

'It worn't my kit he looked at.' Kirkby's lips trembled as he worked with a handkerchief at both frames of his glasses. 'It was yourn, Seaton. We'll swop back in the train.'

Filled and squared according to regulations, their packs were identical, but Brian dreaded those little wheels in the customs officer's mind suggesting that all might not be well. Or was it only another of Kirkby's games to pass the dog hours? The pack leaned against his case. He could be right. Packs were no more alike than snowflakes or people, though he was glad when they were dressed by the right and marched to the train.

Kirkby was in the last carriage. 'I knew they wouldn't search your kit. You look honest, the backbone of the King's Air Force.'

Woods and fields were all the more cherished because soaking wet. He wanted to throw him out into the undergrowth of a cutting where, more's the pity, there were no tigers to make a meal of him. But his vicious mood went, and he merely felt like cutting his throat, disposing of the body in bits, and taking potluck on his capture by Scotland Yard.

Kirkby sat by Cheshire for protection, but looked at everyone as if contempt wouldn't melt in his mouth. 'It was only a lark. I thought I'd have the bastards on a bit, and knew you could take a joke.' The Burma cheroot was bigger than any Brian had smoked. 'Cough on that. It'll do you good.'

'His kit's full of drugs and God knows what else.' Selby held on to the luggage rack. 'We ought to shop him. It ain't right to smuggle stuff like that.'

A few tins of fags or cigars did nobody any harm, but he didn't like the idea of opium, because five years in jail would make his stint in the air force no more than a long weekend, and would be no way out of his problems. He stood in the corridor to finish his smoke. As a kid he'd played draughts after school with Jim Skelton, when the teacher took on the winner. For Brian it was one long rearguard action, defence to the death, but he held on, always looking for a way out, plotting two moves ahead, though aware when one tactical fiasco followed another that the teacher was thinking three if not four moves ahead. Setting the pieces back in their box, Brian remarked that he had lost because he was not very intelligent. The teacher smiled, surprised to hear such a word, and Brian felt as much of a fool then at trying to impress someone, even at the expense of his self-esteem, as he had at having allowed Kirkby to use him for his smuggling.

So what? Tomorrow he'd get a civvy suit and a railway warrant for going home to Nottingham. Back at the Mullinders', where Pauline lived with her mother, they would put themselves down for a council house. On the waiting list, time would fly – and if it didn't he would soon earn enough to rent a couple of rooms where they could be on their own.

He slipped off his webbing – waterbottle, bayonet and small pack – and opened the ration box given out at the docks. No longer interested in well-rounded Wiltshire fields, he ate bread and cheese, hearing the singing from next door:

'She'll be wearing camiknickers when she comes . . .' as the train sent smoke into the dusk. A spam sandwich, a Bakewell tart, an apple and a bag of toffees – and beyond the chalk cutting a few bars of red had replaced the fiery purple of Malaya.

'When I get my girl on the settee,' said Durham in his singsong voice, pulling a letter from his tunic, 'I'll give her all I've got – after two years in the house of the five-fingered widow.'

'Mine was a block of flats,' Selby said mournfully.

'She's got somebody else,' Kirkby told him. 'She was so busy she didn't have time to scribble a note. Dropped the pencil when she came, I expect.'

'Get stuffed. I sent a telegram from the ship. A shilling a word. So BURMA, I said. ITALY, I told her. I'll slip it around her left ear.'

The air dimmed with fag and cigar smoke. Selby's head knocked against the glass, and Durham's gobstopper eyes stared in front. Four to a side and some on the floor, others lay in the corridor on heaps of kit. The train turned a wide bend, and he spotted the glittering Big Dipper but not the North Star. A lit station showed marks of dust and raindrops on the window, and he wondered how many trains the porter had waved to.

Was it Newbury, or Oxford? Huddled buildings melted into the earth. Dim lights meant power was short. He'd meet his old self crossing Slab Square on Saturday night, though maybe he would stay as the person he had turned into after his absence, never feel the pang of recognition. Closing his eyes, Pauline's face showed up no better than an old photo. An imagined smile would not clarify her features. What did you do while I was away? Talk would help. Yes, I suppose Gary was a handful. Did you go to the pictures? What about my mother – did you see her? You never said so in your letters. Or did you only sit by the fire staring at the flames? Two years were like twenty. Hard to imagine going home to a wife he had blundered into, and a kid he'd never wanted. The horizon rocked, as if he was still on the troopship.

Kit was given in, signatures collected on the final clearance chit. He stood in line with his vest off, a smell of sleep and pungent sweat after the all-night train. The machine clicked in a production-line medical, the steel plate cold against his chest. Earlier numbers were going out, suitcases in one hand and a cardboard carrybox in the other, a demob gleam and a wide disoriented smile beamed on no one in particular as they went through the gate.

He sat with the signals mob for a last meal of pie and trifle, Cheshire calculating money due at the final pay parade. 'Four weeks' arrears from the ship, and six for demob leave: in shekels, akkers and pice that makes twenty-eight quid – more or less. We'll be rich beyond the dreams of average.'

Durham asked how much it was in french letters.

'Not all that fucking much,' Kirkby said.

'That's why you did a bit of smuggling on the side. Opium's oozing out of your boots.'

'He was diddled,' Selby said. 'It's toothpaste. That Chink must be cackling to himself. They cheat twenty swaddies a day like that, and now they've chalked up an air force wireless op. They're even laughing about it in Hong Kong.'

When Stacey hooked a mug over his middle finger and went to the hatch for more tea he sent back a piercing whistle in the dots and dashes of morse, signifying TRIFLE. Those who couldn't understand looked up as if he'd gone crackers under the strain of being demobbed, but the signals wallahs roared the word in plain language as they flooded down the aisle, plates and irons poised to scoop up the pan of extra dessert put out by the cooks. The unity of the group divided them from those who didn't have a secret language, and they came back with huge helpings before anybody else could get a look in.

'Lousy wireless bastards!'

Cheshire licked his spoon. 'Oh yes? Who used to tell you when your number was coming up for the Blighty Boat?'

The gulf separating them from civvy street was deep, the parting sharp, and there was no saying what impact they would make on the world when their badge of a clenched fist emitting sparks unlocked its fire.

The iron stove shone on a polished floor, colder than the rain which pelted the windows. He scrutinised the bare woman in *London Opinion*, then read the newspaper. The Airlift was in full swing. Sixteen thousand were on unofficial strike at Austin car works. Cigarettes were scarce in the shops. Was it for all this that he had wanted the boat to roll across the sea?

The man in his wet cape fished a scrap of paper out of his pocket. 'Anybody called Leaton here?'

He stood. 'You mean Seaton?'

Waterdrops bubbled his glasses. He took them off. 'I suppose so.'

He preferred his name on a sheet of paper with a dozen others – though maybe they're sending me home today because I'm married, a rush job on compassionate grounds.

'The MO wants to see you.'

7

Nor did he like his tone, in spite of the Lancashire accent. He probably lived at home less than ten miles away, biked to camp and back, or did it by tram in bad weather. He had square-bashed at Padgate, and never left the country. 'What the hell for?'

They stepped through the rain. 'Search me.'

Such self-satisfied bastards never give anything away. Humps of cloud came from the sea, but there were gaps of blue, and the rain was sweet and fresh as they walked between rows of admin huts by the parade ground.

Adjusting his cap, he went into the office and saluted. The MO stopped scribbling. Faced with a puzzle, Brian thought nothing, empty brain. A clock said fifteen-hundred hours. Greenwich Mean Time. Or near enough. If I leave in an hour I'll still reach home before dark. Change stations in Manchester, and at Derby get on the Nottingham line. He knew the drill.

The MO was tall and thin, thirty years old, a hawkish face and dark hair. He picked up an X-ray plate. 'Stand at ease.'

A fly bounced off the clock, and Brian agreed that time didn't move fast enough, wanting to hit the wall as well.

'The fact is, Seaton, your X-ray isn't as satisfactory as we would like it to be.'

The language was of a formality unknown among his mates on the troopship. At the time he didn't realise the change, except insofar as he repeated the words to himself as a buffer against his exasperation.

'You have some scars on your left lung.'

He was meant to understand something, but if that was a flicker of irritation on the medical officer's face, he needed more clues. Scars healed. To be considered dim pushed him even more into thoughtlessness, as if the boat trip had been a stint of unceasing labour which had left him too tired to understand even the plainest message. 'Scars, sir?'

'There are a few on the right, as well.'

The X-ray plate illuminated his bone structure, and he smiled at the secrets of his chest laid bare, a series of volcanic hills on an imperfect map. 'It's not a pretty picture, on the left particularly. See how it's pitted down there?'

Did he bring me here to tell me that? The MO was tactful, kindly even. There was something wrong with his lungs. Energy rushed back. He had never felt healthier. He was on his feet, and had no intention of falling, so how could anything be wrong?

'Take your shirt off, and we'll have a look at you.'

The cold mouth of the stethoscope slopped around. He held his breath after expanding the lungs, and the irritation made him sweat.

'Do you cough much?'

'Who doesn't?'

'How much?'

'Not much.'

'What about sputum?'

A new word.

'Phlegm.'

He was chagrined at being held up for something so unimportant. 'Now and again.'

'Have you ever spat blood?'

'No, sir.'

'Have you lost weight lately?'

If he falsified his answers the MO might let him go for lack of evidence. But he told the truth, not knowing the direction in which to lie. Weight lost in the jungle had been put back on.

'No, sir.'

The MO felt the ends of his fingers. 'Do you have any indigestion?'

He belched a lot, but they'd belched in his family for generations.

'We call that flatulence. Do you get tired easily?'

A few minutes ago he had felt on top of the world. He put on his vest and shirt, collar and tie and tunic, with an alacrity suggesting that such covering would protect him from whatever threatened.

'We can't let you go yet. There may even be cavities. I'm afraid it's going to be a matter of treatment.'

Straightforward but weightless, he reasoned that if your X-ray wasn't right you had only one thing. 'Treatment for what, sir?'

'Things aren't very good in that left lung. Nor in the right. You need to be looked after for a while.'

He saw himself wheeled off to a green-walled lazar house for the rest of his life. 'How long will it take?'

He seemed to consider the matter. 'It's hard to say. You're under no obligation to take any treatment, but you'd be foolish not to.'

The silence, short though it was, seemed pitiless. He wanted to die on the spot or break into pieces, too weak to do anything. He didn't know whether he had felt like this for months, or only for as long as he had seen the X-ray.

'We'll give you ten days' leave.'

He had expected to be walled up at once, and couldn't be ill if they were sending him home. 'When you come back you'll have more tests, and then we'll decide where to send you for treatment.'

Not even a hope that after the tests they would find nothing wrong and would send him home for good.

The rain smelled so clean he wanted to lick it up. He splashed through pools on the path, shaking his head. Better never to move again, but a month's pay, a railway warrant, and ten days' leave was good. Thoughts were more tormenting when he stood still. He sorted his kit in the hut.

'Going out today, then?' Thompson called from his bed.

He held the kitbag so that everything fell out. 'I go on leave tomorrow.'

'What did they want you for?'

He lit a cheroot and sat down, a coincidence that every breath felt as if claws were scraping the inside of his chest. He wanted to say 'lungs', but the word was obscene, pink and spongy stuff fed to the cats. 'Something's wrong with my medical.'

'You don't say?'

X-rays, like bullets, have your name on them, but mistakes can be made. Babies got mixed up in hospital and nobody was any the wiser. A stupid medical clerk had slipped the wrong tab on his X-ray while reaching for a mug of char. The dam wall was flimsy, and if the waters of tribulation poured through he would plug the hole with his head as the Dutch boy had with his finger, till the world changed or the water went away. 'There were marks on my X-ray.'

'Somebody wanked on it,' Thompson said. 'I wouldn't put it past them.' He would be away in the morning, to his job as a steward on Scottish Island Airways. He might start, he said, before his demob leave was up. He wasn't sure. A grandmother in Aberdeen had left him some money, so maybe he wouldn't go back to his old job. Being uncertain didn't worry him, it was a way of life. Pondering the options, he blew smoke rings towards the ceiling. Air stewards were only glorified waiters handing out coffee and biscuits, he said, but it sounded the sort of work Brian would like, instead of standing at a capstan lathe in the old shed-like factory in the Meadows, doing so many hundreds a day for ten quid a week.

But who would want to set him on, even in a factory, with such marks on his lungs as he had seen written out as plain as words in the Bible? He felt like Daniel, only waiting for the lions to be unleashed. 'I expect I'll get a job when all this is over.'

Thompson, picking up a tone not usual in a mate from the signals section, returned to his musing. Brian was ashamed that his voice had given him away, so to avoid more danger he lay on his bed pretending to doze, worn out without knowing why. He had only ever slept during the day after a fourteen-hour night watch in the hut beyond the runway, and then for no more than an hour or two before sprucing up and going to the NAAFI for a bottle of Tiger and a steak sandwich.

Back from the last meal of the day, Thompson handed him a mug of tea and a piece of cake. 'You were sleeping, so I left you.'

He wasn't hungry, but tea washed the bile down. He got into his tunic. Buttons, cap badge, buckle and shoes gleamed from being set to go home since morning. He was always unwilling to look scruffy to the world. 'Pubs'll be open soon. Do you fancy a drink?'

Thompson leapt off his bed as if a tarantula had bitten. 'I'd better bull myself up as well, or the blokes on the gate'll turn me back. It's discipline and good order right to the end in the air force.'

Waves hit the sand. 'Our blood's thin after Malaya,' Thompson said, on the deserted promenade. 'I wonder what December's like? They should put Britain on a raft and push it south.'

He couldn't care less what happened to the country and its climate. 'I can't get over that bloody X-ray.'

Concern made the Scottish accent more pronounced. 'It might not be as bad as you think.'

Two years' active service counted for nothing. A terrorist bullet would have been better, even if he had lost an arm. And if he had been killed he wouldn't have known about it.

'You might have lost your dick, though,' Thompson said. 'Then if you heard a joke you wouldn't be able to piss yourself laughing.'

The pebble-dash pub was a friendless place, as if business had been bad for months. The bartender's withered face was morose, strands of grey hair arranged over his pink skull. Brian asked for two pints of bitter, laying half-a-crown on the counter. He remembered that after basic training they had celebrated in a similar pub before going on leave. He'd had an attack of hiccups, and suddenly a dry biscuit was in his mouth, a cold key down his back, and a call to hold his breath for as long as possible. 'That'll cure it, lad,' a woman said.

'Laugh and the world laughs with you,' Thompson said, 'but cry and you die alone.'

Thirsty, he expected to knock the jollop back, but there was a soapy wash against his palate. 'Not like the old Tiger Beer, eh?'

'We'll never guzzle that again.' Thompson finished the pint too quickly to notice the vileness, but Brian slid his back on the bar. 'My thirst's gone.'

Atlantic clouds loomed beyond the sea wall. Waves formed with senseless persistence, throwing up green froth, so that he didn't know whether his face was wet from spray or tears. On the troopship England had been so remote that he could not imagine picking up his existence where he had left off. Being away from a routine of duty had paralysed his will, though he didn't think that such a thing as will had anything to do with the past being so obscure and the future reluctant to show itself. He kept them apart as if they were two wings of an army trying to concentrate into a whole that would crush him. Alone on the highest deck, standing by the rail, he couldn't care less. Teeth set, face pale, it was no longer 'Beyond the Blue Horizon' but 'Fingal's-bloody-Cave' with a vengeance. Spray stung his skin, he was happy because without land or people there were no troubling thoughts. Anticipation of the new being better than the sliding away of the old buoyed him up, though he still couldn't care less because hadn't Corporal Knotman said it was useless to worry about the future, since whatever happened would never be what you expected? He felt drunk. Fear and joy came from looking at the sea that, within limits of the full moon's influence, knew no law, and produced a sensation he had no name for, and if a word existed he didn't wonder what it was, because he preferred the freedom of being at the sea's mercy.

Water flowed through defences made of sand, and Thompson put a hand over his shoulder as they walked back to camp in silence.

Chapter

❧ TWO

She sat behind the counter, made up with powder and rouge and lipstick. Her hair was grey, a hairnet over her curlers. When they came out she would have a good time singing in the pub. Cards were arranged for a game of patience, and he was tempted to tell her which one to move. Three years ago he'd called to buy french letters for his first home leave, thinking that one kid was enough for any man's lifetime.

Ash fell from her cigarette when he asked for a Sunday paper. There was no reason why she should recognise him. He had been away. She had been nowhere, and served scores of customers a day. He had bought french letters since he was fifteen, but there still seemed something furtive in the transaction. What else did she sell from under that long counter? If she had recognised him he would have denied being the same person.

A packet of San-Toy cigars would eke out the cheroots left in his pack at the demob centre. No need to take everything, since he would be going back. He picked up his kitbag and suitcase for the mile walk across Manchester. For once it wasn't raining, and he was determined not to show the weight of his luggage, his left arm swinging as if on the march. He stopped to adjust his cap rather than rest from the burdens, and got to the Central Station with half an hour to spare.

In the tunnel before Millers Dale he saw his face in the

glass. Gaps into daylight revealed weekend cycling places. From Matlock he climbed the Hills of Abraham and Isaac for the view, green crests rolling away to the sombre memorial of the Sherwood Foresters at Crich.

The old gang from Radford wheeled their bikes out of backyards on Sunday morning, and as far as Eastwood the run was easy, but beyond the Erewash the slow climb began, and they waited for the girls to catch up at Ambergate. There and back over fifty miles left them shagged, but after a plate of dried egg and bacon for his tea he would bike to Tapley and call on Pauline, and in the woods they would get shagged even more. On Monday he had to be careful not to get blown out of a window when the machinery was switched on and the belts began rolling overhead. He wanted the smoking train to go in circles so that he would not have to explain to those at home why he hadn't been demobbed.

From Derby he stood in the corridor, but a couple got down at Attenborough so he took their seat and looked out at rubbish tips and factories, then the long grey building of the university on a rise of green land. The Castle was squat on a hillock of sandstone, its parapet known as Suicides' Leap because it was death by the time you hit the railings a hundred feet below, arms outspread, gliding off the low stone wall, legs together and falling till the body curled into a ball, before sleep without end.

With twenty pounds in his paybook it was barmy to worry about a few trails of fly shit on an X-ray plate. His body had never lied when it said he would live forever. An X-ray couldn't lie, either, you might think. And yet, if he got on a bike he could reach Matlock in three hours. In three more he would be home again. Who was right? He could work fifty hours at a lathe and feel none the worse at the end of the week. So who was right? He could dig the garden, and redecorate the house. There was nothing he couldn't get his body to do. So who was right? But if he did all those things he might cough himself to death in three months.

Nonetheless, he felt on top of the world. But who was right? The red-bricked grain warehouse loomed along the side of the train. Aunt Ada worked there during the war, sweeping the place out when it was empty and before more grain was dumped in. She chased rats into their holes with a sweeping brush, to keep them from precious wartime supplies. They were bigger than moggies, she said. We put cats in, but they ran away. The rats ate their kittens. Rat turds as big as marbles got into the grain. There was rat shit in the bread all through the war. That's why it tasted so good. Dave was on leave from Germany with a row of medal ribbons: 'That's why we didn't give in when the Gerries cornered us.'

Ada got tired of being attacked. 'You needed a machine gun to keep 'em in order. I hit one with a brick, and it screamed.' In fact she got the sack for selling grain to a man who kept chickens. Stopped at the gate one day, a hundredweight fell out of her bloomers.

The smoke of Midland Station brought memories from the old sock of the past as he loaded himself up to mount the steps on to Carrington Street. A trackless took him to Slab Square, where he switched to a petrol bus, going upstairs for the view. The reek of oil and stale fags never changed, and neither did the stench of sweat from other passengers who, he thought, should burn their clothes and get new ones. A daily shower or bath since joining up, and several a day in Malaya, set him apart from his previous self when he had gone once a week to the public baths – otherwise stripping to the waist in the scullery after work, so that he must have ponged to others as they now did to him.

The same grub and rubbish shops lined Alfreton Road, scruffy streets falling away on either side. As a kid he'd lose any pursuer in the yards and double-entries, or cobbled alleys cul-de-sacked against factory or warehouse wall. Familiar with every landmark of pub and chapel, picture-house and pawn shop, cop station and public library, the area reminded him of that in *Les Misérables* where the barricades were defended to the last, though he couldn't imagine a revolution here, everybody in work and with other things to think about since the war.

Beyond Bobbers Mill was the restaurant from which he and his cousin Bert plundered chips and fish batter left on the plates. Gorged to the hilt, they collected beer mugs from the Nag's

Head yard next door, and the publican gave them a packet of chocolate biscuits, part of their stray dog itinerary when there was nothing to eat at home.

Bert in desperate times put on a starvo face and called at the back doors of newer houses, begging something to eat, and when Brian was afraid to come he said: 'Well, yer've got to live, ain't yer?' returning with a carrierbag of loaf-ends or old cakes, apples and an orange, and a tin of milk which some good woman took from her larder.

He got off the bus, no turning back, no thunderbolt to blight him to a cinder simply by hoping for it. Excitement pounded his heart, and he walked so decisively along the pavement that a couple of kids playing marbles swore as he scattered them from his track.

Shabby council houses were still better than the old dwellings in Radford, but the latch was hanging off and about to fall, so he forced the screw in as far as it would go with his jack-knife, then closed the gate behind him, standing for a moment to wonder where he had picked up such habits. The rank lawn had a hole in it, a wooden spade broken in two. He walked to the front door instead of going around the back, but knocked before going in.

'Who's that?' Pauline shouted from the kitchen.

Bits of paper and cigarette packets lay in the fireplace. An odour of soot meant that the chimney needed sweeping. Lace curtains were dirty. So were the windows. He supposed it had been the same before joining up, but he hadn't noticed. He dropped case and kitbag. 'It's me, Brian!'

She was tall, with sallow face and brown eyes. A tail of dark hair down her back set off the same luscious figure covered by a white blouse and grey skirt. Her legs were bare, feet in carpet slippers, a stranger perhaps, but someone whom he had known since he was seventeen now given back to him, pressing her face against his shoulder as if wanting touch more than sight to prove he had come back.

'I wrote and told you I'd arrive about this time.'

'You did, I know you did.'

He sat on the settee. Like poles repel, unlike poles attract. The magnetic flux had them in its grip, no power strong enough to keep them apart. 'I should have got here yesterday, but we were delayed.'

'I thought you'd missed the boat and wouldn't be here for another month.' She wiped her eyes. 'Oh, I am glad to see you, duck. You've still got salt on your lips! How long was you at sea?'

'Over four weeks.' The voyage was a dream, broken out of to ask where Gary was.

'His grandma took him shopping. It's a wonder you didn't see 'em.'

He'd wanted to name him Victor, or Harold, but Pauline liked Gary Cooper on the pictures – a daft idea he hadn't argued against. She held his hands. 'You do look well. I suppose it was all that sun.'

'Must have been.' His advantages had been greater than hers. Everything had been provided, and he'd forgotten the struggle of ordinary people. 'Did you manage all right?'

'Oh yes. Mam's got her pension, and I had mine. Maureen goes to work and pays her board. Nobody's gone short. I worked at the greengrocer's two days a week, serving cabbages and taters. That brought in a bob or two. Mam looked after Gary.'

He kissed her. 'Have you been lonely?'

'You talk a bit different than before you went.' She looked into his eyes, as if to find something he didn't want to tell her about. He was more of a stranger than seemed necessary, his voice halfway to being posh. Perhaps he didn't love her, otherwise he would have spoken the same as before.

'When you join up, you change, and so does the way you talk.' Not everyone did but, speaking by telephone to the control tower, you had to make yourself understood.

'I'm not different, am I?' She was proud at having stayed the same.

'You'll never change.' Kids screamed as they played on the pavement. She was different by two years, but twenty thousand miles had altered him far more. He drew her close. 'I love you more than I ever did.'

The words vibrated her eardrum. 'Now I know you're back. Do you remember all them times we went up Strelley and did it in the fields?'

A bus trundled along the drive. 'I thought of it every minute.'

She whispered, her face hot, 'I often did, especially in bed at night.'

'I thought about you all the time, and about Gary.' It wasn't true. She came and went. After a while she went more than she came. Absence made the heart grow fonder, though not if it went on too long. He had written once a week, but her letters came by the month, clumsy writing he could just about read, telling little more than in a telegram. Her moist lips kissed him.

'Let's go upstairs,' he said.

'Mam'll be back soon.'

The heat came through her clothes, and he put on the old accent to coax her. 'It don't matter, duck.'

She walked before him up the golden hill. Blankets and sheets were intermixed, the yellow and orange stippling of the wall as if colour had been sprayed by a typhoon. On the dressing table was a pot of cream and a box of powder, two tubes of lipstick and a comb. The window hadn't been open for weeks. She had slept in the double bed, Gary in a cot by the wall.

The odours sharpened his desire, as she unhooked her skirt and let it fall, and he folded his trousers over the rail so that the creases wouldn't spoil. The lino was cool to his feet. She looked at his deliberations, wondering what had been done to him. He would soon throw off his clothes, and jabber as he had done before. She undid the buttons between her legs, and when he took something from his pocket she wondered who he thought he was having it with. 'What are you using one o' them for?'

She didn't want him to put it on, and he couldn't understand why, so there was no answer except to go into her, hoping she would forget about it, because he didn't want to fill the house with kids, and though uneasy at her surprise, nothing would deter him after that long horny trip on a troopship. He was a sailor, home from the ocean, making love to his wife, loving her more than himself, and wanting to keep on, and never let go, though aware of cars passing and kids shouting out on the drive.

She clasped him. 'I don't care if you don't use one. It don't matter, duck, honest it don't, not for me' – moved under him to prove it, the squeak of real springs instead of a croaking rope bed. In as far as he could get, pushing but unable to reach the ice cold part of himself so that he could hold back, she was closing the glove of home over him, and he forgot everything, to make it last as long as possible, till he was wrenched free, let go of, and she cried out, knowing that he had shot, and pulled at his shoulders, and bit into his lip on feeling his release like a spring snapping shut deep inside.

'Why are you sweating so much? You're soaking me with your sweat.'

'I always sweat a lot.'

'Not like that, you didn't.'

He balanced on one elbow. 'You must have forgotten.'

'I don't forget owt like that.'

'You sweat a lot in Malaya.'

'You shouldn't a gone, then.'

A globe of light showed him as sparks on a pinnace when he took the place of the regular wireless operator who had gone sick. They were laying out a bombing range off the coast, and his morse from the old Marconi transmitter with coloured dials and clickstops reported its progress to Kota Libis. In the morning, when orders were sorted out for the day's work, he flashed the Aldis lamp to the tug where the naval officer was quartered, and to a landing craft that stored the buoys.

Most of the day he lay by the donkey engine, out of the way of the crew who worked the boat between the islands. He smoked, or drank tea provided by dark-haired, amiable Irish deckhands padding the boards in bare feet and ragged shorts. The sergeant-skipper, seven years in the Merchant Navy and fourteen in the air force, had a half-mad expression as he barked at the deckhands who regarded him with affection nonetheless. He threw Brian a rope from alongside and told him to tie the dinghy up, but such a bungle was made of the knot that he jumped on board to do it himself.

'Do you want to lose the fucking dinghy? Get out of the way.'

They anchored for the night near an island that was no more than a half-orange of jungle, and on anchor watch he would sling a leadweight every few minutes to make sure they weren't drifting towards the shore, taking soundings more often than he had to, the others undisturbed by the constant plash of the lead falling among grey jellyfish.

Dawn came from behind the escarpment of Gunong Barat, and he relished the last cool air before burning sunlight rushed over the water. The coxswain handed him a mug of tea by way of thanks, the only smile of the day.

The doorknob sounded from downstairs and Pauline jerked away. 'Didn't you hear it? Where were you, in your dreams?'

'I don't know. Thinking, I suppose.' Maybe he'd been asleep. He couldn't tell.

'We'd better get up. It's Mam. She's come in with the shopping.'

She would see his cap and tunic, and know that he was home, and if she didn't realise what they were doing it was too bad. He held her firm, kissing her. 'It's all right.'

'Oh come on, duck, let's get down.'

He was hard in her and wanted it again.

She moved away. 'You'll have to wait.'

He supposed he would, but didn't care to be told as if he was a stray youth she had just met, shook his trousers straight before drawing them on and buttoning them up. She fastened her skirt. 'You didn't have to go to Malaya, did you? You could have got out of it because you was married.'

'I suppose so,' he smiled. 'Anyway, here I am.'

'Are you?' She didn't yet know what he had brought back, and he didn't know how to tell her. He didn't even know how to tell himself, but assumed he would have to know how to tell others before he could do so. And maybe he didn't want to inform others because then he would have to take it in himself, and being the last person who wanted to know, he didn't give a damn whether he knew or not. The time in Malaya had been the best thing that had ever happened, but there was nothing good that you didn't have to pay for.

Jenny Mullinder's black hair once went down her back, much like Pauline's, but since Ted Mullinder had been injured in the pit, and during the illness before he died, it had turned grey.

After his death she joked about dyeing it black, for she was tall and straight, with brown eyes and smooth skin, and young for her forty-odd years. She touched his arm. 'Maybe things will get right now there's a man in the house. It's never been the same without one, I can tell you.'

The front and back garden was a rubbish dump. The hedge needed cutting, the windows wanted cleaning. Why hadn't they done it? The prospect of such labour seemed like an adventure, and he couldn't wait to start. 'Where's Gary?'

'I left him in the street with a neighbour's girl. She'll bring him back soon. We expected you yesterday.'

He looked around, and she sensed his thoughts. 'I do what I can, but I get no help.'

'Not even from Pauline?'

She took off her coat, and he followed her into the kitchen with the carrierbags. 'Not enough.'

He wanted to go to Radford and call on his parents, who might be glad to see him. 'You've been shopping?'

'To get the rations. But it's never enough. We're not too bad off for money, but I can't understand why the war's bin over three years, and there's still nowt in the shops. I reckon this guv'ment likes keeping us on coupons.'

He stacked plates in the sink to be washed. 'It's a Labour Government. You voted for 'em.'

'But it's a bit bloody much, in't it?' she said bitterly. 'There's allus plenty on black market for them with big munney.'

He emptied his kitbag. Two tins of cheese, four of fish and a tin of sugar from the camp mess and shops at Kota Libis fell on the living-room floor. The cheese was meant for his parents, but he still had a scarf for his mother and a tin of fags for the old man.

'It's corn in Egypt.' She struggled with a tin, so he took it from her and ran the opener around the rim at both ends, the rich smelling cheese dropping out like a pudding. 'I'll get the tea on, and we'll have some sandwiches,' she said. 'You must be hungry.'

'Starving.'

Pauline stood by the door.

'You ought to be happy now.' Her mother's tone suggested

it might not last long, he didn't know why, but he smiled and put an arm around her, and she kissed him.

'Maybe you won't go out so much,' her mother added.

'I only went to the pictures.'

He kept quiet.

'Yes, I know you did.' She took milk from a cupboard under the sink and forced the cap off with a bottle-opener. 'I'm fed up looking after Gary. I've got a life of my own. You forget that, sometimes.'

He leaned against the table thinking of Jenny's hard life – as hard as all the women he had known. Jack had brought his wages home and didn't booze, but a truck underground jumped a rail, crushing him against a wall. He screamed to be put out of his agony, but no one could muffle Jenny's as she stood on the platform waiting for the Sheffield train, to witness poor Jack in the hospital inching day after day back from death.

Her old flame Terry Mackin got off the London express, all spruced up and carrying the smartest suitcase she'd ever seen, a mackintosh over his arm as he greeted her, shy at the hand-shake to enquire after Jack. She told him, no tears allowed, and he held her close to kiss her lips, saying how sorry he was, and she must be sure to give his best regards to the luckiest man in the world who had married her.

She endured, and Jack was never a proper man again, though you had to be grateful for small mercies, she said to Brian, when Pauline was out buying fish and chips for their suppers and Jack slept in the front room.

She washed cups and plates. 'Don't you think you ought to go and get Gary in for his dad to see him?'

Pauline was angry at being told what to do. 'I don't want to stop him playing. He'll be in soon enough.'

'The last time I saw him,' Brian said, 'he was no bigger than a doll. I won't know who to look for if I go out.'

Pauline slammed the door as she went, and he wondered what he'd said wrong. 'She's often like that,' Jenny told him. 'I can't think why.'

The sandwich reminded him of breakfast at the wireless hut – the same cheese, the same hunger, but without the anxiety. 'Is that why she had to go out a lot?'

'You don't mind, do you?'

Curiosity had prompted him. He hadn't realised how separated he was from normal life. 'I like people to enjoy themselves.'

'You can take her out now.'

'I've been looking forward to it.'

'I'm sure you have.'

'Hasn't Pauline?'

She sipped her tea at the living-room table. 'I can never tell what she thinks. She's not like our Maureen.' They had hoped Maureen would stay on at school, but at fifteen she went off with her pals and got a job. 'Once a gel gets an idea into her head there's no shifting it. If Jack had been alive she might have stayed on.'

'I wanted to,' he said, 'but I didn't pass the scholarship.'

'You're clever enough. You ought to have done.'

He didn't know about that. If he'd been clever he would have passed. He had been brought up on comics, and only knew about machinery and wireless. She glanced at his suitcase, and the emptied kitbag. 'Didn't they give you a demob suit?'

The dreaded question always came, or why would you dread it? The revelation seemed to have been with him since birth, but his mouth was blocked with concrete. 'They've given me ten days' leave. Then I've got to go back.'

She was indignant. 'Ain't they got enough chaps, without 'anging on to a married man like you?'

'I failed the demob medical. They want to give me more tests to find out what it is.' She hunched, her half-bitten sandwich back on the table. Telling her would make it easier to explain matters to Pauline. 'I had an X-ray, and there were scars on it.'

'Scars?'

He nodded.

'Are you sure?' She reached for his hand.

Her concern gave him courage. 'They can't be certain till they've done more tests.' I should have jumped off the platform at Derby when the express went through. Instead, he had enjoyed its thunder, the smell and balm of smoke. He pulled his hand away and, a grown man, stood up, took the half-bottle of Johnny Walker from his pack and poured a good measure into her tea, wondering if the crooked smile would ever leave

24

his face, though it was surely better than the expression of his true feelings. 'I'll probably be discharged a week or two after I get back.' He stood as if on parade. 'You can see how fit I look.'

She was convinced. 'Was it nice out there?'

'We wanted for nothing.'

'So you said in your letters.'

'Did Pauline read them to you?'

'Bits of 'em. She said she'd have been frightened of all them snakes.'

He'd never mentioned any. What few he'd come across hadn't bothered him enough to write home about. She'd seen too many daft films. 'Did she save my letters?'

She looked up. 'I don't think so.'

He hadn't kept hers, and was glad that she had dropped his into the fire, a sudden wish to have everything from his past destroyed, as if it would obliterate the evidence that he had got something as deadly as TB. Throughout his working life he had believed in machines, and the classes at radio school had taught him much, so nothing of what the X-ray said could be undone to suit himself.

Pauline led Gary in. 'I had to drag the little bogger miles. He was running after the ice-cream man.'

He snapped free, and went to his grandmother, a two–year-old in leggings, with dark hair and brown darting eyes, looking at this strange man holding his mother's hand. His face was smeared with toffee, though not so much that Brian couldn't make out the Mullinder features, while detecting something which he thought might belong to him.

'Go to your dad, then,' Jenny said.

He wouldn't wrench free, and Brian didn't take him.

'He likes his grandma, don't you, duck?' Pauline cried. 'He never leaves her alone.'

He felt a surge of ownership. 'He'll come when he wants.'

'He can be a stubborn little devil.' Pauline was puzzled at the stillness. Brian pulled the straps through the buckles of his suitcase, found a key and opened the lock. 'Wait till he sees what I've brought from Malaya.'

Gary's face observed the box drawn from the most protected part of the case. Brian wanted to cover him with kisses whether or not he protested. Gentle contact would be less contaminating. Pauline was irritated by the slow unwrapping of the gift, a model fort, with a palm tree, ten lead soldiers poised at the crenellations.

'Puppy dog,' Gary said.

'I kept telling 'im you'd bring 'im a puppy dog from Malaya.'

A fat white animal popped its head from his tunic, joy all round. It would lie on the floor licking its belly and they'd laugh at the show. We'll electro-plate its name on a collar, and buy a lead to take it to the park. In Malaya a full-grown dog wandered close to his hut and he shot it dead – sorry when it was too late. He should have bought one in Manchester from the woman with the hairnet.

'I had to tell him summat,' Pauline said. 'Especially when that was all he wanted. I can't think why you don't pick him up, though. Anybody 'ud think he worn't yourn.'

He wouldn't get close in case he infected him. Gary was vulnerable. His clothes were dirty, and he was unwashed, but kids were like that. Send 'em out neat and clean, and the next minute they were filthy.

He didn't know what the fort was, stood like Gulliver, tapping the portcullis with his plimsoll so that the palm tree and two soldiers fell over. Eyes were heavy with unshed tears, yet shone at the gift. Brian picked him up, unable to hold back from what he had rehearsed with almost as much feeling as clasping Pauline. But Gary didn't like being so high above the familiar rug, and screamed to be put down.

Pauline told him not to be silly. It was only his dad. 'I sat him on a wall last week to tie his shoe lace, and he wriggled so much he nearly fell off. He was that frightened to death.'

Brian plonked him on his knee, but he squirmed free and set the soldiers in different positions around the fort as if his spirit was inside and he would defend it to the death. On the ship he had been a fortress unto himself. A reek of fuel oil and cooking stew lay over the decks day and night, no matter how hard the wind spat salt. He sprawled near a lifeboat reading *Sevastopol* by Leo Tolstoy. Lost behind the walls of that fortress, he couldn't be bothered to decode the lamp of a steamer on its way east. Big guns belched at British and French troops struggling at the walls, the placename familiar from 'The Charge of the Light Brigade' read at school by a teacher whose emotion was so hot that his voice quivered, and tear marks appeared behind his glasses because the six hundred of his battalion in the Great War fell in a lot less time than the Light Brigade.

They went back to their meal. 'You seem awkward with him,' Pauline said. 'I can't mek you out.'

Jenny poured more tea. 'He's got good reason for it.'

He should have gone to his parents first, because telling them would have been a dummy run for informing his wife and mother-in-law – hard enough, but he might not have been so paralysed. He pulled himself together. Three years in uniform had taught him to keep himself to himself when necessary, and to restrict his speech to those few words essential for the preservation of discipline and good order, external or otherwise. 'I'm not going to be demobbed yet.'

He'd said in his letters that he liked being in the air force, but only because he didn't want her to worry. Even when things were bad he'd said they were good, though they had never been bad enough to remark on it – disliking those bods who groused that they weren't having sugar put into their tea and stirred up by their mothers at home.

She assumed he found life in uniform so wonderful that he might make a career of it, and then where would she be? She had been right not to stint on going out and enjoying herself whenever she could. 'So you've gone and signed on?'

'He's not that daft,' Jenny put in.

'We had a medical yesterday, and they found marks on my X-ray.'

Her response signified that he didn't look ill, and he was gratified. The more people were surprised, the better he would feel. But her continued stare told him that his thoughts were off centre. Her lips closed tight. 'I knew summat was wrong.'

He had been prepared to argue. Maybe they'll let me go in a few weeks. Perhaps they made a mistake. When I get back they'll see I'm as fit as I feel. The marks will disappear, even if they're deep. Perhaps they've never been there at all.

'What did they tell you?'

'The left lung's got scars on it.' He wouldn't mention those on the right. 'I've got to go back for more tests. If they're no good, I'll have to stay in.'

Gary clutched a soldier in his fist, and walked towards his knees. Pauline called him back. 'Did they say for how long?'

'They can't tell.'

She kissed Gary so hard that he cried to be put down. 'I knew you wouldn't get demobbed. I could tell summat was wrong. I felt it all last week.'

She was shit-scared he would get too close. Billy Tomkins died of TB at seventeen, and his mother who was forty had no other kids. Her husband was away at the war, and every day she stood at the gate, tall and gaunt, waiting for Billy to come home from school, or staring at the pavement where he used to play hopscotch.

He swore to himself, and stood out of range. Wanted, dead or alive, Brian Seaton, last seen travelling on a bus to the City Centre, smiting all passengers with a foul disease. He laughed at his joke.

Pauline jumped to her feet. 'Oh yes, I know you think it's funny. It's all right for you. I expected you to come back and get a job so that we could live a proper life again. But what's going to happen now?'

She was tearful, and nobody could blame her for that. 'Are you sure about it, though?'

He loved her and hated her at the same time. It wouldn't have been difficult to make her happy. I'm kept back for the Berlin Blockade. Planes can't fly without wireless operators on the ground to back them up. But the X-ray hadn't lied, so neither would he. Nor did he want to. Lying was meaningless. He kissed away her tears. 'I don't know how bad it is, but the MO showed me a lot of black areas on the X-ray.'

Gary began to cry, and ran to his father, but Pauline pulled him free. 'You'd better stay away from him, until we know.'

I've got you under my skin. He remembered all the things you are. He put on his tunic. He reached for his greatcoat and cap. He took up the presents for his parents. He went out of the house, and the gate clattered as he walked down the drive.

Chapter

❧ THREE

Buttons and belt buckle glinted in a plate glass window. He noted the uncertain angle of his cap, and the face beneath. Let a dozen Lincoln bombers rap out for bearings, and he would form them into a queue, deal with them one by one. The signals officer had congratulated him for his behaviour under stress.

Sweat ran down his face. He craved to wake up and find he had been through the demob machine without the knowledge that made walking twice the effort. But if thought was pain, motion proved that he had power over himself, and the quicker he walked the emptier his mind became.

From the cigarette mills of Players' drifted the odour of maturing tobacco which as a kid he thought came from the most wonderful pudding on the boil. Not even the Christmas duff at his grandmother's cottage had fulfilled the promise of that rich smell.

In the dell behind the church, opposite the school that was now demolished, the teacher showed them sycamore leaves and seed pods, hinting about the basis of life, and in that walled space he first noticed the smell of the earth. Ada's son Dave went to the school as well, and one day wore his mother's old coat to keep warm in the snow. Because the headmaster mocked him – the same headmaster who gave Brian a penny for counting to a hundred – she walked in next day and hit him so hard he fell behind the blackboard.

On Lonsdale Road he had looked into an enormous hole on his way home. Cobblestones had been broken and planks hammered in to shore up the sides, and through a space he saw men shovelling soil on to a platform, while more men on a ledge above spaded it on to the street, and still more men heaped it on to a lorry. The smell of fresh planks blended with that of pebbles coming out of the depths, and with petrol from the lorry's exhaust as it moved to make room for another. He asked what they were doing down in the dark, and a man said they were putting in new drains. They were boring a hole to Australia, a lot of work to get so deep into the earth.

Every day he wondered whether water had been struck. The click of spades and a barked word from labouring shadows in the half dark made him want to be down there and find out why they were really digging. Men came up splashed with mud, blinking at daylight, as tired as if they had been fighting with horrible reptilian things in driving the tunnel where the gang-boss wanted it to go. Harold Seaton went to ask for a job, but no more hands were needed, and he came home so enraged that everyone had to get out of the house.

He crossed from the picture house to Harry's the newsagent's, knitting patterns still displayed outside, as well as detective magazines whose lurid covers had sickened him as a kid. Hot steel from the bike factory ponged with gasometers by the River Leen, and locomotive smoke from the station.

'I see you're home, then.' Mr Beasley had grey wavy hair, a neat and handsome man. 'You can't beat it, can you?'

Ma Bull at the yard-end gave him a hard look. He didn't care. He was back, and happy at being alive even if only because the terrace seemed about to be swept away with all who lived in it.

His father sat at the table rolling cigarettes, lips pursed to a march thumping out of the wireless. His broad and swarthy face showed shock, not at seeing Brian after two years away, but at the click of the doorlatch and the thought that a stranger had invaded his privacy without previous announcement.

'Hey up, Dad!'

Seaton stood, short and stocky, in badly fitting trousers, shirt without a collar, waistcoat open, slippers cut at the sides to ease his bunions. Brian had rarely seen him in a suit, and never in one that was tailored. Labouring since twelve, his arms were ungainly, and he walked with a sailor-like sway that suggested one leg was longer than the other, so that Doddoe's kids referred to him behind his back as Oddlegs, a name Aunt Ada had coined after Seaton had hit her sister Vera over the head with a *distance* shoe. Blood poured into a bucket from the wound, but Seaton was now a mild man in his middle forties, who since the war had created less fights about lack of money.

Brian was taller, though doubted he was stronger on feeling the grip of welcome. 'I've bin worried every minute yer've bin in Malaya,' his father said.

'It was a holiday camp.' He unbuttoned his tunic. Perhaps he ought to shoot a line to the effect that things had been grim, otherwise he might be called a liar when he mentioned the X-ray.

Seaton put the kettle on. 'There was a lot of blokes killed out there, worn't there? Me and yer mam heard it on the wireless. I'm glad yer got back, though. You can get a proper job now, and settle down.' He put a cup and saucer out, and a mug for himself. 'You can't beat your own country, I'll tell yer that much.'

On the odd day trip to the Lincolnshire coast, Seaton sat on the sand and stared at the sea, and never wondered what was on the other side, except to tell himself he didn't want to go because he liked being where he was, and that even if he didn't occasionally like being where he was he at least knew what it was like and so was a damn sight better than whatever was on the other side of the sea because he didn't know what it was like which meant that he wouldn't like it even if he got over there, which he never would because he liked being where he was thank you very much.

He couldn't read or write, and Brian had tried teaching him. To start with pen and ink and a smooth Woolworth's pad, instead of a pencil and a bit of lining paper, would seem too serious, but even so the nicotined fingers finally laid the pencil down, and he would stare at the few letters wrenched out against his deepest will. At least he was able to sign his name, and bluff people into believing he was not illiterate when collecting dole or wages. At the point of abandoning the lesson he

31

pulled the paper towards him and scripted his name in such copperplate style that anyone coming across it would not think him the numbskull that Vera called him in their quarrels. He pushed the signature towards Brian without a word, then went into the scullery to mash some tea. Brian, having known the lesson wouldn't last, though he had wanted it to, realised that Seaton didn't care to relinquish his ignorance and be like everyone else, but to stay in the shelter of illiteracy he had got used to since birth.

'How have things been?' Brian asked.

Three saccharines bubbled in his tea. 'We still can't get the real thing.' He loved cakes and sweet things, but as soon as he had money to buy sugar at the beginning of the war it was rationed. 'I've got a job, I go out for a drink on Sat'day night, and get to the pictures now and again. So I don't suppose we can grumble. This bleddy guv'ment wants upending, though.'

Brian looked into the yard. 'What happened to my bike?' Maybe they had carried it upstairs to stop it rusting in rain or snow.

'Well, my owd lad, your mother got a bit short one week, and a chap asked how much we wanted for it. Mind you, it worn't much cop by then. The back tyre had rotted, and the brakes was none too good.' He had put a bit by from his wages every week for a year, but there was no point in complaining. 'I knew you wouldn't mind,' Seaton said. 'It was cluttering up the yard as well.'

The doorknob rattled and his mother came breathlessly in. 'Mr Beasley told me he'd seen yer, so I nipped straight home.' Face hewn out of rock, he saw her as if for the first time, never having been so long away – sunken cheeks and shapeless nose and lined mouth, but hair carefully rolled as if in that department at least she'd tried to do something. 'How are you then, duck?'

'All right.'

'Was it nice out there?'

A dog barked from the line of lavatories. What could you say? 'Marvellous.' It had given him TB – but that was something else. He would have gotten it anyway, wherever he'd been, something that had always been waiting to jump on him like an invisible tiger out of the burning bush.

She poured tea with a shaking hand. 'I wish I'd a gone. I'd do owt to get out of this rotten country. Don't suppose I ever shall, though, a woman of my age.'

'You know you love it here,' Seaton scoffed.

'I never did. I'd love to go to another country. Look at our Brian, how healthy he looks after all that sun.'

'A lot o' bleddy good it'd do yer,' Seaton grumbled.

In two minutes they would be cat-and-dogging it, and knowing they would calm down if left on their own he went upstairs to look at his old room.

At the top of the landing stood a common piss bucket so that you didn't have to go across the yard during the night. The window of the room which his sisters slept in looked over the backyards, from where you could see anyone going out for the evening, or coming back from a day's work, or on their way to the lavatory, or hanging their washing, so that you'd know what people wore right down to the underwear – if they had any.

The front room he shared with his two brothers looked over the cul-de-sac of the terrace, where the doors had numbers and letterboxes, used only by postmen, debt collectors and policemen, or someone looking for the long-lost member of a family. The opposite houses were a few yards away, and the railings that had defined individual gardens had been taken away for scrap during the war.

The suit left on a hanger behind the door had also gone to the ragman. Most of the books had flown from the cupboard, but he looked under the bed in case any had been put there in a sack. Spirals of fluff made him sneeze. They had cleared nearly every trace of him. All the same, it was a familiar place, with a small table to sit at and a cupboard for books. The bed he had slept in with his brothers was a geological landscape waiting for the surveyor. Only in the air force had he found the luxury of sheets, and a bed to himself.

A plate of ham, lettuce and tomato, bread and butter was on the table. He had no appetite, but she wanted him to show his appreciation by gobbling every scrap. The ultimate her care could go to was in feeding them, because often she had not been able to, and lines of misery at such failure marked her face. Her arms were folded over her chest, as if thinking that he also wanted to hurt her. 'Aren't you hungry?'

He managed the ham, and drank the tea because he was thirsty. 'I had something at Pauline's.'

She took a packet of Park Drive from the shelf, and lit up. 'She don't come to see us anymore.'

'I thought she did.'

'Can't think why. We ain't done owt to her.'

'You wain't be up to much if you don't get some grub down yer.' His father implied that whatever he had eaten at the Mullinders couldn't have been either copious or suitable.

'She ain't been to see us the whole time you was away,' his mother went on.

'She's a funny gel, though.' Seaton shook his head. 'To think I'm a grandad, and she don't bring Gary up to see me.'

Vera nudged him in the ribs. 'A right grandad yo' are!'

Maybe Pauline grudged the bus fare, or even the time. 'I asked her to, in my letters, but she was busy, I suppose.' He tamped a cigarette against the table, and lit it. 'Did you go to Tapley and see her?' He couldn't think why she had stayed away. People seemed too tired to do anything after work, and he hoped such a blight didn't descend on him now that he was back.

'I expect she'll look after you,' Vera went on. 'But she'll never look after you like I've done, will she, my owd duck?' There was pride in her voice, yet also a hint of doom, the only way in which she was able to put deep meaning into her words. 'I allus said eighteen was too young to get married.'

Seaton nodded. 'Twenty would have been all right, but not eighteen.'

Brian liked the fact even less. Everyone had warned him against it. 'Anybody who gets married asks for all they get,' Len Knotman said in Malaya. But he hadn't got anything, except Gary, and he wasn't sure he had him any more.

'Have you made up your mind where you're going to work?'

'There's something wrong with me. I've got to go into

hospital for some tests. I caught it in Malaya.' What could be plainer? He had told them, and it was easier this time.

'I allus said them places was bad for yer,' Seaton said. 'You should a done as I towd yer and not gone. The war's over, in't it? They'd never a got me to go to Africa.'

'Asia.'

'It's all the same.' He was a stranger to a map of the world, *Mappa Mundi* but Brian had grown up with one in front of his eyes, even when they were closed.

'You look well, though,' his mother said, 'so it can't be all that much.'

Seaton, happy to see his firstborn son, slapped him on the back. 'Course it ain't. He's come home, that's one thing. There's a lot as didn't, by the time the Japs had done with 'em. No wonder they used the atom bomb on the boggers, after all they'd done.'

Brian remembered their prisoners, short healthy men labouring at the airstrip. They travelled on the same lorry, and he handed out cigarettes, because you couldn't smoke and not offer them, but a sergeant on the gate shouted him black and blue: 'Did you see Changi jail when it was liberated?'

'I had an X-ray, and they found something wrong. So I've got to go back in ten days.'

They must have understood, yet lived in their own world, which he wasn't part of. Any world an inch from their eyes was foreign, and his was further than that. Not that he could blame them, because he had always kept the gap as wide as possible.

'Them X-rays aren't healthy,' Seaton said. 'They give you all sorts of things. A van come to the factory on'y last month and the gaffers wanted me to get one. But wild 'osses wouldn't get me in front o' one o' them things. They give you an X-ray for bogger-all these days, and I'm sure it don't do you any good.'

'In my case,' Brian smiled, 'it was orders.'

'Course it was. If you join up you have to do as you're towd, don't yer? That's why I never let 'em get me.'

That's why we'll never understand each other.

'When you go back you'd better write and let me know

what's wrong.' His mother had been overloaded since birth with so much privation that a wall had been built around her. Only a small matter would release the sea of misery, so she protected herself with as much indifference as she could muster, and he didn't want to upset her, in case he upset himself by seeing that it wasn't possible.

Seaton put an arm over him affectionately. 'Sounds like you've bin up to a bit of hanky-panky with them black women. You should a bin more careful. Still, my owd lad, they cure owt these days. You'll be back on your owd job soon, and nobody'll be any the wiser.'

He registered his father's picture of a swaddie queue outside a tin shed in Benghazi, or some such place. A dose of the pox would have been no slur, and curable in double-quick time, but all he'd had was Mimi, and he'd certainly picked up nothing from her. The only way to deny he had caught the pox was to yell that he had TB, consumption, tuberculosis, take your pick – because they wouldn't accept anything in less than *Daily Mirror* headlines, and maybe not even then, unable or unwilling to understand. Perhaps they were right. For how could one X-ray be absolute proof? Cigarette smoke caught in his throat as he straightened his cap at the oval mirror above the fireplace.

'You aren't going, are you?'

'I'm off to the Meadows, to call on Dave and Colin.'

'If you can find 'em in.' His father detested them. 'I expect they're out robbing somebody or other.'

'I'll see Aunt Ada as well.'

Seaton hated her even more.

Vera switched on the wireless. 'Remember me to her.'

Someone sang 'All the things you are' as he went through the scullery and up the yard.

Chapter

❧ FOUR

His first time on foreign soil, two turbaned men wanted to tell his fortune. Being broke, he had to say no, so one of them jeered that he had 'snake eyes'.

The fortune tellers of Ceylon made a mistake. Snake eyes see everything. Fate never catches a snake off guard. He'd laughed at their remark, but thinking back on it, maybe they knew what they were saying. Snakes see only what is close to the ground, so Snake-eyes was about right, because he had lived blind and would pay for it, though not yet knowing what he hadn't yet seen, he didn't know what price he would have to pay when he did see something.

He passed the school: playground wall and red-bricked tower, tiers of windows. Since leaving, each year had been as long as ten. From fourteen to twenty-one the key-to-the-door had been work, eat, sleep, enjoy yourself, but there should have been more than that, because everything he hadn't learned pressed like pitted buckshot against his lungs. His attitude to the truth had been that he did not believe it, and everyone around thought the same, because it was the only way to protect yourself from the world. If an outbreak of the Black Death was announced on April Fool's Day – and this is Alvar Liddell reading it – you'd laugh at the idea and carry on living.

A poster advertising IS GOD DEAD? made him wonder when He had lived. Whether He had or not had never been relevant, and strange that it might be to others, because whoever needed to ask such a question must be stone from the neck up.

He had money in his pocket, clothes on his back, and wasn't hungry. What more could you want? A bus passed, and he envied a cyclist – while daydreaming he was on a foot-wide ridge, water on either side miles deep and lapping at the path, as if any second it would wash him into an endless sea. Lucky to be alive, he was carried by the left-right-left of footsteps through familiar territory, the clean air of the Park area, a beautiful morning that had turned into afternoon. By the Castle his mind switched into a locker of consciousness where no one could follow, and he wondered whether this separation from his normal self was due to an exhaustion never before experienced, or a force over which he had no control, until he recalled descending the forest of Gunong Barat from the highest point, and laying out a camp by the short drop of a waterfall. He scoured among surrounding trees with a kukri to collect dead wood so as to keep a fire blazing through the night. Mess tins of stew were cooking while he laid his groundsheet in the undergrowth, hung a mosquito net – and suddenly he wasn't with five others in the jungle, but was boxed within a stockade of himself alone, only connected to the world by the sound of water travelling the path of least resistance in the dusk like static in a radio, strengthening the wall that cut him off.

He was as unaware of the changing scene, walking the last mile to Ada's house in the Meadows, as he had been all his life oblivious to what had gone on around him. Using the footscraper by the back door brought him back to consciousness, as had Corporal Knotman's voice in the jungle telling him to come to the fire and eat.

He knocked before going in, the combined smell of pumice and cracked drains not far from the odour of mangrove swamps. Pots and pans were stacked by the scullery sink. 'Who is it?'

'The rent man!'

'I'm not in!' She laughed, a tall woman of over fifty whose once reddish hair had turned grey.

'Where is everybody? Have the coppers bin for 'em?'

She pulled him close for a kiss. 'I *am* glad to see you.'

As a kid he loved her more than his mother, probably because she fed him when there was nothing on the table at home. He'd often shared a bed with Johnny and Dave and Bert, fighting for clothes against the night cold. They sat at the table. 'Doddoe's gone somewhere on his motorbike. He allus manages to get petrol off the ration. Are you on leave then' – she nudged him – 'or have you deserted?'

If he had, she would shelter him, he was sure of that. 'I'm just back from Malaya.'

'Yer mam towd me yer was out there. You look a bit like death warmed up, though.' She peered at him. 'Is owt wrong?'

He loosened his belt. 'I feel all right.'

'You should look sunburned and healthy after so long out there. But you don't. You're a bit thin.'

She would understand, but he wouldn't tell her. 'You're nice and bronzed while you're on the ship, but as soon as you walk down the gangplank in England the air rubs it off like a flannel.'

'You do talk daft,' she said. 'But I suppose that's what a uniform does to you. No wonder our Colin and Dave deserted.'

'Bert and Johnny didn't.'

'I'm glad as well, when I think of the misery Colin and Dave went through. I don't want them times back. In fact I don't want any times back. Things are better now everybody's back at work. At least I don't jump out of my skin when there's a rap at the door. I don't know whether to laugh or cry when I think of it. Dave came in one morning with his trousers soaked in blood because he'd fell on a wall of broken bottles getting away from the coppers. I was all day picking bits o' glass out of his arse. Even I'd never heard such cursing. He didn't let go of a leather attaché case, though, with sixty quid in it. Another time they wheeled a safe home on a pram. Dave said he left the baby in a cardboard box among the geraniums, but it was only an owd one they found on some waste ground. A bit of shrapnel hit our Colin on the way back so I had to bandage him up as well. He daren't go to the hospital in case they asked for his Identity Card. When they dragged 'em back in the army they never had such a peaceful time.'

Doddoe, the ex-bombardier of a husband, pawned her underwear and the sheets off the bed just before her confinement – because he wanted a few pints of ale. 'To get a bit o' money to buy summat for the table me and your mam used to doll oursens up and go down town to get what we wanted. Doddoe and Harold caught us at it once, and there was ructions, all up and down Long Row – and you know what that means. Well, you're old enough to know. Not that Doddoe and yer dad worried too much when we came home with money in our handbags.'

Salmon and cucumber smelled of Sunday afternoon tea at the Nook with his grandparents. She spread thin bread with butter. 'Our Jane works at a shop, so we don't go short. When I was a gel my dad got me into service, and the woman of the house used to put a cake on the table for tea. She had eight kids, but woe betide any who took too much to eat. She just shaved a piece off for everybody, then locked it away in a cupboard. Mean as bleddy 'ell, she was, but they had plenty o' money.'

He ate a piece of cake. Generosity was her nature, but she'd had a hard time bringing up Doddoe's eight delinquent kids. In her house during the war they heard on the wireless that Goering had ranted: 'Bomb the cities! Bomb the poor!' and she'd turned pale with indignation.

'Things is better now,' she said, 'but Doddoe's never forgiven me for what I did, and it's more than ten years. I don't know why we're still together. If he'd left me then he wouldn't have been able to keep on being a bad 'un to me. I suppose that's why he'll never leave me.' Misery turned to a mischievous laugh. Enough men found her attractive to make life worthwhile, and whoever she married would also have a hard time. 'Maybe I want to punish that bogger, though,' she laughed. 'Besides, I might end up with somebody worse.'

He stood up to go.

'Tek care o' yoursen,' she said. 'You don't look well to me. Are you sure you're all right?'

'Never felt better.'

His foot tapped the bar rail of the Eight Bells saloon, black toe caps against mock gold. A hand clutched his shoulder. 'I didn't expect yer back yet. I thought that leaky old troopship 'ad sunk. If it was owt like that one I went to Belgium on it would.'

His cousin Bert, closer even than a brother, gave a berserker grin at the chance meeting. Eagerness had been part of his expression for so long it had become a permanent feature – resembling avidity. Impossible not to be friendly, though Brian trusted him less as he grew older, as if they knew too much about each other, or there was a lot about Bert that Brian could never know – hard to decide which.

Bert was a few inches shorter, stocky and strong, his short fair hair faintly waved. Blue eyes glittered with concern, but hid a steely base to be wary of. 'I'm glad you're back, though. You want to get out of that uniform, and stay out. Still, I enjoyed it while I was in, especially in Germany after VE Day. Had a marvellous time. Fucked every nationality in the world except Eskimo. I expect yo' 'ad some slit though, in Burma, didn't yer?'

They sat by the window. Someone was trying to play 'Roses are blooming in Picardy' on the piano. 'Malaya,' he said.

'I never 'ad Chinks or Blackies, but I 'ad everything else. They'd do owt for a packet o' fags or a bar o' soap. "It's all I've got," I used to say. "Tek it or leave it." And they allus took it. They could swap it, see? You worn't supposed to fraternise, but I'd do owt for a bit o' cunt. It was *verboten*, but the Redcaps was gerrin all they wanted, and so was the officers.'

Unless he was drunk (and he was never that drunk) Brian couldn't imagine shagging a woman he didn't think he was in love with. A woman with grey eyes, silver rinse and shapeless nose, wearing a smart New Look costume, sat at a table with a man who had blue-veined cheeks and a Brylcreemed quiff, a folded mackintosh across his knees. He adored his fancy woman, but she was more interested in other people, for which Brian could not blame her, her sharp ears picking up all Bert said.

'At the end of the war you laid your hands on whatever you could nick from the stores, and bartered it on the black market.' He'd flogged petrol in Italy, fags in Germany, and watches in Blighty, but after a year in civvy street he was as stony as ever. 'I get ten quid a week, driving for a cardboard box firm. As if that was what I joined up for. Still, I worn't killed, and that's all that matters, in't it?'

Brian stood. 'I'll get some more ale.'

'That's my pal.'

'I'm courting now,' Bert told him. 'She's a lovely girl, called Nancy. Lives up Sneinton. I was in bed for a week six months ago, getting over a rupture, and she used to come upstairs. See to me, if you know what I mean.'

'And you're going to get married?'

His mouth set firm. 'You had to marry Pauline, didn't you?'

He felt even more trapped now than he had at the time, when Bert advised him not to. 'You'll be done for. You'll be hooked, finished, skewered and knackered. Why don't you do a bunk?'

Leaving her in the lurch with an illegitimate kid would have been better than putting her through what was bound to come. She'd be married to somebody else and a lot happier. But he had thought he was in love, forceput or not. Maybe he wasn't. But he was full of love – for someone – and Pauline happened to go with him into the fields.

'Her old man's a big beer-swilling bastard,' Bert said.

Like Doddoe. Brian was unable to resist some of his own back. 'Why don't you vanish? They'd never find you.'

A shade of panic went over him. 'I couldn't live anywhere except Nottingham. Anyway, I'm twenty-three, so if it ain't her, it'll be somebody else.' He groaned. 'She's so fat it's like fucking a football.'

Brian laughed in his beer. 'Just fine for you.'

'If she was as good-looking as your Pauline it might be different.' His look turned lecherous and sly. 'That's somebody I could go for. She's got lovely legs, and a smashing figure.'

Her legs were disfigured by varicose veins, and after having Gary her shape wasn't so good, but Bert saw every woman he couldn't have as better than one he could. 'She's not for you, and that's a fact.'

A gang of youths wailed in tune with the pianist about a slow boat to China. 'Maybe she ain't, but I saw her in The Peach Tree a month ago with that pal o' yourn who went in the Signals. You used to go out with him before you joined up. I forget his name.'

Albert Lomax had worked on the next lathe at Edgeworth's. They'd gone to the same youth club, and argued about communism being the best system in the world. At election time they pinned a Labour poster on the factory wall, till Edgeworth took it down. 'So what?'

'Well, if a wife of mine was in a pub with a soldier while I was serving abroad I'd give her such a pasting she wouldn't get out of bed for a month.'

'They bumped into each other in town and went for a drink. She told me about it.'

She hadn't, but he didn't want to live in the kind of world Bert was trying to push him into. He'd seen enough of that at home, and so had Bert.

'She was dressed up to the nines. I'm just telling you what I saw. I said hello, but she looked at me gone-out, as if she didn't know me. He was sitting in the snug drinking a black-and-tan, and she had a glass of mild. I'd called in for a last drink before they put the towels on.' He emptied a pint in one long travail of his throat. 'Women are like that. As soon as you turn your back they shit on yer. Tek you for all you've got.'

Brian didn't know. 'It depends how much you've got. Some don't have all that much.'

Bert took this to signify that he wasn't worth robbing or shitting on, and he didn't like being reminded, even though he might, for the moment anyway, be just about flat broke in every respect that mattered.

'All I mean,' Brian said, 'is that I haven't got a lot myself right now.'

Bert was mollified. 'You've got brains, at least, which is more than I'll ever have.'

True or not, he didn't feel less close to his cousin, and when he came back with two more pints Bert said: 'Do you remember the time I nicked that book for you? Stuffed it under my coat in the shop when nobody was looking?'

After Bert's success he had taken a few himself, but he was ashamed of Bert's thieving, ashamed of his own, and then ashamed of his ingratitude. Well away from the shop, Bert waved that little red book with the flexible binding, waiting for him to reach so that he could snatch it back, emphasising the favour. It had gone to the ragman, with his bicycle and clothes.

The one similarity the ale had to Malayan beer was that if you put enough back you became fuddle-headed, though he'd drunk only two pints. He recalled how Bert at sixteen stopped him in the street: 'Look at all this money! We'll put our best clothes on and see Joe Loss at the Empire.'

'I ain't got any best,' Brian said.

'I've just robbed a couple of gas meters, so I'm rich. We'll find a pawnshop and buy you a coat.'

They sat in the front stalls, eating choc-ices, Bert tapping his feet to the music of Joe's wonderful band.

'I'll get off home, or Pauline will be wondering where I've got to.'

Bert scoffed. 'Don't let women rule yer. Let's go to the Langham and get a nobble on. There's allus lots o' talent in there.'

It was eight o'clock but felt like midnight. He had woken at half past five in an almost empty hut, a reveille different from any other. There was no going back to sleep, or not believing in what had happened, but by drill he got up, by drill he washed and dressed and went to breakfast, and by drill he packed his kit and made tracks for the station.

Bert's expression hinted that he was the most disloyal pal anyone could be lumbered with. If a pal wain't come to the next pub after you've been good enough to sup two of his pints – or was it three? – then don't bother to talk to me again.

Brian stood. 'I'll see you in a couple of days.'

'I've heard them promises before. You'll go on your own somewhere, and forget all about me.'

'If I say I'll see you, I will.' He put on his greatcoat, to protect himself from people in the street. 'I'll walk you through Slab Square.'

Bert laughed at his concession, as if to say that he had won, or at least hadn't yet lost. After a couple of stints at an approved school and a dose of borstal he had worked on building sites as a labourer and dumper truck driver. Adding a year to his age, he joined up and saw action in the infantry. Bert could give him lessons in survival, but Brian didn't think you could learn from anyone else. You couldn't help yourself to their flesh, or to their spirit, because their flesh and their spirit didn't fit your flesh and your spirit. It belonged to them and them alone. If you wanted to survive you had to do it by yourself. You had no right to

44

think you could get anything so vital from anybody else and not have to pay for it. Whatever you get from yourself, you have to pay for that, too, but at least you were both the borrower and the lender, and beholden to nobody, and learned more surely for it.

'Anyway,' he said when they were outside, 'why aren't you with your lady-love?'

'I'll be with her enough when we're married.' He swung into a walking gait. 'I won't be bored, though, not for the first fortnight, anyway.' He dug his elbow into Brian's ribs. 'If you know what I mean. I've been bored to death since I left the army. It's funny, but I was never bored in the army, not even when everybody else was. If we had to wait somewhere for days in the rain or snow I didn't get bored. I don't know why. Maybe I was happy at watching the other blokes get bored. But me, I'd cadge a fag from somewhere, and have a quiet smoke. I knew there'd be a brew-up sooner or later. I had a uniform on my back, so I could wait forever and not care. I'd got nowt to worry about, that's why. Even when the shooting started I didn't give a fuck. I could run and duck better than anybody else, and I allus kept my bayonet clean for if any fucking Gerry got near me. How can you get bored when you've nowt to worry about? You get your few bob a day and all found. But now I've got to go ter work every day and worry about the weather in case I wear my boots and clo'es out, or whether my wages at the end of the week'll be enough to live on. I'd rather be dead than bored.'

He was a skiver, and a thief, though when his back was against the wall there could be no doubt about his tenacity as a soldier. 'Why didn't you stay in the army?'

The two cement lions on either side of the Council House looked staid in their authority. The one on the left resembled their Grandfather Merton, the blacksmith who had tolerated Brian but driven Bert and his brothers away because one of them stole something from the parlour – or Merton thought they would if he let them in.

'I had ulcers. Then I had a rupture. I got fixed up but they still wouldn't have me. Anyway, I joined the Terriers last month, and now I'm a gunner in my spare time. We'll be going on manoeuvres soon, and that means a bob or two in my pocket. When you get out of the air force why don't yo' join? I'll tek yer to Hucknall and introduce yer.'

Halfway up Market Street Brian stopped, as if a giant spike from the sky fixed him to the ground. He wouldn't be able to join anything ever again. No air force would have him, no navy, not even the army – not even the Terriers. The body on which he had relied so absolutely that he had never thought about what it might one day do to him had broken. He had never considered himself at war with his muscles. Whatever he thought of doing, his body had done. When he had demanded the utmost, his body had given it. But somewhere along the line his body had also wanted some consideration from him, a signal he hadn't recognised at the time, so that eventually he had made the body do something which in fact it could not do. He had no idea what it was, nor when the crucial conflict had taken place, but if that was the case, there was no justice in it, and though he had never thought that the notion of justice applied to him, he considered it at Bert's suggestion that he join the Terriers after he was demobbed.

'What's up, duck?' Bert wanted to know.

Blue sparks flashed where the trolleybus wires joined those overhead. A contact had fallen off, and the driver was trying to fix it back with a hooked pole. 'I've got TB.'

A surge of foul beer rose in his gorge, but he felt glad at informing Bert so painlessly. If he couldn't tell *him*, he couldn't tell anybody.

Bert didn't go to one side as if he might catch something, but looped an arm through his, then grasped him by the shoulders and looked into his face.

'I wish it was me. A mate o' mine had a touch of it and went to Newstead Sanatorium for a year. You'll be in a nice hospital. You'll have all your grub brought in on a tray. You'll live like a lord, and you'll be washed by lovely good-looking nurses who'll make your bed and tuck you in every night. You've allus bin a lucky bastard. I wish I could go down with a nice dose of TB, and not have to lift a finger for a couple o' years.'

If a lorry hit Bert and he lost both legs he would measure the catastrophe in terms of bread and butter. And why not? Nothing was tragic as long as you were left with a beating heart and breath in your body. Yet there was something else as well, and he didn't know what it was, but in trying to decide whether Bert's attitude was valid or not, now that he had reached this vital fork in the road, Brian felt that the world had showed him its right face at last. Bert's kind of life was cut off from him, because he had never been part of it, even when seemingly as far in as anybody could get. Running by his side from some escapade when they were kids, he had looked on, both at himself and Bert, with no real attachment to either.

Bert put the arm back on his shoulder. 'You never know what's gonna happen till it happens. All I know is that everything's allus gonna be all right, until it ain't. If you don't think that, you might as well jump off Castle Rock.'

There was nothing he could say, and he surprised Bert by a quick march down Parliament Street towards Chapel Bar, when Bert had thought that Brian's confession was the prelude to a long evening of talk about old times.

Darkness was coming, a pink glow above the rooftops. He had seen that kind often, and took comfort because such light provided a thread between the time when he had been too busy to think, and the time, which was now, when to think about what had struck him was the only way of staying alive.

Chapter

❧ FIVE

Brian dabbed Gary's nose with the brush. Gary watched him clip and screw the three-piece razor into action stations. Gary watched him shave. Big-eyed Gary watched the cotton-wool face coming back to pink.

Gary watched him polishing his buttons, as if he was the lodger. Brian gave him the button stick to play with. Gary threw it away.

Brian spread his best uniform trousers on the table to sharpen the creases, but Mrs Mullinder snatched the iron as if he were insulting her. Pauline had gone out, he didn't know where, but he wouldn't have expected her to be his batman anyway. The only automatic right was to darn his own socks, sew on buttons, wash underwear and shirts – when he had to. He felt almost as insulted at Jenny Mullinder doing his trousers as she would have been if he had prevented her.

When in a cul-de-sac, go back into the wind that tries to bottle you up. Pauline did not know where he went or what he did, but at least he was where he could be no bother. Putting himself in her place, she prayed for his leave to be over. It was plain a mile off. So did he. He wasn't wanted, so had to go out. Everything had been said between them, and if it hadn't, Pauline wasn't going to say it. Neither was he.

You could hardly go back off leave before your time. 'Got no home to go to, airman?' 'No, sir.' 'Find one, then. Leave is an indulgence you are obliged to take advantage of.' He didn't have the sort of money for a stay in London, whether or not he lodged at the YMCA. He would be broke in three days.

The uniform protected him, in that he belonged to the world yet was set aside from it. Therefore he was himself. He carried his folded greatcoat in case of rain, the sky as blue as it had been in childhood, walking by Tapley Hall and down Colliers' Pad, the Cherry Orchard obliterated by an estate of pre-fabricated government offices. At six he had run across humps and grassy hollows to the Arlingtons' cottage on the edge of Serpent Wood, a jungle still untouched for kids to play in.

He leaned against a fence and looked towards the trees. Brenda Arlington had said she loved him, run across the field and into the wood, leaned over the pebbly brook because she liked to look at water. Her two mouths moved. Beetles swayed and flitted between the stones. One set of lips went down, and a greedier mouth came up in a drinking kiss. The water went through her throat, as it did his by her side, and they drank the mirror between them.

Her mother had said that she would get frogs in her belly drinking like that, but you only found frogs in pools of twigs and slime, not in a running brook. 'In't that right, Brian?'

He nodded. She ran across the Cherry Orchard, sun high, wet in the heavy dew, rooks rattling like a bag of beads in a tin, a skylark chasing a crow as if the crow had done something unforgivable. A rabbit zig-zagged like a brown cat towards the lane.

She fell, rolled into a hollow.

'I love you,' she said.

Merton's place had vanished in a wash of new houses, as had the garden, and the well-top his uncle staggered from, yoke on shoulders, splashing a trail down the path. No taps, or gas, or electric light, but coal and wood and oil lamps, and a steel scoop to drink icy water out of the bucket.

There was a bookcase in the parlour, and a gramophone with records. He read or drew maps. He tapped the first of a domino line on the mahogany table, no feeling for the last one crushed under their weight.

He walked the sunken lane to a three-street area notorious

for rough-stuff and thievery, poachers and illegal bookies – the smell of bacon from backyards making him hungry though he had just had breakfast. No one knew him through the disguise of his uniform. Two women talked outside the beer-off. In the beginning was the word, but it was different everywhere: Tom Pinder had been caught on Pillicock Hill after robbing houses at Strelley. 'The coppers must have waited for the daft bogger.'

A young fair-haired woman lifted a hand to push hair in place, a hole in her jersey at the armpit. He could look without seeming to. Maybe she was Brenda Arlington. He wouldn't know, hadn't seen her for fifteen years. Faces never came back as you had known them. Memory was a fairytale. Altered too much, it became a lie, though a lie was less painful than the truth. You only found out the truth when the mind was ready for it.

All in all, he couldn't care less as he turned by the Crown and headed towards Radford, revelling in the walk, the march, the swing towards home that he no longer felt part of. His mother was talking to Mrs Bull at the yard-end, but came into the house after him. His return from Malaya had been an occasion, but dropping in now was somehow out of place, so she made him coffee instead of tea.

He gazed into the firegrate, father and brothers already at work. Nobody was offended by silence, or expected you to talk for talking's sake, unless the silence had been present before your arrival and they had been waiting for you to break it. His mother stared with him, knew what loneliness was, part of her nature to stare with others. In spite of Harold and five kids she lived alone because she had never been allowed to be herself. He felt he should say something, but all words had gone, a weight he could not lift, strange when he had set out from the Mullinders in love with the world.

'I thought I'd call and see how you were,' he said, as if only now he had got back from the East. 'I came by the Cherry Orchard, but there's not much left of it.'

'You walked all that way?'

'It's only a couple of miles.'

She laughed. 'You'll wear your shoes out.'

'That's what they're for.'

50

'You look as if you don't know what to do with yourself.'

'I'm on my way into town.'

'Has Pauline chucked you out?' she joked.

'It's not come to that.'

'I expect she wants you to get a job.'

'I don't know what she wants. But I can't do anything about it till I've got rid of whatever I've got.'

'Did they tell you what it was, then?'

'They just took an X-ray.'

'A bit of pleurisy, I expect,' she said.

'That's what they thought.'

'I had it when I was young. You do feel bad, for a month or two.'

'I suppose that's all it'll take.'

'They don't look after you in the air force. Not if you get pleurisy.'

'I don't have any complaints.'

'You'll be a lot better out of it.'

He didn't know about that. No prospect was pleasant.

'The trouble is,' she said, 'people don't know when they are well off.'

'They're daft if they don't,' he smiled.

'There's a young woman up the street called Lillian Verney. She's got TB. Bin in bed years, though she's allus cheerful. I was talkin' to her on'y yesterday. She can't get out of bed because of her TB, but she don't grumble. She said how lucky she was to be alive.'

'Is she religious?'

'I don't think so. She's only your age.'

He wasn't interested – not even in himself, as far as that went.

'You ought to nip in, as you go up the street.'

He was amazed. 'Me?'

'Call in, and remember me to her. The poor gel don't see anybody from one day to the next. Her mam looks after her, but she can't be there all the time. She's got a struggle, with a daughter like that. I don't know what I'd do if it was me.'

About the same, he surmised, standing to put his cap on.

'She'll be glad to see yer, though. You pass on your way to the bus stop.'

'I'm not calling.'

'Just pop in. It's number eighty-seven. Tomorrow, if you can't go today.'

'Are you trying to get me off with her?' he laughed.

'Not with somebody like that, duck. She's a nice gel, though. It's a shame, when you think of some varmints runnin' around. But she likes somebody to ask how she is, laying there day after day. Remember me to her mam if you see her.'

Better things to do, he walked by the plain lace-curtained window, a young woman inside with TB, couldn't go by quick enough, as if part of him might die with her if he knocked at her door. She'd take one look a him and twig what his X-ray had revealed.

Clouds were high, the air fresh. A passing trackless was a miracle. No battered taxicabs or rickshaws with skeletons short-coughing at the shafts, no overburdened sampans out on the water. Glad to be in town, he forgot all tribulations. After his dinner at the servicemen's club he sloped into a lounge chair to smoke a whiff and read the *Daily Mirror*.

Kirkby walked in, banged him on the back. 'Don't your demob suit fit you?' His good quality cloth was hung neatly, non-utility, with stylish turn-ups, a gold tie-pin and fancy cufflinks. 'A tailor ran it together in forty-eight hours. Greased his palm. Fucking had to. Nobody does owt for nowt these days.' Must have sold the smuggled stuff from his big pack, whatever it had been. 'You got your ticket, though, didn't you?'

He told him. 'Failed the medical. I've got to stay in for a while to see what it is.'

Kirkby settled in an armchair opposite. 'What does that mean?'

'I'll be in hospital, under observation.' He puffed contentedly, as if he might enjoy a bit of incarceration.

'You'll be in sick quarters?' Kirkby's eyes enlarged behind thick glasses. Hadn't had time to get gold frames.

'That's about it.'

He drew closer. 'You're certain?'

'What are you getting at?'

'Are you sure you'll be in sick quarters?'

52

Brian picked up the newspaper, not caring to have the fact of his affliction rubbed in. Kirkby eased the paper from his face: 'Do you want to earn summat?'

'Drop dead.' But he was curious. 'How?'

'White Market. Know what I mean?'

'You tell me.'

'Well, if you get pally with a nurse, or an orderly, and you slip 'em a few quid, they might let you have some drugs or medicines. I'll tell you what to ask for.'

'You're a real fuckface.'

'You'd earn more than eight bob a day as a wireless operator.'

It wasn't so much that he objected to being a go-between and getting Kirkby some drugs – though he did – and certainly not to earning extra money, but the idea of gaining the confidence of people he might not normally care to know, just because he wanted something, was a course he could never take.

'You'll regret it,' Kirkby said.

'I won't.'

'Well,' he smiled, 'you might.'

Brian leaned forward, didn't like to be threatened. 'The only thing I smuggled back from Malaya was an eighteen-inch bayonet, and if you cross my path again with a proposition like that, I'll rip your guts out. I mean it. I wouldn't think twice.'

Kirkby patted him on the shoulder. 'Forget I mentioned it.'

Brian felt a fool at such emotion. 'Go to hell in your own way.'

'I'll see you halfway there, pal.'

'Right.'

'Let's have a whisky, though, for old times' sake.'

'Sure.'

The air was fresh away from Kirkby. He walked down Wheeler Gate and jumped a bus to Radford for a pint in the Jolly Jugglers – no troubles, no past, no expectations, only to sit, and sup, and suppose he would always be what he was, at ease, blank, biding his time, alone, untouched, almost invisible. The pong of Oldsock Twist from a man's pipe made him cough, but it was soothed by a gulp of ale.

The tinkle and thud of a fruit machine was worked by his Aunt Emily. He stood behind her, and she gazed, the wheels of recognition turning. They said about her that though the penny hadn't dropped you could at least hear it moving. You could even see it, Brian thought, if you looked into her pained eyes. 'Are you winning?'

She pulled the handle so hard the machine rocked on its base. Spinning wheels settled at two lemons and a damson, and a dozen pennies clattered into the steel scoop. Half the pub looked up from their tankards as she counted the money into her red handbag. 'You brought me luck.'

She was known in the family as Batchy Em'ler, his mother's backward sister occasionally taken up by rages of bitter passion if she thought someone was mocking her. Her feelings were never to be laughed at, for the strength and conviction of her blacksmith father, mixed with the sentimental passion of her Irish mother, would turn her from a half-sinking dugout canoe into a battleship of the line, the *Rodney* or the *Hood* at least, steaming full speed ahead with a broadside prepared.

He nodded towards the snug. 'I'll buy you half a jar to celebrate your winnings.'

'You've bin away a long time.' She sat down. 'We missed yer.'

'Only a couple of years.'

She tutted. 'I wonder how our Nimrod is, I kept asking Lydia. I think I got on her nerves at times.'

'If you go on like that I'll buy you a gin.'

'I wonder what everybody thinks, me sitting here with a nice young chap like yo'?'

He touched her hand. 'They'll think I've clicked.'

'Did you like being in America?'

'Malaya,' he said.

'Do blackies live there, like in Abyssinia?' She was staring at a respectable clerkly man with a glass of stout beside his *Evening Post*, sitting across the room. 'Yes,' she cried, 'you can look. He stands need to look, a swivel-eyed gett like that. You'd think he'd got nowt better to do than stare at me. Yes, yo', I mean yo', with glasses on. Looking at me like that. You'll get this glass between your eyes if you don't effing-well stop staring at me.'

Brian was embarrassed by her foul mouth, and ordered her

54

to sit down, like a sergeant set to look after her, but she yanked her arm loose. She had worked in the war, when no employer was particular, but even so, she was sometimes out of a job due to her temper, and was then kept in food and pocket money by her sister Lydia.

'It's on'y owd Em having a turn,' someone said at the bar, but the man got up and left.

She sat down. 'Tell me about Malaya, then. I'm ever so interested.'

He described the jungle luridly, till she shivered with horror, and was in no state to complain at being stared at, which was just as well, because he didn't want to get into a fight if anyone objected to her frantic tirade. She put her hand on his wrist. 'When do you go back?'

'Next week.'

'Shall you be gone a long time?'

'Not if I can help it.'

'I wish I was a man who could get called up,' she said. 'I went to join the ATS but they wouldn't 'ave me.'

He stopped himself laughing at the idea of anyone needing poor old Em, and when she looked into his eyes he turned away in case she detected the pain he suddenly felt for her. Even her own family weren't allowed to stare. He jigsawed the story together from innuendoes over the years how at twenty she worked in a hotel as a chambermaid and was raped by one of the guests. Emily was primed to damn him in court, but when someone gleefully told her he'd get sent down for at least five years she wouldn't give evidence. Or the man had a good lawyer. Or both. She was taken in. She was too simple. The child died at birth anyway. He pressed her hand. 'I've got to go. But don't put any more dosh in that fruit machine. You'll only lose it.'

'I know, duck. But I like a bit o' fun. I don't lose much.'

At the door he was impatient to get away. 'Remember me to Aunt Lydia.'

She looked at him. 'Will you write to me?'

He couldn't bear her gaze. She didn't know how to read or write. 'If you like.'

'I've never had a letter in my life.'

55

He put on his greatcoat against the rain, fresh air going straight to his toenails, knowing exactly where he was, where he lived, who he was, who he had been. The night was young, but he stopped himself whistling, for the world was old and so, he felt, was he.

Even Pauline cared enough to ask, when he walked in: 'Where yo' bin all day?'

Her tone implied that though she was glad he hadn't been at home she wasn't very pleased that he had enjoyed being away from it.

'Out,' he said. 'Where did you go?'

She answered with the same word, and there was no more to be said except: 'I'm not staying in tonight, either.'

'Let's go downtown,' he suggested. 'We can sit in Yates's for a while.'

'No thanks.'

'What about the pictures, then?'

She was washed, combed and scented, a ribbon to hold her dark brown hair, five years younger but no longer for him. 'I'm going out on my own. You look after Gary for a change.'

To cajole would be like hitting a wall with your fist, the mood she was in. Telling her about the X-ray had been a mortal insult from which she wouldn't recover while he was in her sight. He'd failed to protect her, and she would never forgive him. But she might have been like this anyway, he thought, remembering Bert's revelation about seeing her with Albert in a pub. He supposed she was off to meet him now. 'Who are you going out with?'

She turned from the mirror. 'It ain't got owt to do with yo'.'

'It has.'

She drew back at the menace in his tone. 'I'm only going to see a pal I used to work with.'

'Where does she live?'

'Cinderhill.' She answered too easily. 'I go every Wednesday. We talk about old times.'

He would soon be gone, and she could perish for all he cared.

'Gary's asleep,' she said. 'If he wakes up, give him a slice of bread and jam. Then he'll go back.'

She looked happy. If she was doing it on him he couldn't

complain, after his long bout with Mimi in Malaya. All the same, he wanted to strangle her, except it would bring them closer together.

He went upstairs and looked at Gary, who had Pauline's dark hair, and a snubbed nose that could have come from anyone.

He sorted the books in his old room. His mother stood in the doorway. 'If there's any you don't want, give 'em to that gel I towd yer about. She likes books.'

He put aside some novels by Walter Scott. 'Take these.'

'It's little print, in't it?'

'Not too little to read.'

She picked them up, unfamiliar with books in her hand. 'Littler than the Bible.'

'If she doesn't read them, she can stand a plant pot on them.'

She held them out. 'Just drop 'em in, on your way by.'

If he didn't she might think he was scared to catch something. In any case he could see what state he might be in if he refused all treatment. 'Why not?'

Books under his arm made him conspicuous. Walking up the street, he intended continuing round the corner to the bus stop and into town. Leave them on her doorstep rather than be troubled, where they would be found and taken in, or washed away by the rain. Books were never thieved around here, he knew, knocking before he realised it.

Like the postman, he rapped again and, poised for a final hard rhythm, heard a bolt go clack, the door scraping over a piece of matting.

A dark-haired, startled woman came to the step. 'Couldn't you have gone round the back?'

He retreated to the pavement, telling her who he was. 'I brought these for Lillian.'

'She's not well.'

He thrust the books at her, wanted to run. 'Can I leave 'em?'

She was worried, her mouth trembling. 'You might have woken her up.'

'How did I know?'

'Yer mam should a towd yer.'

'She did. It was my fault. But I thought I'd say hello.'

57

'Who is it?' a woman's voice cried.

She drew back to close the door. 'Only somebody with some books.'

'Let him come in.'

Her mother relented, as if Lillian's word was law. 'All right. Just for a minute.'

He noticed little about the darkened room except a smell of perfume and medicine, saw her white face, and black hair going over a pillow like the courses of rivers.

Every breath was a shallow cough. 'I'll look at 'em tomorrer.'

He stepped away, guided to the door, her mother wanting to be rid of him. Lillian smiled, a hand out of the sheets that he pushed his way back to touch, unable to speak.

Walking, sleeved by the squalid street, only the lack of books under his arm told him it hadn't been a dream. Her pallid face shielded his eyes, and she had gone into him, the last kind of influence he needed, wanting to go back and tell her he had got TB, so wasn't frightened of catching it from her. He wanted to ask questions, observe closely, listen to her talk, and maybe speak some of the words that were scorching his soul.

Chapter
 ## SIX

He laid his possessions on the table to remind himself who he
was: a wristwatch, a fountain pen, a Bible given to him at
school, the map he had drawn for the expedition to Gunong
Barat, and the waterstained notebook used as a diary. Parts of
the map had worn away with sweat and rain, and he pressed it
to his nose to bring the odour back, opened it and traced the
sinewy hairlines of blue water falling down jungle slopes to join
the stream along which they ascended. Boots sank into rotting
undergrowth, and he drank after holding his bottle under the
water, then watched himself clamber through tangled jungle
laden with rifle and pack as if in a moving photograph of years
ago.

Memory abandoned him, and he stared at the wall, wondering how he came to be where he was, why he couldn't get out
of the trap he had fallen into. Thought was eternal worry,
because he could no longer think and act at the same time.

At half past six his temperature was taken, pulse read. The
orderly had fair wavy hair, seemed asleep under heavy lids, lips
curling as he wrote the score.

'Been in long?' Brian asked.

'Too damned long. Six months, and can't wait to get out.'

'Is it that bad?'

He clinked the thermometer into a glass. 'A waste of my
life.'

'Where did you work before?'

'I didn't. Lounged around in my father's office – for six pounds a week.'

'A skive, eh?'

He rubbed his hands down the white apron. 'You could call it that. I used to bind like hell, and now I wish I was back.' Brian was puzzled at such grumbling, though he had done the same in his time. The orderly walked away: 'I'll send in your tea.'

He put on his dressing gown to go to the bathroom. All his life he had wanted to be alone. Now you are, he told the shaving mirror, so like it. The situation was too interesting to feel lonely. To be alone was to die, but he could not feel dead. An invisible blade severed him from what he had been. He had never been alone, not even for a day, hardly for an hour, yet had always wanted to be, without knowing what he craved. It was one thing to walk alone through forests, and even then, for better or worse, other people would be somewhere, and nature all around. Being free and healthy you were never alone, for in that case there were two of you, and one could talk to the other. In an isolation ward there was too much space to talk to yourself and feel sane.

He spun out the minutes till breakfast: cornflakes, bacon and sausage, bread and butter. On his fourteen-hour nightwatch beyond the runway the nightsweat journeyed between shoulder-blades while his tea cooled, a paraffin smell where the primus flame had licked. Doors were closed because he did not want to be a sitting target for terrorists. The responsibility for life and death lit up his solitude, and he listened for any last message from a kite on a crashlanding course towards the cauliflower tops of the jungle. Through strangulations of static he clicked out a message to Singapore or Bangkok, and the rhythmical squeak of reassurance that he wasn't alone bounced back into the spherical drum of his earphones. Winding the handle of the field telephone, a voice answered from the glow of the control tower a few hundred yards away, and standing at the door he would hear wind hissing in the elephant grass. In kids' talk with Bert they had agreed how good it would be to live in a hut far from folk or family, and now he looked on the reality of his wireless hut as an ideal existence, never to be taken from him as long as it was not forgotten.

He read, or wrote letters. At half past ten the orderly came in with coffee. He picked up a book called *Many Cargoes*, and while he read the walls receded, and he made his own film out of the stories. A day was like a year. The grey dressing gown was a new garment for him, in which he walked up and down like a convalescing soldier, glancing left and right to ensure that none of the empty beds had been stolen. He paced the ward five hundred times, for whatever the tests proved he had to convince himself that he was not ill, to replace the pressure of the steel claw at his brain with an ache in his legs. If an orderly looked in, he would stroll back to bed as if finally bored by the view from the window.

His bed, third on the left, was made daily, while the eleven that were vacant stayed ready for other suspects of contagion. He sat in his dressing gown, staring emptily. Dud thoughts like inferior fireworks burned for a second and went out, disturbed when his dinner of vegetables and roast beef, currant pie and custard was brought in. The meals were small, but he wasn't hungry afterwards, because food was fuel, neither to be praised nor complained about. Waking from an after-dinner doze he reached for *The War of the Worlds* and read until tea and bread and butter was set before him.

Similar huts surrounded his own, hard to say where he was, clouds running between eaves like sheep, could be anywhere in England, though he felt no connection, occupied his own cul-de-sac, body and spirit balanced on the razor's edge of a path, an endless sea to either side, talking to no one, as if everyone ever known, out of consideration for his feelings, had left him to hang on to life by himself.

Supper at six was spam fritters, boiled potatoes and salad, stewed prunes. The orderly collected his plates: 'It's better than we get in the mess.'

Between life and death you had no choice, could not avoid breathing, existed in a time-scheme so looked at the clock – and wished himself out of it. At thirteen, in the woods with his pals, he climbed a tree, swung up from the lower branches, glorying in distance from the ground. Leaves shivered and clouds elbowed by, his grip sure, plimsolls slotting into each separation of twig or stump, a kingdom he controlled absolutely. From the upper branches his body hit the ground, shaking every gram of blood, his mates astounded at the thump of his flesh bomb. A false footing had been made, and the half stun of his fall shook the memory out of him. Maybe nothing was sudden, though it seemed everything was. They laughed when he stood up undamaged.

His body betrayed him then as it did now, and the question as to what had caused it was repeated over and over, a carborundum wheel grinding his brain to powder, though the brain was continually renewed and wouldn't leave him in mindless peace.

After a mug of Ovaltine he looked forward to lights-out, when he could accept the luxury of oblivion. In the morning a paper cup was set on his bedside table. 'What's that for?'

'You're to gob into it,' the orderly said. 'They'll test you for TB.'

'When do I know?'

'A couple of weeks.'

'Why does it take that long?'

'They've got to culture it.'

'I see.'

'You're due for another X-ray this afternoon.'

They still weren't sure, as if in a few days the jovial Welsh medical officer would come into the ward and say get dressed, you can go, we're sorry we made a mistake, but we had to be sure, and don't hold it against us, it was all for the best, the air force looks after its own, especially those who did their duty in Malaya. The words were endlessly repeated, but like a leper he spat his soul into the paper cup.

A dark cloud with an edge as sharp as a chisel lay against a white cloud as if to slit it open. He smelled fresh air, then shut the window. Water beat at the panes, new off the ocean, dividing the ward even more from what was outside.

In control of life's decisions, he was a jailer and a prisoner because he was free to request his clothes and walk out, a fact more tormenting than the iron claw which gripped his temples when he endlessly discussed whether to go or stay, a contest so even-handed he sat gazing at the green wall which, when he blinked, changed to a pale wash of blue.

The ward was a prison, his affliction another, himself and the affliction in eternal conflict. Opening his Bible, a lion plodded around the pit with Daniel in its mouth. No one could say who he was if he did not know it himself, and because of the enormous clothbound ball that pressed on him he knew even less who he was, became so many different people that nothing mattered except whether it rained or not. He had no calendar but kept account of the date, knowing that he had been in the place three days.

In Malaya a Sunday boat took them to a beach on Tiger Island where they swam. They passed a row of leper colony huts between palm trees, curiosity silent as they sailed by. He never saw people, they were hidden away, forced into seclusion lest they infect, or shock with their wounds.

The effort of trying to speak the word distorted his lips. In summer when he was eight he leaned over the fence at the Nook to watch Aunt Lydia's bloke coming up the lane, a tall and bewildered man wearing an overcoat and white scarf, helped along with a stick, dying from TB.

Shame fanned him like a blowlamp, and he craved the time when he had not been tainted. Without the X-ray he would have gone obliviously back into the factory, but he had made his own way into isolation instead of being carried on a stretcher bleeding to death from bomb or bullet – which was like strolling into prison instead of being handcuffed and driven in a Black Maria.

He dozed against the infiltration of the afternoon, body and mind locked in futile attrition, blaming each other for the disaster that had pole-axed him. He had fallen from an enormous height, couldn't understand, struggled to discern cause and effect even while manoeuvring the parachute of hope to land in the green comb of the Wiltshire hills.

He paced as close to the beds as possible, the rectangular shape of his walk an alteration that gave an illusion of free will. Countless circuits later he stared out of the window at the emerging moon. The almanack said that when he came a week ago the planet Venus was at its greatest elongation. At the same

63

time a new moon had formed, and the moon now in its first quarter had Jupiter in conjunction, so that Venus and Moon and Jupiter beamed on him as he opened a pack of foolscap pages to write about Gunong Barat, map and diary recalling progress towards a summit never reached.

Knotman and I first thought of the idea and discussed the practicability of it over a cup of coffee in the NAAFI, one night towards the end of March. The possibility of it grew more and more real as our discussion progressed, and we concluded on a note of high determination to carry the idea to its practical end if we could obtain the co-operation required.

What we had in mind was to organise an expedition of approximately six men from the camp, who were willing to accompany us to the summit of Gunong Barat, a mountain isolated from the main range of mountains forming the background of Malaya, situated twenty miles north of Kota Libis. The actual summit, which was nearly four thousand feet high, took the form of a jagged piece of rock, visible from the camp when not obscured by cloud.

Within a short space of time the whole form of the expedition took shape. We were assured of the backing of the officers of the station, and had no difficulty in obtaining six men to form the expedition. Knotman and I paid a visit to the Survey Office on Muong Island, and obtained a one-inch map of the area, and at the same time were fortunate in having an interview with the Chief Surveyor. From him we gathered that the seventy square miles of the mountain area were covered entirely in dense jungle. Apart from this, the information on the map, and some scanty notes on its geological structure, obtained from Muong Library, very little else was known on the area. In an interview with the District Surveyor, who had climbed Gunong Barat in 1939, he said that it would be impossible to ascend the mountain from the south, as we proposed, because the jungle was extremely thick and the ascent very steep. Also, he informed us that tigers were known to inhabit the jungle on its slopes. After this interview, two things were decided upon. First, that we should go armed, and second, that we should attempt the Peak from the south.

On the morning of June 12th there was a slight breeze blowing in from the sea, as a fifteen hundredweight lorry with six of us on board left RAF Kota Libis at eight thirty and travelled north. Apart from myself our party consisted of Jack the Welshman, Kirkby, Flt/Lt Odgeson, Corporal Len Knotman, and Baker, all of us from signals except Odgeson who was a dental surgeon.

I'd drawn several maps on an enlarged scale of the area to be explored and also supervised the collection of navigation instruments, while Knotman organised all other stores, knives, firearms, and numerous items of essential equipment. All members received a typhus inoculation and took anti-malarial tablets for fourteen days before, until fourteen days after the expedition. We tried to secure a portable wireless set to take with us, but unfortunately this extra safety precaution was not to be had. The Station Catering Officer provided our party with a comprehensive scale of rations. The armoury let us have two .303 service rifles and a twelve-bore shotgun, with fifty rounds of ammunition for each.

We arrived at the Dam, which lay at the Southern Approaches to the Mountain, at ten minutes to eleven, and waved farewell to the lorry, which returned to camp, and began loading our packs. Our dress consisted of bush hats, bush shirts, slacks and mosquito boots. Also, we wore full webbing, with water bottle and small pack attached, besides carrying a shotgun, rifle or machete, and ammunition. Each of us carried two dozen tins of food in our big packs, which made them full to capacity and extremely heavy. The total equipment of each man must have weighed something in the region of seventy pounds.

At eleven fifteen, with our packs on our backs, we moved forward in single file, northwards, along the rocky bed of the stream. Progress was extremely slow, this state of affairs being brought about by the fact that the weight of our packs, and the slipperiness of the slime-covered rocks below the surface of the water tended to make our balance somewhat precarious. Within the first hour, several members of the party, including myself, had overbalanced and floundered with full kit into nearly a foot of cold water. Also, I had to dispose of the drawing board on to which the maps were pinned, as it was hindering my progress.

The shallow stream was still wide enough for the sky to be seen between the trees. By half past twelve we came upon a small island of rocks formed by two arms of the stream, and decided to have some lunch. Wood was found in abundance, and we soon had a blazing fire, on which rested two tins of meat-and-vegetable, and mess tins of water for tea. After this repast, we rested and smoked cigarettes. Knotman had been in the jungle before, and so Odgeson said he would be in charge of the climb from now on.

By two, we continued our trek along the bed of the stream, but after a short time called another halt before a waterfall, at the foot of which was a large pool of inviting, crystal clear water. The temptation was not to be resisted. We all stripped down and spent a glorious half hour swimming.

All too soon, about three o'clock, we dressed and pushed on. After half an hour, the stream took shape into a deep ravine. As a pathway, it was unnegotiable, so we were forced to bypass it by cutting up through the jungle to a height of two or three hundred feet, and advance parallel to the stream below. Just after quitting the stream to execute this plan, it started to rain, not heavily, but a light continuous drizzle, which soaked us to the skin during our upward climb.

During the trek through the jungle, our machetes were in constant use. We literally hacked a pathway back to the stream. The going was rather strenuous, and we rested several times. By five o'clock, we had passed the ravine, and emerged from the jungle, wet, covered in a dark brown soil, and very weary, to the stream.

We found a relatively flat piece of rock just by the stream and decided to make a camp for the night. From the nearby jungle, we collected as much wood and bamboo as possible, in order to keep a fire going all night.

On unloading our kit, almost every item was found to be either wet or very damp. Several tins of cigarettes and many boxes of matches were ruined and had to be thrown away. Taffy found that he had lost two of his pipes in coming through the jungle and had broken his third and last one; however, he mended this by using some sticking plaster from Odgeson's first aid kit.

After a meal of potatoes, meat-and-vegetable, we took off some of our clothing to dry. We found several bloated leeches on our bodies, but got rid of them very quickly with the hottest end of a cigarette. The next task was to make two beds, to sleep two men in each, the other two being on guard. Each consisted of two groundsheets, on top of which were two blankets doubled to sleep on, and one to put over us. Above all this, suspended from overhanging vegetation, were two mosquito nets, and so, at seven o'clock, thoroughly tired, four of us (the other two mounting guard) turned in for a few hours' sleep.

During the changing of the watch at midnight, a large cat-like animal was observed on the opposite side of the stream, about fifty feet above the camp. We fired a few shots from the rifles in its direction, and it slunk away into the jungle.

The following morning, Sunday, 13th June, I, being on guard at the time, aroused the camp at half past six. While the others proceeded to cook the breakfast, I took the compass, and managed to take a bearing on Bukit Karong Besar, a mountain lying to our south-east, thus confirming our position to be some thirteen hundred yards up from the Dam, at a height of nine hundred feet.

After a breakfast of beans, bacon, biscuits and hot sweet tea, we broke camp and fastened up our packs, and at nine o'clock were on our way upstream. Within the first half hour, we all had our feet wet. Soon after, we came upon the first waterfall, after which we came upon others which we either scaled direct, or bypassed by cutting up through the jungle. All of us had long sores on our backs where the tins of food in our big packs had rubbed. Fortunately we were blessed with fine weather, but the going was still arduous, and progress slow. We decided against having a midday meal so as to save time in unpacking and repacking the kit. The meal scheme was a light breakfast, with biscuits, water and a little ration chocolate at various times during the day, and a large evening meal upon making camp in the evening.

Having found a suitable space on the right bank of the stream at half past four in the afternoon, we called a halt and made camp.

There being no known terrestrial objects in view upon which I could take any compass bearings to define our geographical position with any degree of accuracy, I estimated, taking our rate of progress into consideration, that our present camp lay some thirteen hundred yards upstream from our last camp, thus placing us some fifteen hundred feet above sea level.

Having found an abundant supply of wood, we lit two fires, some twenty yards apart, with the camp in between, having one sentry at each fire. After an extra big meal of meat-and-vegetable, carrots, potatoes, peas, fruit pudding and tea, again thoroughly tired, I turned in. Baker and I were on guard between twelve and two during the night, each sitting down near a fire. Suddenly, while I was feeding the fire with wood, I heard a scuffle, followed by the report of a shotgun from the direction of the fire at which Baker was standing guard. Upon enquiring what was the matter, it appeared that a snake of about four feet in length had uncoiled itself, rather foolishly, near his feet and promptly received the attention of the business end of Baker's twelve-bore shotgun which he always carried.

The day was Monday, 14th June, and by half past six the camp was astir. Breakfast consisted of a mug of tea and a piece of fruit pudding each. We spent some time boiling water with which to fill our water bottles, because we had run out of water-sterilising tablets.

At half past eight our northward trek was resumed, through jungle and upstream. Better progress was made. At one place during the morning we caught a glimpse of the Peak, two thousand feet above us, but lost sight of it after a few minutes as it became obscured by cloud. Later, while resting, Taffy took a shot at a sparrow at a hundred yards' range with a .303 rifle, and brought it down. When retrieved, it was found to have been hit through the neck, almost severing its head from its body.

Just after midday, we found ourselves at the base of a series of imposing waterfalls, rising vertically skywards for several hundred feet. We stood and gazed in awe at this sight of might, beauty and majestic splendour, of water cascading from the sky, falling down a green limestone cliff from ledge to ledge, to finally form a pool of lusciously clear water where we were standing. Several shots were taken with the camera, but unfortunately the film was damp and could not be developed, although I doubt that a camera could convey any idea of the grandeur of the scene.

After a somewhat prolonged rest, we undertook the task of hacking our way through the jungle, and climbing upwards in order to outflank the waterfalls. Fallen trees that blocked our path were cylinders of purple soil under the bark. Our boots went in. They were completely rotten.

When we finally emerged from the jungle, Taffy, who was the first one out, saw a lizard-like iguana, some three or four feet long from head to tail, but before anyone else had time to see it, it disappeared into the undergrowth.

Later on in the afternoon, we had another glimpse of the Peak, which seemed considerably nearer than when we saw it in the morning.

By five o'clock, we found a camp site on a ledge of rock overlooking the valley of the Sungei Bujang. The stream itself was by now a mere trickle, but adequate to supply our needs for the night. In the surrounding jungle there was a noticeable shortage of dead wood for the fire, so we had to manage on live wood as well, and even then had only enough to keep a small fire for the night. Our position, calculated after the conclusion of the expedition, was eighteen hundred yards beyond our last camp on the Sungei Bujang, at a height of some two thousand two hundred feet.

The first hot meal for thirty hours of hard going was cooked by Len Knotman. By seven, when it began to get dark, four of us turned in, and I for one fell asleep immediately. Before it got dark we found a large insect, resembling a grasshopper, with a body about two inches in length and one inch in diameter. From this nucleus, coloured light green, were spread feelers several inches long. It was crawling along a slab of rock on which we intended spreading one of the beds, so it was found necessary to get rid of this unwelcome visitor. Len Knotman hit it with the butt of a rifle, but it only squeaked, and continued to roam over our camping space. Baker solved the problem by firing at it with the twelve bore. That was the last we saw of it.

In the morning, Tuesday 15th, the whole camp arose at six o'clock so as to move off as early as possible, as on this day we were to leave the stream and make a determined assault up the escarpment and attempt to camp that night on the Peak itself.

After breakfast, and filling all the water bottles, we advanced up the trickle which was the Sungei Bujang. A lot of trees had fallen across it. By nine o'clock we left the stream bed which was dried up, and cut off in a north-easterly direction for the Peak. The vegetation near the stream was extremely thick and thorny, and during our upward climb, through this and away from the dry watercourse, we sustained many cuts and scratches. The cuts and scratches sustained on our way through the jungle on the lower reaches had made four of our party incapable of wielding a machete and so progress was rather slow.

However, as we left the stream further behind, so the vegetation thinned out and we were climbing at a faster rate than at any other time so far. For the next five hours we climbed vigorously, resting occasionally for a swallow of water and a biscuit. We made jokes about the escarpment in *The Lost World*, and seeing pterodactyls floating around. After midday, we really began to climb, being now on the main escarpment, rising up to meet the Peak. In places, the vegetation disappeared to reveal sheer cliff, which we circuited, making sure to keep to the vegetation as much as possible so as to avoid unnecessary risks. At one place we came across a belt of almost solid thorn undergrowth. We could find no way around it, so we were forced to spend over an hour hacking through it.

By half past four in the afternoon, we found ourselves at a height of three thousand nine hundred feet, only some eighty feet or so below the ultimate objective of the expedition, the summit of Gunong Barat. But we found ourselves unable to climb any further because it was sheer rock, and we needed climbing gear to scale it. We had anticipated finding vegetation almost to the Peak, and then after a little rock scrambling, to find ourselves on the summit itself, but this was not so. I took off my pack and did a little scouting, but could find no path to the Peak. It would have been possible to have reached it by descending a few hundred feet and approaching it from a different direction, but this would take time, probably more than a day, and then we may still be forced back, and there was one ominous fact to be considered, that of water. Since we left the stream the same morning our supplies of this precious commodity had slowly but surely dwindled and if we rationed ourselves very carefully we had only some eighteen hours' supply left in our water bottles for all six men. In view of this situation, we decided upon falling back to the nearest supply of water, which was the source of the Sungei Bujang. We were bitterly disappointed at not being able to reach the actual Peak, but did derive some consolation that, had we been in possession of the proper equipment, it could have been done. Thus it is not impossible to scale Gunong Barat from the south.

We acted immediately on our plans to retrace our tracks to the water, and by four thirty began the descent, so as to get as much of a start as possible on the race for water which, we estimated, we should reach by the afternoon of the following day.

At five o'clock we came upon a ledge several feet wide, and decided it was as good a camping site as we would be likely to find on the escarpment, and so took off our kit and began making the beds. To do this, we had to stamp down the undergrowth and level the area off with rocks. Then we put down the groundsheets and made two beds in the usual fashion, only tonight there would be three men in a bed, as it was unnecessary to maintain a guard, and also impracticable.

All the surrounding vegetation was wet, and we had no paper, so it was impossible to light a fire. We put our mugs under some moss on a bit of cliff, and water dripped into them, but not much. It began to rain, a fine drizzle. We were cold, and to sustain ourselves opened a tin of jam to go with the hard tack biscuits. Then we opened a tin of carrots to share out, and drank the water from the tin, but it was salty. Despite the cold, and our bed of rocks, we managed to get a little sleep.

I was lying awake in the undergrowth at half past five the next morning, waiting for the dawn, after one of the most uncomfortable nights I have ever spent. For breakfast, we ate some biscuits and the remainder of the jam, with a little water. Later, we were able to obtain a very fine view of North Malaya. We took photographs of this, but they did not come out either.

When we had taken up the ground sheets and bedding, we found an adder lying there. Apparently we had slept on it all night, and it was quite dead!

We began our dash for water at half past eight. Going down naturally proved much easier than the ascent, and we made fine progress for the first hour or so, following the trail we blazed coming up. Unfortunately, we lost this later, and found ourselves on the brink of a precipice, falling sheer away from us in a several hundred foot drop. The trouble was that you couldn't see these obstacles until you actually stumbled upon them, because the vegetation, although not so dense as on the lower slopes, prevented you from seeing more than a few yards.

On the ascent, we were continually 'making easting' to reach the Peak from the watercourse, and so on the descent we would need to 'make westing' to hit the water, but apparently we hadn't made enough westing, and found ourselves with sheer rock stretching below us, and also rising up about three hundred feet to our right, thus blocking our route to the west, and water.

To overcome this, we had to undertake the exhausting task of reclimbing several hundred feet until we found a small ledge across the rockface. The scanty bushes which grew out of the rock helped us a little. Len Knotman was the first to attempt the crossing. We stood watching him, literally feeling his way over. The rockface fell away for hundreds of feet. Small bushes of heather grew out of the rock itself in certain places. Above him, broken only by ledges similar to this one, was the same scenery.

There was the sound of the sliding of studs on granite. He had slipped. The rustling of dry shrubbery. We could see his head. He had caught hold of some heather, twenty feet below the ledge. Tortuously slow, with beads of sweat breaking out all over his face, making footholds in seemingly impossible places, he clawed his way back to that precarious ledge, and felt his way over to the other side. Then he made several more journeys across and we made a human chain until every man and his equipment was safe on the other side.

We scaled many minor cliff-faces during the expedition, but this was by far the most dangerous. In many other cases Len Knotman, poet and adventurer, from Vancouver, Canada, showed examples of resource and sacrifice, scaling rockfaces first, and always carrying the heaviest pack.

Having overcome this obstacle, progress was much faster and more straightforward, although our thirst was by now intense, having had little water since setting out in the morning. We had to go carefully with the water, in case we had difficulty finding the stream. Slithering down through the undergrowth, I saw the tail of a brown snake getting out of the way.

At about half past two, after cutting our way through thickening vegetation, we came upon the dried up bed of a stream. After following it down for just over half an hour I, being at the head of the file in which we were advancing, carrying the compass and trying to follow a bearing, spotted water gushing out of the earth, and volubly flowing down the stream-bed. This sight was greeted with enthusiasm. We discarded our packs and webbing and proceeded to drink our fill. We ate a few biscuits and some ration chocolate, and had a fifteen minute rest. The position of this spring on the map is 096.157. Knotman said he now knew how Moses felt. I said that my navigation had got us to it.

We tramped alongside the stream and the water became more voluble as we progressed, with a few tributaries joining here and there. Later, we cut through the jungle to avoid the series of vertical waterfalls which we encountered on the third day of the ascent. After bypassing a minor waterfall, we came upon a few square yards' clearance in the form of a bed of rocks, having the appearance of an island, being almost surrounded by two arms of the stream.

The time being a little after half past four, we decided to use this as the camping site for the night.

Upon discarding our webbing, we all set about various tasks, gathering of wood, making the fire, fixing up the beds, and later, preparing an extra special evening meal, being the first hot food for forty-eight hours. We sat around the fire smoking and talking until dusk, then, except for the guards, we turned in. I was lying on my back looking up at the stars, then I was asleep. It rained a little during the night, but not enough to disturb our sleep. Baker and I, being on guard at dawn, made tea, and roused the others at six thirty with same. For breakfast, we opened a tin of pears and a tin of cream.

Feeling absolutely fit after some hot food and a night's sleep, we began to make our way down the stream bed by eight o'clock. We more or less retraced our tracks down the Sungei Bujang. I checked the tributaries off on my map. Progress was good, and by eleven we sat ourselves down for a rest at the site of our second night's camp.

At midday we cut up into the jungle to avoid some sheer falls, and then the rains came. It rained as it can only rain in the tropics. I think we all felt pretty grim. Absolutely wet through to the skin, half hacking, half slithering through the rotten stinking vegetation, blinded by that torrential downpour of rain. In this area of mountain jungle, there is not one native inhabitant. It is understandable.

At one o'clock, the rain had ceased, and we emerged from the jungle to find ourselves at our first night's camp. We rested here, and stripped off our upper clothing to burn off some of the leeches. The rain had caused the stream to swell considerably. A silver Avro Anson flew overhead, on its way to Burma, we thought. We waved, but knew it couldn't see us in this forest.

Half an hour later, we set off again, and had to enter the jungle once more so as to avoid the deep ravine which we encountered on the first day's ascent. The subsoil was almost all washed away by the rain, and made our downward path treacherous in the extreme. However, with the help of the undergrowth, we eventually found ourselves back at the stream, at its lower reaches, not far from the Dam.

Our progress was again impeded to some extent owing to the stream being so swiftly flowing. We had the water swirling around our waists in places, instead of around our knees. By half past three we felt hungry, so stopped for a cold meal of biscuits, meat-and-vegetable.

From now on it was plain sailing, and just after four o'clock we had reached the Dam, from where we had originally started our assault on the Peak. We must have looked a bedraggled crew as we emerged towards the native house just beyond the Dam. Our clothes were mudstained and torn. Our arms were covered in scratches, and my boots at least were almost off my feet. Six days' wear had rotted them through. We still had some tins of food left.

There was a telephone in the Forestry House, so Flt/Lt Odgeson contacted RAF Kota Libis for transport to come and get us. Then we began the monotonous and weary walk of three and a half miles through the Bukit Tupah rubber estate to the main road where, after a few minutes, a truck arrived to take us back to camp, where we arrived less than an hour later, weary and tired, but in high spirits.

The scratching pen, the trail of script, the inky smell that never changed – writing took a week, each word properly spelled, every step of the trip measured – as far as it was possible to recollect. The idea of the excursion had been mulled on during long night watches in the paddi field, before talking to Knotman and Baker. He collated lists of equipment, calculated supplies of food, worked out a route from the map, and solicited the CO's permission to form a team that would search for the crews of any plane that crashed in the jungle. For the Kota Libis Jungle Rescue Unit the expedition to Gunong Barat would be a dummy run. The CO told them he did not want any responsibility for them getting lost or injured. Brian said it was unlikely they would go missing if they had a compass, and with the maps he had drawn. But the CO had flown over the area: 'It's as rugged as hell. There could be accidents.' Knotman gave his advice, and promised to look after them – as if they were kids. The CO saw they were keen, so talked Flight-Lieutenant Odgeson into going with them. He also stipulated that they take wireless so as to keep in touch by W/T. They must also apply for leave, and go on their own responsibility. No one would carry the can except themselves.

The Malayan Emergency started while they were away, planters getting popped off by terrorists all over the place, so the CO had to report them missing to SEAC at Singapore. An Avro Anson was sent to look for them. Just the CO's luck. They couldn't have cared less. They were all right, Jack. The radio hadn't been ready, so they had left without it; panic and flap was the order of the day. A lorry of Malay Regiment blokes was sent to look for them, but they went to the wrong place, and after a hundred-yard dash into the forest blowing whistles they turned back.

He had marched up and down the room with Fred's Diana air rifle, wanting to be one of Custer's men, a Bengal Lancer, or a Sherwood Forester in France. Some talk of Alexander and such great names as these, of Hector and Lysander – but Fred punched him for playing with his gun. Then he wanted to be a surveyor, a tin miner, a rubber planter, to live in half-explored regions out of touch with England. Compared to expeditions in Borneo the excursion up Gunong Barat was like an afternoon's outing in Serpents Wood, and he felt abashed at writing about it, but at least he had slept in what was marked as jungle on the maps, dreamed of since that first childhood book whose lore burned into his soul and said that a crowded hour of glorious life was worth an age without a name.

Steel claws gripped his temples like those in the glass cage at a funfair that you manoeuvred over a heap of novelties in the hope of clutching a prize. But you never got one, because the claws were weak, the aim too random. Now, he himself was inside the glass, though he was not such a prize that the claws would crush him. He kept a hold on himself and endured, took one step at a time, and never considered any matter unless it could help him to be still without burrowing under the earth to escape from himself. He got through the day by dodge and subterfuge, giving a tactical consideration to each minute so as to pack hours out of the way, time once gone never to come back.

Unable to sleep, he dreamed of creepers and decomposing trees, and blades of water waving down cliff-faces enlarged by memory's infallible magnifying glass. They grasped at bushes to get their laden bodies up, then slithered their way down through red mud back to the stream – to the softened drone of a searching plane.

The jungle was a place where you could be as much at home as in any maze of streets. The struggle to reach Gunong Barat had been so arduous that the spirit was ignored, whereas writing about it wiped out all awareness of the physical self. But stringing words together so as to bring back reality caused

74

irritation rather than a sense of struggle. The jungle had inflicted a deadly bite by drawing him through the valley of the shadow, and had scarred him with something that would change him absolutely.

The thought passed quickly, but not before telling himself that he would never struggle to gain understanding. Even more than your body might die if you entered into a struggle, a mean and petty contest, because though he may have struggled all his life, at least he had not been aware of it.

Light decreased in overhead bulbs as if the generator had been drained by too much demand, but his essay on the climb up Gunong Barat became a powerhouse never to vanish in the darkness.

The black-haired Welsh doctor, laughing eyes in a gaunt face, a regular finger-flick at his left ear as if to castigate it because he was fed up with the things it heard, said that the X-ray had not changed its spots. 'It's a leopard of an X-ray,' he smiled. 'They mostly are, I'm afraid.'

He made the same daft joke to everyone, but since he was a flight-lieutenant you couldn't give him any cheek. 'How much longer will I be here, sir?'

'We'll wait for the sputum result to be cultured, but I wouldn't set much hope on that. You'll know where you stand, at least.'

He was a doctor, so might well know what he was talking about.

'Are you being looked after all right?'

He said that he was.

'No complaints about the food?'

'No, sir.' He fixed the MO's eyes, insubordinate or not, couldn't care less. 'What will my treatment be?'

'Bed rest, I believe. Bed rest, and then more bed rest. We won't know for some time. If you respond to bed rest, and it clears up, maybe you'll need nothing else. Otherwise, we shall have to see. I can't say fairer than that, though believe me, I would if I could.' His restless eyes saw the sheets of writing on the table. 'A long letter, is it?'

'Yes, sir.'

'Keep at it, then. We'll know in a few days whether you'll

be going to a civilian sanatorium, or to our own hospital in Berkshire.'

'I'd rather not go to a civilian place, sir.'

'You wouldn't? Well, well!'

'If there's any option.' Nothing would hold him should he be cast among ordinary civilians in a shabby lazar-house.

The MO sensed his horror. 'We'll see what we can do, Seaton.'

Maybe the MO was right. His narrative would become the longest letter he'd written if he put Dear So-and-so at the head and tacked Yours Sincerely at the end. He'd ask the orderly to get him a big envelope, and think of someone to send it to.

Edgeworth who owned the factory he had worked in before joining up was a first class mechanical engineer. The same as his workmen, he'd left school at fourteen, and had been taught by his father. Brian had never been in awe of him, because Edgeworth wore a boiler suit like the rest of them, viewing finished goods, or turning out some special piece on his own gleaming centre lathe just inside the door.

He was bulky and bull-headed, straight grey hair combed back. The factory was set at the end of a cul-de-sac of small houses, by a railway line in the Meadows. Edgeworth's wife came in to work because she was bored, and had to contribute something to the war effort like everybody else. Thin and severe-looking, she was so pale you would think she was bloodless, though when Edgeworth walked across and laid a sud-stained hand at her waist she said something that sent a crimson rush to the back of his neck. The lads said she only came in to see that he didn't get off with that lovely Portuguese refugee who hardly talked to anybody.

Brian made pieces on his capstan lathe, and when the Cincinatti machine replaced the clapped out British object, the piece of work for Rolls-Royce had to be modified. Each operation usually came with a blueprint, with measurements to work from, but the toolsetter hadn't bothered to get one from Derby, or Derby had forgotten to send it, so Brian, knowing it was a rush job, took the piece home, cleared the kitchen table after supper, spread a sheet of graph paper, got pencil, pen and ink, ruler, compasses and protractor, as well as a depth gauge and micrometer borrowed from the bench, and in a couple of hours made a blueprint to pin before his machine. Edgeworth asked if he'd thought of going to night school to learn mechanical engineering. 'We can get you into a reserved occupation. Then you won't be called up, providing you keep up your attendances.'

If he had agreed he might now have been a toolsetter earning a good wage. Maybe Pauline wouldn't have got pregnant, and so we wouldn't be married. I wouldn't have gone to Malaya, and ended up in a transit ward wondering whether I'd go to a civvy sanatorium or a military hospital.

But here he was, and his letter to Edgeworth would say: 'I thought you might like to read the enclosed, and I hope all is well, and is Nottingham the same wild place on Saturday night, and just as dead on Sunday morning?'

He would mention that he was ill, but not that he'd ever call to see if he could have his old job back. He'd be lucky to get set on as a nightwatchman, because from now on he was separated from the world like oil from water, dots from dashes – the sick from the fit. Why he chose Edgeworth to send his manuscript to he couldn't say, except that it would have to be to someone who hadn't been to Malaya, who didn't know the jungle, who wouldn't get bored after two lines and chuck it out with the rubbish, and who might envy him the experience and halfway thank him for having written the account at all. In any case, he knew no one else to send it to.

The bed was a better sleeping place than a shapeless patch of jungle, or a friendless palliasse, or a ropy charpoy, or a canvas hammock, or the sagging marriage bed in which two people had never any hope of becoming themselves. Its plain mattress was his last refuge and, stretched out for sleep, he was on a beach of ash and clinker beating time to the sluggish waves with a piece of stick. Belsen pyjamas were plastered to his skin with sweat, the button of the sun almost the same colour as the sky.

The orderly put his morning tea on the bedtable. 'You're going tomorrow.'

He sat up. 'That's sudden.'

'It always is.'

'Where to, then?'

'Berkshire – a land flowing with milk and honey. Very sunny – when it's not raining.'

'You don't say?'

'The MO just told me.'

'Is it a civvy place?'

'No. It's the best RAF hospital. I almost wish it was me. My folks are in Reading.'

'Do you want to change places?'

'Like in *The Tale of Two Cities*? I'll have to think about it. But you'd better stay up the rest of the day and get the use of your legs back. You'll be taking the train on your own.'

The smell of air at the window reminded him of spring, primed with hope for the long summer, the sort his body had sensed as a kid, unable to put it into words. After weeks of wet feet, and cold misery at home, he would get up one morning and smell mild air even through the fixed windowpane, air telling of spring and optimism, like now – until he remembered that it was autumn, and that winter was on its way.

Chapter

❧ SEVEN

Half a dozen airmen climbed over the back. He didn't know what made him look. Anything that moved was interesting. A pilot officer stepped from the cab, and the other ranks drew out a coffin draped with a Union Jack, and marched with it ceremonially on their shoulders through the station entrance to an open luggage van on the platform.

A civilian, with briefcase and walking stick, took off his hat. Brian stood to attention and saluted, the cloudy autumn day playing the 'Dead March' from *Saul* in his brain, and making him feel good to be alive. Someone had died, beyond care or caring, no doubt an old sweat who had filled in his final clearance chit, or a pilot who had pranged his kite on the aerodrome, its gleaming belly sliding up the runway into death. He asked a bod getting back in the truck what had happened.

'He died, Tosh.' Straightened his cap. 'What they all die from up there.' He gave a cough. 'He was only nineteen.'

Brian offered him a cigarette, while the officer got a receipt for his cargo. 'You're stationed at the hospital, then?'

'Yes, mate.'

'What's it like?'

'A cushy billet, I suppose.'

'I'm on my way there,' Brian told him.

'You're a patient?'

'I expect I shall be.' The man was smart and well-creased, his moustache a mark of long service. Brian was split between envy of his unthinking attachment to air force life, and pity for the person who no longer had any problems because his body was loaded on to the train for going home. Not knowing who he would rather be, he did not have to be either, so was luckier than both.

He idled around the town, knowing he wouldn't be back for a while, bought a clothbacked ordnance map so as to mull on the landscape as he lay in bed, and a paperback of *The Odyssey* – drawn by the title and brown cover. In a café his last Malayan cheroot tasted of hot sun and the mangrove reek of over-ripe bananas. A man at the next table reading a racing paper sniffed as if it was a crime to enjoy it. Cigars were for the well off, and ponged of old socks and horse shit. He went on smoking, thinking that if he told the waitress where he was going she'd break his cup and saucer.

The bus hauled its carcase up the green–sleeved road, showing round a bend at the top water towers and billets and hospital blocks among neat lawns and the crestline of the Downs.

An RAF standard flew from a pole, the familiar rig of a camp, and a corporal by the guardroom pointed him to a reception office. The general duties clerk turned to a shelf and collected white shirt, pyjamas, bedjacket, socks, dressing gown and eating irons.

'Ward Eleven.'

The extreme desire was – to be on nobody's list, nothing to receive and nothing to sign for. 'What sort of a place is that?'

'TB negative. They test you, classify you.'

He wondered when they would stop fucking around and say whether he'd got it or not. A month since the first X-ray, if they didn't know by now, how could he? He was tempted to drop the items he'd signed for and run, over the Downs and far away. The dream of a fugitive played itself out. You didn't do anything you thought about. He should know by now. As soon as he started to think, he knew he wouldn't act. He didn't think about continuing to stand where he was, so that's what he did. Nor did he consider following the clerk to Ward Eleven, and that too was what he did.

The clerk carried his kitbag and case between the flowerbeds, beyond two-storeyed blocks to a zone of prefabricated barrack wards where he imagined 'All hope abandon, ye who enter here' engraved in spooky lettering above the lintel of the one they stopped at. Pans and cutlery clattered, and the sound of voices as if coming from a pub, with Richard Tauber singing 'Long ago and far away' on the wireless.

A stout blonde nursing sister in a grey headdress showed him a locker in a sideroom for his uniform, told him to take what he fancied from his kit. 'You won't be needing much for a while. What's your name?'

'Seaton.'

'I mean your first name. And you address me as Sister, by the way.'

Bollocks, he said to himself. 'Brian, Sister.'

'When you've finished I'll show you your bed. We kept a meal for you, though you should have been here earlier.'

He hoped she would go, as if he had slopped his last ten dinners and was ashamed to be seen taking his tunic off, which he was, in front of a stranger. She had broad features but her lips were finely shaped, and her chin was dimpled. 'I got delayed.'

'Most of you do. Funny place, Bristol.' She smiled. 'You can't tell whether the trains are coming or going.'

He disliked her being so right, and wanted the last word. 'It was Crewe, as a matter of fact – Sister.'

'I don't care where it was, but next time, get here punctually.'

You only came into a place like this once, so he picked up her humour. Medal ribbons showed she had been to the Middle East and Northwest Europe. She was about thirty, and must know a thing or two. 'Were you in radar?' she said, seeing his sparks badge.

Those bods did a six-weeks course, not twenty-eight. 'I'm a wireless operator' – a twinge at his misplaced pride.

'You'd better hurry or your supper will get cold. I'm Sister Middleton, by the way.'

Her blue-grey eyes seemed dead as if, should you try to plumb them, no leadline would come back with the fathoms marked. He undid his braces as the door closed, in the machine, could only do as he was told, being *hors de combat* – an exact

French term culled from the shabby dictionary half-inched at the transit camp.

The ward smelled of floor polish and disinfectant, stale food and dead flowers, ointments and tobacco smoke, a soldier's ward, not a civilian sanatorium. He set his Bible, dictionary, map and Penguin book on the locker. His Malayan notes and the old wireless log in which he wrote whatever came into his mind about Gunong Barat went on an inside shelf with shaving tackle and money. A letter from Pauline in his paybook said she hoped he was getting better and would come back soon, but in the meantime they were managing all right, so he wasn't to worry. It had come the day before leaving the transit camp, in response to three of his – or was it four? Not a word about Gary.

His mother said in a letter that Lillian wished to be remembered to him. She was poorly, Vera went on, and might not be long for this world. He smiled at her phrases, sorry that the girl's time was up, if up it was, though if it was there'd be nothing anybody could do about it – the same for him if his time turned out to be up as well. He didn't know whether it was or not. Too much to think about from minute to minute to bother, too busy not knowing whether his time was up to care.

He got into the high bed with laundered sheets, and a male orderly brought supper. Hunger had left him, but he ate the pudding, then lit a cigarette. There were fifteen beds to a side, and a long table in the middle with two patients playing draughts. A bedtable could be swung to his chest when he rested against the hillside of pillows. To his left lay a bony-headed flight-sergeant with glittering eyes, thin lips and a pencil moustache, angrily telling a black-haired Lancashire man across the way that in London a porter had carried his suitcase from the train to the taxi, and when the flight-sergeant said thank you, the porter snarled back: 'We can't live on thanks, mate!' The flight-sergeant appealed as if to Solomon's court: 'I didn't have any change, and he gets his wages, doesn't he?'

Maybe he didn't, Brian thought, or if he did it wasn't much, but he didn't chip in, being new at the place, and him being a peppery kind of sergeant, who in any case stopped binding when he realised no one was listening. He probably missed being on the parade ground, though he wouldn't for much longer, because no one tainted with TB stayed in the air force.

Adjusting to a new situation, after so many camps, troopships, staging posts and now hospitals since joining up, meant that all decisions were out of your power, nothing you could do about it except thoughtlessly settle in like others on the same posting. Uncertainty extended to your finger ends, but you let no one see it, the only truth being what they could see plainly, and not what you yourself felt inside, suggesting that the only way to stay sane was by being two people, a device which kept you level-headed and easy-going. He took out his notebook, but the idea faded as soon as he unscrewed his pen. Lights walked like yellow crabs along the ceiling. Sister Middleton stopped at his bed. 'Anything more we can do for you, Seaton?'

He would be out on his neck if he told her – which might be what he wanted, but that would be handing the decision to them, instead of solving it himself. 'No thank you, Sister.'

She placed a paper cup with a lid on his locker. 'Cough your sputum into that before you drink your tea in the morning.'

The regal stiffbacked presence floated away, head in the air, and he wondered whether, against all the odds, there wasn't a smile in her heart – if not on her face. He willed it to appear, but suddenly gave up, though instinct told him it might well exist, which made him hope that she had received a similar message from him.

The man in the bed to his left said: 'Where are you from, Shag?'

He told him, and his name.

'Mine's Ernie. I'm from Brum.'

'How did you get into this place?'

'I took ill on square-bashing. Pleurisy, it was, but it left shadders on my chest. They'll chuck me out, I reckon.' He leaned on his elbow, gaunt and fair, the rattle of breath through his open mouth. 'I spat in my cup yesterday, but it'll be a week before I hear if it's positive.' He grinned. 'As long as they send me home. I want to go home. I never wanted to come in the air force in the first place. I was all right at home.'

The flight-sergeant wondered why they had put him in the same ward with a pathetic National Service conscript. 'Why don't you stop whining? You're at it from morning till night. You're starting to get on my wick.'

'Bollocks,' Ernie said. 'I've got a right to whine, ain't I? Everybody's got a right to whine if they're in hospital. If you can't whine when you're in hospital when can you whine, is what I'd like to know. I like whining, anyway. It does me good!'

He spoke, rather than whined, his tone suggesting that it had been his ambition since birth to get into hospital and have a good whine, and that if when you got there you didn't whine you wouldn't get better.

A smile even crept on to the flight-sergeant's lips, though he was quick to crush it. Ernie was eighteen, and Brian didn't doubt that he had been just as outspoken at that age.

'Anyway,' he went on, 'you'd better be a good lad and spit in your cup for Sister. I'd do owt for her, she's got such lovely tits. She smiled at me this afternoon after the rest period. I suppose she saw that pyramid under my blankets. There wouldn't be any bloody nonsense with her, though, but she knows what's what. Last week a chap was told to spit in his cup, and he couldn't do it. Sat half an hour while his tea got cold, hawking and scraping, and bugger-all would come up, not even a bit o' cuckoo spit. So he goes off to the toilet and wanks in it, then hands it in as proud as if he'd coughed half his lung up. Them daft sods at the lab wondered what it was. They didn't catch on for days. When they tumbled to it there was all hell let loose. The MO came up the ward red in the face waving the report, and shouted the bloke black and blue. But the bloke just laughed at him. He was one o' your lot, Seaton, a wireless operator from Malaya. Or 'appen it was India. He was round the bend and halfway up the zig-zags. Anyway, he got chucked out, which was what he wanted. Dishonourable discharge, it said on his papers.'

In three days you could get used to anything. The previous existence was rubbed away. When asked if he wanted a morning paper, to be paid for at the weekend, he hesitated because he couldn't imagine being in Ward Eleven more than a week, expecting changes to come without warning.

But one week led into another. People came and went. He was wheeled off every day for deep X-rays. Sputum had to be drawn out by the sickening process of a tube being pushed in at the nose and down into the stomach, because he wasn't able to get at the real stuff by spitting. Time was needed to see if the tubercle bacilli would grow, and he could only think that if they didn't discover him to be so ill that he would soon be dead it wouldn't be for want of trying. Lying in bed made him an invalid whether or not he was ill.

Flight-Lieutenant Fox walked up the ward, and you couldn't tell who he was coming to see, because his expression suggested he was on an open plain, and the horizon fifty miles away, and he was curious about what lay beyond. Tall and thin, sallow-faced and slightly stooped, he might also be a patient coming off leave after too much nooky and booze. Maybe he worked too hard. The one medical officer who looked halfway healthy was Squadron-Leader O'Dowd, in charge of TB cases at the hospital, but it was said he only went to see those who were dying. Ernie joked that if he stood at the end of the ward laughing with the sister you'd better ask yourself how you were feeling, because if he started walking up the ward towards you you should put your head under the clothes till he had gone by. And if while your head was in the dark you heard his heavy black shoes stop at the end of your bed, you'd do better to cut your way through the mattress, floor and wall, and make for the road outside the camp, and not stop running till you dropped, when your troubles would be over anyway.

Flight-Lieutenant Fox's protuberant eyes set for the horizon didn't deceive Brian, because as he advanced up the ward, a clipboard firmly under his arm, he knew who he was coming to see.

'The results of your tests have come through, Seaton.' Deeper X-rays revealed cavities, not just scars or marks. The most obvious perforations were on the left lung, but it was too early to say how bad they were on the right, though the indications weren't good. And the sputum tests had come out unmistakably positive. 'In view of which,' Fox said, standing close, words

85

for him alone, 'we'll be moving you to Ward Fifteen this afternoon.'

Nothing to say except thank you. A ton of evidence could not be wrong. At least they had made his descent into the Inferno gradual, the dread of a Positive Ward partly offset by the fact that they were justified sending him to it, though because he didn't feel ill there still seemed to be a joke in it somewhere.

He sat in a wheelchair, belongings piled over his knees, a mode of transport in keeping with his status as an invalid. A book fell from his lap by the office door, and Sister Middleton picked it up, telling him not to make a mess of her clean ward. 'Homer, eh? You'd better be careful, or a nurse might get a crush on you.'

'I hope so.' No such luck, because who would fall for a consumptive – a catching disease as rabid as any known?

'Don't think you've seen the last of me,' she said. 'I'm due to work over that way soon.'

'I feel better already.'

She put her hands to her hips, superb sarcasm. 'You make my life worthwhile!'

He went out laughing.

The orderly wheeled him into the foggy October dusk, away from the two-storey hospital blocks to a pre-fabricated single-floor ward with lower ceilings. The mist lay in wide hollows between the camp and the hills, a season of short daylight and shut windows, with little noise from outside.

The orderly had two tries at bumping the wheelchair up the entrance step, so Brian stood and pushed with him, then got back in so that he could make the expected entrance. He was stronger than the weedy orderly. The world had turned upside down, the gyroscopic axis of the universe unstuck, and he was helpless to right it.

Chapter
❧ EIGHT

The door closed and he didn't know when he would go back into the world. He did not care, glad to imagine that the hostile outside no longer existed. Cut off in a lighted place of even temperature, he hardly knew who he was. Who he had been up to then had died, his old barely remembered self fading under the erosion of quarantine.

Though his spirit dissolved so that he no longer knew himself, his senses were sharper than they had ever been. He was nothing, yet knew that he was everything; dead, yet vital and alive. While everyone knew him to be nothing, only he knew himself to be everything, from within the body that kept his secret safe. Behind the layers of his disablement he was intact, but felt so dead that all he could do was lie still until he could come back to life.

There was no future, hard to imagine when he might return to full spate, walk any amount of miles on his own two feet. Forget time, he was told, tear up calendars, chuck away clocks, lie doggo and heal yourself with a long-term poultice of peace and quiet. Squadron-Leader O'Dowd had a way with words, spoke as if the body was detached from the person who looked through its face – and how right he was – suggesting that if the body didn't do the work expected of it, there were ways of making you heal.

Michael in the next bed was six feet tall, and his feet were continually pushing the sheets and blankets from the bottom of the bed. On her temperature and pulse round in the early morning the night sister grumbled at seeing his legs in the cold air, a serpent of bedclothes pinning him to the mattress.

Brian tried to guess how tall some of the others were. Allowed to get up for an hour a day, as a reward because the body had responded by doing what was expected of it, or throwing a book at the bloke opposite and leaping out of bed to get it back, someone he had imagined of medium height strode across the ward like a pyjama-clad pit prop, while a man he had decided to be as tall as a pole stumped along like a dwarf. Not until the person was helping the orderlies to serve meals, or dusting window ledges before Matron's inspection, did some personality emerge from a covering of sheet and blanket. You often couldn't say, from rumpled bedclothes and a face on a pillow, what length the concealed body was, like talking to someone in the window of another building across the street whom you never met until you saw them out walking one day.

Not supposed to get up, every morning he put on his dressing gown and, looking ahead but craving invisibility, walked to the end of the ward. His legs didn't buckle, nor his pulse rate flutter, and in any case he would rather take longer over his recovery – if he had to – than have screens put around to use a bedpan.

Breakfast plates collected, slops emptied, bundles of cutlery dropped into compartments on the trolley top, counterpane smoothed and everything shipshape, all you could do was take a cigarette from the locker, and by the time the stubbed end lay in your ashtray, watch Rachel come on duty, or wait for Mike in the next bed to call for matches, and toss them across so that he had to lean forward saying: 'Your aim gets better every time.'

'I expect it'll improve when I've been in five years.'

Remarks on something done for each other, or a straight answer to every question, killed speculation or curiosity. Words exchanged depended on supply and demand. After a brief life-story there was little to say. Frank had been a clerk before joining up, then trained as an airframe fitter, and anything else about his life seemed to come under the Official Secrets Act. He wasn't interested when Brian mentioned Malaya.

The past was something to be forgotten because it had led to this, as if to recall anything would be too painful, or uninteresting, he couldn't always tell which. Perhaps they shrivelled the past because if allowed to stay active it would consume the spiritual fuel necessary for recovery.

He accepted a bottle because it saved getting up in the night. The orderly pushed a couple of beds close so that they could play a game of solo, but told them to keep the pennies hidden in case the sister showed up. Others unhooked earphones and listened to the wireless. Some embroidered tablecloths or made raffia mats. A sergeant-airgunner who had been in three years built model aeroplane engines which he posted away to be sold. Brian preferred to read, and sleep when he felt like it.

Harry was trying to rid his windpipe of a button, his face the colour of a jellyfish, cheekbones like sticks in a sack. He wiped his damp skin and fell back with a moan against a high backrest of pillows, waved Brian away when he got out to offer him a drink: 'A tickle in my chest.'

Harry was only free from coughing when the newspapers came at ten, and Brian folded *The Times* for him to hold close and do the crossword. The pencil slipped in his excitement at solving a clue, and Brian handed it back so that he could sort out another anagram.

Harry had been a map clerk at Middle East HQ, and one afternoon coughed a lake of blood on to a desert area that wasn't even British. 'I liked it there,' he said. 'I was having the time of my life. But they shipped me here, worse luck. I wanted to chuck myself in the drink on the way back.'

Brian tried the crossword, but for weeks could make nothing of it. Every day he studied the answers to the previous puzzle, and noticed how Harry circled the letters of an anagram so that they might fall into place and provide the answer. When the solution to a clue was a missing word from *Hamlet* or *King Lear* he went on a clandestine trip to borrow a Shakespeare from a bloke called Summers at the other end of the ward.

'Keep it for a while. I've read it a few times. Besides, I'm busy with this.' The book open on his bed was *The History of Western Philosophy*, so Brian took the Shakespeare, and read a play in order to complete the quotation, and by the time the Scottish newsvendor charged in with next morning's edition a bridgehead of answers was established between the black squares. Soon the empty spaces represented the last centres of resistance, and sometimes even those were eliminated, though often after a long siege.

He couldn't compete with Harry, who finished within the hour, face made ageless by a fight for life. Brian was uneasy at being near the worst case in the ward, because the rest were active, noisy and – you might say – healthy. When he looked into those sunken far-off eyes, at tears which fell during a bout of coughing, he saw the end of the world, and of his own world as well. He was disturbed because at such times a fervour for living took him over, as if the sick man kept the blood pounding through his own veins, and he would be able to recover as soon as the other man was dead – as Edmond Dantès had been able to escape from the dungeons of the Château d'If only when the Abbé Faria had perished.

He sheered off the possibility as if gnawed at by a scorpion. It was a game. While you coughed, you lived, and there was always a chance that health would come back, despite what the medicos assumed, or what Harry himself might believe when he fought for breath and cried for oxygen in the night. Life was embedded in his body and soul, and Brian hoped that nothing would be able to wrench out such tenacious roots.

Fevered by Iago's villainy, bewildered at Othello's blindness, he shut the book, to see her as on every evening walk into the staff room to change into a white overall, emerging with the temperature and pulse book, and giving a signal that might be for him. He waved back, nothing to lose, a motion so slight that she would hardly notice.

She had dropped her watch last night and was waiting for it to be repaired, asked the first patient to lend her his, and Brian envied the position of his bed. Her progress up the ward was slow, so he re-read the letter from Edgeworth. Mail was rare, and when the large envelope landed on his bed he thought it was meant for Mike. Readdressed from the sick quarters of the demob camp, the writing was unfamiliar – never having seen

Edgeworth's hand – but his name and number were plain, and inside was his account of the jungle climb typed on good paper.

'Dear Brian, I was surprised to get your letter. Of course I remember you. I was sorry to lose you to the air force, and I'm sorry to hear that you're in hospital. I hope it turns out to be nothing serious. You know your old job is waiting for you as soon as you get out. We might even find you a better one, because things are booming now. The government contracts are finished, but there is more work than ever.

'My wife and I were pleased to read about your adventures in the jungle. It'll be a bit tame in Nottingham after all that, but I'm sure you'll be glad to settle down. I know I would be in your place. We liked what you wrote, so I got my secretary to type it up for you.

'You don't say what your illness is, but I guess it can't be much. Maybe being in Malaya wasn't so good for you after all. Anyway, I enclose something to help you along in the meantime. A serviceman always needs a bit extra in his pocket. I know I did in the last war. Write to us again, whenever you have got the time, and let us know when you'll be back.'

He thought it peculiar – refolding the letter with its two big five pound notes and replacing it in his locker – that his main interest in life had always come out of jobs he had done. Work was the only thing that demanded all he had got, and to which he had given everything that was in him. Interest and knowledge had come from work, the basis of all experience, enriching his life because it effectively helped him to escape from it. Standing before a capstan lathe had made existence tolerable by providing the ambition to excel at what he was doing.

Such dreams were finished, because Edgeworth would be shocked to hear that he had got TB, wouldn't so glibly offer him a job, and without the possibility of occupation you were a cypher. No one in the ward talked about what they were going to do when they left, as if they would go over a cliff or vanish into thin air.

He read advertisements in *The Times* for people who were wanted in the colonies as surveyors, district officers, forestry wardens, even radio operators, to work at tin mines or on rubber estates, in the police or on the railways, and he mulled on each possibility as a story for himself, living a tour of duty in sun and freedom.

He sheafed through the typed account of his trek up the slopes of Gunong Barat as if the essence of his life was printed there, read it slowly, hardly able to believe it wasn't written by someone else, took up a pencil to alter an occasional word, reluctantly spoiling the immaculate copy.

'Is that your last will and testament?' Rachel held her hands peculiarly close, as if she would have clapped with glee if she hadn't a thermometer in one and a watch in the other.

'No. It's something I wrote.'

Her brown eyes darkened, almost violet under the light, as distant from him as when glimpsing his own in the mirror. 'Better not talk, or you'll have a mouthful of glass.'

He enjoyed a perfect view of short wavy hair, full cheeks and a small but shapely mouth. He stroked the flesh and kissed her nipples, a fantasy while she held his wrist and looked at the watch, thinking himself unnoticed, but she saw his thin face, harrowed and rougher than the sort she had been brought up with, though not – she said later – more so than some types in the ward who had done service overseas.

While he stayed mute, to let the glassed-in mercury register the heat in his body, her lips muttered the pulse rate of his blood, a special and positive connection, in spite of her doing the same with thirty others. If you willed something intensely, it came about, but he could think of nothing to say, absorbed totally by her pale face, and bosom moving with her breath, while she observed the watch, his appreciation telling him that she did not have a face, but a countenance. Her features glowed, but did they light up, making it a countenance, only when he looked at her? Or was he the only one in the ward who saw her face as a countenance because he had never been so close to such a face and was in love with her?

She shook the thermometer vigorously for the next person, and set it in the bowl of Lysol. 'So it's something you wrote?'

He had said too much. Talk, and you eat glass. But what else could he have told her? 'Life's a joke.'

She surprised him by taking his remark seriously. 'Why do you say that?'

'I'm lying here, and you measure my pulse and temperature. Who would have guessed we'd meet like this?'

'I don't see it as a joke.' She wasn't wearing a brassiere, the nipples of her plump breasts showing faintly. Or so he imagined. You couldn't see them at all. She pushed the things on his locker to one side, and set her paraphernalia down, making his bed the halfway station of her round.

'Maybe not. But it's a strange way of meeting.' When she had gone he would slide his feet to the warmth she was bound to leave, a prospect which left him less able to impress her with talk.

'It's only my job,' she teased.

'If anyone told me a few months ago that I'd be in hospital and meet a marvellous person like you I'd have said they were round the bend.'

She pushed a strand of hair into place and drew her grey stockinged legs in towards the bed. 'I suppose everyone could say that.'

The lit cigarette was a proxy kiss, which she took as if he gave her one every evening. She hardly smoked, puffed uncertainly, the sort of carefully brought up young woman he'd never yet spoken to. 'What did you do before you joined up?'

She had difficulty smiling, preferring to laugh openly – if he would say something funny. Her aloofness was a form of protection, though he liked to think it was because she couldn't fathom him anymore than he could plumb her. Unfortunately all the jokes he knew were dirty, and in any case she only seemed aloof because anyone with such a delightfully clear accent would sound so to him.

'I lived in Hampshire,' she said, 'and worked in an office. Then I decided to join up. I like it better in the air force. But I wanted to leave home. That was the main idea.'

The next best thing to making her laugh was to ask about her life. Questions got people talking, and everyone liked to talk. 'What did your parents say?'

'There's only my mother, and she didn't mind.' She stood up. 'I must be off, or Sister Middleton will be after me.'

He touched her hand. 'See you tomorrow?'

'Sooner, I expect.' He followed her course down the ward, noting that she stayed the minimum at each bed to make up for the time with him.

He clamped the earphones on, Beethoven's 'Leonora' going into his brain like calipers to gauge his enjoyment, the opposite to the poison funnelled into the ear of Hamlet's father, pure sound, not liquid, reviving instead of stupefying unto death, but hard to bear the suggestion of freedom from within the prison of a bed.

Sister Middleton, white cap, starched apron, hands on hips, indicated by her smile that she could see more than temperature, pulse rate, nature of sputum, sediment rate of blood, X-ray shadows and hidden cavities; might perhaps like to see also what was on his mind. 'How are we tonight, Seaton?'

The earphones fell to his neck. He would only know how he felt if he ran to the end of the ward and back. 'Fine, Sister.'

She picked up his board. 'Your pulse rate is high.'

No wonder.

'Don't sit up too much. And try not to exert yourself – in any way.' She flicked a smile. Or did she? Her look lasted a moment longer than necessary, as if there was a further question to ask, or as if he ought to have something to say to her. Couldn't tell which. But he was sure some words were about to move her lips.

He went back to the nine o'clock news, telling of the Cold War, by no means freezing in Berlin, and definitely hotting up in Malaya, announcements from another planet he felt so little connection, a long time since he had worked on the Marconi direction finder, guiding Lincoln bombers on to bandit lairs.

Talk was livelier before lights-out. Rachel came with the spirits bottle to rub the sore bones of those who lay too long in one position, and Brian thought some wheedled her attention only for the pleasure of being attended to. As for him, the less bother he was the sooner he would improve so that they would let him go. Even if he were more ill he would scorn such treatment, happy only in being left alone – which he suspected was a system of pointless obstinacy brewed from a fuddled kind of hope.

Back bent, she worked the lotion into Harry's limbs, eased

him over and fastened his pyjamas, till Brian regretted he wasn't sufficiently stricken as to get the same consideration. But her smile on going by hinted that she was glad he hadn't used up her time.

Darkness brought the niggling comments of two people who had read the same book, or backed different football teams, or suddenly remembered a joke. Sister Middleton's plimsolls squeaked on her bedcheck, a torchbeam across closed eyes. Talking became a murmur and, the craving for freedom unimportant, he was only troubled by the void of having no worries before being pulled into sleep.

Chapter

❧ NINE

In his dream he dreamed that he was awake. But his eyelids were fastened together. Struggling to reach daylight, he couldn't signal for help till his eyes opened, and then he wouldn't need to. The ward was silent until he could see. If his blindness was noticed he would be ill enough to stay in the place forever.

He had to fight in silence, no matter how desperate, or how much alone, how far from help or, what was worse, how close to it. The struggle went on long enough to threaten that it might not end even if the grip on his eyes relaxed. His body had betrayed him, and his spirit was unable to defeat the force that kept him blinded.

He wouldn't see the world again, even in his own blind way, until his eyes were opened. Trying to force them, to find where he was, to enjoy a tree, a horse, a house, a river, fields and hills, kept him as a dead man with neither arms nor vision, but he fought his way back, eyes washed with salt, stung with energy. Thus shall the eyes of the blind be opened, and soothed by the magic ointment of a view.

He touched his lids with relief, light filtering through. Eyes that had been inexplicably shut were suddenly free, he didn't know how or why, but he lay still, marvelling at a release from the prison of his nightmare that no one would understand, would consider him insane if he told them he could see for the first time.

He lost the wonder at pristine sight, back from a tunnel, seeing everything as normal, the damp sweat that matted his pyjamas being the only sign of the dream receding, and thanking God no one would come to check his temperature while rusty nails burned in his lungs at each deep breath to see how much life was left in him, spit out the salty cough wondering how it had been possible for his illness to get worse by lying in bed and trying to cure himself, the reverse to what had been intended, treading to get out of deep water, to reach air but sinking into the depths.

The sight and noise of the familiar ward returned, and he was tormented by wondering whether in spite of rest and good food he wasn't worse than if he'd accepted no treatment. The free life might have rid him of the disease, but now the cough burned as if his mouth would fill with blood. He didn't care that his number was stencilled on the X-ray as on a bullet, imagined it was still his decision whether to live or die.

In Dante's Limbo, he was defined as a patient because impatience anguished him. The shame of having to lie still, of not paying for food and breath by work, took away all pleasure of freedom. Poets and composers with the same disease had lasted till thirty or forty, old age from the vantage of twenty-one, but he was here to dream the days and nights away, because it was natural to drift, easy to dream, comforting not to think, pleasant to doze, to drift, to dream, float from past to present and Greenwich to Singapore, from what he had been to what he might be, but free, and drifting, and dreaming – though thought leapt from the unbearable as a finger from a hot poker.

He had drifted at school, which he had loved and dreaded, but hadn't been able to dream in the factory, where he'd laboured till worn out and able only to eat and sleep, but never hating it because he'd been free to carry on or pack it in. As a recruit at hour-long square-bashing sessions, when the rhythmically accurate body performed with two hundred others (the mind in love with the body like Saul with Jonathan, never to be divided, and from now on never to be trusted), part of your mind could drift, though rarely for long. A wireless operator listened to the sky from Hong Kong to Darwin while static roared through nightdreaming thoughts and you heard the sombre theme of *L'Arlésienne* coming from maybe as far as Sydney or San Francisco but, for all that, the dreaming and the drifting was always close to an anchor such as the teacher's fist, the foreman's exasperation, the drill sergeant's howl, or the squeak of morse from a plane above the cumulonimbus whose navigator wanted to know where he was and for God's sake tell me quick.

In the hospital you had an unquestioned right to dream, would be all the sooner out of their hands if you were set on some extra-terrestrial feat of psychic navigation, keeping still, dreaming, away from the main run of the universe. Do anything as long as you appear to dream, smoke (though not too much), read, drink your beer, embroider, stare into space, consider yourself free as long as you dream and drift and devour yourself in anguish between the sheets.

Impossible to get behind others' eyes, test the quality of their dreams, compare them to yours, find out what fluid notions or daft fantasies went on. They spoke, laughed and joked, told a yarn, or cursed – the closest to a quarrel in their helpless state – winked and waved their hands, played chess or ludo, clock patience or draughts. He couldn't tell them about his dreams anymore than they would find a motive to inform him. In this they were united by the common illness, isolated from each other by being perfect jailers of their dreams. It had been the same even in the factory or signals section, a matter of degree perhaps, but here they were at the bottom of the pit, even those allowed up and back into uniform for two, four or six hours a day.

Whatever their hopes or dreams, encased in the same situation, they were far from familiar, and he too was as different from anyone as it was possible to get. Since childhood, school, factory, active service, he had been set apart from friends, brothers, parents – everyone. He was different now, but the difference came as a revelation because the other thirty bods were reduced to such similarity by the state in which they lived that he had been forced into realising his absolute difference, not better, or worse, but different in a way that it was a matter for rejoicing rather than regret.

In the days when he had not realised his difference he had

still been different. He had been at one with life and locked into the rhythm of his world, in tune absolutely with himself, so there had been no need for his spirit to realise any difference. Thought had not disturbed the equanimity of his daily turmoil, life perfect because unruffled by any sensation of difference. Nothing extraordinary had occurred to remind him of the difference as clear as that which gripped him now.

That difference was an anchor to cling to through his dreams, a steel that set his compass to rights instead of spinning the needle in chaos. The magnetic field of the brain was in alignment with the backbone. There was salt in his throat, and nails in his lungs, but no return to previous confusions.

Having discovered his difference to everyone, he could admit what similarities existed, accept the fact without perishing from shame that he was ill, and no longer expected the MO to come up the ward waving his X-ray and say a mistake had been made, a fantasy finally disposed of not through despair but by an ingenuity absent from his former life.

Hope was no longer an unmitigated torment, nor despair a tool for survival. He could wait without using the subterfuge of surrender, and while he waited live by a formula which did not shatter the stiffnecked spirit responsible for landing him here in the first place, and which would surely provide the mechanism for getting him out. He had opened his eyes on himself and, while wondering why it had taken so long, knew that it could not have happened sooner or in any other way.

Rachel sat on his bed after lights-out, and he moved his leg so as not to be oppressed by the weight. Cutting away from sleep, he opened his eyes and caught the sweet odour of her make-up. She leaned close. 'Are you awake?'

He lifted himself on the pillows, moonlight showing rows of white counterpanes pulled up like the snowy mounds of un-marked graves, everyone silent or asleep, sick and waiting to recuperate, yet maybe not sick when 'prolonged illness was nothing more than a premature old age, and old age nothing more than a prolonged illness' – as he had read in a book about the life and death of a tree.

Her hands were warmer than his own. 'I've been asleep for hours!'

She laughed softly. 'I wondered if you had a cigarette.'

Hardly breathing, he was in a far-off place alone with her. But he let go of her hand. 'They're in my locker.' Every few days she would leave a packet on his bed, to make up for what she borrowed. 'Light one for me.'

His leg rested against her thigh through several thicknesses, warming his flesh in other places. He tasted lipstick on the cigarette, would ask her to take her clothes off and come into bed, but she wasn't the girl who would do that sort of thing, might see him as uncouth and walk away, never talk to him again. He pressed her hand. 'Get my uniform from the store-room and we'll do a moonlight flit!'

He explained what he meant. She wasn't a girl from Radford, so he had to travel more circuitous routes to get what he wanted. She closed the window as if he might fly out and vanish. 'I'd get shot. And so would you. Sister comes around at twelve.'

'We can go to the village pub. It's only a mile over the fields.'

'You're supposed to get better, not kill yourself.'

He drew her close. 'I love you. I've never loved anyone so much.' His heart banged away, every limb vibrating, impossible that she could love someone who was so sunk into insignificance, though she would never know the downward fathoms he had travelled.

Her small full lips trembled as she looked into space. 'I love you, too.' The kiss was brief, and she drew away, her face stern, as if she had let go of a deadly secret that might destroy her. 'There's something about you. I don't know what. You're different, I suppose.'

He could hardly believe what he heard, but didn't want to break the spell, only to live without memory or expectation, bask in moonlight and silence. She loved him, had met his own announcement so openly that even being ill had been a godsend for leading to it.

Back from leave she brought some of her mother's books, and he envied her being born into such a house. He mulled his way through something called *The Withered Branch*, which seemed to be about the death of the English novel. Rachel showed him *Alice in Wonderland*, a favourite from her childhood, which he knew of but hadn't read. She must have talked about him to her mother, another sign that she cared for him. 'There's this airman who reads and writes all the time . . .' 'Well,' her mother said, 'maybe you can let him borrow these. Let him get his teeth into this one – if he can.'

It was *The Critique of Pure Reason* by Immanuel Kant, in which the first fifty pages were devoted to proving that if you moved a chair, the space which the chair, now absent, had occupied was still there. It amazed him that such difficult writing was necessary to prove something so obvious, though it was exciting to realise that nothing was as simple as you thought. Perhaps all simplicities needed to be wrapped up in tortuous language if they had to be explained for the first time. In philosophy Kant's premise was as important as the invention of the wheel, Summers told him, and he saw the point of it, pure reason being a tool of the brain as vital as any machine at Edgeworth's factory. He certainly knew, when Rachel sat by his bed, in her pressed uniform with glinting buttons, that when she went away the space she had occupied was still there, and that as far as he was concerned she was in it for as long as he looked at it, or thought about her, or indeed until she came back to reoccupy it. His brain manufactured its own lighted way through intricacies scattered in his path, an intoxication of discovery without the sickness of being drunk.

On visiting day Michael's mother came from Liverpool, twelve hours on the road to be an hour with her son. Harry's wife travelled from Southampton. There were rarely more than a dozen visitors, but most patients saw someone once a month. Brian neither regretted nor expected anyone. His mother had written to the MO to find out what was wrong with him, unable to make head or tail of his half-truths. 'Why didn't you let your mother know?' the MO said.

'I did, sir, but she didn't believe me.'

'Very strange. Well, now she knows.'

Pauline never mentioned a visit in her letters. Not possible. Couldn't afford the fare. Gary would be a handful. She'd never travelled on her own. Might get lost. Her mother couldn't come with her, because there would be no one to look after Gary.

And children weren't allowed in the House of Contagion. She could lift him up and show him at the closed window, so that Brian would see him at least. But time and money kept her away. She didn't need to explain. He didn't want to see her and she knew it. She hadn't come because he hadn't asked her to, and he hadn't asked her because she didn't want to come. He knew. During his sick leave they'd had nothing to say, deadened by a silence that deepened the longer they went without speaking, no contact even in bed because she was horrified at the idea of his illness. Her coldness crippled him, wasn't even part of her, or part of him, came between them because neither could overcome it.

Jenny Mullinder nagged Pauline to pull herself together and shake it off, begged Brian to ignore it, said that true love never ran smooth. He tried to talk, to smile the blight away, but against such silence, and her fear which stopped him touching her, he had no chance. Maybe he should have spoken more, made her laugh, but he felt angry and wouldn't talk until she did. The day before leaving he forced himself to be as normal as he was able. But she held out, with stiff lips and glistening eyes, her determination impossible to defeat. He lost hope, knowing she had dished him forever. Dressed for leaving the house, kitbag ready for hoisting, he laughingly asked, after a last kiss for Gary, if she would visit him in the hospital, as if to give her the opportunity of making a promise she would never keep, proof indeed that it was the end. After a while she said without looking: 'Yes, duck. I'll come and see you.'

So he was glad there would be no visitors, because they'd embarrass him at being seen in bed. Accustomed to his new life, it suited him to hide behind a barrier of distance or indifference. He only wanted Rachel to visit him on Sunday, should it be her day off. On duty she was close enough anyway.

But suddenly in a vision his cousin Bert sway-walked along the middle of the ward as if he owned the place, his short and compact body and double-breasted suit in harmony with the polished floor, gazed at by those without visitors as he passed. He smiled widely, and punched the air a couple of times to signify the delight he felt at having tracked him down.

'Hey up, then, yo'!' he called, in the Radford accent Brian

had hoped never to hear again. Yet at Bert's appearance he came back to life. The hemlock stone of his childhood with its adventurous suffering still lodged in him, and his hand went out for the shake, as Bert lunged at the bed and came down to embrace him, carrierbag falling to the floor. 'How are you, then, our Brian?'

He told him. All well. 'Drag that chair up and sit down.'

Bert turned his stare on to the sister coming towards them, and when she drew level asked, as if not believing Brian's assurance, but really as an excuse to talk to her, his pale-blue, almost white eyes piercing her buxom presence: 'How is he, then, Sister?'

She smiled. 'We'll pull him through.'

'Like my old rifle,' he quipped.

'I expect so. But I don't think he appreciates it.'

'He doesn't know when he's well off,' Bert said. 'If you want any 'elp, Sister, just let me know. I'd give you a hand any day!'

'I'll get in touch if we need you.' She was attracted by his exuberance, as if she would rather have a ward full of Berts than the quiet lot she had to put up with.

He felt in his pocket for a pencil. 'I'll give you my address, Sister, if you give me yourn!'

He was going too far, but she laughed and walked on. 'We have all the help we need, at the moment.'

'Get dressed quick, and let's change places,' Bert said. 'I'd love to see to her. Did you see that look she gen me?'

Michael's visitors turned away, though the mother smiled.

'They'll throw you out if you aren't careful,' Brian told him.

Bert scoffed. 'Naah! They're good sports. Nurses allus are. The things that went on, when I was in dock once in Germany. I daren't tell yet. I 'ad my share, though.'

Rachel smiled as she walked by, which Bert took as meant for him. 'Did yer see that? What a lovely wench!' He opened his carrierbag. 'Still, I didn't come to see her. Here's some fags, and here's a pork pie, me owd duck, and here's some chocolates. I would 'ave brought you some grapes and flowers, but Dave couldn't find a lorry for 'em to fall off!'

Brian had some beer in his locker. 'Help yourself, but I've no opener. Ask the bloke opposite.'

Bert put them against the steel rim under the mattress, snapped the tops off and drank from the spout. 'I'd love to be in 'ere, and get stuck into them nurses, especially the one as just passed. I didn't even look at her, and she smiled straight at me. Christ, I've got an 'ard on already.'

'I don't think you'd get far with her.'

Rachel wasn't like the easy girls Bert had known, otherwise Brian wouldn't have fallen in love with her. And if she had supposed for a moment that he thought she was (if she was able to imagine that kind of thing) she wouldn't have fallen in love with him, either. One brash move and her mouth would tighten, eyes glaze over, and she'd walk away frostily never to return.

'Not get far?' Bert laughed. 'That ain't like the old Brian I hear talking. You must be barmy. She's longing for a bit of the old mutton-dagger. I don't know whether that look was for you or me, but I know what it meant, and if I knew what it meant you did as well, so don't tell me you didn't.'

Rachel was too far off to hear, but he imagined her ears burning, and thought it better to say: 'How's Nancy? Did you get married, then?'

He wished he hadn't asked. He liked Bert, his life-long pal, the only visitor he was likely to get. Bert's expression changed, as if he had drunk a bucket of gall before realising it wasn't beer. 'No. She lost it. Or she was never preggers. Or her monthlies started. I forget which. But she still said I'd got to marry her, and so did her old man. I towd 'em to get stuffed. He came to the house, and mam set on him. So did Doddoe, as well as Colin and Dave. Me and Nancy sneaked out to the pictures. When we come out we went up Strelley Woods, and everything started again. I'm as soft as shit where women are concerned. Spin me on their little finger, they do. Still, as long as I get my oats, that's all I care about.' He looked around, the bile gone from his system. 'If I was in this place I'd get plenty, I'll tell you that. I bet yo' do, though, eh?'

'I'm supposed to keep still.'

'You don't have to *move*,' Bert said, 'unless you want to. Let her do it, you idle bastard. I'll bet you get all you like – though you wouldn't tell me about it. You've allus been a sly bleeder.'

It was an uphill battle. 'How did you know I was here?'

He set another bottle on the locker top. 'Went to your mam's, but she worn't in. I guessed where she was, and found her in the White Horse with Harold. She had your last letter in her handbag, so I wrote down the address. She asked if I knew what was wrong with you. I said it was pleurisy or bronchitis, or idleitis – or summat like that. Harold bought me a pint, and when I said I might come and visit you they said I shouldn't bother because it was such a long way. I asked Vera if she wanted to come, but she couldn't leave Harold on his own, and she'd see you soon enough anyway, when you got home, which she expects before too long. You know what they're like.'

He did, they did, both knew each other knew, words eddying into the past that needed no elucidation. Bert's eyes and the cast of his lips showed it was nothing to complain about. You couldn't hold anything against them, were lucky in fact to be left alone, fed, clothed, looked after, in no danger of dying, though if you were you knew the rescue procedure would go into action.

'The grub's better here than in the officers' mess in the army,' Bert said. 'Nowt but the best for the Brylcreem Boys. In the poor bloody infantry it was pig swill, if you was lucky.' He laughed, fussy and pleased. 'You'll be as *fat* as a pig soon. And even if you shag all the nurses they won't get pregnant. They know a thing or two, nurses do. And they won't want you to marry 'em, either. Just a bit of bang-bang, and it's all over. Lovely!'

When Rachel brought a double amount of bread and butter and jam so that Bert could have tea Brian was horrified at his hand seeming to slide across her arse. 'Will yet cum up to London with me, duck?'

'I'm too busy.'

'Next week, then?'

She laughed, and went back to the trolley, seeing to other patients and visitors.

'She's not your sort,' Brian said. 'Nor mine, it seems.'

Bert brushed crumbs from his chin. 'I'd have her in a week.'

'I'll bet you wouldn't.'

'Two weeks, then. No more. If a woman's got lovely tits

like her it teks ten days. If a woman's got small tits it on'y teks a week. That's about it, in my experience.'

'How's Doddoe?'

'Same. Drinks twenty pints every Saturday night. He works all the hours God sends on the building sites, then swills his wages at the weekend. I don't say owt to him, unless he gets on to mam. He threatened to paste her a month ago because she looked at another bloke in a pub. Luckily me and Dave was there. He might be our dad, but we'd put the boot in, and he knows it. One day he'll get killed on his motorbike.'

'Don't say that.'

'It'd serve the bastard right. Even when he's tanked up with ale he rides home as if he's sober as a judge. The trouble is, mam gets on the back, so if owt 'appens to him she'll cop it as well. We're allus telling her not to go on it, but she's had so much booze she don't care, either. It worries me to death. I'd die if owt happened to Mam.'

'Ada's indestructible.'

Bert grinned. 'You're right there. She'll see us out. But if owt did happen to her on that motorbike, and Doddoe's still alive, I'll finish him off, even though he lost both legs.'

Visiting time over, he walked down the ward, moving step by step backwards to the door. Brian saw him talking to the sister, fancied he heard them laughing, then he'd gone.

He felt as tired as if he had walked ten miles, and lay back, Rachel touching his hand when she took the plates away. Drifting into sleep, he heard a thump at the window, and saw Bert's face framed in a Bela Lugosi grin, half laughing and half to strike terror, his dental plate in one hand so that the few remaining teeth made him look like a demented old man. Rachel screamed with laughter, till Bert waved a final farewell, lowering himself inch by inch as if falling off a cliff in slow motion. Then he came up with the dental plate slotted back, and vanished across the misty grass.

When Rachel came on supper duty she asked who that funny little man had been.

'An old oppo from Malaya. I'll tell you about it later.'

The real story he would never spin, either to her or anyone, because it was part of his life, and he would bleed to death in

106

the telling. It was almost as if he had dreamed Bert's visit, not good these days at remembering recent events. They hid. Or he hid them, if they had too much significance. In Nottingham Bert had been put away, goodbye forever. Brian didn't know why, had done it without thought, yet however final the parting, it hadn't been final enough, because when Bert clowned up the ward it was as if the decision to get him out of his life had been no more than a fantasy, and he was glad, because if you cut away part of your flesh you surely would bleed to death.

After her own supper in the mess Rachel came back to sit by his bed. 'He was in the army,' he told her. 'When the Emergency began in Malaya he was in a platoon stationed in the camp. They put their tents up under the palm trees.'

She pressed his hand. 'Another jungle story! Oh goody!'

Her warm lips were close. He would tell lies till the cows came home if she kissed him for every yarn. 'The swaddies used to go on patrol, searching for bandits, but mostly they stood guard over us Brylcreem Boys. They'd lounge on the beach, or play Tarzan in the bushes. We signals types had a boat, and often sailed it to Muong Island two miles away. One day I took it out on my own. About half a mile from the beach I saw this bloke swimming, and waved as I went by. When I headed back for the beach, getting on for teatime, I expect, I spotted him again, waving and shouting. I thought he was larking about, but he'd got cramp. I reached him just as he was going under for the count. The sea was choppy, but I had a rope, and how I got him in I'll never know, but I did, and rowed as quick as I could to the shore.

'He asked me not to say anything about it, because he'd be in trouble if his CO got to know he'd swum that far out. Next day he left a hundred fags on my bed, as well as a note saying "Thanks for saving my life". From then on we were pals, though we didn't have much in common. He said it was a miracle he'd been rescued, but it was only by chance I'd been close at the time. After Malaya we kept in touch, and I met him on my last leave. When I told him what I'd got he said he'd visit me. I didn't think he would, but I should have known he wasn't the sort to go back on a promise.'

'He was funny,' she said. 'But nice. Looks like the life and soul of the party. When he went out I heard him telling Sister Middleton he was your cousin.'

He laughed. 'We got a bit tight together in a pub, and he shouted to everybody that we were brothers.'

'It must mean something, to save someone's life.'

'Well, I didn't think much of it at the time.' It also meant something when you told a lie, though they made better stories than any concerning his childhood, which might seem even less believable – but which in any case he did not know how to lie about.

He was wary when she became too serious.

'God must have been happy,' she said, 'when you rescued a drowning soldier.'

'Well, He let me do it.'

She kissed him. 'That's true.'

'Do you believe in God?'

'Don't you?'

She would be shocked if he said no. 'I'm not sure.'

'I do, when I go to church.'

He knew nothing about her. 'What, with your parents?'

She straightened on the chair, the tips of her fingers touching him. 'At boarding school you had to go. On leave I go with my mother.'

'What about your father?'

'He died when I was ten.'

'In the war?' It must have been earlier.

'No. He had cancer. Afterwards my mother got a job, and sent me off to school. My grandparents paid.'

'What did your mother do?'

'She was a housekeeper for my uncle, who owns an under-wear factory. He has a big house in Hampshire, and I used to go there for holidays and exeats. But I hated it. I had to make sure I was never alone with him, because he would really try it on, if you know what I mean. I couldn't tell my mother because she would make a fuss, and then we'd have to leave. Even now I don't like going home, but he doesn't try it anymore.'

'Sounds awful.' Her face was set with misery. 'I'll tell you what, me and Bert'll put on khaki and blacken our faces, and lie in wait around the house, for a week if necessary. Then one day when your uncle's taking a post-prandial stroll we'll give him a good hiding. He'll never bother you again.'

She was laughing, which was something. 'I think I'd rather have another jungle story.'

'About how I shot a tiger? Or that time I bagged a terrorist with my jack-knife?'

She stood. 'I'd love to hear it, but I must go and write a few letters. I'll come after lights-out.'

A stocky orderly, Maureen, had short fair hair and tartar eyes, mere slits which made her look as if she was always grinning. She was resentful in her work, and if anyone wanted a bedpan or bottle she took ages about it. The male orderly on duty was called Clive, and when the sister wasn't around they sat in the office brewing tea and dealing the cards, leaving those patients who were fit to fetch and carry for the strict bed cases.

Another orderly was Jenny, a Scottish girl whose Glasgow accent made her hard to understand. She wore glasses, had red hair and was slim and tall, a hard-working girl who chose Joe from Liverpool for a boyfriend, so that after lights-out their shadows merged as if a curtain was drawn around them. Sister Middleton came up the ward one night and found Jenny closer to Joe's bed than she should have been, the flash of her light on Jenny who was just standing up. Brian thanked God that Rachel wasn't with him at the time. As it was, Sister Middleton tore her off a strip, and though there was no proof, because Jenny made the excuse that she was by Joe's bed because he'd called for a bottle, she was put on another ward for a couple of weeks. Brian was sure Clive had opened his trap, though there was no proof about that either.

Reading an advert in the papers, he ordered a box of fifty whiffs for Christmas, an occasional cigar reminding him of midnight smokes in the radio hut where, when he opened the doors, which he did before danger from bandits, the noise of mating bullfrogs battled with atmospherics from his earphones.

But it was no longer any use thinking about Malaya. Enjoy today, and tomorrow will look after itself. He forgot the ward, forgot even Rachel. God doesn't give a written guarantee at birth of three score and ten. Maybe your seventy years would slow down and take you through a lifetime of ninety, or they would race like mad and leave you with only twenty-five. You just had to accept the rate you were destined to live at.

She was beside him, touched his ear with her lips. 'I've caught you brooding – what about?'

He didn't know. He supposed it was an accusation in the family she came from. 'I was thinking about you.'

She kissed him. 'You shouldn't.'

'I want to get out of here.'

Moonlight marked the polished floor. She sat on his bed instead of the chair. 'My father walked out of the hospital. He wouldn't put up with it. So mother had to nurse him. But he died in three months.'

Strange that someone in such a family should die. He had enough to eat, fresh air, few worries – or so you would think. 'What work did he do?'

'He was a draughtsman. And an artist. He drew pictures, and got them into magazines.'

'A good job.'

'Sometimes he earned a lot of money. Often not very much. What does *your* father do?'

He had taken a risk, knew that you couldn't ask without being asked. 'He works in a factory.'

She lifted her head. 'How wizard! What do they make?'

'Those funny things that you ride, with pedals and handle-bars. Bicycles. I'd ask him to send us one, so that we could fly as fast as we could from this place, but they're for export.'

'Really?'

'They go to Africa, and places like that.' He held her arm, smooth skin under her blouse, reaching her shoulders and pulling her till she was lying on the bed, face level with the opening of his pyjama shirt. Her skin had a foreign temperature, warmer or cooler he couldn't say, the state of heat varied against legs and hands, between the pillow and the back of his head, wishing his hands long enough to reach her thighs. Trembling, she moved away, but he sensed it was only for form's sake, so eased her back, whispering into her ear what loving words came to him, white with longing and cramped by the anguish of a love he had never known.

The blankets were down, her face close, warm breasts shielding him from the night air. She was so still he thought she had fallen asleep, kissed her hair, face, neck, but she stopped him unbuttoning her shirt. 'I'm going to the storeroom,' she whispered. 'Follow me in a few minutes. You'll have to cope, though.'

Over her shoulder stretched the wide lane of the ward. He heard a cough, a grunt, the cry of someone falling in their sleep down an unexpected cliff. From beyond the billets a car stopped at the camp gates, then set off back to town, changing gear on its descent of the hill. He was no longer tired, waited calmly, knowing what her words meant.

Reaching into the most secret place of his locker he took out what he had bought as a bird of passage between stations in Manchester the morning after he had learned about the X-ray, from the woman who played patience.

Chapter

❦ TEN

His skin had been broached by a surgeon's knife for the first time, payment of dues for the One Lung Club. As a kid his head was split often enough by stones when gangs clashed in open ground beyond the railway, and part of his leg had been scooped out by a piece of bottle, but here the cutting was done under local anaesthetic so that the knife could enter and sever lesions connecting his lung to the pleural wall. A couple of thousand cubic centimetres of air were pumped in so that, flattened into rest, the lung no longer had to work. He breathed on one, no strain if you were lying down.

Trolleyed back from the operating theatre, he got into bed by himself, sparing the orderlies the effort of heaving his dead weight. In any case, the mere prick of the cutabout had only turned him into one of the walking wounded, so that settling into bed he reached for a bottle of beer and a cigar. Expected to go to sleep, like others before him, he felt an electric current lighting him up, thermionic valves, inductances and impedances, earth and aerial connected. He showed two fingers up against the unseeing stare of the world, needed to celebrate his crossing into the unknown, beer and cigar smoke creating exquisite fertiliser to enrich the furrows of his apparent well-being.

Sister Middleton raised her eyebrows but said nothing. It wouldn't have made a blind bit of difference, though at that moment he felt no divide between them, and wouldn't have objected if she'd held his hand. He belched, and for four hours floated in white space without distinguishing marks or topographical features. He was supposed to lie flat for three days. Clive looked at him with a smile, didn't mind when he made his way on a slightly zig-zag track to the lavatory.

After a week the lung began to come up, and he was wheelchaired to the doctor's office, another rush of pure air into his upper innards forcing it down again, setting him on course for a future of periodic needle pricks to remind him, Rachel said, that he was no longer like those who walked the outside world.

Beds were dragged to the middle of the ward. Every day the great cleaning was done, the ward left without mote or blemish. Even Sister Middleton wiped and washed, emptied ashtrays and collected rubbish. He watched the motions of her strong arms, breasts moving under her shirt. The inaccessibility of her fabulous body gave him a hard on reserved only for Rachel, but he seemed to have enough for more than one person.

A breeze blew away early morning smells, scattered petals from vases on locker tops, spring coming after the long winter. Clive and Maureen buffed up the floor space till you could see your face whether you wanted to or not.

His bed was pushed back to its place, away from the line of sunshine. A whirring lawnmower sent in the juicy smell of cut grass, the civvy worker from the village whistling a tune as he emptied a full bin, shouting good morning to someone going along the path. Windowframes looked glassless, ready for the matron's ten o'clock inspection. Maureen collected the clothfooted brooms, and Clive scooped up the tins of polish.

Joe saw her at the end of the ward. 'Here comes the Captain, lads! Sleep to attention!'

She was a dumpy woman with a block face, wore medal ribbons, and might indeed have been capable of harrying a clipper around Cape Horn. Squadron-Leader O'Dowd seemed awed, and Sister Middleton walked rigidly behind. But in spite of her aspect she didn't pass a bed without some encouraging words, which Brian considered himself well able to do without. He disliked people assuming from across the great divide that they had a right to comment, or thinking you craved their interference and should feel grateful to them for making your life more tolerable.

'This airman had an artificial pneumothorax a month ago.' They stood at the end of his bed. 'He's getting on quite well.'

'Good for him,' the matron said. 'I'm sure you'll be out soon.'

The man at the lawnmower went back to his singing, and birds fought on the opposite eaves. The waiting world gave strength and hope, closest to it on those nights when he went with Rachel to the empty side room, where the exertions which should have impeded his progress produced mystifyingly good results, in that his blood sediment rate had descended to almost normal.

'You seem to be on the mend,' Sister Middleton said. He scorned such remarks – though glad to hear them from her. Perhaps she was right. Fitness must be scientifically proved, and he only had to wait, wondering what exactly he was on the mend from, since he had not been broken, one day following another so that if it wasn't for dates ticked off in the diary that his sister Margaret sent him, they would go without trace.

Hands on hips, she stood as if waiting for a word of appreciation at her concern. He had nothing to say, mouth blocked, no connection with her, though the silence intensified his stare. With a vague movement of incomprehension she left him to his reading, and to his irritation at having been so mute.

He read advertisements from the Crown Agents offering posts in the colonies, salaries up to a thousand pounds a year with overseas and clothing allowances, riches beyond the dreams of Croesus, once almost open to him, now closed forever, but such work and money was fabulous to mull upon. As consolation he cheerfully did the crossword to exercise his brain. He noted the title, author of each book read, good or bad, and from the *Radio Times* marked what Third Programme plays and music he wanted to hear. Like Candide he cultivated the garden, but of the mind, and when Rachel was on leave he wrote to her, and even on her days off, letters overflowing with love like milk left too long on the fire. He was getting to know her, but she didn't seem attached either to herself or to him, and he didn't know whether this was because she was so young, or because a type like him could never get to know anyone like her. He didn't care, and during their meetings felt his backbone shoot ecstatically into space. When his french letters ran out she bought more from the chemist's, something he couldn't imagine Pauline doing. 'What do you tek *me* for? Get 'em yourself. I'm not *that* sort!' Such a fact pointed to one more difficulty of understanding Rachel, though it soon seemed natural that she should ensure his supply of whatever would stop her getting pregnant. He marvelled, all the same, at something even Bert would find hard to believe.

In the side room, they stood against the wall, held each other, savoured their kisses and murmured about love, so that he felt fifteen again, or that she was, or that they both were, he couldn't tell, wanted to get the mattress from the cupboard so that they could lie on the floor, though sometimes she was more impatient, because for him the long kisses and closeness of their bodies while standing lulled him into a pleasant stability of desire that, something new for him, he could maintain forever. And then if he wanted her to lie down she might say her period was on (which he'd already guessed), but still make sure he didn't go unsatisfied back to bed.

They stood to the side of the door which, should anyone walk in, would conceal them until they thought of an excuse, though both knew there would be too little time. The sister (who was very Sister Mattick, quipped Rachel) came on her rounds at one, but he was asleep by then.

After making love they went across to the kitchen, and in the light he saw her, like a blind man who has just regained his sight, with her pale tired face and exquisite brown hair, set the tea kettle on the spirit stove hemmed in by tubes and bottles. He lit two cigarettes. 'Shall I get some beer from my locker?'

She stood away, and leaned against the table. 'You drink, and smoke – and do the other thing. How do you expect to get better?'

'I think I'll manage. All I want to do is get out of here.'

'And then what?'

He couldn't see that far ahead, thought only about the past, and not much of that anymore. 'I'll know what to do when it happens.'

'You're married, aren't you?'

He had mentioned it, his records were in the hospital file for everyone to see, and who knew if Pauline wouldn't come walking up the ward one day? 'She doesn't write anymore, which means it's finished.'

'It's surprising she never came to see you. I was hoping to see what she was like.'

The idea horrified him, but her curiosity was understandable. The image of them together made him want to make love again, though the reality didn't bear thinking about. 'What for?'

'To get to know you a bit more.'

He put an arm on her shoulder. 'Ask anything you like.'

'It's harder to ask, than for you to tell me.'

There was nothing to tell. Nothing he *could* tell. 'Such as what?'

'If I knew I wouldn't ask.' She sipped her tea. 'That's why I wanted to see your wife.'

The word sounded strange on her lips. 'I'll write, and insist that she visits me.'

'Will you?'

He'd cut his throat first. 'Why not?'

'I knew you didn't get on very well,' she said, 'otherwise I wouldn't have let you go all the way.'

Such primitive calculation surprised him, yet seemed elementary compared to much of his. He had lost the ability to communicate, except among people he had known since birth, and with them there wasn't much to say. Nevertheless, if he didn't tell her something she might lose interest. 'We got married at eighteen.'

She looked concerned. 'Did you love her?'

It would be dishonest not to answer plainly. 'She was pregnant.' I was a sack of iron filings spilled around a magnet, got caught in the lines of force, and couldn't escape. Same with her. We were young, and I loved her, though I don't think I was in love with her. 'It happened four years ago, and seems like a century. At that age you do things by instinct.'

'You talk like an old man.' She touched his hand. 'You seem too bright to have fallen into something like that.'

'I was out for a good time, and got more than I bargained for.'

'You've changed.'

Though not much caring whether he lived up to her expectations, he would try because he thought it might be good for him. She wanted to think well of him, yet he felt as if he had committed a crime somewhere in his past, an action of which he would be ashamed every minute of his life if she found out about it. 'It's impossible to say what I'll do when I get out.'

She took a long draw of her cigarette, and the expression of stony puzzlement did not make her less beautiful, though her voice lost all tone. 'I'd like to give up nursing, I'm sure of that.' He was wary of her changes from a tragic mask to an open smile, with little in between. 'But I do the football pools,' she added. 'Perhaps I'll win a lot of money.'

He couldn't shake away the idea that she had survived a catastrophe, whose details he was unable to imagine because her life had been so different. She had seen her father in agony, bones sticking out of his skin – and couldn't get over it. He did not know what led him to say: 'Let's go back into the side room.'

She crossed her legs, so that the apron lifted to show more stocking and rounded calf. Then she jumped as if a spring was inside her.

He had expected a refusal. If she couldn't get over the death of her father, maybe he had said the right thing. Perhaps it wasn't that at all. Had the uncle gone further than she'd admitted? Or did the uncle really exist? Whatever it was (and he had no way of knowing), the chances she was willing to take surprised him. If they were caught, nothing much could happen to him, but she would be thrown out in disgrace, 'dismissed with ignominy'. The responsibility was his, but he took her hand and drew her across the corridor, an initiative that made her more than usually passionate after he had closed the door. Or so it appeared.

She evaded his kisses, pushed his hand away, and ran to the door. He heard her cross the corridor, and wondered what he had done wrong. She was horrified at his way of managing things, though he couldn't think how he had failed her. He caught the squeak of Sister Middleton's shoes after the bump of the outer door. Even his good lung hardly breathed. Rachel

117

was answering questions, the clink of a bottle to make her words convincing.

He waited for the door to open, the argument to start, the rapid creation of lies. 'I couldn't sleep, so I wandered in here. I've misplaced a photograph of my wife. Thought it might be in my tunic pocket, hanging in the wardrobe. The nurse doesn't know I'm here. I can deceive anybody by my silence. I'm very good at that. I wonder where the photograph is? I'd better go back to bed, though. My teddy bear will wonder where I am.'

Not much use trying to kid Sister Middleton, slack to think so, the overbearing fact of his illness smothering the smaller matters of the instinct. In Malaya his fine-tuned caution had surrounded his hut with tin cans and tripwires when the terrorist troubles began, kept his bayonet sharp, loaded rifle close, but here he had relied on Rachel for protection, and look where it had got them.

He read the sounds. The sister had finished talking and gone into the ward, shining her torch at the beds, up one side, down the other. He had left his bedclothes and pillows so that a quick flash of her light would show nothing wrong. She was often cursory, because it was unthinkable anyone could be missing. But he expected her to call: 'Where's Seaton? He always was a queer fish, and now he's bolted.'

Then she would try the door he stood behind. He waited. Life had become a pleasant kind of death, but he vowed to regain his usual alertness, if it was not too late, even if only to prove his concern for Rachel. He always fought back his coughs, no impulse irresistible. If he coughed, they might think he had TB. He was in an asylum, acting normal to prove he was sane. Coughing was a badge of noise as isolating as the leper's bell.

The rage to ease the irritation in his throat was hard to block, and he sweated like a prisoner in hiding during an enemy search, coloured flames dancing with the effort not to give himself away as Sister Middleton stood outside the door telling Rachel that all was well.

She had gone. God watches over you, his grandmother would have reminded him, if his grandfather had not been close. There was no cough. Impossible to understand. He wanted to laugh. Rachel hurried him to his bed.

Sister Mattick must have thought her visit hadn't been thorough enough. As soon as his head was down she came back, as if she had known, and given him time to get where he belonged. Her light was a knife over his eyes, not held momentarily, either, to let him know that an old hand like her could not be deceived. She wanted him to open his eyes, and acknowledge that he knew she knew. But he didn't. Step aside from my life. Work it out yourself. Let her call him cunning if it made her feel better. But he liked her, at that moment seemed closer to her than Rachel, a kind of love, though not quite the same. He was tempted to make a sign so that she would not get on to Rachel about his misdemeanour against King's Regulations, but he kept quiet in case she had nothing positive to tax her with. Work that one out as well, he thought. He was a grown man, and the game was infantile.

The light turned away.

Chapter

❧ ELEVEN

The pay sergeant filled his palm with pound notes and coins in exchange for his signature. Strange to get eight bob a day for lying in bed. 'The air force looks after its own,' Joe laughed. 'You'll have to get used to it, like the rest of us.' No trouble at all. What money he didn't need his mother put into a savings account at the post office.

The script of his expedition to Gunong Barat was hatched with additions and crossings out, and he craved to see it as orderly as when it came from Edgeworth. Summers offered to lend his typewriter, but Brian ordered one from a smooth-faced bespectacled traveller who came round offering reconditioned machines – cash on delivery.

He asked his mother to draw twenty-six pounds from his bank and send it by registered mail, to reach him before the salesman returned with a Remington Portable. He knew typing from his telegraphist's trade, and the excitement of owning such a machine made up for fewer solo meetings with Rachel, for since Sister Middleton had twigged he wasn't in bed when he should have been, they chanced it no more than once or twice a week. 'But I've always got on well with her,' Rachel told him. 'She asked what school I'd been to, and it turned out that one of her sisters went there as well. We must take care from now on, though.'

Being in love, he no longer craved to escape his durance.

There was always something to look forward to, apart from Rachel's visits and turns of duty, even if only a blood test, X-ray, sputum result, or the next refill for his pneumothorax. He had no option but to follow the rules, no matter how irritating, and look on his recovery like a game of ludo, every move a few more careful steps towards the winning post and then, he supposed, falling into oblivion like a discarded tiddliwink.

Sergeant Brent, the airgunner who made model aero-engines, told him as he went by his bed that he might be eligible for a pension when time for demob came. Brian laughed at the idea. Only those wounded in battle got pensions.

'You were in Malaya, weren't you?'

'Nearly two years.'

'So you'll get forty-five bob a week, and twenty-six bob National Health pay. A hundred per cent disablement.'

'You're joking.'

'Three pounds eleven shillings. Better than a poke in the eye with a bit of burnt stick.'

The future seemed unreal, and a pension even more so. He hadn't expected anything.

'People live on less.' Brent beckoned. 'Come closer.'

Brian sat by his bed, and the airgunner put down the tiny file with which he was scraping at a piece of metal over an ashtray. 'When the demob officer comes to talk to you about your case, he'll ask you where you think you caught TB.' He spoke softly. 'So what will you tell him?'

'That I got it in Malaya.'

His expression turned to despair. 'If you say that, it'll lead to a dispute, and if it leads to a dispute they might try to prove you got it one day when you were on leave. Or they might not, but you never know. So when he asks, just look dumb and say you don't know. I don't suppose you'll find it difficult.'

'Why not tell the truth?'

'Because there's no such bloody thing, Tosh. You'll only be giving an opinion, and in this mob it pays to keep your opinions to yourself. Why do you think they suddenly get friendly and invite you to give an opinion? Just listen to an old sweat who's heard a thing or two in his time.' He scratched his short black hair, brought a few iron filings out in his fingernail. 'A life of

121

idleness and leisure will be much to your liking. From now on we're all pensioners – not decked out like ancient Chelsea blokes in red coats and funny hats, but pensioners nevertheless; not going around with a hook, a crutch and an eye patch, but careful of every breath and footstep nevertheless; Trenchard's shadows, a hundred per cent disabled but without a mark on us, except where the flies have been. The children of the Gods – eh? As for passing the time, there's always self-improvement and self-education – instead of self-abuse and self-degradation – to make a better man of you – Gunga Din. Ever thought of going to university?'

What a gift of the gab some sergeants had – though maybe the TB fever made him like that. 'I didn't even go to grammar school.'

'Neither did I. I shan't go to university, either. But you look as if *you* could, always having your head in a book. Me, I'll earn more this way. But if you want, you can go to night school to learn Latin. All them dud kids at Eton do it, so I don't see why you shouldn't. Then you can get a university grant as an ex-serviceman. Everything's coming your way, provided you don't cough your lungs up. But then, you can't have everything.'

You certainly couldn't. Red patches flushed up Brent's cheeks as if death the invisible man was dabbing rouge there. He had already lost three ribs, but still went in and out of being positive. If anyone deserved a pension, he did. Two, in fact. Brian felt in his prime by comparison, and poured him a glass of water to still the hacking beast. Sister Middleton, whose ear was so finely tuned she could pick up a cough ten miles off, came and took away his work tray, and persuaded him to rest. 'You'd better go back to bed as well, Seaton. I know you're not supposed to be up.'

'I was on my way back from the bathroom, Sister.'

'I know. But don't tempt fate.'

The registered envelope from his mother had eighteen pounds instead of twenty-six, though her letter said the full sum had been sent. He had enough in his locker to make up the amount when the salesman brought the typewriter, but what had happened to the rest? He wrote to ask, and meanwhile speculated that having so much cash in hand she had been tempted into a Saturday night out. His father had seen her putting it into the envelope. 'What's all that money for, duck?'

'It's our Brian's. He asked me to get it out of his bank and send it to him at the hospital.'

'What does he want all that for, lying in bed? He's got nowt to spend it on. Let's go and have a jar or two at the White 'Oss. He wain't mind. Just write that we wanted a bit o' fun at the boozer.'

It made no sense. She would have told him. Maybe they were in arrears with the rent, though his father earned enough, and they didn't need to be. The rent man had threatened to bring the bailiffs and have them thrown into the street. They wanted eight quid to save themselves. 'He'll understand,' his father said. 'We'll send a quid a week out of my wages for the next two months to pay him back. I'm sorry we have to do it, but we've got no option, have we Vera, duck?'

He would have given it to them, if that had been the case. They were feckless enough to get into such a situation, but you couldn't curse human nature, at least not theirs. On VE Day his father had been so blindoe he had lost his false teeth down the lavatory when he was sick, so Brian gave him nine pounds to get another set.

Yet to rob him now that he was in hospital was uncharacteristic. They'd never robbed him, so he didn't complain in his letter, but only asked Vera why she hadn't sent all of the twenty-six pounds. Something was wrong, he didn't know what. The registered envelope had been sealed, the blue cross of pencil indelibly intact, and guaranteed by the Royal Mail, so he would never know how he had been robbed.

He didn't worry. He didn't care. Don't care was hung, his grandmother called out, but there had to be a cut-off point, because worrying got you nowhere, and what else could you worry about if you'd already got TB? Life was so simple he laughed himself to sleep.

His mother wrote by return of post. Watched by Harold, she had counted the money into the envelope. She went back to the post office and kicked up a row, but the woman behind the counter, whom she'd known all her life, swore blind nobody had touched it, because registered letters were as safe as houses, though she would forward the complaint to head office.

Eight quid gone, and he felt guilty, as if he had doubted his mother. But why eight, instead of nine, or twenty – or all of it? Registered mail came to the office at the end of the ward, and the orderly on duty signed the chit before handing it out, a plain infallible procedure – which he was too busy with his typewriter to mull on. An officer from the RAF police came asking who had lost money from registered letters, and it turned out that he wasn't the only one robbed.

Corporal Knotman's time was up, and he was passing through Blighty to Canada. Late for the boat, the air force had flown him to Lyneham in a York, his aerogram from Singapore signifying that he was on his way.

'Surprised? Don't get up. The sister with the big tits and one eye told me you weren't long for this world, so I told her I was from the Air Ministry to take statements about your heroic actions in Malaya. Said you were up for a gong – the Air Force Medal, at least. She told me you got back from Malaya by the skin of your teeth. At one time they were planing the planks for your coffin. Now they're saving it for somebody else. "Though we've still got our eye on him," she said.'

Brian last saw him wearing khaki drill, bush hat, mosquito boots and crumpled socks, knees well brown and on his way out of the mess to say goodbye. He wore a full moustache, and was often unshaven, grizzled sparse hair like a low cloud descended, a firm chin, wide mouth and sparkling grey eyes, a hefty figure of a man. He'd often lost his stripes for slovenliness and cheek, but now he wore a grey suit, waistcoat, tie, mackintosh over his arm, trilby in hand, polished shoes – and a shaving cut under his left ear.

'I've never seen anyone in bed who looks so well. You must weigh two stone more than after running around in the jungle.'

'They feed us on meat and beer.'

'I wouldn't have known you if that sister hadn't pointed you out. I think she's in love with you, by the way, but being English she'll never say so. You'd have to hit her with a shovel first. What have you been doing to her? You've got yourself a very cushy billet, a change from sleeping in the undergrowth with a tin of cold stew under your belt, and a Dyak's doxie you grabbed from the trees. I know where you'd rather be, though, eh?'

'What about you?'

He looked up and down the ward, as if to an escape route, meaty hands resting on his thighs. 'It's back to the wide open spaces for me.'

'What are you going to do with all that poetry you wrote?' Brian had read some of his verses at Kota Libis, cynical–lyrical love stuff about the women he'd shagged from Ramree Island to Car Nicobar.

He showed his broken teeth in a smile. 'Well, I wouldn't stay in this rundown country. Rationing, in 1949! What kind of socialism's that? You're living under a dictatorship. The socialism of surfeit's what I believe in. To every man according to his wants. The jab of ambition is everyone's right, so I'm going back to where they're felling timber and sinking oil wells and shelling out a hundred dollars a week. That's the stuff to write poems about. I brought some back from Malaya. The rest I burned.'

'Do you think you'll get them published?'

'I write 'em for myself. They don't go much for poetry in Canada.'

'If they're good, they will.'

'Bullshit. I just want to get home and see snow. See that door at the end of the ward? Go through it. You don't belong here, I don't care what's wrong with you. Write a poem about it, then scat. Come to Canada. They still need wireless operators up north. I'd piss blood and shit rocks if I had to stay in a place like this.'

'They don't let people into Canada with what I've got.'

'Change your name. Forge your records. What sort of moral being have you turned into? You never lacked initiative, airman. Without you that whole Gunong Barat fiasco would never have got off the ground. A crowded hour of glorious life is worth an age without a name. Remember? If you were sick and couldn't move, that'd be different. Get a job on a farm in Canada. That'll fix you up.'

125

Brian could only smile, and inwardly wonder why the hell Knotman had come to see him. 'I'll be out in a few months. They even talk about giving me a pension.'

His walrus roar turned into a laugh. 'A pension book in one hand, and a ration book in the other! The key to the door at last! And when we talked socialism in the NAAFI you said you were going back into the factory to convert everybody, and sail the *Battleship Potemkin* up the Trent! I can understand you backtracking on that little option, because in the Revolution troublemakers like us would be the first to get shot. We're romantics, who only *talk* about socialism, but as for living under it, excuse me while I get out my Monopoly game. I'm an anarchist in a country of one, off to the only country where you can work and be left alone. If you let these Limey bastards pension you off you'll be eating out of their hands. Nothing is for nothing, especially in this country.'

Such words warmed him with expectation and hope, but he was no longer part of Knotman's world. 'I'll go out under my own terms, when I'm good and ready.'

'Well, don't mind me sounding off, but if anybody had told me you would end up in this human cattle pen when we were in the jungle, I'd have put them at the hot end of a blowpipe. Even I couldn't have seen you like a patient anaesthetised upon a table. Still, when I heard you were knocked up with TB I was envious. He'll be a poet before I am, I thought. As for writing anything, I ain't had time the last few months. While I'm staying in London I'm going with a woman who won't leave me alone, but that's because I won't leave her alone. The women are the best thing about this country. They're the other side of the coin to the weather.'

He was the same old sweat from Malaya, a veteran pushing thirty, and with only a few days in London to enjoy himself he had spent time to come and see him, bringing half a dozen of his favourite Malayan cheroots in a tin so that they wouldn't break on the journey.

'I wrote an account of our trip up Gunong Barat,' Brian said. 'For something to do. And so that I wouldn't forget it.'

He had also written a few poems in his old logbook, read some to Rachel and to Summers at the other end of the ward,

126

but he couldn't show any to Knotman. Summers, with the pink moon-round face, eyes that seemed almost Chinese, told him they didn't scan.

'What's scan?'

'Make a certain rhythm. We did prosody for School Cert. Poetic grammar. Tells you about it at the back of this selection from Wordsworth. I come from Grasmere, so I carry it with me. You can borrow it.'

Nothing was what it seemed. Even poetry had rules. Dactyl was Greek for finger, a long and two short beats, which in morse became D for Dactyl. Iambs and anapaests, trochees and spondees weren't so simple, though knowing morse made them easy to remember if you read them aloud. He learned about rhyme schemes, length of line, differing shapes and forms, all of it easier to comprehend than physics at radio school. Poetry existed before rules were made. Take the rules away and the poems were still there, much like the chair of Immanuel Kant.

'The earliest poets hadn't heard of prosody,' Summers said, 'but it's useful for you to know it, then you can see how poems are constructed.'

Plenty of knowledge was coming his way. Rachel had given him a Tennyson Selection for his birthday, and now that he had learned prosody, a word like hendecasyllabics was teaching him to count in Greek.

'Not long after you left,' Knotman said, another scornful look up and down the ward, 'I led a group to the top of a mountain that made Gunong Barat look like a pimple on a giraffe's left testicle. We went after a kite that pranged, and got two bods out alive. Gunong Barat was no height at all. Mind you, I thought I'd write about it as well, but I don't know how to tackle it.'

'I start my account on the evening of the fourth day,' Brian said after a silence, 'when we got to the cliff and couldn't go any higher. Then I switch to the beginning, and when I reached the cliff again I carried on to the end. I typed a carbon copy, so you can take it if you like.'

Knotman put the papers in his pocket. 'When you get out, and feel like making a new start, scratch a few lines on a piece of slate and send it to my mother's address. It's useful to know somebody when you land in a strange place. I could say some awful things about Canada, but at least it's big, and that makes up for a lot.'

Rain splashed at the window, and Brian watched him striding across the lawn – which was forbidden – mackintosh flapping, hat cocked to signify his general liking for the world because soon he would be free of the air force, a unified person impervious to difficulties. Everything came to the man who acknowledged no split between body and spirit. If he had toothache, a bad back, sore feet, a hangover, they never stayed long enough to ruin his outlook.

Brian, living from day to day, wouldn't see him again. Tears pressed, but he held them back. To stay behind and rot in bed was painful, but he couldn't move except to straighten the blankets and shift position so as not to seize up with cramp.

A different picture of Knotman behind the moustache might be one of misery, of pain that caused him to brag, of uncertainty that drove him to woman-chasing. He reached for his pen.

> I don't know where I'm going
> I only know where I am,
> But Fate will get me, like a fox
> That knows how to open a hedgehog
> Like a child its toy-box.
>
> I've got a key to the door
> But somebody's altered the lock.
> The door was made of wood
> And now it's turned into rock.
> If I don't know where I'm going
> Will the door open or not?

Rachel laughed, waking someone who still slept. Life was good. He had every reason for staying, and better the place you knew than one you didn't. He would show her the poem, whether or not it scanned. She set down his tea, a squeeze of the hand and a larger dollop of jam. 'See you after supper.'

They would be together in the end room – impossible to sign himself out of paradise.

Drowsy from dawn to lights-out, hours dissolved like butter under the sun. Strength lurked somewhere but indolence was pleasant, and he preferred to let time do its work. No longer bored, he didn't even care what impression he made on Rachel. They held hands, happy not to talk, in which silence he felt more like himself than otherwise.

He was mendable, said O'Dowd and, looking at his case notes, gave him permission to get up between ten o'clock and midday, so that without any subterfuge he could put on his dressing gown and talk to Summers about poetry, or natter to Brent on future prospects.

Maureen and Clive didn't turn up for duty, and everyone thought they had deserted, being so passionately involved. Instead, they were under arrest in the guardroom, because Cunning Clive and Marauding Maureen had steamed open registered letters and extracted cash, gluing down the flaps so that nobody would be any the wiser.

When the camp post office had been cleared of suspicion the police had gone to local pubs and watched anyone spending more than their few bob a day, and after observing Maureen and Clive had sent a decoy letter which in their blind greed the orderlies could not help looking into.

Eight pounds filched was more than a fortnight's Group Two pay. 'It's a good thing I'm not in charge,' Brent wheezed. 'I lost fifteen quid.'

Brian wondered what they had done with the cash.

'Stayed at the best hotels in London. Or basked on the beach in Devon. Maybe they stashed most of it away, and they'll share it when they get out. They'd better not cross my path. Hanging's too good for 'em.'

The Scotsman whirlwinded newspapers right and left. 'Dinna yer pay me noo, laddie,' he called when a recent arrival reached for his cash. 'See me on Saturday.'

Sister Middleton followed the coffee trolley with the morning mail, handling it herself after the fiasco of looting. 'Nothing for you today, Seaton.'

Sometimes it was hard to say which of her eyes were dead. Behind her ward-sister exterior was an eagerness which he could not explain, in the glint of an eye, the shapely lift of her lips, both beyond her control. But he noticed it, and suspected that she knew he was the only one who did, which might explain her few seconds of hesitation before going on to the next bed. She wanted him to mention what he had so acutely observed about her, knew that he couldn't, but was invariably disappointed when he didn't, as if he knew something about her which she didn't even know herself.

'Maybe tomorrow.'

'I don't suppose you mind.' She spoke as if suddenly disliking him. Or so it seemed, but he could have been as wrong about that as he was about so many other nuances. 'At least the mail's safe these days,' he remarked.

'Well, we couldn't help it. Can't be everywhere at once, you know.'

He was surprised that such a confident impregnable person should think he was blaming her, and even his smile didn't mend matters by the time she swung away to someone for whom she did have some mail.

Chapter
❧ TWELVE

Around the block and through the married quarters, he got over the perimeter fence on the opposite side of the camp to the guardroom. An Avro York grumbled towards Lyneham. Three fields lay between him and the lane a quarter of a mile away, but he couldn't care less what anybody thought as he paused to take in the fresh air like cooling snow, a twinge in his chest from yesterday's refill.

Vivid buttercups leaned against Queen Anne's lace whose thick stalks had outgrown their strength. Behind the nettles a medley of vegetation buttressed a hedge which, except for short gaps, gave cover on his way to the village.

Allowed up four hours a day, he could put on his uniform, though instead of a blue collar and black tie the hospital dress of white open-necked shirt would make him easy to spot beyond the environs of the camp. 'Going to visit a friend in Ward Eleven,' he told the orderly, who said all right as long as you get back before Sister Middleton comes on her inspection.

A fluting cuckoo sounded from the woods as he went through a field of green wheat. Standing, he felt dozy and vulnerable. When he moved, he felt safe.

At the lane a slim-legged horse came across the field and stood at the fence, an arched but ample back, a white line down its long head merging into the left nostril, mane parted by the breeze.

Scattered houses began four miles away, a smoking train heading for the station, the squeak and clank from marshalling yards carried on the wind. He spoke to the horse and patted it, a picture of sensible endurance at the bothering flies. Almond eyes beamed rather than looked, ears twitching like aerials. A sideways push against his arm demanded attention, the first creature to meet him on his foray out of bounds. The horse craved to abandon its unthinking state for his, sensing the barrier without knowing how to cross it. He could do nothing for the horse, its neck arching towards the grass. A horse would always remain a horse, and he lacked the power to turn it into anything other than what it was.

He tugged at succulent grass, but it preferred to chew his hair. When he pulled away it licked at the sparks badge on his tunic. Grandfather Merton, a craftsman farrier two years dead, would calm any horse with secret words, and cure their sicknesses by lotions to rub on them or make them drink. For himself when out of sorts he would take a bottle of the same piss-like jollop and, shaking the contents into a foam, turn back his head and drink the lot. His eyes spun. He pushed a hand up his features as if they had turned to rubber – then went to work.

A dose of the same medicine might scorch away every trace of TB, though without obliterating the spirit that had put it there. His divorce from the real world had been fated since birth, but it was as well he hadn't known that the Sword of Damocles swung like a metronome above.

Merton would not have advised him to walk out without being cured, might even have visited him. He had been lousy to his own children, and never called at their houses when they had kids of their own, but Brian was different, a living commodity motivated perhaps by his grandfather's peculiarities, and set for the future after he was dead. Merton would have thought that way.

A sunken lane descended the hill, grey stone walls supporting the gardens of thatched cottages. He wanted to live in one with Rachel. Rain slashed at the windows, the room warmed by a coal fire. They would make love to flashes of lightning under the beamed ceiling, and thunder howitzering between the clouds, the first time since the troopship that he had imagined a future.

Two men at the bar who recognised his dress thought that if he got close they might catch something, but to give them what he had was beyond his power, so he took his pint to the window, hoping the landlord wouldn't get on the blower and complain to the hospital that one of its inmates was loose. An affectionate Labrador came over to sniff but was called gruffly to heel.

Too early for appointments saved you from the sin of being late, but eventually a smart airwoman with shining buttons and cap badge got off the bus, and those at the bar had something to stare at. He stood to greet her, fully dressed and back in action with the sort of girl he had never dated. She smiled at seeing him in a public place. 'Been here long, darling?'

He got her a gin, and the pub noise hid their speech. In the room at the end of the ward they had whispered about a holiday together in August. 'I got a list of boarding houses from Devon, so we can book ourselves in for a couple of weeks.' He had more than enough for fares and spending money. 'After reading *Lorna Doone* I want to visit Oare and Ilfracombe.'

She held his hands, eyes widening as if she couldn't properly see him. 'I can't wait.'

He drank the beer. 'It's thirsty work, breaking out of camp.'

'Quiet,' she said, 'or they'll carry you back in a straight-jacket.'

'Another experience.'

'Write a poem about it.'

Two flies were making a hell of a buzz over a bit of nooky on the window glass. 'I'd rather get you another drink.'

'Don't I knock it back?'

Her lips hesitated before tasting, and with a delicate movement the gin was gone. 'When I go home I'll scrounge more books from my mother. She's got a whole set of Dickens.'

'Bring *David Copperfield*,' he said. 'I haven't read them yet, though my father loves all Dickens's works. In the Great War he carried a little red book in his tunic pocket. Do you know what it was?'

She didn't. Mention of any father reminded her of hers who

was dead. He held her hand. 'A little red book called *A Tale of Two Cities*. Saved his life when a bullet hit him. He had to buy another copy, though.'

The lie came uncalled for, a device for prolonging talk which signified he had too much to say, meaning that nothing possible or important could get a look in. He couldn't choose, fought for words because he had too much to hide, but when he thought of talking about what he had previously wanted to hide he decided it was too ordinary and not worth bothering with. The positive act of talking made him conspicuous no matter what he said, betrayed his character and gave the person to whom he was talking power over him, though he had no idea what he had to hide, or what he had done in his past that would shame him if he spoke without rehearsing what came into his mind. With his mates in camp the give-and-take rattled from one to another, as it had in the factory or between him and his girlfriends before joining up. But in the bridgehead of *terra incognita* with Rachel he had to choose his phrases before letting them go in a supposedly free flow of talk.

Often when he made the effort to produce civilised conversation for the sake of good manners his success was taken as natural ebullience. He appeared at ease, but felt so full of anxiety that he wondered if he had been like it all his life, and saw how important it was to achieve the same ease with Rachel as in inner conversations with himself. Maybe everyone had the same problems. Often, not caring whether he talked or not, he spoke with ease. Or Rachel might say something, and his response would set them going like a tennis match. When they sat by his bed not caring to talk, holding hands and kissing, he was embarrassed by the silence before she was, and would say anything to break it, occasionally misjudging the moment, and realising that he should have kept quiet.

'The other news,' he said, 'is that I got a letter from my wife.' Pauline was settled in with Albert, his one-time pal who was out of the army and had a job in an office downtown. He'd also got his own house, now that his mother had died. 'I left some of your books and clothes at Mam's, so you can collect them when you get demobbed. I'm happy, so hope you don't mind. Gary's happy as well, with his new dad.'

134

'When things get sorted out she'll want a divorce. I think her new bloke dictated the letter, because it isn't in her style.'

Rachel's cheeks were slightly swollen, the mouth more shapely, eyes shining as if close to tears, an expression often presaging a coolness which took a day to evaporate. 'Does it make you sad?'

'We gave each other up even before I went to Malaya.' He had said too much, too dim to realise that seriousness of any sort made her unhappy.

She'd be going on leave in the morning, she said, and dreaded bumping into that awful uncle. He got another drink hoping to cheer her, third round lucky, and told her about the horse in the field eating his hair. 'I go riding at home,' she said. 'The horse in my uncle's stables knows me as soon as it sees me.'

'What's its name?'

'Jackson.'

'I'd like to see you on a horse.'

He told her about his grandfather. 'He was blind in one eye, where a spark hit him.'

'Was there a spreading chestnut tree outside his forge?'

She was a bit tiddly.

'He worked at the pit when I knew him, shoeing ponies underground. Then motor cars came in, so he couldn't compete. He had eight kids.'

'Poor man.'

It was dusk, and time to go. 'I mustn't push my luck.'

The lane was dark, neither moon nor stars, the breeze carrying a smell of grass and mellow wheat when they stopped to kiss. 'I love you, darling.' She whispered, as if people might hear. 'Write to me like you did on my last leave. I love getting your letters.' Did she throw them away, like Pauline, or treasure them, as he did hers?

Rain splashed the asphalt, and at the top of the lane she left him, to go in by the main gate. He climbed the fence and walked along the hedge, every gap memorised, disturbing birds as he worked towards the perimeter. Crossing a lighted area in the camp he trod quietly, as if no sound meant out of sight, pictured strolling on Exmoor with Rachel, and having breakfast after a night in the same bed. Sweating and breathless, he pressed

135

himself into a doorway, while a camp policeman went by, such evasions nothing to someone brought up to avoid hostile gangs, or acting as Robin Hood in fields around the Nook. He smiled at his guerrilla skill, and walked on.

Sister Middleton came out of the office. He could have gone in the back way, the door was often unlocked, but he didn't think. Hesitate, and you're lost; look before you leap – not knowing why he hadn't been ready to dodge her.

'Where have you been?'

'In Ward Fifteen, Sister, talking to a friend.'

'The roof must have leaked.'

He could barely stand. 'I had a stroll on my way back.'

'And now you're dripping all over my clean floor. I was about to phone the guardroom and report you missing.'

He wasn't a kid, to be slammed in this way. If she said much more he'd tell her where to go, and it wouldn't be half as nice as the place he'd been to.

She smiled. 'Was the pub full?'

He motioned with his hand. 'Nearly.'

'You'd better dry yourself. I'll feel responsible if you get a fever.' She shook her head. 'You think you're invincible, but I've seen people up for eight hours a day and ready to be discharged, then they do something foolish and they're back on strict bed. We wouldn't like it to happen to you, so look after yourself. You're worth a lot to us, believe you me.'

She spoke as if she cared whether or not he killed himself, thought he was fragile. He laughed as he undressed in the spare room, hung his trousers by the radiator to keep the creases in.

The news went up the ward and back again. 'Who got a dressing-down from Sister Mattick?' Joe called.

He flashed a fuck-you sign.

'Lucky bastard,' Harry said.

An hour to go before lights-out, he flipped through his notebook, dreaming of Rachel. The sister set a mug of Ovaltine on his table. 'You missed this on your travels. Drink it up, and get to sleep. Your poem can wait till the morning.'

'I don't write poems, Sister.'

'That's not what I heard. Come on, lean forward. Your pillows are like sacks of walnuts.' She was close enough to kiss, to stroke, to slide into, an odour of cleanliness and perfume the only barrier. Proof of her goodwill was in hammering his pillows so that they would be soft when his head went down, and such care gave him a feeling of love, robbed him of his backbone. He didn't deserve it, it was wasted on him, it wasn't necessary to have pillows softened, hot drinks provided and tenderness delivered in order to go on living, something he'd given up with babyhood, if ever he'd had it – which he supposed he had. But this strange woman in white headdress and shoul-dercloak looked after him in such a way that he doubted he'd been tended like it before. Not that he was singled out, because all had their turn, and if she was intrigued by his escapade tonight, she would find something of interest in another patient tomorrow.

'How's that?'

'Thank you, Sister. No more walnuts.' Am I a painting? he wondered, when she stood back to look at him, or an ancient bloody monument? 'I was going to crunch them all up in my fist.'

'You don't look as if you'd get very far. If you visit your friend in Ward Fifteen again, choose a night when it isn't chucking it down.'

They said she had a glass eye, but he was certain she winked. 'Yes, Sister.'

'And don't let that drink get cold. I had it made specially.'

He followed her legs in white stockings down the polished floor, then went back to his notebook, the poem about Rachel transformed into one extolling her.

His body burned like a fire in a nightwatchman's bucket. He lay in bed, temperature up, blood sediment rate likewise, his spirit down. He was full of salt water, which for three days fought the fire. Sister Middleton was right. He ought to treat his body as if it belonged to someone else – his equal in prowess, and capable of knocking him down if he unthinkingly abused it.

Nothing could obliterate the fact of his being useless to the world, though survival was possible because he had long since stopped caring. As after a bout of malaria, however, fever came back to harrow when he had imagined the disease beaten by his resilient system, and after nine months the blow was still like the stone Sisyphus dragged forever up the hill.

He only had strength for a page to Rachel, ashamed that a walk in the rain had pole-axed him. He wanted to tell her why his letter was so short, couldn't make his pen obey, because even with her, who would understand, he was embarrassed at being ill.

Sister Middleton smiled, going by to deliver a bedpan. Coming back, he knew she was aware of passing his bed, but she was unseeing, eyes as if sweeping the floor in front of every mote of dust. She returned soon after: 'I hope you're a bit better today. You look it.'

He glanced from his book. 'Thank you, Sister. Fine.'

Since his relapse he had found more favour with her, as if he was the only patient needing care. He didn't know why this was, liked it and didn't like it. She seemed to pick up his thoughts. 'Well, it's only a chill. You'll be back to normal in a day or two, I suspect.'

He was going to say he hoped so, but there was no need, felt she only wanted to say things to him, needle him at his fall. Under a sudden wave of noise from the beds roundabout she said: 'Please watch yourself from now on.'

He wondered if he had heard right. 'I shall.'

He couldn't make her out, but then, nobody could. You weren't supposed to try. She was herself, so there was nothing to make out. When she was off duty, and observation was slack, he got up to test his legs, to regain their use for when Rachel returned.

She walked in after her leave, surprised to see him in bed. 'He got caught in the rain coming home from the boozer,' Joe shouted. 'Or whatever it was. Went down with the flu.'

She blushed. 'Did you?'

'Sister Mattick took him to task.'

He preferred to tell her himself. 'Pipe down, Scouse.'

She had brought him two novels by Dickens, poems by Rupert Brooke, a book on psychology, and a tin of sweets from her mother. 'They'll keep you quiet while you get better.'

'She shouldn't have sent these. They're still rationed.'

'Well, she did.'

'I'll write and thank her. It's marvellous of her to think about me.' He would meet her, the educated woman he'd never known. 'Did you have a good time?'

She looked straight ahead, no kiss, as if she had become shy during the break. 'I went riding with my mother. My horse killed a hedgehog, but it couldn't be helped. It was by a wood at the top of a hill.'

A french window opened on to a lawn, and Rachel walked across. Her mother, dark-haired but slightly grey, about forty years old, sat reading on the terrace, waiting for her daughter to come from the stables before they had tea. A narrow river flowed nearby.

'I told her about Devon.'

What a daft thing to do – though he couldn't say so.

'She doesn't want us to go.'

Her mother ran across the lawn with an umbrella, to save Rachel from the deluge. Her uncle lurked in the bushes – grey wavy hair, moustache, red cheeks, and unblinking blue eyes.

'She said it wasn't right.'

Argument would be useless. 'That's that, then.'

'I'm sorry. It would have been wonderful.'

The only prospect was marriage, but he was hooked already, and a divorce would take years, even if he had the money. There was no point suggesting that they go and live on his pension.

Now that the Devon plan had gone bust he felt that her love was waning, but she swore never to leave him, to love him till the end of her life. He said the same, and in his longing, when they got to the empty sideward, he wanted to pull off his french letter so that she would get pregnant, to be Fate itself and change their lives, shoot himself home in one exquisite flood so that they would indeed be one flesh, as it said in the Bible, nothing between them, and the baby would come out of her nine months later, an agonising launch from the estuary between her legs, the first of many, but watched by the miserable face of her squeamish mother, a notion which drained him in a way that kept her safe, because he hesitated in those few poised moments, and she would never know. Such an achievement eluded him

139

as had the summit of Gunong Barat, when he stood in the wet forest and couldn't gird himself for the final perilous climb. Perhaps you only learned by failure, by pulling back from the impossible. His backbone melted and flowed into its cul-de-sac, and she clung to him as if they were more than one flesh.

Even so, he acted as surely as Fate by not causing a disaster which would have destroyed their love. Her mother knew that if they went to Devon she would get pregnant, so she had saved him as well as her daughter, though for what? From now on it was as if he spoke to Rachel through a hole in the wall, divided from her like Pyramus from Thisbe. No lion would threaten her, nor would he do away with himself in supposing that it had, but a full meeting of their bodies and minds was impossible, and even while kissing her he sensed the renunciation of a quest which was not part of his nature.

She was moved to another ward, unable to dole out kisses or extra butter. The shift was sudden, as if a new boyfriend had crossed her path, and he didn't see her for a week, until the next cinema show, when she came to sit with him. The kiss was cursory, and she barely touched his hand.

Beds were pushed to the middle so that everyone could see, the film a broken-backed tale in which the man who seemed marked as the hero at the beginning was crossing a railway junction, and when he paused to look about him the changing points trapped his foot, and he was killed by an onrushing locomotive.

Rachel's eyes glistened at the satisfying tragedy.

'Tripe,' Brian said.

Everyone liked it.

'What was wrong with it?'

He should have used words which did not imply that she lacked judgement and taste, ought to have kept his trap shut instead of allowing a small difference of opinion to drive her away. She looked as if he had smacked her face, and didn't stay for the evening drink.

She came to see him once more, as if to convince herself that he wasn't worth carrying on with. Books were on his locker for her to take away. He was stiffnecked, unable to apologise, couldn't even think of an amusing lie to make her laugh. When she had gone he looked into his Bible.

'He that hath no rule over his own spirit is like a city that is broken down and without walls.'

Chapter

❧ THIRTEEN

Cattle stood by a clump of trees on the crest. In a dip behind lay the black hangars of the aerodrome, a windsock limp at its mast. In a month, if the tests stayed good, he'd get six weeks' leave, go to Nottingham and lodge with his parents. Then he would come back for the final tests before demob – the real one this time, and no mistake.

Clouds of horseflies hung over the hedge parsley. A track went directly to the summit, but he took a path which ascended gradually, avoiding waterfilled tractor ruts, a faint rattle of crows somewhere behind. A straightbacked set-featured man wearing a black cap and brown jacket rode by. He nodded a greeting, and the sleek horse carried him to the top of the hill, like Alexander on Bucephalus. He cantered around the site of the Saxon fort as if chasing the sun, then descended into a re-entrant – maybe a farmer on his daily run keeping an eye on land and cattle, a master of settled habits with a family, a car, and a house which had a parlour and a shelf of books.

The grassy area was surrounded by a ditch, and Brian descended between green walls. Holes barely big enough for your fist led to rabbit burrows where feverish life went on. He climbed the ramp into the open, stuck his cap in his belt, and sat down, couldn't rouse himself to read anymore of *Little Dorrit* though he wanted to know who would live and who would die. A large crow watched from a distance, wings uneasy with thoughts of food. Deciding he was not dead enough, it launched off into a thermal.

Someone was striding up the hill from the uninhabited Downs of the south. He didn't own the land, so anyone could walk by, though maybe whoever it was would pass on the opposite slope and not disturb his solitude. The break with Rachel had been so final that he was empty. They hadn't even met by accident to joke in a friendly way. Weeks had gone by, and he no longer cared that she hadn't answered his letters. The ludo game of recovery was being played, so what did it matter? He was on a one-way track to the winning post, and puzzlement about Rachel seemed only to help in banishing the TB from his system.

She stopped at the gate to search the sky with binoculars, so he turned away in case she might think he was looking at her. The sun warmed him, and he took off his tunic. Anxiety subsided, and smaller worries that pestered him even in sleep did not oppress as much as the gnats. Lighting a cigarette to disperse them made the open air more enjoyable.

Clouds were high, but you never knew when they would close ranks. He followed the angle of her binoculars to the large black crow with a flash of blue in its tail, watched it strut awhile and then take off.

She recognised him. 'What are you doing in these parts? Communing with nature?'

A grey mackintosh was folded over her arm, white blouse buttoned to the neck, a shoulder-bag matching her brown laced-up shoes.

'With myself, I suppose.'

She lacked breath, and smiled uncertainly, a headscarf to stop the wind scattering her fair hair. On the ward she was harassed and tight-lipped, and passing her quickly on the street he might not have known her, as if a uniform and the running of a ward disguised her real features. 'Don't look as if I'm trying to pick you up!' she laughed.

When he stood to explain his surprise at meeting her, they were the same height, though she was more robust. 'I didn't mean to.'

'It's lovely around here – strange more patients don't come up to sample it. You're the first one I've seen.'

A light plane stuttered towards Mildenborough. He'd look at that with binoculars, not birds. Silence again. In the air force you were obliged to salute an officer even if he was in his bath. She also was commissioned, and seeing her in such a place would be worth more than the price of a salute. He put his book away. 'I come up here a lot – unless it's raining.'

'We often wondered where you got to. It's a nice spot for writing poems.'

He wished she'd go on with her walk. 'I like to get away from people.'

'So do I, come to that' – her tone implying that he should be more polite.

'I thought you were the advance guard of a search party,' he said, 'seeing your binoculars.'

She circled her foot through the grass. 'I don't know who's supposed to be out of bed and who isn't, half the time. I only knew when *you* were.'

'I was ready to tumble into the ditch and make a run for it.'

She stood back to look at him. 'We should have found you, don't worry.'

I don't think you would, he said to himself.

'I hope you don't mind if I sit down. I've walked miles.'

He made room for her. Skulls and rusty swords were no doubt buried deep down in the mound. A compass would make widdershins. 'You must have seen what funny manoeuvres the birds do when they pass over.'

'I love to watch them. They don't even notice, if you're discreet.'

He offered a cigarette, but she didn't smoke. 'I'll bet they do.' Her body was close, and she couldn't know that his heart banged as loud as if he had run up the hill. 'Birds aren't really free,' he said. 'They have a struggle to exist, though I wouldn't mind being half as free.'

'That's a pretty tall order. Life just isn't like that.' It seemed that neither could end the silence, and looked in different directions. 'My name's Nora, in case you didn't know. While I'm off duty, anyway.'

'Well,' he said, 'you know mine.'

'No one else in the ward seems to need your kind of freedom.' She laughed as if to neutralise her disapproval – which she thought might have gone too far. Like everyone, there was more to her than was apparent. He saw the hole in the street, passed and repassed as a child, where material was brought to the surface by a painstaking construction of levels. Maybe to get into the depths of a person's mind you also had to build as intricately going down as you would if erecting a tower that you didn't want to fall.

'My father was a vicar, and there were five girls.' She followed a crow's progress into the dipped land towards the hospital. 'He just packed us off to earn our keep when the time came. Nurse, secretary, teacher – he didn't mind, as long as we were out of the way, though he certainly loved us and took care of us. But all he wanted was to read his old books in Greek and Latin. People said his sermons were good, though.' Her binoculars moved across his face. 'I got these when he died, and the books.'

'You must have been pleased.'

'As well as a cottage in Kent out of the money he left, where I can put my feet up. I'm afraid they're a bit mildewed after the winter – the books, I mean.' She turned from the sun, the deadness of her left eye accentuating her humour. Her lover was probably some squadron-leader at the airfield, unless she looked so lively because she didn't have one. 'I'm free inside,' she said, 'which is what matters. Isn't it?'

He hesitated, not knowing what to say. 'Would it be the same if you got married?'

If she didn't like him becoming personal he had no doubt that she would let him know. He would gladly answer such questions from her. They seemed far enough apart to tell each other anything.

Her tone made him regret his question. 'I don't think I'm cut out for that kind of life. In any case, the man I might have married was lost on operations, five years ago.'

Death was in the soil, grass rich with corpses. He was lucky

145

to be alive, though sitting by Nora Middleton was surely an experience which would never be repeated. 'I'm sorry about that.'

'I got over it. You do, you know. So many good people died. I've been with men since, but no one I'd dream of marrying. I can't be as free as the birds, but at least I can be that free!'

He wanted to touch her face, stroke her, comfort her. The gloss of her life would come away on his hands, like pollen from a flower. He didn't know whether that spark-gap was impossible because she was the sister of the ward, or because she was thirty and too far beyond him. Her confession had made a barrier. She knew how to protect herself. 'I was married,' he said, repaying her confidences, and to let her know that his life had not been without its events. 'But my wife was so shocked I'd caught TB that she's living with someone else now, though I think it was finished anyway.'

'You're a man of the world.' The laughter was about to break through faint lines at her eyes, but she held it back. 'Married, and separated already!'

'It leaves me feeling at a loss.'

'So what are you going to do?'

'I can't say.'

'I wish I was twenty-odd again.' She had access to his records, so knew about him anyway. He hoped she'd made a point of looking. After his bedraggled return from the village she had warned Rachel not to see him anymore, then got her transferred to another ward. Every situation had more than one story, so he could have been wrong in his assumption. 'I'd like to be a writer' – a notion so unreal that he hadn't even told Rachel.

She turned, and took his hand. 'Then you will be. I thought you would be, anyway. So much scribbling, I told myself, he's got to be.'

A grasshopper danced over his shoes. Other people lived for her, helped her to make life richer. She stood, keeping hold of his hand, so that he also got up, wondering what the hell was going on.

'Let's walk into the moat. I've never dared to go on my own. It's a bit scary.'

A lane ran up to the Nook, under a long tunnel-like railway-bridge, through which his robust Aunt Lydia had been afraid to go in the darkness, and got him to come with her on a winter's evening when she had needed something from the shop. The memory came back because he was being invited to make love to Sister Middleton. She couldn't add to her comment, hardly needed to: No one will see us there, except the birds, and they don't count, free as they are. 'I'm tired of life,' she said, holding his arm and pausing halfway down the slope, her cool cheek against his. 'If I want something, I take it.'

You couldn't believe anything till it happened, which was why he was where he was, and he knew when the green walls reared on either side that such a state would have to alter, so that he could get where he really wanted to be, though whether that would ever be better than where he was at the moment, as they stood and kissed, was impossible to say.

understatement

Chapter

❧ FOURTEEN

She couldn't speak to him in the ward. Even the air was
different. He couldn't talk to her. They were conspirators,
eating each other's messages. He did not know that he liked
such a system, though felt it was natural to him. Best not to
look. With Rachel, everyone had known, but there had been
less risk because they were equal in rank, while Nora could be
cashiered for carrying on with an airman. After four years in
the service he knew the score, so arrangements were made with
hardly any words, both beyond suspicion.

The ward was emptying. Mike had transferred to a civilian
sanatorium. Liverpool Joe had gone home. The airgunner
signed himself out, others were on sick leave, or had been
claimed by the natural attrition of recovery. Summers' family
had paid for him to go to Switzerland. Fewer erks were coming
off the boats with TB.

Soon he would go on leave, a time impossible to imagine in
the days when he was in thrall to that first fatal X-ray. An
altered person stared at him from the bathroom mirror – sceptical, uneasy, curious, no longer sure of himself – though the
same opaque blue eyes blocked off anyone from guessing his
thoughts.

Along the well-marked bridleway, he swung his jacket over
his shoulder, neither hut, barn, nor building visible. Clouds
were low, the air close. He thumbed a stone from his shoe, and

hoped it wouldn't rain. With blue patches to the south, and the wind against him, he was optimistic. He had fetched his civvies out of the store because Nora said it would be best for him not to meet her in uniform. She was staying the night in Mildenborough with a woman friend, and tomorrow would go on leave to her place in Kent. 'So come and see me. We can have tea in the Red Lion. You can tell me your plans.'

Did she think he was Field Marshal Montgomery? His plans were no more than urges, or instincts, or bare necessities, notions without hope or substance. She would go one way, and he another – that's what would happen. He flattened an insect against his forehead.

Ideas filled his notebook, a hundred scraps of pen-and-ink jigsaw slots that might one day cohere. Or they might not. He didn't care, and by not caring he was just as likely to make them into something durable. Not to care was the great cure-all, the one wise command to treat the mind as his servant, and the body as if he had the use of both lungs like everybody else. He'd walk three miles, four, eight, no place beyond the radius of his feet.

'You'll never be able to carry a suitcase again,' Squadron-Leader O'Dowd said, his mock-sombre pep-talking voice resonating the tannoy. 'Pick up one inadvertently, and it won't only be the sleeve of your jacket that will tear. If you have a hill to climb, rest every so often. Sit if you can. Try not to get into a crowded bus, where you won't find a seat. Stay downstairs if it's a double-decker. From now on you're fragile, as wounded as if you had been patched up after a battle. You are, as the French say – who always have a word for it, bless 'em – blessé. Don't forget it, for the rest of your lives, you're blessé! No more Hail Marys from me if you don't look after yourselves.'

The rolling downland was pitted with tumuli, scratches of ancient settlements in the wilderness – enough space to remind him of the world's size. He found it more tiring to go otherwise than at his normal quick pace, but on his first forays he'd had to rest when tackling the two hundred foot slope, almost added his bones on the surface of the Saxon fort to those under the soil. But he advanced. You'll kill yourself. No, I won't. You'll crack. I'll do what I like. You'll kick the bucket. 'I'd snuff it even sooner if I shirked like an invalid,' he said aloud, heady at being out on his own, weightless and wanting to sing, no more of the nagging anxieties which he had always felt with Rachel.

He dodged a couple of lorries smoking their way towards Reading. A woman in drab green behind the bookshop cashdesk settled her glasses as if to make sure he didn't nick anything. He paid one-and-sixpence for a magazine of poems with neither rhymes nor capital letters, nor any metre that he could pick out.

The hotel on the main street, with black and white beams, and a cobbled arch leading to the garage, advertised dinners at three-and-sixpence. A man wearing a checked jacket and derby hat came out as if blindoe. The tall anaemic woman at the reception desk who had so many rings on her fingers he was surprised she could lift her hand asked in a severe tone what she could do for him. You can go and drown yourself, since you ask. He had to sit down after walking seven miles. 'I want to have tea, please.'

The place smelled of sweat, carbolic soap, beer, cold mutton and tobacco, as if somebody had done bayonet practice on the cushions, releasing the stench of centuries. The assize judge ate his dinner after sentencing a few peasants to hang, and sending Captain Blood to be a slave in Virginia.

He went into a panelled side room of dark tables and straight-backed chairs. The print wouldn't hold, and he wondered how long he'd stay if she didn't turn up, though it wasn't yet four o'clock. A door thumped in a far off part of the inn, and he waited for a lawksamussey shriek as the maid dropped a tray and skedaddled because she'd seen a ghost.

Nora pulled out a chair before he could get up, called for the woman and asked for a full afternoon tea. Her presence brought on a feeling of excitement, and he wondered why he responded to one person and not another. 'It seemed such a long shot, me walking over the hills, and seeing you at the end of it.' They were meeting properly for the first time, and he couldn't even hold her hand. Prohibitions made something stir, and his glance hinted at the state he was in. 'I'd like to be with you. You know that, don't you?'

A flush indicated that he shouldn't have said so, but he didn't care, looked at her pouring tea from a large earthenware pot, and setting out the jam and scones. 'Don't think I don't know what you mean, but it isn't going to be possible this time.' She turned her left eye away. Her skin was incredibly clear and pink, breath sweet. She wore a pale green jersey and a cream skirt, hair tied back. 'You must visit me, then we can be together.'

A man and his wife came in, and a young couple whose motor had broken down. The food revived him. 'Do you mean that?'

Well-built, she worked too hard, continually on the go, burning energy like fat off a candle. She ate half a scone at a time. 'Don't look so startled. I'm flesh and blood as well, you know.'

The moat around the Saxon fort had been another kind of battlefield, dodging spears and axes, two electric cells scorching for each other but never quite meeting. They'd both needed courage to push it through – but not anymore. 'I'd like to, believe you me.'

'I'll give you my address.' She put a couple of fingers into her well-organised bag. 'You leave the hospital in three days. I'll be at my cottage, with ten days to go.' Her eyes sparkled, her whole face lit, fanatically rejoicing, he thought, in possession. 'You can listen to music. I'll let you wind up the gramophone.'

'My arm won't ache.'

'Well, I'm not cradle-snatching you.'

He was older than she might think. 'I worked in a factory before joining up.'

'A lot of people had to. What a change the war made. They're all classical records, though – Bach, Mozart, Haydn, Handel.'

He was, even so, in a different landmass, though he didn't see it as so important that their two worlds might not close. 'They're my favourites.'

'I'll order more sandwiches. You'll need them to walk back.'

A flycatcher hung above the fireplace, a bluebottle buzzing itself to death. His grandmother had used the same sort at the Nook, the sticky band unwinding out of a cartridge. 'I've eaten enough. If I catch the bus I'll be back in time for supper.' The

151

next few days would be a hundred years by any reckoning. 'If I eat anymore I'll weigh a ton.'

'They all do,' she smiled. 'It's Air Ministry policy. Feed 'em up, and chuck 'em out! You were thin when I first clapped eyes on you. We'll soon change that, I thought. And we did. Or the cooks did. Yes, I saw you brooding away and hoping you'd die. Not a chance.' She laughed, one of her side teeth made of gold. 'I notice everybody, but you were the only patient who looked at us with the same intensity that we – or me, rather – were looking at you. You carved out a patch for yourself, and wouldn't let anybody in. That's when I made up my mind that you weren't going to enjoy being alone too long if I could help it.'

He sweetened his tea, a full basin of sugar, in spite of rationing. 'How did you lose your eye?'

She twitched her nose. 'Nobody asks me that.'

Only her boyfriend. He wished the bluebottle would die. 'I hope you don't mind.'

'I was riding my cycle through a wood. Flying, more like. The front wheel hit a rut. Through the air I went, and when I woke up: no eye. Just a headache – well, and some pain. I didn't want to upset father, who was writing a sermon, so it was a good job a friend was with me to raise the alarm, or I'd have lost the other. Still, it doesn't miss anything.'

'So I've experienced.'

'I'd got my SRN, and the war was on. I was still useful.'

They chatted a while. Keeping his distance, he basked in her. 'And I fell for you,' she said. 'But I didn't show it – of course. Still it's time for you to go. I promised to cook supper for my friend and another sister from the hospital. Can't think what they'd say if they knew who I was with.'

His wallet was out. She took a pound note from her bag. 'Me now, you next time. It's only a few bob.'

The possibility of a next time made it easy to relent, but her smile of tenderness pained him, in case she expected something he could not provide. 'So come and see me, all right?'

He promised. They parted like brother and sister – without a handshake. The uncertainty floated him so much on air that it was impossible to sit in a bus with others. He walked around

152

the green moat of the Saxon fort, unable to recall who had made the first move. She had. He had poured his soul into her without a word. Was that love? It was all he had wanted, nothing else in life, but would he be so infatuated if he got to know everything about her? With Pauline there'd been so little to know that he hadn't even been jealous when she packed him in and went off with someone else.

He made as if to lift binoculars and bring a bird close. But that was Nora, not him. He wanted to be her, ached that she was so far away. He had always wanted a pair of binoculars, and craved them now, but he brought up the excuse, seeing as how he didn't have them, that you couldn't buy them, or that he had seen none for sale, or he had forgotten he wanted them when they had been displayed in the gaudy shopfronts of Kota Libis, or he hadn't enough money in his pocket at that particular time, or when the opportunity was there, when he had money, and the desire, and even the possibility of making a bargain, he turned his back on them for some reason he could never understand, pulled out of the situation as if he didn't need the binoculars after all, telling himself they would be a waste of money, he had other things to buy, but perhaps afflicted by an unacknowledged feeling that he did not deserve such a fine instrument, or that he did not want to add to the amount of his possessions for fear that one day he would not be able to carry everything at the same time, as an airman should. Whatever the reason, he regretted not being able to look more closely at the landscape of the Downs, as he hadn't also at the mountains of Arabia when passing through the Red Sea – jagged cardboard cutouts one behind the other, as if someone had opened a child's toybook at Christmas.

Clouds turned purple, underbellies mauve and pink. Late for supper, he would hold off a search party with a machine gun. Elgar's Cello Concerto was to be played on the wireless, and he didn't want to lose it. The air was damp, and he tore out a clump of grass, dark and green, already cool. He had walked too far, and pain seared his lungs. When he coughed he spat salt, the Arctic Ocean mixing with a Madagascan sun.

Nothing mattered except being alive. He should have stayed with Nora at the hotel. All the mistakes in his life had come because he hadn't spoken. But she wouldn't have agreed. Their association depended on as few words as possible, and too much speech would destroy it. And don't you forget it, her expression said, a system which threw up too many uncertainties.

His face in the mirror while changing into his invalid rig was as pallid as the chalk he had walked through. After a sluice of cold water he strolled into the ward, the usual dressing-gowned picture of himself. In Nottingham he would find a woman who would talk the hind leg off a donkey, ask no questions and give no answers, wanting only to get drunk and be taken to bed as a diversion from her labours at the factory. Or he would go on a pub crawl with Bert, there being, he decided, much to be said for the good old days.

A letter whose writing he did not recognise glided on to his bed, the envelope halfway between blue and green.

'My dear, I hope you got back all right. I felt guilty dragging you all that way, though you did insist on walking. I suppose it must have been dull being with me, but I want to say that I miss you very much. I couldn't sleep that night. When we were having tea I knew how much I was going to miss you, but I couldn't mention it, under the circumstances. Perhaps I shouldn't tell you, even now, though I don't see why not. I hope you aren't going to do anything silly like going straight to Nottingham when you go on leave. Love, N.'

Pausing in the wheatfield to read again and again, he wondered who she was and, even more, who he was. The same horse came over from the stable to be comforted.

Chapter

❧ FIFTEEN

The grey rockinghorse sea stretched as far as France, the only
country he would rather be than where he was now. Queen's
Bay was a collection of chalets, bungalows and fishermen's huts
below wooded cliffs. Dandelions grew out of drainpipes, fences
were rotten or half down, some places boarded up, gardens full
of nettles and brambles.

He had expected a stranger, but her appearance sharpened his
perception as if a light glowed behind a magnifying glass and
she was no longer the starched and preoccupied sister from the
hospital. She was smiling and relaxed as she came towards him.
'Half a pint of lacquer doesn't go very far.' She led him along
a dusty track between two cottages. 'People don't even have
the leisure to come for the summer. Nothing's back to normal
yet.'

He switched his case. 'I sent most of my stuff home by rail,
so that I could come straight here.'

'I'm glad.'

His chest was tight from yesterday's refill. 'I often wonder
what "normal" is.'

'I bought some strawberries for tea. At least they aren't on
the ration.' She carried his typewriter in its smart black case. 'I
suppose I'm normal. Aren't you?'

He laughed. 'If I ever was, I can't remember. Still, I suppose
I must have been.'

'Don't talk, or you'll get out of breath.' She picked up his case. 'Is it full of books? I can't think why. I shan't let you read them. This way.' A narrow walkway turned into an unpaved road by an area of gravel dunes and scrub patches. Waves came in sluggishly, one grey fist after another thumping as if on to a long pub bar demanding a drink. The superstructures of ships floated between low cloud and the horizon. 'You'll soon taste salt on your lips. It's a healthy place for someone like you.'

He wondered why he had come. She wasn't a stranger, yet made him feel a stranger to himself. Someone like him. He was used to it, as if such words were often said. The idea was laughable. Yet he felt at ease, wondering if she would justify the promise in her letter, or whether, ashamed of what she had written, no reference would be made. This is your room. Mine's across the landing. I do hope you'll be comfortable.

'I'm sure I'm going to like it.'

She didn't notice his irony. 'Here we are.' But she did. He caught the movement of her lips. She wore brown slacks and a white blouse, a cream cardigan over, breasts slightly shapeless, as if only a vest held them to her chest.

A small clapboard house behind a plot of overgrown garden wasn't exactly the shed she had led him to expect. A window denoted a bedroom under the angle of a slate roof. 'My sisters don't often come. They prefer the fleshpots of London.'

From manoeuvring high up, gulls descended to the water, playing at dive-bombers. 'They must be beautiful to watch through binoculars,' he said.

A wooden porch at the front door had a seat on either side. 'They're a damned nuisance. Can't get *them* to use bedpans!' She walked in, no unlocking necessary. 'Not done to use a key, though I do when I go away.'

I would, even if I went to the shop for a newspaper. He hung his mackintosh in the hallway, then went into a parlour as small as the one in Radford, though the furniture was neater, a floral-patterned sofa under the window, a glass-fronted bookcase, a table folded down, armchairs before the fireplace, framed pictures of ships and birds – not magazine illustrations which his father put behind glass and bordered with black tape, but real canvases and varnished wood.

A row of records in brown paper sleeves slotted underneath the gramophone cabinet. On the shelf were pot coats-of-arms from various holiday places, the room reminding him of his grandmother's parlour, though slightly less packed. 'Looks comfortable.'

'I'm glad you like it.' She rested a hand on his arm. 'I bought the place while the shells were coming over. The only damage was a hole in the roof, and I got permission to have it fixed. You wash while I make some lunch. We'll go to the Food Office in Dover tomorrow for a temporary Ration Book.'

There was no bathroom, but an inside lavatory near the back door led to a mildewed yard. He took off his shirt, wondering how long he would stay. If he had gone straight to Nottingham he wouldn't have escaped its web so easily, and Nora might have forgotten him if he'd waited till the last week of his leave.

'I'll throw your shirt in the tub, with some things of mine. Then we'll be married in the soapy water!' He rubbed himself dry, embarrassed at her close watch. 'Don't be shy. I've seen more than you think.' How was she to know? He passed his shirt. She looked at him, with which eye he didn't know, a statue of probity to when they had kissed on the Downs.

They ascended between bushes of yellow furze to the cliff top, the rifle range below. Looking at her old ordnance map provided an excuse to get his breath on the steep path. Inland was specked with woods and farms. Along the coast he identified Stickland Bay and the Isle of Gannet, and she pointed out the Ingle Lightship. 'When I'm on duty at the hospital, and thoroughly fed up, I think of all this. I often come up on my own.'

'I wish I could fly across to Boulogne – like Blériot.'

She squeezed his arm. 'You've just got back' – as if she wouldn't care to follow. 'Anyway, France isn't far.'

'Well, it would be a start.'

She went in front between tall thistles. A black and white butterfly hovered over the hedge parsley.

'Will you come with me?'

'What would we do?'

'Just live, I think.'

157

She leaned against him. 'Be idle?'

'Why not?'

'I suppose you've got the right, for a year or two.'

They went by the coastguard station, and beyond the golf course. Grass grew to the edge of the cliff, and he didn't care to get too close.

'Why not?'

'I might jump off.'

'For God's sake, why?'

She thought him a fool, but death would be even more sure than leaping off Nottingham Castle. 'It's wonderful being with you. Out of happiness.'

'It's the last damned thing I'd do. Don't say it again. It makes me feel afraid.'

He had got her to say something heartfelt, and she walked on the cliff-side, taking his other arm as if he really might do it. Stems of grass waved, silhouetted, and space was beyond, a two hundred foot fall into the sea. 'Is it too much for you?'

'I'll walk to Dover, if you like.'

'Let's go back.' She used the rain as an excuse, but it was only a shower. A line of breakers fell softly on the beach, cats' paws chasing mice. 'I haven't seen such gentle water since Malaya.'

'In the winter it comes in as if it's going to carry the house away.'

Driftwood littered the edge, pieces worn smooth and pale grey. 'We'll make a fire.'

They got back with their arms full, and he sawed the bigger pieces so that they would fit the grate. Clouds were low over the sea, rain spraying the scrub and beating at the window. The air was damp, and he laid a fire, splintering small pieces for kindling. 'You'll eke out my ration,' she said. 'The coal man only brings a hundredweight a week.' A thunderflash burst over the sea, illuminating the parlour. 'I'll batten the hatches, and get us some tea. I love storms.'

The burning driftwood made him sleepy. She came in with a tray, pulled the chairs close. 'I don't know how many times I've sat here on my own. It's nice to have you.'

Green flames in the fireplace, his grandmother said, were devils dancing in hell. He reached for her hand. 'I wasn't sure you wanted me to come.'

'You'll never know how much it took me to write that letter. I didn't know how you'd take it, but I hoped you'd understand.' She poured the tea. He wondered whether she brought other airmen to her cottage. He had observed her for months in the ward, correct, icy, inwardly turned.

'I fell for you,' she said, 'when I saw the way you smoked a cigar as soon as we tipped you back into bed after your operation. Then you snapped the top from a bottle of beer and drank it off. O'Dowd laughed about it. We'd never known anyone do that before.'

He pushed a stump of wood to the middle of the fire, scorching his fingers. 'I wanted to make love to you, but didn't think it would ever be possible.'

'I often caught you looking at me from your bed as if you would like to try picking me up. We'll see about that, I thought. I didn't know I'd fallen in love with you, but I suppose my curiosity was the same thing. You can't imagine what a thick skin I have, though I did hope to spot you on the Downs that day, which is why I took my fieldglasses. You were sitting as lonely as a cloud, and thinking poetic thoughts.'

'My head was as empty as a pint pot at closing time.' He stroked her hair. Perfect kisses were those which you could not remember who gave or who took. The embers were like fires in a bombed city. He put on all that was left, no reason to conserve, always more where that came from.

He was half with her, half far away, dull from exhaustion yet sharp and feverish. Her bosom pressed against him. 'I'll show you where we sleep.'

A dark-wooden bed, a chest of drawers, a chair and a small wardrobe filled the room. She pulled the curtains across as if to keep in the odour of damp bedding and face powder. He stood in the doorway, diffident about entry, listening to the rhythm of the rain, but she drew him in, closed the door and untied her headband. Hair falling made her face raw, vulnerable, as if pleading for him to consider her fairly. Then she smiled, to hide shame, embarrassment, or whatever it was, he thought, that she uselessly felt. 'Gets chilly underneath these cliffs. But we'll be warm in bed.'

On the Downs they'd had no say in the matter, but here she sat to unclip her stockings. 'Why don't you get undressed?'

'It's wonderful looking at you.'

Her eyebrows lifted. 'Going to write a poem about it?'

The journey had once been long between a woman clothed and a woman naked. A hand would find an interstice, and so would the only part of him that mattered. The way to heaven was paved with bad intentions, said a motto on the back of a matchbox, so he knelt and kissed her, never done in that way before. She liked it as if she had hoped for it but hadn't been able to ask. On the bed he found more reserves than with familiar girls at home. She was never still, kissing or being kissed, and he was divided from himself, looking on at her, viewing them both, her features lost as if she was being devoured, and wondering nevertheless whether she also felt separate from him. He used nothing to prevent consequences, no division of the flesh. He loved her, as near as he could get to believing it, words and thoughts burned clean. Only by belonging to her and to this room could he be one with himself but, as on the slopes of Gunong Barat, it was exhaustion that finally told him who he was.

He sat at the table, she in the armchair, curtains drawn. 'Are you keeping a journal?'

'I'm writing a poem.' To admit it so readily was an indication as to how far he had come.

'Can I see?'

Every word crossed out or put back was a fundamental decision. 'When it's finished.'

'Well, I can't see it before, can I?'

In the cottage on her own she would gaze into the lifeless fireplace. 'I feel I should talk to you instead of writing,' he said.

'I want you to feel easy with me. Not many do, I don't know why.'

Pots were being washed, chairs scraping in the kitchen. A clock ticked away time that would never return, comforting, the sooner it went the better.

She came and stood by him. 'Don't let me stop you.'

He kissed her. 'I love you more than I've ever loved anyone.'

'More than Rachel?' she teased.

'There's no comparison. And I wasn't really in love with her.' Maybe he had been, didn't know, couldn't say.

She sensed his betrayal. 'I hope you never say the same about me.'

Better not to talk. The necessity and the impulse for a kiss joined so neatly that it fuelled a response from her. 'I won't.'

'When I caught you coming back in the rain I knew where you'd been, but I didn't say anything. I couldn't very well, could I?'

'Were you afraid to?'

'Well, I'm not afraid of anything, but I saw you were in a funny mood. You were so pale you had me worried, so all I could do was get you into bed – as it were.'

'I felt fine.'

'People do, unless they're in pain. It's Nature's plan to get them into the grave. The greedy old thing can't have enough. You'd be surprised how hard it is to keep certain patients alive and kicking. They recover in spite of themselves, though we lose one now and again. Not all that many, considering.'

'And I was one of those you didn't lose?'

By surviving the valley of the shadow he had handed them a victory. It was good to know. When the troopship steamed up Southampton Water his existence entered a cul-de-sac, every prospect unthinkable, impossible to go back to a factory routine and a flat marriage. Something had to change, so his spirit had induced the body to lie him low, and then cast him so many fathoms down that he could only surface into a half-charted country which he nevertheless had a right to inhabit, because he had always felt in his dreams that such a land belonged to him.

She sat on the rug. 'You were a piece of cake! You didn't care, you see. All I had to do was stop you doing anything foolish. The only time I was worried was when you came back from the pub in the rain. But it only confirmed that you were special for me. I suppose God was looking after you.'

God, as his father had always raved in his anguished moments, was a bastard, implying that His only pleasure was in making things worse if you were daft enough to call on Him. At the best He was mute, distant, and indifferent – qualities which could hardly be mentioned to Nora. When he came back from the pub with Rachel's hot kisses on his lips he had looked after himself. Even so, there was a mystery, which had led to this room, and a love that could not be explained except that it hemmed him in like a cocoon from which he didn't want to break free. 'I felt it as well,' he said. 'I love you so much that it almost makes me afraid.'

'You don't need to be. I'll see that you look after yourself.'

He hadn't meant that, would get sick in the soul if anyone pampered him. If he came to enjoy being treated as an invalid he might lose all idea of himself, till his only identity was that of being ill. She looked at her watch. 'You've had a long day. You should lie in tomorrow.'

'I've been up at six every morning since I was fourteen.' He screwed the top on the ink bottle. 'So I'm used to it.'

She put an arm over his shoulder, not wanting him to become normal too soon, his illness even more important to her now that he was away from the hospital. It was an experience he needed to forget, but his uneasiness was solaced by the truth that no love could be perfect.

Buildings and tall chimneys were so packed together that the streets could not be distinguished, yet the cityscape was familiar. The smoke of exploding bombs came towards him, houses and offices folding into dust and flame. He waited for the roof on which he stood to crumble.

A voice called above the engines of war. She leaned over, breasts warm through her cotton nightgown. 'What is it?'

'A dream I suppose. An air raid.' There was no pungent smell of soil as in the Anderson shelter in the back garden, a sack over the entrance to stop the candle showing. Fear was damped by exhaustion, and you slept sitting up, praying no bomb would blow you to pieces or bury you alive.

She kissed him, then used the pot under the bed. 'You woke me. Go to sleep.'

The moon shone in. A similar dream came back. On an

empty plain black globules of petrol fell from the sky, columns of fire and smoke erupting around him as he ran.

A cup rattled on its saucer. 'It's nine o'clock. I suppose you ought to get up.'

Instead of the long ward, where he had wakened for nearly a year, he was in a box-sized bedroom, propping himself on the pillow. She put down the cup. 'Sorry about your nightmare.'

'So that's what it was?'

She watched him drink. 'I hope you didn't overdo it yesterday.'

'No fear of that.'

'I liked your poem.'

He'd left the book open. 'It's only scribble.'

'You can read it to me later.' Her grey blouse and skirt put her back in uniform – except for the string of orange beads. 'There's an egg for your breakfast, and potatoes. So come downstairs, and I'll serve you.'

The area behind the harbour was a wasteland, bushes growing out of basements, blackened glass on the causeways. 'They stopped quite a packet around here,' she said. 'Mostly gunfire.'

The patched-up town centre functioned more or less, busy compared to desolation behind the harbour.

The hotel dining room was full so they found a café, a plate of soup set before them as if they had to rush back to work. She didn't belong in a place that reminded him of British Restaurants where factory workers could get a cheap midday meal. 'I hope you don't mind.'

'I've been glad of worse, believe you me. You have to eat where you can. Things won't get better till we throw out this horrid government. Everyone's fed up to the teeth with austerity.'

He couldn't disagree, but reminded her that the people had voted Labour in.

'And they'll vote them out again. You'll see.' Meatballs, mashed potatoes and boiled cabbage were followed by sponge pudding and custard. He smoked a Goldflake with the weak coffee, and she asked why he hadn't stayed on at school.

'My family needed the money.'

'You were brave. Can't think what I would have done. Much the same, I expect.'

163

He paid the five-shilling bill, and left a shilling tip.

'You act like a millionaire. Sixpence would have been ample.'

He held her coat. 'Plenty more where that came from.'

'I hope you're right.'

It was a delight to eat with her in no matter how crumby a place, then walk arm in arm to the beach. Water licked dreamily up the shingle, and a ferry was sliding out of the dock for France. He told her about Matthew Arnold's poem. 'I'm afraid my education wasn't very good,' she said. 'We read a lot at school, but I've forgotten most of it.'

'I only read comic books, and the *Radio Times*.'

'Lucky you.'

'But I'm doing my best to catch up.'

'So we noticed.'

The idea jolted. 'I was a fish in a bowl, was I?'

When she laughed he saw the tiniest wrinkles on either side of the bridge of her nose. 'We had no better amusement. Do you mind?'

'I'm flattered.'

'No you aren't.' She straightened her skirt. 'Now I'd like to hear your poem.'

He unfolded the page, torn out of his notebook:

> We find the driftwood,
> watch it burn:
> the sea gives up its fuel.
>
> The dry wood burns,
> we watch green flames
> fingering the soot.
>
> The sea gives life
> and you award me love:
> we watch the driftwood burning.
>
> We search the beach for wood
> and when we kiss
> we kiss the sea.
>
> Driftwood burns in you and me
> flames the sea can't move;
> the salt is saving us for love.

She pressed his hand. 'No one's ever written me a poem.'

To swim out and drown would not obliterate his embarrassment. He helped her to stand, and she kissed him quickly as if someone might see. Up the curving tree-bordered road by the Castle, and on out of town, a hazy sea spread for a moment beyond the wireless aerials. He felt incomplete because he couldn't know whether or not she was thinking about when she would have to go back to the hospital, or about him as he was thinking about her. When he reached for her hand its grasp convinced him that she expected it, therefore he knew what she had been thinking. They occupied each other, and the poem in the inside pocket of his jacket, close to the only place that mattered, gave him that familiar sensation of being in love for the first time. Lean your head against my shoulder, he said to himself, and she did, even though the bus was full.

Chapter

❧ SIXTEEN

She was ten years older, but he felt in no way younger.

'Don't flatter me, though what's ten years between friends?'

Unnecessary to discuss it, they had to talk about something. Age did not matter, and intimacy had never bred contempt. She was as far removed from Pauline as he from his parents, no connection, everyone an individual, which he resisted saying, in spite of the silence as they sat on the cliff gazing out to sea, in case she thought he was embarrassed by his past.

A gull hit the water like a shot-down fighter, came up with a fish in its gullet, and skimmed through a cloud of squealing competitors. She was silent, and he asked if she was bored.

'I never am. If I don't speak, I'm tired. Mostly I work jolly hard, but I like being here, and it's twice as good with you, my love.' To hear her speak of love – it would be the same with any woman – except in a whisper, seemed unnatural. Hard to accept that the distance between them could never close, even when they were in bed. She also realised that they were incapable of a complete meeting. If she didn't, her love was more profoundly given, though if so why, in that case, did he alone feel it? The remoteness that kept them apart may have been when she was thinking of times past. There was no end to such ruminations, from which neither would benefit. His brain recoiled as from a swamp, ill equipped to plough through.

After lunch he couldn't wait. Neither could she. Her kisses

smothered him. She had two identities, one dressed, the other naked. Clothes made her different from other people, but when she was nude, she was as raw as anyone else. The love hovered, was lost and found again, between dressed and nakedness. He found love by tracing her form like a blind man memorising a relief map in order to find his way to safety.

'I've never been intimate – so often. I hope I'm coming into my prime!'

Nor had he. 'Let's stay forever.'

'There's nothing I'd like better.' She leaned towards him. 'But duty will call. My father used to say that duty came second only to God. I was a bit of a Bolshie in those days, but now I think it might be true.'

'Doesn't love have a place?'

'Certainly, but not a name-rank-and-number. It just is, and I suppose we mustn't forget it. When I'm back on duty I won't be able to forget *you* for a second. I'll want you in the ward so that I can see you all the time – though I expect you'll be wallowing in the fleshpots of Nottingham by then.'

She kissed him, and he felt her sadness. Duty was a state wherein you made hundreds of minor decisions, and let the big ones take care of themselves. He had fallen from the paradise of duty, never to return. 'I wish I was going back as a wireless operator.'

'Well, you can't. And you've done *your* duty. I'm sure no one did it better.'

'One long holiday.'

'So you say.'

It was traditional to belittle it, and she'd have been surprised if he hadn't. 'I'll get a divorce,' he said. 'It's got to come sooner or later.'

She sat up. 'It's a mucky and expensive business, so I hear. Takes years.' Gulls squealed in the sun. 'Funny, though, being an adulteress! We're breaking one of the commandments, but I don't care. I've never been so alive.'

He traced a map on her back, till she turned. 'What beautiful breasts you have.'

'I suppose they should be feeding ten children.' The notion gave him a hard on. Her warmth was life. She lay naked under him, but there was an expression of modesty in her closed mouth, eyes unable to meet his gaze, a complexity which slowed his advance, called for more subtlety. He stroked her neck, brushed her stomach with his palm. She put on a show of modesty as a test, and if he hadn't recognised it she would have thought less of him. To have ignored it would have suggested to him that he was as much in thrall to his upbringing as his cousin Bert.

On the footpath towards Deal, a man exercising his bull terrier wished them good afternoon. She wore a white blouse, a red tie blowing in the wind, and a grey skirt. Waves were white at the lip, folded into large lily leaves as they came in. 'Sometimes I think I'll leave the service. Call it a day. Another twenty years, and I might end up as a matron, or sitting behind a desk, and I'm not sure I want it. The trouble is, though, I don't like making decisions, and just want to carry on with what I'm doing. Provided I'm doing good, of course, which I hope I am.'

Such a code, so straightforward, seemed aimed at his insta-bility. 'I suppose if you do good to others you automatically do good to yourself.'

The barb jolted her. 'Well, maybe. That's not the reason I work. That would be selfish. But perhaps I will pack it in, in a year or two. What do *you* think?'

He was pole-axed at her looking so far ahead – and even more at the possibility that she might change her way of life for him.

'Not for you. Though I might do it for us.'

He wasn't afraid of changes, but liked to recognise them on looking back, so as to decide where and when they had occurred, and whether or not they had been bad for him. To know at the time that a change was taking place would make him feel trapped. Decisions had to be made by fate or chance.

She sensed the reason for his silence. 'I'd have to go on working, but there's plenty to do in my profession.'

Quitting the service might be the ultimate proof of her love, but he didn't care to be responsible in case it wasn't. And if it was, how could he deserve it? A ship steamed at such an angle to the coast that it must be heading for Ostend. Visibility was down and the Ingle Lightship blinked, as if another moth had

flown in for lunch. He would apply for a passport, a step up in
the world, a mark of identity – and an inducement to travel
when to be in England felt like imprisonment. 'I'd never go
anywhere, though, unless you came with me.'

She nodded, and held his arm. 'It would be nice to go to
France for a day or two. How's your French?'

'I learned some from a book I picked up for tuppence.'

'We did it at school, but I don't remember any.'

A new harvest of driftwood had been thrown along the beach.
'I used to go on the tips as a kid to get kindling for the fire at
home. As well as anything else I could find. I'd often stay out
all day.'

'Did your parents mind?'

'They knew where I was.'

'We used to dream about being free like that, but we weren't
allowed out of the garden. It was quite a big one, though, with
a paddock and an orchard.'

Clumps of reedgrass, sea kale, red flowers, rusty tins or the
odd bottle littered the shingle. He picked up a broken shovel.
'A stoker on the SS *Mayhem* got drunk one night, and had an
argument with the chief engineer. The stoker was a chap called
Ted Bullivant, the uncle of somebody I knew at school. The
chief engineer chased him all over the ship, till the first mate
told them to pack it in, but instead of going back on duty Ted
fetched his shovel, to whack the chief engineer. But the chief
engineer was a tough old bird. He got hold of the shovel and
threw it overboard.'

He spun it out till they got home. After supper she wound
up the gramophone to play the 'Kreutzer' Sonata, and he told
her about the story by Tolstoy, read on the troopship.

The days of anguish and of love went on, and he was not
conscious that there would be an end until he stated the fact to
himself, words painful because he wanted the end to come.
Since it had to be, it had already happened. Therefore he didn't
care that it was going to happen. He expected her to accept his
departure in a brusque, ward-sister manner, and when she
didn't, as if finding the idea intolerable, he became easy-going,
assuming an indifference he hoped would dispel her sadness.

Sometimes he did not know whether the ache at leaving came

from his heart or the collapsed lung, sat by the window looking through a curtain of rain at the green surf and wondering whether he would ever again be where he was now, not wanting the present to become a memory. Memories don't come back, she told him. 'I didn't expect it to be so hard.'

A week would cure her of all she felt, inconvenient to be mooning over someone ten years younger, a patient, what's more. He killed the notion. 'I can't bear the idea of us parting, either' – his true feelings out in spite of himself.

She spread margarine and date-jam on their bread, using a willow pattern tea service from the glass-fronted case. 'If I let you out of my sight, you'll vanish.'

'That's silly.'

'I know, but it can happen.' She smiled wanly, thinking about her boyfriend who had not come back from a sortie.

'The war's over.' He didn't want to obtrude on her privacy. Everyone had a right to their troubles, otherwise how can they get rid of them – or learn from them? She was welcome to share any of his if it made her feel better, though he wouldn't share his troubles even with himself, if that was at all feasible, but would stand aside to see what effect they would have on him – or in the hope that they would go away.

Tears at the eyes of so strong a woman moved him to say that he loved her, comforting her so as to quieten himself. What he said and what he did divided him neatly, and he drank those tears which proved her love in order to prove his love, her lips cold but her body burning. He knew that passion could be cool, and misery hot, and as for partings, they took place all the time. So did reunions. 'What would you like us to do?'

He searched for what she wanted to say, then said it himself so that she would not have to. 'I'd like us to live together. I don't suppose you want to, but it would be heaven.'

He didn't intend to put a lock and chain on himself, no matter what she might want, and he knew there was little danger of such an arrangement. 'Heaven takes some organising,' she said. 'We won't see each other for five weeks.'

A lot can happen. How many tides would come and go? The misery was exhausting. 'I'll see if they can sell me a bottle of something at the pub.'

She was glad he had broken the mood. 'Take your mac, though.'

'The rain's stopped.'

'So it has.'

He went out with a basket. A couple of jeeps were parked on the shingle, and a bored soldier supped from a pint bottle, his beret resting against the windscreen.

'No whisky, sir.' The bar was crowded, mostly army types from the range. People slid empty tankards forward, but the landlord finally got back to him. 'What'll it be, then?'

'Something to take out.'

He leaned forward. 'What about a bottle o' rum, for a couple o' quid? Best Jamaica.'

'All right. And two of lemonade.'

He went in with the bottle wrapped in newspaper as if carrying the loot of Babylon. Attending to the kitchen table, she was her own preoccupied self. Or so it seemed. 'When I'm with you I feel that the rules I live by don't apply,' she said.

The liquid came out like crude oil from a tanker. 'Is that good?'

She wore a short-sleeved frock, a summery pattern of blue flowers, and touched his wrist. The lighter her gestures the more passionate she would be. 'It makes me feel like my real self.'

He topped the glasses with lemonade, stirred them with a fork. 'If it burns a hole in the side of my face, bandage me up and wheel me into the sea for a cure.'

'I hardly ever drink.' She touched the rim demurely with her lips. He knocked it back. So did she. He didn't believe her teetotal tale, had seen empty bottles of White Horse in the dustbin when he arrived. She had a few shorts in the mess after a bout of duty. He stroked her arm, but she went to the stove to cook fresh herrings, potatoes and cauliflower. 'We must eat supper.'

When the bottle was halfway down, she asked: 'If you were free, would you marry me?'

Only when I'm pissed. He was thinking things he didn't want to say, and saying things before he thought them, unreal for him, but everything was always unreal, and even without alcohol he never felt less than drunk. 'Like a shot.' He leaned across to kiss her. 'How about you?'

Her eyes filmed over. 'We're old enough. It wouldn't be too idiotic.'

He draped his jacket over the chair and sat down to eat. Nothing they said had any meaning, so he could say anything that came to mind. So could she. He said that because of the white moon over the sea they could also do what they liked. She was as rigid as a tree, drink having the opposite effect to what he'd hoped. But there were many sides to her, and he was after one she hardly knew about – a snake pulled out of the stone instead of Excalibur.

She didn't realise that her words slurred. He suspected that his did. Listening, he decided that they didn't, though if they did how would he detect it? Being drunk, they would get to know each other. But he was surely drunk to think so. He told her how he had first got drunk, wondering whether she would disapprove. 'At the factory when I was fourteen we put money by for a couple of months before Christmas. During the last dinner hour we went to the pub, men, women and boys. I slept in the store room for the rest of the day, then staggered home.'

Moving her arm, she didn't notice when her glass bounced on the rug. But she did, picked it up a moment later. 'I feel a bit tiddly. I don't know what you must think.' She dissected the fish neatly, lifting out the spine and laying it on the side of her plate.

If she doesn't know I'm also half seas over she must be blind. He poured more rum. 'Don't you and the other sisters ever paint the town red?'

'We sometimes go to the hotel and come back in a taxi. Just for a bit of fun.'

'And now you're having a bit of fun with me?'

She looked at him earnestly. 'You don't mind?'

'It's part of being intimate – getting merry together.' He wanted to give her an experience to remember him by, as if taking her to bed wasn't enough. A smack in the chops would bring retaliation, though he imagined she could cope. He was at a loss. He loved her. 'A single kiss from you makes everything worthwhile.'

She responded after a pause. 'No one has ever said such wonderful things to me.'

Plenty more where that came from. 'You bring it out because I love you. No person has ever been so delicious to be in bed with. Even looking at you stiffens me.'

'Don't say that, please.'

He drew her close, kissed the sickly flavour from her lips. The return embrace almost cracked his ribs, but his arms went even tighter around her, the iron grip from four years in a factory in spite of his gammy lung. 'Eloquence uses all kinds of words, so forgive me if I become crude.'

'You say exactly what's on your mind. So do I, come to that.' She giggled. 'When there's anything on it.'

He kissed the back of her neck, slackening his hold, feeling her shiver. The sea was never still, the swish and thump as if a nearby house had turned to sand and collapsed. 'My mind's chock-a-block. Poems come and go before I can write them. The ones I catch by the tail are often the worst. But when I'm not with you I'm dead.' If she wanted talk she would have it, a luxury he could not often produce.

'When I'm happy,' she said, 'I begin to feel desperate. It's very strange.'

He fetched the bottle of Camp coffee from the shelf – wasn't where he should be, fluid filling his lung if he stayed much longer on such a strange continent. The purest love kept him, nothing to say and less to think. 'Make a strong cup, while I put a match to the wood we collected.'

She pulled her frock down, set the kettle on the stove. 'It's too warm for a fire.'

'We'll lie in front of it.' Not much to remember her by, since he couldn't be sure it hadn't happened to her before, but it was better than nothing.

Forgot the sea, forgot the swaying flames as she unbuttoned his waistcoat and shirt and trousers, unlaced his shoes, like a doll in her nursery, agreeable nonetheless, knowing that if he moved he would fall, in spite of the bitter stiffening of the coffee. He unhooked her skirt, ran his fingers up and down her thighs, around the elastic of her drawers, would marry her any time, bigamy no object – which made her laugh, ticklish lips running down her calf. 'I've been in love with you since I was born.'

He had said it before, couldn't remember who with, meant it every time but now even more, no other life as she gazed into the fire, warming her dead eye. He released her breasts, gentled the nipples till they became engorged and purple. You're magnificent, didn't say so, kissed each breast. 'Help me with my corset.' Unlaced, the marks were on her skin. He sent his tongue along the happy valley, fingering her throat. She didn't talk, the only time he didn't care what she was thinking. I'll ram you till I disappear. And I'll follow you, she said, wherever you go. If she walked along the backyard towards the house where he had lived most of his life he would fuck her there too, didn't care, finished drawing off her stockings, parted her ample cunt with his tongue, wondering about everything that had happened to her before she found him as she ran into his mouth and he licked her, custard and prunes, intimacy knowing no bounds, which he'd never done before but instinct, perversity, desire – a blindness to her feelings or opinions led him accurately on, to wrench and squeeze and kiss and finger all respectability out of her so that she would end up being her fundamental self and for a few moments at least belong to him.

He could do what he liked to make her come, do what she would not forget, could not resist, would feel when he wasn't there. She embraced him, and he speculated on what her closed eyes saw – she had two when the lids were down – and what she felt, divining everything her senses needed so as to glut his own enjoyment now that he was in the Land of Fire, looking at the Beautiful Horizon, exploring the Holy Land, plodding through Bangkok, eating the Sandwich Islands, swimming off Madagascar, trekking the five-fingered forests of Gunong Barat – a stiffening tongue till he made out her response, sure she had never asked anyone, and then he went into her, round the world again in eighty kisses so as to hold himself back, combing the map for places where people made the only kind of love, out of alliances formed by something they didn't need to understand, stroked her in two vital places at the same time and, legs drawn back, she came with such intensity that even the coast of France must have heard the sound of love pulling his backbone into flight.

She had left her corsets off, wore a voluminous blue dress, a cream-coloured snood, small golden ear rings. There were shadows under her eyes, kissed when he embraced her. 'What a night we had.'

'I'll never forget it. Goodness knows, I'm sore enough. I can't think what you did to me.' Tears wetted his shoulder, but when he was out of sight the mask of duty would go back on her face, as the ice had entered his heart even before waking. 'You'll feel better when you're home,' he said, meaning her room at the hospital.

Perceptive one minute, and so clumsy the next, made her wonder about his sense of humour. 'This is my home. That's only my billet.'

They had the bacon ration for breakfast. Hanging will come next, but this wasn't the time to say it, split as he was between the pain of leaving, and pleasure at heading for Nottingham, which in her present state she would not understand, unless she did already, her misery more intense than his. Her unhappiness wasn't justified, though he didn't reassure her because her tears were a more credible proof of love. He wanted to convince her that he was equally upset, but for him to weep as well would be comical, and she might think he was poaching on her terrain. His anguish would only surface if she put on an off-hand show at his departure. 'We love each other, and we'll meet again soon.'

She calmed herself, made sandwiches, filled a flask and put sugar in. 'Stupid of me to get upset. I know things'll be all right.'

Hard to prevent his voice breaking. 'I'll write to you every day.'

She gave him a telephone number. 'Try it when you can.'

'I'll be sure to.'

'How are you for money? I get nearly two pounds a day.'

The bus would leave in half an hour, not enough time to go to bed. 'I don't need any.'

'I shouldn't have offered.' She wouldn't allow him to make her feel ashamed. 'But I was only being practical.' She gave him a key to the door. 'In case you ever want to be here alone.'

'If I get fed up, I'll come back to write a novel.' It seemed unlikely, her frozen features said, as if he was going to his death, or she was staying to meet hers. Tears meant leaving, never to return. But he would come back. He had walked out of his parents' house with little more than a wave. There were tears when he left Pauline for Malaya (and tears when he came back, till she knew what he had brought with him), but never had anguish been so prolonged as now. He wondered what premonitions she wasn't letting on about.

She carried his typewriter to the bus stop, her aspect altering once they turned on to the path between the cottages. The red flag at the range signalled a crisp uneven Lee Enfield rattle. A gull strafed someone's garden, shitting as it went.

They reached the main road. 'Anyway, let me hear from you.'

'I certainly will.'

'Goodbye, then.'

176

Chapter

❧ SEVENTEEN

Nora had followed him. He rested on the station steps, wishing she had. 'Thought I'd catch you up when you put your luggage down!' Worse for those who stayed behind, but she was too busy to mope, her leave ended, normal existence resuming – though for him there was nothing normal anymore, wherever he went, no matter how long he lived.

The yoke of case and typewriter was lighter than the water buckets his uncles had carried from the well behind the Nook, so it was a matter of honour not to use a porter, and the excitement of a gamble made his burdens easy, but because the bus would remind him too much of coming back the first time, decades ago, he opened the door of a taxi.

The young driver wore a collar and tie, a parting down the middle of fair wavy hair. 'Been on a trip, sir?'

'To Malaya.' He settled back in comfort.

The Castle, dead to him. The town was the same, dead in a different way. Everything had changed since before growing up, before leaving and coming back. The world was different, even though it seemed the same.

'I'm off to Canada in a month,' the driver said. 'I'm doing this taxi work to fill in. There's nowt in this country. You can't mek any money. I'm in the building trade normally.'

'Can't say I blame you.'

'Too much bullshit. I've 'ad enough.'

Kids playing marbles on the cobbles ran to the pavement. Liza Atkin and Flo Musson waved to each other across the street. Jack Ecob came out of the bookies, wondering what to say to his wife because he'd lost all his money. She'd lend him ten bob from her purse and make him pay it back out of his wages, the same every week – Mrs Ecob told his mother years ago.

A taxi was rare, but Mrs Bull didn't deign to move when the driver carried his case up the yard. Brian gave him five bob and told him to keep the change. You tip too much, Nora said. So would you, if you were me. I'm just back from Malaya, and don't know the prices. Odours of soot and coal smoke assailed his system, and he wondered what the driver thought a chap was doing, coming from abroad to a place like this.

His mother got up from the fireplace. 'I expected you a bit later. Let me mek yer a cup o' tea.'

He wished himself somewhere else, but didn't know where. All the same, here he was. 'Did my luggage come?'

'Yer dad carried it upstairs.' She laughed. 'Nearly killed him. He thought he was getting another rupture.' She went into the scullery: 'You look a lot better than when you was 'ome last time. You looked bleddy awful then. Me and yer dad was worried to death.'

They'd noticed nothing, he remembered. Why should they? He wasn't sure he would have done. She filled their cups. 'They fed yer well in that 'ospital, by the look on it. Bert towd me how nice it was. Yer was a bleddy skeleton, last time. It broke my heart to see yer. Ada towd me how rotten she thought you looked.'

'I felt fine.'

'You'd never tell anybody owt. If yer was dying yer'd say yer was as right as rain. My dad was the same. He could be at death's door but wouldn't say a word. Not that he ever was, worse luck, or we might have shoved him through it. But if you don't say how you feel, how is anybody to know?'

He ate the cake put before him. She was in a good mood because Harold wasn't in. They had fought like cat and dog ever since he could remember, and he wondered how they'd got together in the first place. The fact that Seaton could neither read nor write should have put her off.

'He didn't tell me,' she said. 'Just after we was married I left a note saying there was summat for his dinner in the oven when he got home from work. I had to go and see my mother at the Nook. When I got back he was sitting like thunder because he thought there was nowt to eat. I showed him the note, but he hit me. I can't tell yer one 'alf.'

But she had, could, did. He'd heard it often. Amazing what he knew. And what he didn't, he put together. He took a five pound note from his paybook. 'Here's something for food.'

'I don't want yer munney, duck. We've got plenty.'

He set it on the table. 'You can't keep me for nothing.'

'Thanks, then. I'll see yer wain't clamb while you're here. Would you like some fish for your dinner?'

When Jim Scarfedale was fetched back from the orphanage his mother was told to feed him bacon every morning for breakfast. 'Don't bother today. I'll get something to eat downtown.'

The wooden stairway formed a dark place between doors closed top and bottom, but he didn't need to feel his way up. He hung his uniform, put books in the empty cupboard. The small table against the wall invited him to unscrew his pen, but Nora was still so close he had no will to write.

He walked up the yard, mackintosh over arm, the hum of the factory filling his ears, rancid fumes of metallic suds impregnating every particle of air, the same smell he had worked in at Edgeworth's – different to the sea-roar and ozone air of Queen's Bay. He ran for the platform of a bus before it pulled away, clambered upstairs for a view of familiar streets, everything as fresh as if just back from the cleaners, or he from overseas, his previous leave less than a dream. A large hut near the entrance to the recreation ground had served as a dinner centre when Seaton was on the dole and there was no food in the house. Small now, it was tucked to one side of the path, but when a dozen children turned up for bread and butter and cocoa at eight on winter mornings it seemed vast and welcoming.

⚘

During the day, and for most of the evenings when the others were out, he sat in the bedroom to write in peace, read, or listen to music. A wireless in the parlour cupboard had been given up for dead, and his trade came in useful, for he replaced a dud valve, adjusted the flywheel so that the needle would fall on the correct stations, and fixed a knob on the volume control.

'You've got yourself all set up in your 'eadquarters,' Seaton said, 'but you'll have to get out a bit, and not sit writing all the hours God sends. It ain't good for you.'

He was glad his father couldn't know what he was writing. Seaton didn't care. But if *he* had been Seaton, which mercifully he wasn't, he would have wanted to know, even though what he was writing had nothing to do with him. Seaton looked as though he might be interested, and would like to know, but Brian felt no inclination to share thoughts which in any case he was hardly able to express to himself. And even if he could he wouldn't be able to make them intelligible to his father, because any connection had been blasted when he had been afraid of his violence as a child.

He walked, more than his father realised, curious to see how places had changed. The San-Eye dumping ground, where he had scavenged base metals as a kid, was covered by factories. The huge incinerator buildings had been demolished, the land levelled by millions of tons of rammel brought by convoys of carts and lorries, and wagons laden with steaming clinker pushed along temporary rails from furnaces which had burned up the rubbish of the city. No one driving on the road that went triumphantly through, or working in a new factory, would realise the miasmic swamp with its banks of putrescent rubbish, and heaps of swarf and steel raked into uselessness by Aggar and his gang of unemployed, advancing week by week towards the canal. Brian had warmed himself at their fires in winter, between raking for bottles or bits of steel, and though everything was buried, the area still smouldered in his imagination.

On other tips, similar down-and-outs scraped as if times had not altered, because they preferred to eke such a living instead of clocking in at a factory, for which he couldn't blame them, since he wouldn't choose to see the inside of one again, either.

He walked to Tapley to collect clothes and books, timing his visit to late morning so as to find Jenny at home. People had aged more while he had been in the hospital than during his two years in Malaya, though after a few minutes she seemed more or less the same, glasses on to read the newspaper. 'Oh, you did give me a fright.' Her hands were shaking. 'I wondered who it was.'

'You thought I was your fancyman?'

'No such luck. But I'm glad you're better.'

He declined a cup of tea. 'How's Gary?'

'Are you going to see him?'

He didn't know. 'I'm not totally cured. You never can tell.' The place looked tidier. She was lonely, should get a part-time job. 'How's Pauline?'

She began to cry. 'She's happy. It's no use denying it.'

'I'm glad, believe you me.'

She was at a loss because he didn't want any tea, dried her eyes on the corner of a towel. 'What shall you do now you're out?' He wore a suit and tie. His shoes shone and he was freshly shaven, hair neatly parted, but she saw him as a desolate abandoned husband, a TB case with nothing to look forward to but drawing sickness benefit for the rest of his life, a moper around the streets getting older and shabbier. Or maybe she didn't, but if she did she couldn't be more wrong.

'Nothing,' he said. 'I'll be too busy.'

'Can you get a job?'

'I have a lot of reading and writing to do.'

She frowned, puzzled. 'Will that bring any money in?'

His tone stopped further queries. 'I don't know. But that's not the point.'

He wasn't the same lad, talked even posher, which she thought must mean summat. 'I don't suppose it is.'

He knew what she was thinking almost before she did herself. 'I'll get my things from upstairs.'

Shirts, a suit and some jerseys were squashed in the bottom of the wardrobe. He put his few books in the case, and told her to throw everything else in the dustbin.

'I don't expect you'll be calling again.'

His father had a brother living in the same city, and hadn't seen him for twenty years. He bumped into him one day in Slab Square. They talked five minutes and went on their way. Maybe she was right.

She hugged and kissed him, and he eased himself out, leaving with a promise to call when he had time.

Books under one roof, clothes in the cupboard – all assets close – helped him to know who he was, and that everything could fit in one case when he moved, the typewriter hanging from the other arm. He rode a bus into town to buy *The Times* or the *TLS* or *John O' London's* from a kiosk near the Mechanics Institute. In the hospital Summers had lent him *The Cossacks* and *The House of the Dead*, so he borrowed other novels by Tolstoy and Dostoevsky from the library. Cheap secondhand copies of Latin and Greek writers soon filled another shelf of his grandmother's old cupboard, his enjoyment undiminished at reading Homer, Sophocles, Euripides or Aeschylus in English – luxuries almost as cheap as music on the wireless.

When the internal pressure relaxed – isobars drifting apart – it was time for a refill at the local clinic, to press the bell of a redbricked mansion, and at the enquiries door show his letter from the air force. After demob he would be expected to register, a leper to be kept under observation, advice which enraged him, because he wasn't one of the herd, happy to guard the wellbeing of others at the expense of his own freedom. Because the clinic had already been notified that he would be needing their services, the temptation returned to let the lung resume its normal work, to have nothing to do with such a soul-murdering procedure, not continue the X-rays and queue every so often with National Health no-hopers who wallowed in being ill because such an overwhelming fact told them who they were – the smell of sweat and ether heavy in the air.

Notices in the waiting room requested you to neither smoke nor spit. So many seemingly middle-aged men and women suggested that such treatment could go on for life. As you lay dying a white-coated Doctor Frankenstein would rush up with a bicycle pump and fill you with three thousand cubic centimetres of air to float you across the Styx like an inner tube. Charon would look on from his rowing boat as you used your X-ray plate for a rudder. And on the other side Cerberus would bark for your blood sediment rate before allowing you into Hades.

A girl sat close to the door, hands folded on crossed knees, face and body thin but legs normally fleshed under white stockings. A flash photo up from his book took in fair hair drawn tightly back under her pale blue headscarf, grey eyes, small nose, thin lips, chin slightly forward – not as young as he had thought, for her skin was dull, there were lines at her mouth and eyes, and deeper scores across her forehead, a hardly bearable expression of endurance. She reminded him of Sonya in *Crime and Punishment*, and when she was called her name sounded Polish. A lot had settled in the area since the war, so maybe she was. He could imagine not being so alone in the world if someone like her walked in similar isolation.

He took off his shirt, stood before a screener, then lay on the table. The familiar stab – and a brutal interior resistance against his breathing, the lung pushed into quiescence for another fortnight. Hardly a word, exactly how he liked it, no time for goodbyes on the production line.

He walked across to the open ground of the Forest, found a bench on the slope to sit and smoke a cigarette, always an exquisite taste after a refill. The space would be covered by the Goose Fair, as it had every year from the Middle Ages, a three-day October whirligig of lights and roundabouts. His tobacco smoke dominated the stink of chips and taste of candy-floss. Don't smoke, or choke to death on booze and unnecessary stress. He couldn't care less. How mean-spirited to be afraid of dying when your time was up, to take minus the full degree of pleasure in the hope of staying ten more years (or months) in life. Smoke mixed with the air, a wedding of lungs and sky, meaningless pleasure never to be foregone.

He finished reading the play. Clytemnestra was dead, and it served her right, but what a lousy bastard Orestes was to murder his mother. Still, the Tree of Atreus was no bush to get tangled up in. Thyestes had been invited to dinner by Atreus the scheming bully, and the sun turned black because Atreus fed Thyestes his own children. So Aegisthus, son of Thyestes (who hadn't been present at the barbecue) got at Clytemnestra while Agamemnon son of Atreus was away at the war with

Troy, and when Agamemnon came back Clytemnestra killed him because, among other things, he had slaughtered their daughter at Aulis. Then Orestes killed her and stabbed Aegisthus. You couldn't do things by halves when the gods were dangling you on their strings.

The junk shop on Alfreton Road that had once spread a notice across its window saying GUNS FOR SPAIN now sold only old crocks and shabby furniture. People shambling around the streets from shop to shop disgusted him, new air tracking the old in his veins and killing it when cornered, to increase the size of corpuscles in his brain and float him so far above the squalid streets and inferior mob that at Canning Circus he felt as if lead had ricocheted against his chest leaving a great bruise. He was borne up from the blackness of a sheer-side pit, unlike any previous sensation, because in the hospital he had been cushioned by routine and bed and the eyes of Nora, so that all he could do was go home and pass a few hours reading in his room.

He put on his uniform to get into the servicemen's club downtown, and have a bath and a meal for half-a-crown, the good life feasible if you knew where to go. The pleasant normality of idleness took charge, his excuse being curiosity, and lack of energy which allowed him to explore without purpose, but never to feel bored.

He didn't know whether Nora was part of his present, wouldn't till they were together again, hard to imagine when that would be. They would walk on the Downs or along the beach at Queen's Bay gleaning wood to produce green flames in the fireplace which would reflect their faces, and he'd look at them observing each other, and then at all four locked in the furnace, perhaps to find out what they were seeing, and guess their thoughts. He spoke as he wrote, and wrote as the interior voice demanded, telling her that unless he was able to look at both, even though he was one of them, he would never set off on the journey that would tell him who he was, or who anybody else might be.

He couldn't put such an idea in the letter, though the words made a plain enough circuit through his brain. They would seem unreal and forced, but he wrote them in short lines that scanned, a poem connecting him to the smell of ether when the needle was driven in, to the invasion of train smoke when he walked into a station, to the homely warmth of a bed two people had slept in. She was listening, her presence close enough to draw his thoughts, which notion rushed his pen through the letter as if the nib was on ice. She'd open the envelope and find sufficient to read the pages more than once, keep them protected in her secret locked depot of corsets and camiknickers, brassieres and bloomers, stockings and vests. What he was doing in Nottingham was a mystery – or a dumb bout of self-torment. The air pumped into him was chasing out the old, bringing in the rage of strange ideas whose meanings he couldn't fathom, too deep and from too far back. Her affection would not evaporate for want of endearing reminders of their love.

He bought an ex-army camp bed for eight pounds, each night pulling it from under the double bed and setting it up on the floor, chilly yet comfortable compared to the undergrowth on Gunong Barat.

Arthur shuffled restlessly on the big bed. 'Brian!'

'What?'

'Tell us a jungle story.'

He didn't answer.

'Brian?'

'About how I shot that tiger?'

'Bleddy liar,' Arthur said.

'Go to sleep. Fred'll be in soon.'

Arthur was nearly fifteen. 'He's out whoring.'

He laughed. 'What do you know about that?'

'As much as yo' do.'

'Better not let Fred hear you.'

'He's after the tarts in Slab Square,' Arthur said.

'How do you know?'

'I saw him once. Had his arm round her arse.'

'Go to sleep.'

'Tell me a story.'

'About how I nearly trod on a black mamba?'

'I don't believe you.'

'It's true.'

'All right. Tell me, then.'

He didn't know who was asleep first.

Nora wasn't in the mess when he phoned. She was on duty, and he was not to contact her there. His letters floated away on a postage stamp, and he waited, communication not yet established – as signals procedure had it – till the other station responded.

In the reference section of the library he read the lives of poets and composers. Tiring of that, he genned up on the flora and fauna of Malaya, amazed at what he hadn't seen at the time with his own two eyes.

His mother set a plate of fried whiting, bread-and-butter and tea before him. 'Do you remember that young woman up the street who's got the same thing as yo'? She's ever such a nice gel.'

He didn't want to know anyone with TB, and that was a fact. As far as he was concerned he didn't have it anymore, though if he said so his mother wouldn't know what to make of it.

'She's on the mend now.'

Harold turned from tearing a newspaper into strips to make spills for his cigarettes, and faced the table. 'They do get better sometimes. If you got it twenty years ago you was a goner. A real bleddy killer it was.'

'It ain't like the old days,' Vera said.

Brian passed his father a cigarette.

'Thirty thousand a year peg out from it,' Seaton went on. 'I 'eard it on the wireless.'

'She's still in bed,' Vera told him. 'In the front room. But she's ever so nice. Her dad died of it years ago, and they say Lillian caught it from him. He painted houses, so maybe that caused it.'

'Sounds as if it runs in the family. It never ran in ours, though.' He turned to Brian. 'I can't understand why yo' got it.'

He preferred to be upstairs writing a letter to someone who did not regard his illness as such an affliction. 'I caught it in Malaya, I expect.'

'Mrs Verney's a nice woman,' Vera said. 'She's got a part-time job cleaning the canteen at the factory, but she gets a pension, and an allowance for looking after Lillian. The poor gel just lays there day in and day out. People think they'll catch summat if they go in and say hello.'

Seaton's fag, smoked to the stump, sped into the fire. 'You can't blame 'em.' He reached for another from Brian's packet.

'I don't care,' Vera said. 'I nip in whenever I go by, and ask her if she wants owt from the shop. You wouldn't think she was badly. She meks hersen up every morning, like a picture. I feel sorry for a young woman like that, but she towd me yesterday that the doctor said she might get up soon. I think she 'ad the same treatment as yo', our Brian.'

'I hear they're going to build a new housing estate up Clifton,' he said.

'What's it called?'

He gave in. 'An artificial pneumothorax?'

'It didn't do any good, so she just had to stay in bed. You ought to call again and say hello. She'd love to see you.'

She's been talking about me – though he couldn't blame her for that, hard to know whether he preferred his father, who wouldn't blab even if wild horses tried to get a word from him, or his mother who'd natter to anyone. She wanted him to promise. 'It's only up the street.'

'Leave him, if he don't want to,' Seaton said.

He'd been at school with Lillian's brother Ben, met him a few times in the White Horse since, a youth with thick dark hair and a sly sense of humour.

'She loves reading books,' Vera said. 'When her mam was badly she asked me to change 'em at the library, but I didn't know what to get.'

Vera called upstairs to let him know there was a letter. The blue envelope rested by his plate. 'Aren't you going to open it?'

He recognised the handwriting and ate his breakfast. 'Later.'

His mother had told Lillian Verney that he would call, but to avoid the house he turned down the street and got a bus by the White Horse, sat upstairs to read the single sheet: 'Dearest, I got back to Berkshire the same evening we parted, and felt more dead than alive knowing we wouldn't see each other for

187

so long. This is the first moment I can write, because a troopship got in from Malaya, and there hasn't been a moment's pause. Perhaps it's best, but you're always with me, so be patient if I don't reply to every one of your letters, which I read over and over because I love you so much. They told me someone phoned last night, and I kicked myself for not being there, because I knew it must be you. I'm so tired my pen won't hold still. Don't forget how dearly I love you.'

He re-read, damning whoever was blasting the equilibrium in Malaya to make his love work so hard, and overshot his stop, so that at the terminus the conductor wanted another sixpence for his fare.

'I asked for Parliament Street.'

'Can't 'elp that, me owd duck. You're miles past it.'

'I didn't know. I'm a stranger here.'

'I called the stop out. Half the people got off, in fact. Mek it threpence, then, and we'll say nowt else about it.'

An anecdote for his next letter. He went back over Carlton Hill to Edgeworth's factory in the Meadows, to look inside the place he wouldn't work at anymore. Narrow streets led into a cul-de-sac, the factory tucked beside a railway embankment.

At the entrance was a small office for the secretary, Edgeworth's cubby-hole opposite. The smell of hot brass, the grip of steel teeth milling into aluminium, the tang of disinfectant, and the slap of power belts rolling above the machines, rushed his youth back as if it had never gone. Shoulders were bent over lathes, tool grinders busy, all on piecework, earning what they could. If he had overalls he'd walk to a vacant lathe and set to with the same old vigour, but he was excluded forever, no right even to stroll into the workshop and say hello. In any case, except for Alf, the round-shouldered old toolsetter who waved to him, different people worked there. Edgeworth at his bench of micrometers, calipers and depth gauges, wiped his hands on a piece of towel. 'You look better than in the old days, no matter what you told me you'd got.'

They sat in the office. 'Things are busy, even though war work's finished. Rolls-Royce haven't forgotten us, and we still make bits of aero-engines, not to mention a few other things.

In fact the country can't get enough of what we can turn out, so whenever you feel fit, come and give us a hand.'

Strange that Edgeworth could see any feature that suggested he might go back to being a mechanic. 'I'm still in the air force, though I'll be demobbed in a couple of months. They say I'm to have a pension.'

'At your age! I'll bet you don't know whether to laugh or cry.'

Edgeworth knew he'd never be back, his offer of a job more out of charity than a need for his assistance. 'There's plenty of work, but plenty of workmen as well.'

'You might think so, but it's hard to get somebody who understands what he's doing. They're too slapdash these days. I check a man's work, and half of it's a few thou' off centre. They can easily get it right, but they want to mek as much money as they can. I work all hours God sends to mek sure we don't send dud stuff to Derby, and if I tell somebody off he asks for his cards and goes somewhere else.'

The secretary, a middle-aged woman with dyed ginger hair, came in with their coffee. She remembered Brian from the old days: 'You used to play football with the others, kicking a tin up and down the street in your dinner hour. It drove me mad when I was struggling to reckon up the time sheets.'

Edgeworth put a hand on his lank grey hair. 'I don't expect you to come back. You can do better, I suppose. But it's a shame we can't keep good lads in trades like this.'

There was nothing he could say. If he hadn't gone into hospital he might well have come to ask for a job.

'Still, I don't do too badly. I've got a few chaps who know what's what, as well as a woman or two.' He pushed a fiver into his hand. 'Get some fags, or whatever you need.'

Embarrassed, Brian laid it on the shelving which served for a desk.

'It comes out of the petty cash,' Edgeworth said. 'If you don't tek it I'll put it in the bloody post, then you'll have no say in the matter. Come out to Cropgrave and have a bit o' dinner with me and Alice sometime. We'll be glad to see you.'

Sunlight through watery clouds emphasised odours of garbage and pumice, moss in the cobblestones, sump oil from a deteriorating motorbike. The War Memorial gardens were another place entirely, smarter houses across the canalised Trent. He knew the city less than he thought. In town, the intimidating Council House on the eastern side of Slab Square had blocked him off as a kid from the area of law courts and Lace Market factories, warehouses and offices. No names from his own family were on the memorial plaques to local regiments in the church. Army service had been something to avoid, and as for the law courts, none had gone into them except as prisoners. Justice was something thrown at you if you were caught, often less severe than expected, but murderous all the same when you got sent down not so much for what you had done but for having been caught. He was amazed that he hadn't been nabbed and sent to a remand home, approved school, borstal, and then prison like most of Doddoe's kids, and he sweated at the thought of how close it had been. But chance had spared him, maybe because he had never thieved with sufficient persistence to become a menace, only nicking the odd thing as much out of mischief as malice.

By British Home Stores a young woman, whose two pre-school kids were well-enough shod, had legs heavy with vari-cose veins. The kid in a pushchair had a tuppenny custard, the other who dragged behind licked at a Mars Bar. She shouted for him to catch up, and Brian noticed half her teeth were missing. Maybe the curlers under her headscarf were rusty.

Even when there was work for everybody the fight went on, all over the world, for most of the people. In Malaya, after war and occupation, consumption was widespread, though he hadn't seen any starvation; but he would write a novel of fifty characters labouring in different countries, a few pages on the daily life of each, a panorama of human beings showing the same universal struggle against oppression, ignorance and nature.

People still lived by pennies rather than shillings, and he remembered how, many a time before the war, the family waited in the dark for the turn of the handle and the drop of a penny sent down the slot on to a bed of coins to provide light; at which dull metallic sound, never forgotten, the house was illuminated again. He had always wanted it to reveal a different room, without the people to whom a penny meant so much,

even though they were his parents, brothers and sisters, by
sorcery to find himself in a house of abundant food, with people
to offer books and learning and warmth, instead of want,
ignorance and cold.

What came out of the darkness was no less than the reality
that had gone in, but at least light had returned, at the cost of
a penny, which would last long enough to let them finish supper
and get up the wooden hill to bed, and still leave sufficient for
half an hour in the morning before it got light. When the gas
man emptied the meter, a percentage of the money went back
to the householder as rebate, a shilling or two with which Vera
ran to buy groceries, and get some fags for the old man.

It was better these days, but people still had bad teeth, short
sight, blue veins, drab skin, thin hair, sunken cheeks, putty
noses, and he wanted to be where he couldn't see them, or
at least set them against a background of different scenery.
Compared to them he was one of the elect, never to be too
close but always to know them better than himself – unless he
got so far away that he forgot them. A few pounds a week for
which he did not have to work already divided him from them
but, even apart from that, the fact was he had been separated
from them since birth, though he felt close enough to the
woman and her two snotty kids to realise that it would always
be possible to cross the dividing line – but never to stay there
in case he perished from spiritual want.

He paid his ha'penny to cross the toll bridge, and went
through Wilford village to Clifton Grove, the long avenue of
trees from where he had gone perilously down the wooded
banks to the river with Pauline, searching out a place to make
love in.

Life with her was over, every strand of the rope bridge
thrown across the canyon of driving water definitively cut. A
woman teacher at the infants' school, brought up in India, told
them stories to keep them quiet. We were moving, she said –
be silent, and listen to what I tell you – to another house up in
the Hills. All our belongings were put on the backs of elephants,
and the heaviest item was a piano. And we can all imagine how
much that weighed, can't we, children?

She was a storyteller, he recalled, sitting on the branch of a fallen tree. A dozen elephants came to a rope bridge over the river a hundred feet below. The first eleven crossed, though they didn't like it, but it seemed that nothing would get the elephant to go over with the piano on its back. At last it was persuaded, and when it got to the middle of the bridge, down went the elephant, and the piano – into the river, never to be seen again.

So don't try to cross a bridge when you know it won't take your weight, children. You see how wise the elephant was? Some bridges aren't meant to be crossed, especially with a piano on your back. If ever you are tempted, remember what happened to the elephant.

Was that teacher of fifteen years ago still telling her kids it wasn't their place to cross bridges? Maybe she was right, though not all were put off, had no option but to get on the bridge and try it no matter what weight was strapped to their backs, wouldn't even know they were trying till they were on the other side. But most would do as the teacher told them and never make the attempt, and some wouldn't try even if she persuaded them that it *was* safe to cross every bridge they came to no matter how rickety, and that it was indeed their duty to cross and reach the freedom they might find beyond.

All you could do was feel sorry for the poor bloody elephant, and the children, but maybe even sorrier for the teacher, because all were in the hands of fate and hardly knew what they were doing. As for him, he didn't think about crossing bridges anymore, because he was already far enough over the other side not to care.

Chapter

❦ EIGHTEEN

Vera called him from the bedroom because she thought he might be interested when two men came to the back door selling magazines. 'They've bin before, but I didn't buy owt because I don't read much except the *Mirror*. Mr Harper in the next terrace shouted that he'd set his dog on 'em if they didn't clear off. Said he didn't want anybody trying to sell that *commonist* muck to 'im!'

They laughed, used to such treatment. Soft-hearted Vera didn't like turning anybody from her door, but was glad to hand them over to Brian, who she thought could talk to them properly.

Percy Battle, a tall thin man with a ruddy face and a short ginger beard, taught at a local school. He'd worked down the pit in the war, then gone to college and become a teacher. He told Vera he was married and had two kids, and that his wife also did a bit for the Party when she could. Both men went around the houses on Sunday morning, and tried to sell the *Daily Worker* in Slab Square during the week. Vera made them a pot of tea, while they laid out copies of *Soviet Literature*.

'You get all the latest stories and poems in 'ere,' Chuck said. 'They're ever so interesting.'

Percy stuffed the bowl of his curved pipe – just like Stalin, Brian noted – then searched his large bag as if to bring out a couple of rabbits. 'Here's a novel called *The Tanker Derbent*.'

The first lines mentioned a wireless operator on a ship in the Caspian, and when Percy asked if he read much, Vera laughed: 'He's allus got his nose in a book. I can't get 'im away from 'em.'

'What about Russian literature?'

He mentioned Tolstoy and Dostoevsky, and Chekhov's plays, at which Chuck rolled his cap as if about to throw it into the air for a game of football. 'Ah, but it ain't *Soviet* literature, is it?'

He admitted he hadn't read any of that.

'You've got a treat in store.' Chuck offered cigarettes, as Vera refilled their cups. 'I never read owt else.'

Percy's grey eyes and tolerant smile suggested that he didn't mind not getting a word in edgeways when on his rounds with Chuck, because Chuck could talk his way more easily into people's houses. He had worked twenty years at Josiah Pentecost's lace factory downtown, and in a reserved occupation during the war had done his bit to defeat the common enemy by making camouflage netting. The cap accentuated his lean face, such features always ready for a hee-haw laugh which showed his false teeth, though his eyes darted protectively, as if to throw out a barrier over which nobody would be allowed to step.

Brian showed a copy of *The Theban Plays*. 'I'm reading this at the moment.'

'Yes, that's all very well,' Chuck said. 'But this Soviet stuff is about people, ordinary men and women trying to build communism, and get the country back on its feet after beating the fascist hordes.'

Brian had followed the Russian campaign every bit of the way, back and forth, until the Battle for Berlin ended the war. Communism, talked about at the youth club, seemed a fair solution to inequalities, but Len Knotman pointed out in Malaya that communism had no respect for the individual. 'You and me would be stuck up against the wall and shot in no time if there was a revolution.' Nor did there seem much sense trying to apply communism to the lives of people in Radford, who had other problems, couldn't be bothered, hadn't a clue what the issues were – though Chuck and Percy tried to convert them with the quiet passion of Sunday school teachers.

'We've got a lot to do, before going home to have us dinner,' Chuck said, standing up. Brian bought a magazine, and a *Daily Worker*, and they lent him a booklet of speeches by Stalin. Vera invited them to call next week, and they said they would, even if only to find out whether Brian liked the stuff they left.

He sat on the sloping greensward of Wollaton Park, a row of cannon on the terrace of the Hall behind, reading about a man on a collective farm who was shown up because he wasn't doing his work properly. The words didn't grip as printed language should, and he couldn't be bothered to go on to the end. A story set in a factory was written by someone who could never have worked in one, because there was no complaining about rates and wages, and he couldn't fathom a firm in which they weren't eternally chewed over. Talk about the glory of the Communist Party, and the wonderful system they lived under, and of life in the future, was all very well, but what were the types of machine they slaved at, what did they scoff in the canteen, were they on piece work or a bonus system? What were their houses like, their clothes, their hobbies? Did they get blindoe at the weekend and, if so, what on? Did they fight after getting drunk? And what about falling in love? Even a story from the war didn't say where it had taken place so that he could look for it on the map. As for Stalin's speeches – phrases sliding in one ear to do a header out of the other, as if wearing lifebelts to save their lives – they were child's play compared to the closegrained sentences of *The Critique of Pure Reason*.

He wrote every day to Nora. They belonged to each other in a way that seemed too intimate to be thought of as love, memories overwhelming him during an evening walk along the bridlepath beyond Strelley. The surface of fields glided downwards in the dusk, their green cover deepening as if in anticipation of a night's cooling dew, bringing to him a feeling of love towards everyone.

He sat by his cool pint in the homely snug of the Admiral Byng, a place he had come to with Pauline, and even girls before her, on summer nights when the smell of cut wheat mixed with the bouquet of fresh drawn beer, and the lingering odours of passionate courtship.

On his own, memories and his sense of the present were as intense as if the land the pub stood on reached to the centre of the earth. He was part also of the fields he had walked through, their breath having followed, never to let go. Thoughts of Pauline came with affection, but only as she had been when they were sweethearts, a state which ended as soon as they'd been forced to get married.

Lillian Verney rushed to mind, whom he had seen once, and dimly, a year ago, the TB girl who lived up the street. He wanted to see her, could not think why, did not know why, unable to find a reason, knew though not quite as strongly that he shouldn't, because he wanted to be alone till he saw Nora, had so much else to do, and couldn't face someone who might care to talk about the only thing they had in common. Troubled and yet elated – the willing victim of confusion – he lost patience with walking, and took a bus home.

Curiosity impelled him – must he have a reason for everything? – though he didn't know whether he wanted to call or not. He would walk by her house and hop a bus into town, where the safest course would be to buy a ticket to Kent and batten the hatches at Nora's cottage, read and write in peace. But his mother had pleaded for him to do a good deed and let Lillian know she wasn't alone in the world, though he was aware, as he rapped the V sign on her door, that he might be doing as much a favour for himself, pushed into it by a force he could neither resist nor understand, and for which there couldn't be any reason.

She had been expecting him, but the door seemed locked. 'It gets stuck,' she called. 'You've got to push it 'ard! I keep asking mam to mend it, but she don't know how to.'

He hid his embarrassment by observing everything about the room, the light dim after coming from outside. 'I thought I would say hello.'

She was far from dying, lively compared to last time, his mother right in saying she was on the mend. Dark hair flowed against a bank of pillows. 'I was wondering if you would.'

On the counterpane lay a half-done picture stretched across an embroidery frame, of a cottage with flowers around the door. Her bed was pushed against the green-stippled wall, leaving room for a sideboard, and a chest of drawers on which her make-up bag spilled curlers. A plate on the chair had an apple core on it, and he wondered if he should make himself useful and take it away. A small oval mirror in a wooden frame lay at the bottom of her bed, as well as a novel by Bertha Stroud whose gaudy cover showed a man and woman kissing. 'I was on my way into town.'

'Well,' she smiled, sitting up, 'it's nice to see you.'

He thought her face might be rouged, but she was only flushed at the sudden meeting. A blue knitted jacket covered her white nightdress, and she held a handkerchief loosely around her wrist. Ringlets had been put in with a curling iron, which she had sat by the fire to heat. Or maybe she had used the gas. Her mouth was subtly lipsticked, and hair spreading from her thin face deepened her forehead. She had taken a long time over it, wanting to look good, even in bed, and he felt her trying to calculate what was in his mind, the faint lines at her mouth showing how baffled she was, lacking the energy to wonder. In a story he would make Percy Battle fall in love with her, whether he was married or not. 'Not all that pleasant being in bed, is it?'

'I'm used to it, duck.' Her lips pursed, before returning to their set ironic smile. 'Why don't you tek that plate off the chair, and sit down? Put it on the sideboard.'

She didn't know what to make of him, but he didn't mind about that. 'How long have you been in bed?'

The reckoning illuminated her dark eyes. 'Up and down since I was twelve – as far as I can remember.'

He sat down, liking her joke. 'A year was enough for me. Nearly drove me round the bend.'

'The first year's the worst.'

They laughed.

'We'll have to get you out of it.'

'There's nowt I'd like better. I can go as far as the lavatory, but that's about all. The doctor says I've got to stay put. We used to live up Woodhouse, but when dad died mam took this place. She couldn't stand Woodhouse after dad died.'

People walked by outside, their talk as clear as if the wall was cardboard:

'*The bogger allus says he don't want to see me when I goo and see him, so I'm not gooin' to see 'im anymore. Let 'im get married if that's the way 'e feels.*'

'*You can't do owt about it, though, can yer, duck?*'

'*No, but I can chuck it ovver 'is big daft 'ead!*'

She held her sides trying not to laugh, her face twisted into a pig's back. 'I'm in stitches, at times.' Pale wrists showed out of her sleeves. If he spanned them with thumb and middle finger like handcuffs her hands would slip through. He wondered how tall she was, but could hardly ask her to stand up.

'The things I hear!' She leaned close, her breath warm, as if speaking softly would stop her from coughing. 'Mrs Leeming up the street told her husband Jack that her brother was going to come and stay with 'em while he found a job. Then he'd get a place of his own. She hadn't seen him for ten years, she said, because he'd been in Canada. Neither had her husband, because they'd only been wed nine. Well, he lived with 'em, and stayed on and on. He got a job on nights, or so he told 'em, which meant he was in the house all day. Being on days, Jack went off to work in the morning. I used to hear him go by. I knew it was him because of his tread, and he allus whistled a certain tune. The same tune! Can you imagine, not changing the tune you whistle from one year's end to another?'

'I can't.' He could imagine anything.

'Then one day Jack faints at work, and the gaffer sends him home because he's got the flu. When the daft bogger staggers into the house he cops his missis in bed with you-know-who. "How can you be in bed with your brother?" he screams. "I'll die. I can't believe it!" He nearly guz mad, but his wife only looks at him. "Brother be boggered! Yo'd believe owt, yo' would." Poor old Jack! Well, the lodger had to go. She'd met him in the pub, and got him into the house by saying he was her brother. Would you believe it? Jack and his missis are as happy as two lovebirds now. Everything's blown over. You do learn a lot, though, lying in bed.'

He nodded.

'People pop in now and again, so I get all the news. I put two and two together. A lot don't know I sleep in here. They think it's an empty parlour, and argue as they go by. Have you noticed how people allus stop walking when they've got owt to say?'

She breathed as if the paperbags she had for lungs had gone on strike, and put a hand to her chest, her dark pupils expanding, shadows under her eyes. 'I shouldn't talk so much. It meks me cough. And Mam gets frightened if I cough.' There was fear and despair in her smile. For a moment he couldn't make out what she was saying. 'She's terrified of blood. Thinks I might go like Dad. But I know I won't. I'll never go like that.'

He held her hand. 'Of course you won't. You'll just have to be careful not to get run over when you cross Ilkeston Road.'

'I'll try not to.' Her breath rasped. 'I'll look both ways.'

He pointed to the books. 'You read a lot.'

'Most of it's tripe. But it's all Mam brings me. I've read *The Card*, though, by Arnold Bennett.'

'What's it like?'

'Ever so good.'

'I'll try it. Have you read *Anna of the Five Towns?*'

'No, but I've read *The Citadel*, and *David Copperfield*.' She shouldn't talk so much, and he was ready to leave, but he didn't think she wanted him to. She saw his glance at the window. 'You won't hear much till they come up from the factory at dinner time.' She had guessed right, so he would stay a bit longer. 'You get the juiciest bits after the pubs close at night. You didn't have it very bad, though, did you?'

Hard to remember. She was deeper into the hole than he had been, but maybe that was because the TB had hit her younger. His strength had never been taken away, though if he'd stayed another six months in Malaya he might never have got home. 'No,' he told her. 'And I'm all right now.'

'I was three years in Newstead Sanatorium.'

He wasn't interested. 'What was it like?'

'It worn't so bad, now I look back on it. We had some laughs, me and the other women. But they think I'll get better just as well at home.'

'I expect you will.' He must force himself out, felt that he had fallen, was floating downstream and struggling to reach the shore. 'You'll have to get up and go for a walk.'

'I can't, duck.'

'I'll call now and again, if that's all right,' hardly knowing why he said it.

She held the bedjacket close, a hand under the sheet. 'I wouldn't like you to see me if I'm not feeling well.'

'I pass every day.'

'I'm sure I've heard you. I'm tired now, though. I like to sleep a lot. Just knock on the door when you come.'

He took deep breaths in the street, the houses closing in, craved space, but hadn't the will to pack and get out. A bull terrier slipped its lead, and a short middle-aged man wearing a white scarf, mackintosh and trilby hat waddled after it, calling for it to come back. His hat fell off, and the dog kept running, turned into the road – where a bus missed it by inches. The man gave the dog a kick, and would have thumped mercilessly if people hadn't been close. 'That'll learn yer.' He tightened the collar a couple of notches. 'I can't even come out and get a bleddy haircut! Yer did that on'y las' week. It's the las' bleddy time yer play that game on me, yer bleddy daft 'aporth!' The dog seemed pleased to be spoken to in any way at all, and even more so when Brian picked the man's hat up by the newsagent's, wagging its tail, the only part still free.

He called at the branch library and chose *Pride and Prejudice*, *Candide*, *Bel Ami* and *On the Eve* from the shelves. Not wanting to pass Lillian's window and have his footsteps noted, he walked up the street from the factory end.

'I found this on the stairs this morning,' his mother said.

The steel key fitted Nora's door. 'I left some stuff in the hospital,' he said, 'and it belongs to the locker.'

Even she could see it was for a door. 'Did you see Lillian?'

The whole street knew already, but he didn't care. 'I stayed ten minutes.'

'Some people have rotten luck. And she's on'y your age. Do you want some coffee?'

'No thanks. I'm going up to read.'

'There's a letter on your desk.'

He stayed in the kitchen, not wanting her to think it was important. She watched the kettle till it boiled, and he read the first page of *On the Eve*, a beginning that helped him not to run upstairs and open the letter.

'Lillian was telling me about how Mrs Leeming was caught in bed with the lodger who was supposed to be her brother,' he said.

She put the cups down. 'There's nobody o' that name in this street. 'Appen she was having you on.'

He was surprised, and annoyed that she had spun a story which was too good to be condemned as a simple lie. Perhaps there was more to her than he'd thought.

'Maybe they lived in some other street,' Vera said, 'though I'd have heard about it, I'm sure.'

He'd been made a fool of, and imagined she told similar tales to everyone. He didn't think he'd bother to go back and find out.

Nora's letter was much like the last one. 'I only want you to know I'm still alive. Otherwise I'm too whacked at the end of the day even to tell you about the work I'm doing. It's all go. My only pleasure is to find those plain envelopes with your letters inside. So keep writing, my love. One day we'll make up for everything.' He stroked the envelope as if it was her skin, the smell as neutral as her ever-clean body, which more than ever made him ache to go back to the hospital before his leave ended.

Rain sluiced over the lavatory slates, filled holes in the asphalt, saturated washing that hung on Monday clotheslines. He read the time away. Bazarov died of consumption, and Elena went to fight for the independence of Bulgaria. Candide worked in his garden, and after *Pride and Prejudice* he was glad of the cynical realism of *Bel Ami*.

Hungry for stories from beyond the world that imprisoned him, he hankered to go to France, as if that was the country his ancestors had fled from. Near the station a cinema showed foreign films and, waiting to go in, he saw a tall dark-haired woman with books under her arm, and a full satchel hanging from her shoulder. She looked at him, and turned away, as if she knew no one, but even so had no care in the world. If they passed again she wouldn't know him, but he would recognise her, watching her walk up the road, before he turned to buy his ticket.

He read the subtitles but recognised odd words because at home he tuned his wireless on to French stations, and had relearned some vocabulary, as well as a few verbs from one of his old textbooks.

When Vera applied for a part-time evening job at the General Hospital, Seaton grumbled, but she wouldn't back down. 'I'm fed up with sitting here pulling a meagrim at the fireplace night after night. It'll give me summat to do. I'll allus make sure and leave you your tea, though.'

Brian said it was a good idea, and Seaton was mollified at the notion of a few more quid coming into the house.

Upstairs, rain wiping at the windows, Arthur was surrounded by a fleet of paper aeroplanes, pages torn from *Soviet Literature*. 'You little bastard,' Brian said. 'You shouldn't do that to a magazine.'

'I tried reading it.' Arthur sat on the bed. 'It's no good. I thought it was a dirty book. Anyway, I'm not a bastard.'

'Well, don't rip anything else up. And never touch the stuff on my desk or in the cupboard. If you want some paper, just ask me.'

'What do you do all that writing for?'

'What writing?'

'In that book.'

'Fun.'

He made a motion of pulling his nose. 'I don't believe you.'

'Scribble.'

'All about Lil Verney?'

It concerned Nora, but Arthur was fishing, hoping his big brother would tell him about her. 'You really are a bastard.'

Arthur gave a zombie grin. 'Dad wouldn't like to hear you say that.'

'Bugger off.'

'Neither would Mam.'

'Keep your nose out of my things.'

'I do. I can't read, yo' know that.'

'That's what you say.'

'Teacher says I can't.'

'Clear out of my sight, or I'll hack your head off.'

Arthur laughed his way downstairs, no doubt to tell the others what he'd read in Nora's letters. From now on he'd carry them in his wallet.

Library books under his arm, he stood in the rain.

'Wait a minute, duck.'

Mr Litchfield wondered what he was doing on a woman's doorstep at ten in the morning. No use lighting a fag he'd throw away as soon as he got inside in case it made her cough, and inspecting a book would make him look like the gasman before going in to read the meter.

'You can come in now.'

He pushed the door hard.

'I 'ad to finish my wash. I looked as if I'd bin dragged through a hedge backwards when I woke up this morning.'

A flannel in the enamel bowl was like a lump of half melted snow, giving off a smell of heavily scented soap. 'How are you feeling?'

'A lot better today. What yer doing with them books?'

No make-up, she looked older, more of a woman, no need to smile this morning. She let him see her plain and unadorned, as if accepting him as one of the family, and he wondered at the significance. 'I'm off to the library.'

Her hand seemed too fragile to hold more than one at once. 'Can I see 'em?'

'I'll take yours back if you like.'

'P'raps I'll read these.' She sifted through, and chose Turgenev. 'What's this one like?'

'Not much cop.' Nearly every book he read these days had someone dying of TB. Maybe she was used to it, and liked stories about people choking to death, especially since it wasn't her, just as a soldier might be interested in war stories while convalescing from his wounds.

'*You've* read it, so I can.'

'Suit yourself.'

He had better things to do, though he didn't know what. But he stood up to go.

'That was quick.'

He backtracked at the needle of pain in her, ashamed of his

hurry. 'I was going to take your bowl away.' He'd done it in the ward to make himself useful, so why not for her?

'You'd better. Last week I knocked it over and it went right through the mattress. Poor Mam. She was ever so mad. While you're in the kitchen, though, ask her to find my library books. Then you can change 'em same time as yourn.'

Mrs Verney sat at the table. 'I heard you come in, so I thought I'd better not disturb. I was just reading the *Penny Liar* before going out shopping.'

She had heard their talk, no secrets in such a house. 'I've brought the bowl in.'

'So I see. Tip it in the sink, while I find Lilly's books.'

Her face was pale, and she had drawn and rather squashed features, dark hair like her daughter's but turning grey. She was afraid of the light, afraid of the night, her eyes tense with concern. Perhaps he was making it up, but she was right to be full of dread. Her husband had coughed his lungs out, so she hoped her daughter wouldn't.

When the water that had washed Lillian's body had gone down the sink Mrs Verney beckoned, a finger hooked for him to get close.

'What?'

'See her as often as you can, my duck.'

His smile said don't worry, of course, I'll do all you say, yet he hadn't crossed the stormy divide to be stranded in a situation he didn't want. Such tentacles would suck his life away, drag him to oblivion. She held his wrist, eyes blank with hopelessness. 'If owt 'appens to her, I'll die.'

His inferior heart, an enemy which refused to be jettisoned, had landed him in a trap not of his own choosing. Her tears were like rain on the valves and condensers of a radio set, causing it to short-circuit and make action impossible. But her mute tears brought out that fatal and shameless sentiment from his mother up through his grandmother and spreading among the women of the family, and therefore by an unblocked route to him, which led him to say, though unsure that he would be able to do anything at all: 'I'll do my best.'

'What are you two talking about, then?' Lillian called.

'Trying to find your bloody books,' he shouted. 'Are you

sure they aren't under your bedclothes?' Mrs Verney laughed silently at his quickness. You should be on the stage, he thought. 'Yer think we've got nowt better to talk about than yo'?' he called, using the broadest Nottingham accent.

He showed her the books. 'Someone must have hidden them.'

'My mother never knows where she puts owt,' she smiled. 'She must have softening of the brain.'

'Like me at times,' he said. 'You as well, I expect.'

Walking up the street, he wondered exactly what Mrs Verney meant. To care for anybody except himself was to lose the freedom it had been so difficult to find. He might manage to stay half an hour now and again to cheer Lillian up, otherwise let her read about how Bazarov died, because who was he to keep it from her? He wasn't in the world to save anyone except himself.

Water flowing down the gutter found a grate. He kept the books under his coat, and this time walked straight in. She was sitting upright in the bed, as if hypnotised or asleep, a flowered headscarf accentuating the length of her face. 'You caught me! I sit like that for hours.'

'You were in never-never land, if you ask me.'

He hadn't found her without make-up this time. She'd made sure of that. 'When I'm stock still I don't cough. Sometimes I hold it back for hours.'

'Isn't it hard?'

'I dream, and think as well, so I don't know.'

'What about?'

'You don't think I'd tell yo'?'

He dropped the books so as not to touch them with his wet hands, and she winced at the weight on her legs under the blankets. She should eat more, and put on weight. 'Doesn't your mother feed you?'

She arranged the books like cakes or flowers. 'Course she does. I get an egg every day, and a stew. I eat lots of bread and fruit.'

'It doesn't look like it.'

'I'm allowed extra rations, being like I am.'

'When I was in the hospital' – he was glad not to say

'sanatorium' – 'I shovelled it in all the time. I couldn't eat enough.'

'Well, neither can I.' She flushed, wondering if he was getting at her. 'Anyway, mind your own business.' A cough broke, and he regretted his roughness, though anything was worth trying. Her breath was like fingernails scraping on tin, punctuated by short coughs, right hand clutching her left shoulder, the other as if holding something in her mouth.

In Malaya, after a meal in the mess, he had let his belches out in the shorts and longs of morse, forming the callsign of Rangoon or Bangkok, to the amusement of other operators. He now tried to decipher any secret message in the rhythm of her coughing, but found none.

The light in her eyes dimmed, accusing him of callousness, fear blaming him for her illness. It was all because of him, because if he hadn't been born she wouldn't suffer like this, and he thought: who else can she blame except someone close to her?

He couldn't stand it, wanted her to stop coughing, leave him alone, or die. Run, a voice said, run, run. But he sat on the bed and held her gently, his lips at her forehead, nothing else to do, her hot mouth against his shirt, heart pounding as the coughing subsided. He willed whatever animal was in her to get back into its lair and perish, his whole mind urging her to conquer the beast, deprive it of hunger so that it would no longer need to eat, anything worth trying to prevent her being torn to pieces.

She seemed to sleep but, unable to detach himself without disturbing her, he wondered if by sheer will he could root out her cough for good, stroked her hair, gently so that she might not notice, another part of the calming process. It was hard to believe she was ill, she was putting it on, no one was ill unless they wanted to be. But why did she want to be? What had cracked her in two so that she hadn't been able to resist getting TB? He wanted to find a way out of her deadlock, do something instead of just holding her till she stopped coughing. 'My back aches, duck. I've got to lay down.'

He arranged the pillows, releasing her against them. There was more colour in her cheeks, but make-up hadn't put it there. 'Is that better?'

Not much else he could have done. She wiped her eyes, and smiled. 'I'm sorry you got wet, taking my books back.'

'Only my mackintosh.'

'It's good to lie in bed and hear the rain coming down in the street.'

He held a glass of barley water to her lips. 'When it's sunny, though, don't you want to be out walking?'

'I do.'

'If the weather gets good, I'll take you somewhere.'

'That'd be lovely.' She reached for his hand. 'But Mam would be frightened. And the doctor would say I couldn't.'

'What does he know about it?'

'It's a woman.'

'She, then.'

'More than us, I think.'

'I never took much notice of 'em.'

'That was different,' she said. 'We aren't all the same, are we?'

Uncertainty shimmered in her features. He didn't want to upset her. 'What are you going to read first?'

She picked up *On the Eve*.

She bloody would, he thought, in a tone which had a harsh echo of his dead grandfather's voice. 'You'll enjoy it,' he said. 'It's wonderful.'

❧ NINETEEN

Vera liked her work at the hospital. 'It's an orthopaedic ward. You should see the poor boggers. They bring 'em in all the time – day and night, it meks no difference.'

'They wheel 'em in, and they wheel 'em out.' Seaton was in a good mood. 'Feet first, I expect – some on 'em.'

Vera folded her arms with disapproval. 'You shouldn't talk like that. It might be yo', one day.'

'Not if I know it. You wouldn't catch me in one o' them places.'

'Well, you never know.'

'I bleddy well do. They either kill you off with the knife, or poison you.' He spoke sharply, always ready for the last word, though he rarely got it these days.

'People get run over, or fall off buildings. It ain't their fault. I feel sorry for 'em. One bloke was a bit mental. He'd tried to hang 'issen, but broke his arm, and they kept him in for observation. The ward's five floors up. Then he jumped out of the window. Killed 'issen. One o' the nurses towd me about it. She's a lovely Irish nurse, big and tall, with ginger hair. There's another bloke there like yo', our Brian – allus reading. He showed me the book, but I don't remember what it was called. He said somebody from Eastwood wrote it. There's a picture of him on the back, with a beard.'

'I don't know who it can be,' he said, had been in all day,

and thought he would call on Bert, because if he didn't at some time during his leave he'd never hear the last of it.

'I thought he'd got married,' Vera said.

'Not that I know,' Brian told her. 'Though I think he was going to.'

'I expect she's left him already,' Seaton put in.

He reached for his raincoat. 'I'll go and find out.'

The streets were fresh after a long wash, a pink haze between the white clouds reflected on windows and slated roofs. He dropped his letter to Nora in a pillar box, wondering why he hadn't mentioned Lillian, though he supposed he would tell her soon enough.

Bert sat by the gramophone, trying to cheer himself up with a record of Spike Hughes. He leapt out of his chair. 'I thought yer'd fucked yerself to cinders in that lovely 'ospital. What yer doin' back in this lousy owd deathpit?'

They walked over the canal bridge into town, and sat in the Eight Bells. 'I heard you'd got married.'

Bert gulped his beer. 'Not likely. I slid out of it. She worn't preggers. On'y said she was. I'm not going steady anymore. Just out for all I can get.'

He couldn't come alive, not even with talk of old times, and Brian remembered him as being far more cheerful when threatened by a forceput marriage. He grumbled that he was broke, and that his job didn't pay enough, even though he worked all the hours God sent.

Brian bought another round, and they sat at a table by the foot of the stairs, the pub crowded on Friday night. A giant aspidistra thrived in the fumes of beer and smoke. 'I'll change my job,' Bert said. 'Plenty o' drivers are wanted, these days. I'd do a long distance stint, that's where the money is, but I haven't got a licence for a big lorry.'

'Can't you get one?'

'I need lessons, and no cunt'll learn me.'

Brian came back from the bar and set the drinks on the table. A tall crop-haired youth who was blind drunk rolled down the stairs and settled at the foot, a noise like a train on a branchline late for its next stop. Bert jumped up to save his beer, the only time Brian had seen him close to panic.

A waiter persuaded the youth back on to his feet, a man and woman leaning over to look, with smoke, aspidistra, staircase and hanging lamp making an unforgettable picture. Bert stood. 'Pissed as a newt. Let's get out of his way before he starts spewing. In any case, it's dead in here.'

After walking Bert home he got a bus for Radford. A light shone in Lillian's window, and he decided to say goodnight.

'Who is it?'

He wouldn't call his name and tell the whole neighbourhood. She got out of bed to turn the key, back under cover before he walked in. 'I was just passing.'

The tin clock on the sideboard said eleven. 'Where've yer bin?' – as if wherever it was he shouldn't have gone.

He told her about Bert, and the pub, and the man falling downstairs. 'I can smell the beer,' she said. 'Stay a minute, though. I couldn't go to sleep till I saw how that book ended.'

'Did you like it?'

'I cried buckets. Mam said: "What yo' cryin' for?" And I said: "It's that book I just read." So she said: "What do you want to read books that mek yer cry for?" So I towd her you'd got it for me, and she said: "He stands need to bring yer books that mek yer cry." "Well, I liked it," I towd her. "It was smashin'! I like books that mek yer cry." "That's your funeral then, in't it?" she said. But while I was reading I didn't cough once.'

'I'll bring you some more like that. Anyway, tell your ma it's great literature. Where is she?'

'In bed. She's allus asleep by half past ten.'

'Aren't *you* tired?'

'Not now you've wakened me. Sometimes I lay awake half the night. But I don't mind. I think things.'

He held her hand. 'Such as what?'

'I daren't tell you. Stupid things, like why I'm here and not somewhere else. I wonder why I was born me, and not another person.'

'We all think that,' he said.

'Whose fault do you think it is?'

'I don't know.'

'I don't suppose it's anybody's,' she said.

210

'I suppose not.'

'Do you believe there's a God?'

He hadn't thought about it, which disappointed her. She expected him to think about things like that. She imagined he thought about everything. And if he did, then he would think about that, wouldn't he? But he hadn't. In the air force you couldn't talk about politics or religion. There were Jews, Catholics and Protestants, but you never argued, so maybe he'd got out of the habit, because they sure used to chew the fat in the factory during tea break and dinner hour.

'Nobody can know if there's a God or not,' he said. 'Depends what you believe, I suppose.' He hoped that would be enough, because it was as much as he could manage after a few pints of beer.

'I sometimes think I see Him,' she said, her forehead like chalk, cheeks flushed, 'when I can't stop coughing, and when I don't care whether I live or die. I know I'm not going to die, not yet anyway, but that's how it feels.'

'I'm supposed to cheer you up,' he said. 'If I don't, your mother will drive me away.'

'Hold me, then, like you did the other day.'

She burned against him, a two-way warmth, her breath clean because she neither smoked nor drank. If God existed He would make her well, but He certainly wouldn't favour him, and neither would anybody else, if he let himself go where his body was pulling him.

'I've got to be off now.'

Her hands slid away, face set against him, lips thin and eyes blank. 'Come tomorrow.'

'Yes.'

'Don't forget. I can't come after yer.'

She sensed no future – he knew the feeling well, having been similarly brushed, but she lived with the fact far more intensely than he ever had. The only event she looked forward to was the dream of being as fit as everybody else. He had never thought of himself as unfit, but he didn't want to be like everybody else, either. He smiled, and bent to kiss her, a sisterly touch. 'You won't need to.'

He closed the door silently so that her mother wouldn't hear.

Glad of the darkness, he went down the street like spring-heeled Jack drawn along by the stars.

Just as he was getting used to being at home he woke up one morning and wondered where he was. The sense of belonging nowhere was followed by the impulse to get away from where he was in order to find out exactly where he wanted to be. He didn't know where that was, he might never know, but sooner or later he must set off and find out.

Braces hung from his uniform-trousers as he shaved at the kitchen sink, and in a corner of the mirror a gull with white head and yellow beak turned left and right, wings outspread, sat on a thermal and floated over the cliff, all nature on its side. If not to Nora's, he would stay at the YMCA in London, and see the sights. The razor slid up and down, and he described what he knew of the river, palaces and museums to Lillian. He drank a cup of tea which had gone lukewarm.

At the servicemen's club he smoked a cigar and drank coffee, read about Malaya, the Airlift, strikes – the world going on in the same old way, little interested except for a glance at the map. As a kid he'd heard of battles in Manchuria, Abyssinia and Spain. The mind became numb. Six years of war had come and gone, though war and conflict would go on as a fact of life till the end of time, because there was neither peace on earth nor equilibrium possible in the individual body. Ideas of Utopia had been squashed forever by the German death camps, so the soul could never rest. All you could do was find out as much about yourself as possible, and keep out of everybody's way for as long as they would let you, while at the same time trying to discover what you could about them.

Having verbalised such a decision, he was in a happy enough mood to lash out a couple of bob on a bunch of chrysanths from a stall by the Council House, thinking they would put some colour into Lillian's drab room.

He walked in, uniform serge crossed by glittering buttons, flowers held high, and cap skimming on to the sideboard, before laying the blooms on her bed. God alone knows what she thinks, he said to himself. Impulses were the cogwheels of action, though he was glad the gift pleased her.

'Mam, bring a vase. Look what Brian's brought me.'

Mrs Verney frowned at a gift either too extravagant or too significant. Somebody must have got off the bus and forgot them. I couldn't leave 'em to die, could I? Funny how careless people can be. Let them speculate. Or she considered it too exciting a gift for Lillian to receive. Or maybe a little bit of jealousy was involved. They sometimes bickered like sisters.

Flowers changed the room, lived for her. 'I sat at the kitchen table this morning and shelled some peas for Mam. It made me feel a lot better, being up.'

'That's good news.'

'I'll stay up a bit longer every day.'

'Don't overdo it.'

'I shan't, sarky. What's that badge on your sleeve?'

A clenched fist shooting sparks, six points of energy and knowledge flashing at the world. If he'd stayed in he'd have got a commission in the technical branch, and been a retired wing-commander at fifty-five – the first time he had thought of it. 'Shows I'm a wireless operator.'

'What did you do?'

'Sent messages to planes about the weather, and got messages back. I also gave them bearings which helped them to know where they were, so that they could bomb bandits in the jungle.'

She frowned. 'Did you like that sort of thing?'

'I'd do it again like a shot' – if everything to do with my TB could be wiped out. She was bored with his rigmarole, so he stood up to go, though maybe she wanted him to continue talking, whether or not it was all Chinese and he was breaking the Official Secrets Act, but he couldn't sit down and pick up where he had left off, mad at himself for not knowing what to say, missing the right moment all along the line.

The matter couldn't be left on such a razor's edge, no way of treating her, so he'd have to come back, though not too soon in case she thought he was courting her. Everyone in the street probably thought so, anyway, an area full of the juiciest rumours.

He packed papers in the bottom and shirts on top. Unreal, a dummy run, yet as if he might at a moment's notice strap the case up and go, because the window was wide open, fresh air blowing in that was not to be resisted. The penny had landed three times on heads, demanding that he go to Queen's Bay and be closer to Nora – eat at the table they had eaten at, sleep in their bed, sit by the fire and see her in the flames, the smell of burning driftwood filling the house.

Arthur walked in. 'Where yo' goin, then?'

'Back to Kent.'

'What for?'

'I want to get away for a bit.'

'Shall yer go back to the air force, then?'

'Yes.'

'Christ – yer must be barmy.'

'I expect I am.'

Arthur laughed, and sat on the bed. 'You've got a woman down there?'

'Belt up.'

'You must 'ave. What about Lillian?'

'What about her?'

'If yo' don't know, I don't know.'

'Clear off.'

'I live here as well, you know.'

'I know that, right enough.'

'Are you going today,' Arthur said, 'or in the morning?'

'Tomorrow, first thing.'

'I still don't know why.'

Brian laughed. 'You don't care, do you?'

'Course I do,' Arthur said. 'You're my big brother. I ain't seen much of you, in all my life.'

'That's the way it is.' Nothing else to put in, so he closed the case and sat down, filled his pen at the ink bottle, aware of Arthur's steady silence behind. He did not want to go, and he did not want to stay, started a letter to Nora but didn't get beyond a few dead words, locked at the centre of the first full stop. Arthur slammed the window, and went downstairs.

A photo transmitter sent Nora's features two hundred miles, the signal unweakened by distance, setting her so firmly before his eyes that all else dissolved, except when he was with Lillian. He wrote, to say that no matter how far apart they were not alone, covered pages because if his letters got shorter she might think she was losing her power. Absent, he did not know where he belonged, so instead of waiting in limbo till he could see her he would stay at the cottage where everything reminded him of her.

His sweet coupons were enough for a pound box of chocolates, a parting gift he hoped she'd eat so as to put on weight. Vera laughed as he went out. She could think what she liked.

He set them on her bed. 'Try a few of these.'

'Oh no, I can't tek your rations.'

'I don't like chocolate. I haven't eaten it for years.' He split the paper and gave her one, the lump in her cheek soon diminishing. 'Now have another. They'll give you energy.'

'What meks you think I need it?'

'We all do.'

As if he lived there, Mrs Verney brought supper of bread and cheese and a pot of tea. 'You need summat to walk home on.'

'I'd take these chocolates away, if I was you,' he said, 'or she'll make herself sick. She's eaten one already.'

'Two,' Lillian said. 'They're lovely.'

He ate in silence, as if his brain had gone into a sludge. Having brought his present, he should now go. Mrs Brown went by with her evening stout from the boozer. 'She walks right against the wall,' Lillian said, 'because she sings to herself, a little tiddly song as she goes by.'

Mrs Verney came in for their plates. As soon as she went back to the kitchen Lillian got out of bed to draw the curtains, moving gracefully, taller than he had guessed, thin but lovely. 'Tell her *you* did it if she asks, or she'll get on to me.' She kissed his cheek before getting back into bed.

'When did you first get TB?'

She combed her hair, curls and rolls springing back into place. They were the same age, but he wasn't sure how much emptier her life had been than his. He felt tormented because of her. 'You've been in bed a long time.'

'I'm fed up with it,' she said. 'I either want to die, or get better.'

215

'You'll get better.' The silence enraged him. 'Don't you think so?'

'I can't tell, can I?'

'If you say you will, you will.'

'The doctor says I've got to be patient.'

'Tell her to get stuffed.'

She frowned. 'Did you say that to *your* doctor?'

'No, but I didn't do all I was told, either.'

'Mam won't let me get up till the doctor says so.'

'I'll have a word with her.'

'She wain't listen.'

'I'll take you to the White Horse for a drink. Or to the pictures.'

'Is that a promise?'

'As soon as you like.'

'I'll think about it.'

'Just tell your mother you're going to get up.'

'I know she won't let me.'

'Get up anyway. You're bigger than she is.'

'Like a beanpole,' she laughed.

'It was a treat to see you standing just now. You're nearly as tall as me. I wouldn't have believed it.'

'My dad was tall – tall, dark and handsome.'

'I remember seeing him, now I think of it, before I joined up. I saw him one day, walking down the street.'

Her eyes glowed, fires fearful of being put out. 'Did he have a ladder on his shoulder?'

'Yes. He smoked a fag, and wore a cap. Very jaunty.'

'That was him.'

'Don't cry, duck.'

'I can't help it. He's been dead four years now.'

He passed his handkerchief, couldn't abide tears, having seen so many from his mother. 'I'm sorry.'

'It's all right.' She swabbed her eyes. 'I often feel he's going to walk through that door. But he won't, I know. It seems like yesterday. You remember when you knocked, that first time?'

'It was the V sign in morse. A habit, I suppose.'

'I thought it was *him*. He'd often knock like that before

coming in, just to let us know who it was. That's why I looked shocked.'

He didn't remember. 'You want to get out of the house. See what the streets look like for a change.'

'I'm sure they ain't altered.'

'You're right there. I'll take you for a walk, if you'll let me.'

She reached out. 'Sit on my bed.' He took care that the blankets didn't oppress her. 'Promise me summat.'

'What?'

'You'll think I'm barmy.'

'Why should I?'

'Well, if yer do tek me out, put your uniform on. I've allus wanted to go out with somebody in the air force.'

Nora would never ask him to do such a thing, but it certainly wasn't much to promise, since he would hardly wear it again. 'All right.'

While telling himself that he could not possibly be said to be 'going out' with her she drew him into a kiss, as if to seal a pledge, one which he knew he couldn't honour. Their lips stayed together, her arms around his neck, eyes open, an anxious expression burning through his stare as if attempting to see herself more clearly, which visage she would plant in him so that he would never be able to go away. But he wanted to wrench himself free, because it was against every human law to be committing the awful sin of deception with someone like her, for which there could be no atonement.

Locked so close, he would have stayed all night if she hadn't let him go, as if she had the right to keep him as long as she chose, that nothing could be denied her because her life had been blighted by sickness.

Her mother came in to say she was going to bed, a knowing look at Brian, who told her he would be leaving any minute so that Lillian could go to sleep.

'Don't leave me yet,' Lillian whispered as soon as they were alone. So, imagining he was old enough to trust himself, he went through the old dodge of going outside, banging the door, walking with a quick clatter down the street, then coming silently back to let himself in.

Sitting close in the dark, she told him how she liked winter, even though it was cold. Her father had died in the winter. She liked snow, thick flakes like scraps of cotton. She recalled how flakes of snow melted when they touched the outside sill, when she shivered and pulled the blankets up, warm and protected against the weather. After a while the flakes settled like dead butterflies, others falling on top, which she saw clearly when she sat up.

She talked, a wonderful woman who remembered being twelve years old. He became the same age with her, listened intently to her even voice. She wanted to talk forever. The glass was grey, she said, white snow flying against it, until a bank formed that each flake melted into, as if there was fire underneath. She wanted to rub the snow on her forehead, to kiss it, to cool herself, to push it into her mouth. There had to be sugar in something that looked so cool. A handful of snow down her throat would cure her cough, make her breath easy and clean.

They lived at Radford Woodhouse, and a train trundled along the embankment a hundred yards from her room, iron wheels muffled by snow, and she guessed it pulled twelve carriages. In sunlight she climbed the fence, frock flying, to see the red green flash and flicker of the black engine under its smoke, but so long ago it was a dream she wanted to go to sleep for and get back to. She could reach any dream by settling her cheek on the pillow and pulling the bedclothes up, but no one came to put on the light on the night she was talking about.

'Why not?' he murmured.

'I don't know.' They drew curtains because of the black-out. Nor did they waste pennies. They thought she was asleep. Her mother was getting her dad's tea for when he came home from painting camouflage at the gun factory in the Meadows. You couldn't decorate houses anymore. It was all war work, but he got four pounds a week, and there was plenty of overtime. Walking between stalls and roundabouts at the Goose Fair with her father, delicious smells of hot oil and candy floss, she recalled how he had held her hand, and joked that the wooden animals on Noah's Ark would bite her, but then he started to cough and a red snake came out of his mouth.

She coughed in bed, and when she woke, her mother stood in her nightgown, holding a candle because she didn't want to put on the light. 'Oh my duck, what are we going to do with you? They can hear you halfway up the street.' Next door banged, Jacob Maddock on his way to the early shift at the pit. 'Your cup's empty. I'll get you a drink of water.'

You couldn't hear people's footsteps in the snow. She lay, to tame the scraping nails inside her chest. Nobody liked her to cough, but she couldn't help it, didn't know where it came from, how it started. Her toe would ache, a finger would itch, her hair would chafe, and she tried to hold it back, but it burst from deep inside. The doctor said it was pleurisy but she knew it was TB. Her dad had it because of the painting he had done, but he was better because he drank lots of milk and had a tin of soup every day for his dinner. And he worked outside instead of in. She would get better as well, especially if a black man walked through the door on New Year's Eve and brought her luck.

Ben her brother came in from school, thumped the scullery door and scraped a chair to the table. What would he have to eat? Toast and jam, and a cup of tea. There would be margarine on his toast, maybe best butter. She liked strawberry jam, not plum. She laughed, and got a sharp pain in her shoulder. During the night it was worse, a steely flash across her eyes, she couldn't stop coughing, thought it was spit, and didn't know till morning when she saw blood on her hanky. She stayed hot, but felt better, a coke stove glowing behind her eyes like the one they lit at school in winter.

They were on the same level through the closed door, between kitchen and parlour, which saved going upstairs if Lillian wanted something, yet when it was important enough to save her life no one heard, so she called louder, and her mother was wiping her hands on a teatowel saying: 'I heard you, but I was busy. Oh my God, all this blood . . .'

She hadn't lived till then, so frightened, that's how it started, a story she could only tell him in the dark, the world asleep, by which time they lay on the bed with arms around each other like two lost people who had met at midnight in a forest, and he knew what had to be done because it was impossible not to, and he wouldn't leave anything to her. She encouraged each slow move, a positive desire in the silence, her expectancy filling the box of darkness. Taking off his shoes and trousers, he got into bed as if he belonged there.

'I haven't had it before.' She whispered, as much to save her breath as to conceal what she was half-ashamed and perhaps afraid of, though whispering took more force than the normal talk necessary to sustain their contact, the intensity generating a pull neither could resist, so that he no longer cared how he came to be in bed with her. She reached for some cream, then held him as her prisoner, a feather the wind might blow away, arms gently around, hips pressed. He stroked the small hot breasts under her nightdress, unable to talk in such darkness, got in as far as he could, until the whole impacted seatide of his many selves leapfrogged into her.

She was sweating. So was he, but he opened his eyes and saw the snow, then shut them firmly to kiss her fiery lips. Her ecstasy cooled him, soothed her. He thought she was asleep, calmed himself, couldn't detect her shallow breathing, imagined she had died on him without a sign, so must ease himself away, run, leave her to be found by her mother in the morning. Silence and stillness in the absolute dark confounded him, and if it weren't for occasional footsteps along the pavement he would have thought them anchored in a room way off in the universe that he didn't have the means to escape from, unable to uncurl his hands and put a foot on the ground.

He didn't know how long they lay there – half an hour, an hour, two hours, maybe only ten minutes – didn't want to pull himself away because she lay as if assuming he never would, a pity to disturb their peace, if that's what it was, but his arm was in torment from cramp. Even so, he tested himself, determined not to move till she did, as if paying with discomfort for any wrong he might have done, a dream from which he would never wake up.

'I must go now.'

She moved when he kissed her. 'I know.'

'Are you all right?'

'I don't know where I am.'

He smiled, but she couldn't see. 'Shall I tell you?'

'I don't want to know.'

'Where do you think you are?'

After a while she said: 'Somewhere I've never been before.'

He was anxious to know. 'Is it a nice place?'

'It's all right. I only know I don't want to leave.'

His arm eased. 'Stay as long as you like.'

'What about you, duck?'

'I'll stay as well,' he said.

'Have you been here before?'

He certainly hadn't. 'No.'

'Was it all right?' She sounded worried.

'Wonderful.' Yet he didn't lie. To lie would be a lie.

'I'm glad.'

'Do you want to go to sleep?'

'I don't care what I do.'

They lay for a time. He was too exhausted to let anything bother him. She called his name. He was drifting. 'What?'

'You're hurting my arm.'

He moved. 'Is that better?'

'What time is it?'

'I don't know.'

'Find out.'

He eased himself away, and struck a match. 'Half past one.'

'The middle of the night. I don't mind, though.'

'Your mother will.'

'She's fast asleep.'

'Are you sure?'

'She sleeps like a stone. It'll mek her happy if I lie in in the morning. She's allus telling me to sleep longer.'

He got out of bed and pulled on his trousers, felt for his jacket. 'I'll have to go soon.'

She sighed. 'I know you will.'

His vest was saturated, and he lit a cigarette, sat with the end glowing. He didn't know whether it was his sweat or hers. Both. Her dark hair flowed away on the white pillow when he put on the bedlight. 'I'll get up tomorrow,' she said, as if it was a sacrifice she'd be glad to make for him.

'That's good news.'

'I really will.'

He knelt to kiss her. 'Just for a while.'

'I suppose so.' She held him close. 'Why are you crying?'

Beads of sweat had built up. 'My eyes are running from the smoke.'

'Funny,' she said. 'I wonder why I said that?'

He drew away. 'I don't know.'

'See you tomorrow, then?'

'I'll call and say hello when I pass in the morning.'

'I'll wait for you.'

The chains were tenuous, yet more than binding. The door closed gently, and home was a waiting prison. Her sharp ears would know he walked up the street instead of down, turned on to the main road where traffic lights worked hard but had no cars to use them. The four corners were a pub, a church, a school and a pawnshop: damnation, salvation, education and ruination. Hence it was called Damnation Crossroads. People had a name for everything, and so had he.

Chapter
❧ TWENTY

'Lillian was asking for you today,' his mother said.

'Was she?'

'Wondered why you hadn't been to see her.'

''Appen 'e's got somebody else,' Seaton laughed. He went to the factory just after seven, and came back at five in the afternoon. For years he'd laboured at fetching and carrying, but now he was a viewer at a bench checking other people's work, which he liked better.

Arthur slopped his dinner down. 'She's got TB.'

'Shurrup,' Vera said.

'I 'eard 'er coughin'.'

He hadn't seen her for three days. 'I'll call as soon as I can.'

'Who do you get all them letters from?' his mother wanted to know.

There was a wall between him and his mother, between him and everyone, which was why he could only keep his trap shut, or tell lies. Three of Nora's blue envelopes had come into the house, and to those who could barely write it was an avalanche. 'A friend of mine, in Berkshire.'

'What sort of friend?'

'An old mate.'

Arthur spluttered into his tea. 'I'll bet it's a tart.'

'Keep your comments out of it, or I'll choke you.'

'I'll choke you back.'

'Go on outside,' Vera said.

Arthur grumbled, slamming the door as he went, the unjust world shadowing him.

'I can't do owt with him,' Vera said.

Seaton took cups and plates to the sink. Strangely enough, he'd never minded washing up. 'I'll punch his tab one o' these days.'

Heaven was one thing, family life another. He hadn't come on leave from the air force to live where the crowd could see every gesture.

Boats were on hire for one-and-six an hour, and two bob deposit. The water was soothing, almost up to the rim as he held a course in midstream, avoiding other craft under the Suspension Bridge. Don't lift a suitcase. No swimming for a few years. And as for rowing, not even to save your life.

The air was damp, suggesting rain, but he had his mac, and though no one could reach him unless they swam, and he was free of worry, everything nagged, the slightest matter causing him to hanker for the wilderness, to pull out of life, yet not die.

He threaded the train bridge, pillars big enough to have rooms inside. Two windows – one east, one west – would give daylight. At night he would draw curtains, an oil lamp glowing. Stars would shine along the silvery Trent when he stood at the window to spit. A table, a chair, a bed and a few books were all he'd need, a stove to make tea on, a bucket to empty slops out of the downriver window, and to fill it from the other side. Absolute peace, except for the rumble of trains overhead, and the splash of oars from boats on the water. He'd wave at girls, and one would come up on a rope he'd have ready. He laughed that a man of twenty-two should have such a fantasy. The railway company would throw him out, and he'd swim ashore. You had to be rich to live on your own.

He rowed through opaque water, beyond the bridge where there were fewer boats. His pension made him close to independent, having only himself to keep. Perhaps his writings about Malaya would be published, as well as some poems and a few stories. Even a pound or two would be useful. A pension would not allow him to keep a woman, however, and he worried that Lillian might be pregnant, because in the murk of his stupid passion, or whatever it had been, he had not used anything, and he didn't doubt that if something had clicked he wouldn't be as determined as Bert in avoiding responsibility.

He saw Pauline with Albert, her new fancyman, a hundred yards downriver from the landing stage. Albert was swarthy and fat-headed, hair combed back as if to keep his eyes free for every chance in the world. He wore a suit, and rowed their skiff towards the main traffic bridge. Gary, turning in all directions, looked for a moment at Brian, who was about to shout hello, how are you all, no hard feelings, but was stopped by a force he could not explain.

Pauline yanked Gary around, as if she had seen Brian from the back of her head. Gary would keep the picture fixed, or so he hoped, though it wouldn't puzzle him for long. Their boat passed under the bridge, people looking from the parapet, erasing them.

The attendant held his oar so that he could get on to the steps. He felt faint, thought he would stifle, another group from the queue jostling to reach his boat. Trancelike, he had seen the last of his son, and Gary hadn't even known. People were queuing on the Embankment for ice-cream. On the main road there were bus queues, so he walked over the bridge where no one was waiting, having stood in enough lines to last a lifetime. Cinema queues had formed downtown. There was another queue outside a café. He was hungry, but would go to any inconvenience to avoid waiting behind the back of someone else.

Seaton was at the table, so Brian didn't ask Percy and Chuck in when they knocked at the door with their bags full of magazines, though he wondered whether he wasn't using the old man as an excuse to keep them on the step.

'I was walking past the Castle this morning,' Chuck said, 'and I thought: One day we'll turn that place into a workers' rest 'ome!'

'It's a museum full of paintings,' Brian told him.

Chuck nearly jumped off the asphalt. 'Yes, my owd, but they're upper class daubs.' He wasn't as daft as he sounded, but was trying to sound as daft as possible because he thought it the only language Brian would respond to, and Brian, wondering why he thought that way, wasn't flattered. 'Pictures of Albert Ball – just because he shot down a few Gerries in France.'

'He was a pilot in the RFC.' Brian talked as if he had known him.

'Of course he was, my owd duck, but he was fighting in an Imperialist war, and that's got nowt to do with working class lads like us.'

The dialogue was not going well, so Percy asked Brian what he thought of the literature they had left on their last visit.

He'd only read half a page, unable to argue about prose which bored him. 'Stalin's speeches were as dull as ditchwater.'

Chuck was offended. 'He's the Great Leader, as far as I'm concerned.'

'Hitler was called the Leader, in German,' Brian said. 'In English it just sounds daft.'

'Everyone needs guidance.' Percy was unruffled. 'Especially the working class. Didn't you get that from the stories you read?'

'I don't know. The people in them didn't seem real.'

'But they was just like you and me,' Chuck grinned. 'Members of the great working class!'

Brian wondered what he was on about, though liked him for being a bit of a card, and a good sort for trying to interest him in a way of life he might have hankered for if he didn't fundamentally distrust it. The word 'literature' made it halfway respectable, and when you thought of how the Russians had ripped the guts out of the Germans during the war, you had to admire them, though when Chuck had the gall to call him working class – Brian never having considered himself to belong to any group or designation at all, except a fully employed and paid up member of the air force – his share of the Seaton bile shifted on its base, though being in temperament far distant from his father he did his best to control it.

Chuck took his hesitation for uncertainty. 'You worked in a factory from fourteen, like me. That meks you working class, or I'm a Dutchman.'

Scraps of grey cloud above the rooftops were like ashy cloths that had been through the slough of defeat but still went gallantly along – heralds of rain. Argument would only convince them that they were right, however skilfully it was done. 'I don't know what I am, and don't much care. If ever I find out, I'll be dead, I expect. It's no use calling *me* working class, because I'm not any class. I'm only sure I am what I'm not, and even that doesn't tell me what I am – nowhere near it. And if I don't know what I am, I don't see how you can tell me.'

'The awkward squad!' Chuck was delighted. 'Proletarian from the toenails up. He ought to join us, eh, Percy? You'd get on a treat at the meetings. All those middle class sods talk theory, but I'll bet yo'd tell 'em a thing or two.'

'Unfortunately,' Percy said, looking sadly beyond the clothes-lines and battered fences, 'you often are what people say you are. Or you become so, especially when they think they're saying something to put you down, or set you in your place. Then you have to become what they say you are out of self-defence. Everybody's got to fight for their rights.'

You couldn't win, Brian thought, but then, he neither expected nor wanted to. Hoping to win, you fell even more into people's clutches. All you could do was turn away, and let their words rot in unresponding air. That was the only way. As for Chuck and Percy, they were well-meaning and harmless, and selling magazines kept them off the streets.

'Blokes like them used to spout outside the factory in the war,' Seaton said when they'd gone. 'Skivers, up on their soapbox.'

'One of them worked on nights,' Brian recalled, 'and spoke about communism during the day in his rest time. He wasn't a skiver.'

'Used to tell us how good it'd be in Russia,' Seaton scoffed.

'That's what they believed.'

'You still have to work, though.'

He stirred the sugar into his tea. 'What do you expect?'

'I expect bogger-all. But somebody in our shop was telling me the other day that if you go on strike in Russia you get shot.'

Len Knotman had said the same. 'Maybe he didn't know what he was talking about.'

''Appen he didn't, no more than them two on the doorstep.'

227

'They say there's a government of the workers over there.'

Seaton lit a fag, swallowed half the tea from his pint mug, and settled in front of the fireplace – taking his time about it. 'Yes, but that'd be as bad as any other guv'ment. No guv'ment's any good. Never tek any notice of any of 'em. It's all propaganda.'

It was just as well that the old man had remained in the house, though no doubt he would have listened to what they had to say; but if they had stayed too long he would have turned nasty, being fractious, full of suspicion, and a respecter of nothing under the sun. The closer you were, especially if a member of the same family, he was to be avoided because of the damage he could do if you gave him half the chance. Brian would help him if he were in need, when in any case Seaton could be jolly and malleable enough to make it easy, and Seaton would do the same for him, but his malicious temper had at one time terrified his family, before his grownup kids learned how to fence him off from his excesses more effectively than any political system.

Seaton, controlled by his own ignorance, was easy to govern, as long as he had a packet of fags, ten pots of tea a day, and a few bob to spend in the boozer at the weekend. Perhaps his only virtue was that he wouldn't let the Russians or Germans or anybody else easily take the country over in case the fags and beer and tea tasted different.

All the same, his father had often been good to him: carried him on his broad shoulders when he was tired; put him on the crossbar of his gridiron bike and ridden him to Beeston and back; taken him to the pictures and been happy at his enjoyment; looked on his avid learning with wonder and approval, and got into debt to buy him a set of educational books – though Brian had to pay off the last instalments after starting work, lest his father be taken to court. Seaton had always been more than one person, however, hatred and love following so close – as with nearly everyone else, he could only suppose – that after leaving school Brian found less of interest in his father as he himself became fashioned by what his own life had to offer.

He looked at the wall. Halfway through his leave, he wanted to get back to the hospital for his last tests – though afterwards he supposed he would go over the cliff and never stop falling.

It was important to forget the blue horizon you could never reach, and certainly not go any way beyond if you did reach it, the only course being to do what you liked and see where you ended up, so after writing to Nora, and telling her about his trip on the river, and spinning out the latest encounter with Chuck and Percy, he went downstairs and announced that he was going for a walk.

Vera winked at his father. 'I'll put the key in the window.'

'You needn't bother,' he said gruffly.

'Give my love to Lillian,' she called as he went up the yard, every neighbour hearing. At Damnation Corner he turned along the boulevard. It was evening, yet there seemed hours of daylight left. He wore flannels and a pullover, his jacket open – finished for a while with the man in uniform – lit a cigarette, looked at cinema stills, walked by the queue for the second house, and followed a homely whiff of beer into The Black's Head.

He got to the bar and asked for a whisky. The taste of his cigarette recalled the days of boozing with his mates after work that hardly pertained to him anymore. Content in his isolation, he was rooted wherever he happened to be, never divided from himself while on his own, though gratified at not having altered so much from his old self as to be beyond recognition .

A woman's laughter at the barmaid's joke showed her white teeth. She had ginger hair tied back, her opened coat revealing a shapely bosom covered by a fluffy mauve jumper. She stared: 'Didn't you used to go out with Pauline Mullinder?'

He admitted it.

'I worked at the next machine. I remember you meeting her outside the factory, about five years ago.'

'You've got a good memory.'

'Oh, I don't know about that.'

'Would you like a drink?'

'I daren't, duck, thank you. I'm waiting for my husband. What happened to Pauline, though?'

Such laughter made her someone he could fall in love with, and she looked as if she might fancy him. Husbands were a curse. 'I don't know,' he said. 'I lost track.'

'She lived up Tapley, didn't she?'

'I believe she did.'

'I heard she got pregnant.'

'Did she?' He no longer felt bothered about the liar in him. The pub became too small. Finishing his second whisky, he walked back through the gloaming to Damnation Corner.

He knocked, and she called for him to come in. There was no one else he could visit, so he was choosing her, though her helplessness had sent messages to say she wanted him, was choosing him, as if she had read the code of his footsteps coming down the street. But he had no intention of being chosen, and from now on he was the one who would choose, though whether it would be her or not he wouldn't take the trouble to decide.

'What do yo' want?' she demanded.

'I thought I'd say hello.'

'It took you long enough.'

She looked like a queen, pale and alert, drawn and angry, hands over the counterpane, as if she had done nothing but wait, though he hoped she hadn't. He turned to leave, glad that something was finished which he had never decided to start.

'Don't go. I ain't seen yer yet.'

He hesitated by the door. You didn't call on a queen without a gift. 'I should have brought you something.'

'Don't be daft. Sit down.'

'I won't stay long.'

'You did the other night.'

'I'm sorry about that.'

'Why? You didn't force-fuck me, did you?'

He blanched at her dead-common way of putting it. 'Well, I shouldn't say I did.'

'I loved it,' she said.

'So did I.'

She held his hand. 'Mam asked what the blood was on the sheet, and I told her I'd scratched myself. Luckily, I've got long nails, so she believed me.'

Her mother came in. 'I *thought* I heard the door go.'

'Can we have a cup o' coffee, Mam?'

'Aye, I'll mek it,' she said wearily.

He offered to.

'You're needed more here than in the kitchen – it looks like.'

Lillian kissed him as soon as they were alone. 'Don't mek it so long before you come again, duck.'

'I thought you wouldn't want to see me.'

'No, you didn't.'

He couldn't respond.

'You're a bit funny. I'll never understand you.'

'Is that so?'

'Have you got somebody else?'

'No.'

'That's good, then.'

She knew what she wanted. He wanted Nora, but couldn't have her – at the moment. 'You know I'm married, though?'

'Yer mam towd me.'

'Do you mind?'

'I wouldn't a let yer go all the way if I did, would I?'

He envied her directness, except that he didn't want to be too close to it. He recounted his day, stories that entranced her only because he had rehearsed them in a letter to Nora. Mrs Verney knocked before coming in with the tray, giving them time to part, though she entered almost at once, unable to resist confirming her suspicions. 'Don't be up too late, then you can stay up a bit more tomorrow.'

'I got dressed today,' Lillian told him. 'The doctor said I could. I wore stockings, and my navy blue costume.'

'She looked lovely,' her mother said. 'I don't know what's come over her. Well, I might, but I'm not saying.'

'You'd better not,' Lillian exclaimed.

'He might blush,' she said on her way out.

'She'll allus mek fun of me. It meks me mad sometimes.' She held a biscuit in her lips and they split it between them, mouths touching, kisses tasting of chocolate and coffee. She clasped him. 'This is all I want.'

'Me too.'

'You set me off. I get so passionate thinking about the other night.'

Hard to talk, but it would be unjust to leave it to her, though the feeling that she might not mind made it easier. 'I'll stay after she's gone to bed, if you like.'

Her eyes were mischievous. 'Can you wait?'

He stroked her breasts through the bedjacket. 'If *you* can.'

'We've got to.' She released him. 'Tek the cups and plates into the kitchen. Mek yersen useful.'

Mrs Verney dozed in an armchair, glasses at her nose end, a newspaper on the rug. He stepped by and set the pots in the sink so as not to wake her.

She stood, and yawned, an unforgettable half-heard whine as her lips came together. 'Are you off now?'

'I am.'

'Tell her to mek sure and lock the door behind yer.'

He went through the same form of goodnight, glad the street was empty. The stars were in their usual patterns, seeming warmer up there than down here. He regretted the impulse of a V-fingered sign at their serene condemnation, and went back in. The dim light was on, and she held out her arms. 'I want to see you with no clothes on,' he said.

'I'm too skinny.'

'Not to me. You're just right.'

'I suppose everybody is – to you.'

'I'm only talking about you.'

Her lips thinned. 'Don't get mad, duck.' She smiled. 'I expect yer was tatered the other night though, worn't yer?' – meaning clapped out, done for.

He laughed.

'I was,' she said. 'I know that much.'

He saw her as a girl in the women's ward at the sanatorium, eyes and ears alert to miss none of their raw talk. 'You're a know-all.'

'You've got to be, ain't yer?'

'I reckon so.'

She looked at him, frowned. '*You* don't know much, though, do you?'

'Don't I?'

'I don't think so.'

'What don't I know?'

'It ain't for me to tell you.'

He met her stare. 'I expect I'll find out.'

'One day you might.'

'Or I might not.'

'You don't say much, that's all.'

'I say all I can.'

He wasn't getting anywhere, had got to know her in order to keep her company, to pass the time, to do he didn't know what while the summer drifted, until he went back to Nora. Not true. Nora was forgotten when he was with Lillian. But he couldn't allow her thoughts to become his, or his hers.

'And that day might be too late,' she told him, waiting to hear what she had already made him say in her dreams.

'Then there's nothing I can do about it.' The hard edge to his voice reflected what he felt, which he wasn't able to soften. Perhaps she didn't expect him to, though he stayed silent rather than say anything he didn't mean – or that would hurt. She hoped he would speak freely but, awkward and guilty, he resisted speech even though tempted to it. If he could say something which had no bearing on what she wanted him to say, he would have been glad enough to talk, but his locked mind lacked a diverting story, and wasn't in the best condition to put a smile back on to her anxious features. He knew exactly what she craved to hear, and it would be easy to lie and make her happy. To do so on such a matter would destroy his integrity, which might also be what she wanted, assuming that if his spirit was so fragile, he would not mind if it was broken. But because his spirit was fragile he cared more if it was broken than if it was made of iron. The fragile spirit was all he had, and while to lie might make her happy, it would put him into a furnace as impossible to escape from as from himself. She had been burned by illness more deeply than him, and a lie would have been better than no word at all, and much comfort to her. The danger was that she would believe him, and turn his lie into the truth.

'I often wondered,' she said, putting the matter aside, 'whether I loved my father more than my mother loved him. We had such nice times together. Mind you, they could be like a couple of lovebirds. She used to heap food on to his plate so's he'd get fat. But he never did. When he nearly finished and couldn't eat anymore he fed titbits to her on the end of his fork.

233

P'raps that was the reason she gave him so much, and not to mek him fat.'

He had seen no such manifestations of marital tenderness in his family. 'Maybe it was.'

'They thought a lot of each other. It's years since dad died, and she ain't got over it yet.'

'It's not surprising.'

'None of us have. Maybe we never will.'

He leaned close to kiss her. She was no more willing to say what she really thought than he was. If he ate her despondency to the last crumb she would be free, empty and unhappy, but he would not let her uproot any words out of him, even though he might never get closer to anyone than he was to her. She must have known that his words belonged to him alone, because she did not rage as she had a right to do, and claw words from his heart with her coloured fingernails.

Her passion was of the same intensity whether he spoke the words she wanted to hear or not. Need was satisfied in a way he desired. The same with her. When he lay with her, the frugality of his consideration shamed him. But he took care to hold back till the ultimate passion passed through her, her mouth open and eyes staring, not knowing or caring who he was. In the empty moments before he rushed up to meet her he was tempted to speak at which, feeling it, she would wipe her tears against him, as reluctant to let him see her expression as he was to allow any words to betray him. He knew, and she knew, that inadequate words would only fester the soil in which they came together.

'I used to be frightened of dying,' she said, 'but I'm not anymore.'

'Don't say that.'

'Why not? I know my own mind.'

'I wish to hell I did.'

'I've allus known my own mind.'

'It doesn't surprise me.'

'I didn't mean it to. I'm only telling you.'

They made love again, the urge on them both, he out of natural desire, she as if not much time was left.

'I could drink you,' she said.

234

He laughed. 'How much?'

'Pints. Don't stop coming to see me.'

'I couldn't,' he said.

'You eat me, and I'll drink you.'

'That's right.'

'It's like being married, in't it?'

'Yes.'

'I never thought we'd be like this when I first heard about you.'

'Nice things happen. To me, I mean.'

'Your mam came in one day and said you'd be coming on leave. But I didn't think much about it. I thought you'd never come to see me when she said she would ask you to.'

'As soon as she mentioned you I knew I couldn't live without seeing you.'

She pressed his hand, a fevered weakness he hardly noticed. 'I thought you was just a rough bloke, even though you was in the air force.'

'Aren't I?'

'I don't know yet. It's funny. You can be both. But maybe that's why I love you.'

They held each other, and became warm together. He didn't want to leave. 'I must go now,' he said.

'Don't get lost on the way back.'

'I'll try not to.'

They kissed, beyond time, the world a few square inches of their lips. 'See you tomorrow?'

'All right, duck.'

'Come in the morning, and say hello.'

She didn't want him to see her only at night.

He promised.

❧ TWENTY-ONE

Uncle George stood aside to look at him, without letting go of his arm, a tall solid man with thick grey hair and an open, ruddy face, one of Merton's blacksmith sons who after the smash of the horseshoe trade worked for the canal company by day, and took care of his allotment garden in the evening.

'Where yo' off, then, Brian? Got a gel to see? Yer mam towd me yer was in dock, but I said there was too much of old Merton in him to stay long in a place like that. Come and let's ev a quick jar in the Jolly Jugglers.'

They crossed the road.

When Brian stayed on Saturday night at the Nook as a kid, and slept in the same bed, George would come whistling upstairs at two in the morning reeking of scent. He'd empty his pockets, money clashing on to the table, undress in the dark and then carefully fold his clothes, still no doubt thinking of the woman he'd been loving up. On Sunday morning George would take him on his bike along the canal, where he sold twopenny fishing permits to anglers so as to make a bob or two for himself.

He got a pint of mild and a whisky from the bar.

'My time's my own now,' George said. 'I just walk up and down the Cut seeing that the locks and the banks are in good order, and mek sure nobody's fishing as shouldn't be. If they are, I tell 'em to clear off, and if they don't I bat their tabs.'

'I don't suppose life's the same now Merton's dead.'

George's pint dropped its level like the Nilometer in a sudden drought. His mood declined likewise. 'He was a miserable owd sod.'

'I liked him, though.'

George's smile showed good white gnashers. 'You was his favourite, that's why. When he was dying he asked where our Nimrod was, and we towd him you was in Malaya. "You mean Abyssinia, don't yer?" he said. "He allus said he'd go there one day. I wonder if he'll get back to tell me about it?"'

'It was one long purgatory, though, living in the same house with him. He led my mother a dance as well. She once caught him in a boozer with another woman, and shouted at him to come home, telling him what she thought of his antics, in front of everybody. Yes, my duck, I'll have another pint o' Shippoes. It's warm today.'

He demolished his second pint. 'Yer know what the owd rotter did? He followed me mother 'ome from the pub, and pulled her out of the house. Then 'e called her all the foul names in front of the neighbours, and gen her such a bang at the chops he knocked three teeth out. The bleddy swine. When you knew him, Nimrod, he was a man o' sixty-odd, so he'd stopped all them games. But he got on to me once for coming in late one Saturday night, and I was thirty at the time. He hit me, so I hit him back – the first time in my life I'd stood up to him. In fact, I hit him so hard he fell down. My own father, lying on the kitchen floor! I couldn't believe it. I didn't know my own strength, I suppose. I was over six feet tall – just like him – and he'd hit me once too often. Mother was screaming for us to stop, and I didn't want to upset her too much, so I bolted, and stayed a couple of nights with a woman I'd been knocking on with, till her husband came in by the back door, and I nipped out the front. I'd got nowhere to stay, then, and when I went home Merton saw me coming up the yard. He ran out swinging a woodsman's axe, and I swear to God he'd 'ave cut me down like a bit o' kindling. So do you know what I did? I ran for my life. I forget how we made it up, but he hardly spoke to me for years, though I came in when I liked after that. We could never understand why he took to yo'. I think he loved yer more than

237

anybody else – except your grandma. But there's a lot o' yo' in 'im. Nobody else spotted it, but he did.'

He had been Merton's shadow, following him everywhere, working for him in the garden, fetching his Sunday ale from the beer-off. 'Maybe he liked me' (if he did: I might have been no more than a toy or pet) 'because I was as different from him as anybody could get.'

'Think what you like. I heard him talking about you to Lydia. "He'll be a bogger when he grows up. I'll bet the woman he marries'll have a hard time!"'

Two pints was enough, unless George bought some, which he wouldn't, even if they sat till closing time, and Brian didn't want to hear anymore against Merton. 'I've got to be going.'

George laughed. 'Aye, I don't suppose she'll wait long, Nimrod, even for a married man like yo'!'

The bus went by the White Horse, and the big grey-walled tobacco warehouse that his Uncle Doddoe had worked on when it was being built; dropped a straggle of lunchtime boozers at the Admiral Byng; climbed by the colliery to Balloon House Hill; and crossed Trowel Moor, countryside at last.

Marsh marigolds and water crowsfoot lined the canal on his walk to Cossall. Across the valley Ilkeston church huddled among low redbricked buildings, in the foreground a loco-motive trailing a muffler of smoke along the underbelly of cloud. He stepped out through the fields, Nora closer than if she were with him, painfully near, Oldpark Wood a silent wedge in the hollow, no noise but that of the birds and the solo pad of his feet.

She had been coughing half the night, so rested a couple of hours after her midday dinner. 'I dream more in my day-sleep,' she said, 'than in the night. Or I don't remember what I dream at night. But just now I dreamed that you and me was on a big white ship with three tall funnels, walking arm in arm. I've never been on a ship, so I wonder where I got such an idea?'

Such dreams made her feverish. Her eyes pleaded with him to stop the fevers, but her lips had an ironic expression saying she didn't need his help and she would be up soon without it, thank you very much. It was nothing – to be feverish. Even fit people could be feverish, and at the moment she was that sort.

But why should she be ill, he wondered, who had never harmed anybody? Though her illness lurked like an animal, waiting for her guard to drop, illness didn't seem part of her. Certainly it wasn't so powerful that it couldn't be defeated and seen off. Something in her lay supine before what illness there was, and he wanted to help her keep it at bay, fortify her spirit against what would drag her down. He said she ought to get the bed upstairs put back where it belonged, convert the room of her affliction into the parlour it had been before.

Maybe his description of the troopship caused her to dream about the sea, though the ship wasn't white. 'Or maybe it was,' he said. 'I forget.'

'I don't care what colour it was. I dreamed it, and that was that. But tell me all about it again: right from when you left Singapore.'

Perhaps it was his doing, after all, his advice taking effect, scorn forcing her up. Mrs Verney fussed over him as if he had brought off a miracle. Lillian had to get up, or he would stop loving her. Or she got up because she thought he did love her. He once had a grandfather, he said, and if he'd been alive today he would have killed or cured any of his daughters who caught TB. As for lying in bed, he would have turned them out even in the snow – especially if it was snowing, and on Christmas Eve. 'So gerrup, then, yer idle bogger!' he said, mimicking the old man's ruthless peremptory voice.

She laughed with him. 'All right, duck. I'll see what I can do.'

Vera creased his trousers, and pressed his shirt. He spent the afternoon with his buttonslide, Brasso and buffing cloths, and he could not have been smarter even on passing-out parade. They would certainly make a well-matched couple going up the street. 'She's a smashing gel. All she needs is somebody like yo' to look after her.'

'What do you think I'm doing?' he said.

'You know what I mean.'

'I'm still married.'

'You wain't be forever.'

'That Pauline never was much good to yer.' Seaton hadn't forgiven her for not visiting them while he was in Malaya.

'I don't suppose I was much good to her, either.'

They went to a restaurant meal and, while eating, talked about the countryside. 'I want to go up Strelley,' she said. 'It's nice up there. Mam and Dad used to tek me and Ben on picnics when we was kids.'

'I know lots of better places.'

She cut into the meat, hardly visible under the thick gravy. He didn't want to go that way in case he met Pauline and Albert. And he'd had it with Pauline in too many places around Strelley. But he promised to take Lillian as soon as she liked. 'We'll go to the Hemlock Stone as well. It's on a hill, so it'll be a dummy run for when I take you to the Castle.' They hurried through the pudding and coffee for fear of being late at the Theatre Royal.

Each day she looked stronger, a normal colour back in her face, eyes losing their darkness the more she got used to walking. On the bus from the Hemlock Stone she asked him to wear his uniform one more time.

'What for?'

'To come downtown with me, to Clumber Street.'

'What's there?'

'Don't you know?'

He did. 'No.'

'If I tell you, you wain't come.'

They sat in front of the camera, four photographs for seven-and-sixpence. She seemed so happy that he ceased regretting his softness by the time they were on the bus going home.

He collected the photographs, and she fixed one behind an oblong of glass, bordering it with black tape, to go on the chest of drawers by her bed. They looked a handsome couple, Mrs Verney said. Hard to imagine it was them. He thought it unjust that she hadn't given herself equal space, looked over his shoulder instead of standing by his side, her vivid face outshining that military deadness which the uniform gave to his.

She spent an hour getting the frame right. 'Do you think this'll do?'

'Sure. But I know a secondhand shop on Mansfield Road. An old wooden one would look good.'

'If you like.'

'I'll rummage around.'

They walked through narrow streets into the Castle grounds. He carried a newspaper so that she could sit on a wall and read when she got tired. As if planning an attack, he eyed the pathways up the slope, choosing one which looped with the lie of the land.

'It don't look like a Castle,' she said, 'does it? I've never thought so.'

'I'll knock it flat and build another.'

'I first came here with Mam and Dad.'

'Sit down, and I'll tell you what I know about it.'

'If they set fire to this one,' she said when they walked on, 'maybe they'll build a proper castle in its place.'

'I'll write to the Council, and tell them my young woman wants one with towers and a moat and battlements and a drawbridge, with flags flying and knights going in and out, and maidens walking along the walls.' Like the one he'd brought back for Gary – an unpleasant memory immediately crushed.

'I'd love it.' She took his arm as they went across the grass. 'Let's go on the path.'

'This way's shorter.'

She was agitated. 'You aren't supposed to walk on the grass.'

'Who says?'

'That notice.'

'We're doing it anyway.'

'Grass don't grow if people trample on it.'

'We're nearly there.' He held her arm, as if to stop her by force from returning to the lawful path. 'And we're not *people*.'

'Aren't we?'

'No.'

'Well, I am.'

'We're you and me.'

He ought to have known it would disturb her to walk on grass when a notice said they mustn't. Maybe he wanted to upset her because she didn't seem properly alive. Nora would be amused in a similar situation, especially if she had led him into it.

A long thin coat and a purple headscarf protected her against the wind, the half-open coat showing a white blouse with ruffled sleeves and a grey pleated skirt. Flat shoes, fastened by a button, were borrowed from her mother because her own were too high-heeled. 'I'd forgotten there were so many people in the world.'

'Is it making you tired?'

'Oh no. It's wonderful to see everyone out and enjoying themselves.'

They took the steepest part of the walk slowly so that she wouldn't get out of breath, and met a homely Nottingham couple coming down. The woman wore a bulging blue frock and had curly grey hair. 'It fair teks it out on yer, don't it?'

'It does,' Lillian responded. 'I've got to go slow, though.'

The woman stopped. 'Why, 'ev yer bin badly, duck?'

'A bit, but I'm getting over it now.'

The woman's husband was swelteringly dressed in a herringbone suit, waistcoat with watch chain, polished brown boots and a trilby hat. She took hold of his arm, and he smiled, putting a hand to an ear. 'What was it, then?'

Brian thought they should mind their own business.

'I 'ad TB,' Lillian told them.

'Oh, I am sorry,' the woman said.

'It's all right now, though.'

'Well, you can get over owt if you're young, can't you?' She put her mouth to her husband's ear and shouted so that the whole park heard, as well as, Brian thought, finishing his eardrum off for good: 'She 'ad TB.'

Lillian tried not to laugh.

'I hope you get better, duck, though I expect you'll be all right with a nice young man like that. Come on, then, Herbert,' she bellowed, 'let's get 'ome for us dinner.'

'I bleddy 'eard yer, Panmouth.' But he grinned at them, an elderly dandy with false teeth. 'That was the on'y reason I married her forty years ago. I knew I'd never lose her, with a mouth like that. As soon as she opened it, there was no stopping me. Mind you, I went to Flanders with the guns, though I still heard her now and again!'

They argued down the path, and Lillian's laughter at last came out, holding her side to prevent a bout of coughing. 'You meet some right people!'

They looked over the parapet at railway yards and the massed streets of the Meadows, where Ada's lot lived, and where he had worked at Edgeworth's factory. Beyond the Trent rose Wilford Hills, with the dark green bush of Clifton to the right. He put an arm around her.

'I'm glad you got me out,' she said. 'It's a long time since I came here.'

He kissed her. 'You'd have got up yourself sooner or later.'

'Still, it's nice having you do it. I love this view.'

There were decrepit old coaches in the museum, and one of Laura Knight's pictures in the gallery was of a plain woman with a naked baby on her knee sucking its thumb. Lillian stood back, then went forward and peered as if she could hardly see. 'Hasn't she painted it well?'

'She lived in Nottingham,' he said, 'at one time.'

Such information took her away from the picture. 'How do you know?'

'I read a pamphlet at the bookstall downstairs while you were in the toilet.' She went back to look at the picture, till he was bored with waiting.

On the hill going down, her ankle ached. 'It was easier on the way up. That's funny, isn't it?'

Every remark had to be answered. 'You'd think so.'

There was a queue at the ice-cream van, and nowhere for her to sit. Outside the enormous gateway he settled the mac over his arm. The sky had been clear, but now there were two ragged eyeholes of blue in the grey swirl, and he wondered whose large and ghastly eyes were looking through, keeping watch on every poor bastard who went into the Castle. She laughed at such an idea.

In the Trip to Jerusalem he got a gin for her and a whisky for himself. They sat at a table in a small sandstone room dug into the Castle hill, and it was dim compared to the light of day outside. 'It's been too much for you.'

She lifted her glass. 'This'll see me right. Here's to you, duck.'

He couldn't refuse. 'To both of us.'

'You know,' she said, 'I remember you when you was little. I didn't realise it till the other day. When we lived at Woodhouse you used to run up the lane to that cottage called The Nook, where the old blacksmith lived. He chased me with a stick once, when I rattled his gate.'

She had broken into his last secret, his only secret, the one most of all he wanted to keep, yet the one he could least expect to hide, especially from someone who was so close, so close that it was unbearable, and unendurable. But his fragmented heart also enabled him to enjoy the intimacy, and he told her all the stories he knew about Grandad Merton, but without mentioning the similarity that George said he'd had with him. 'Funny we didn't meet, when you rattled his gate. I was probably in the house.'

She nudged him. 'We might a bin childhood sweethearts.'

I'd have loved that, he was supposed to say. They'd have had two kids by now, if not three. Behind the horror, he felt the trap of eternal peace and comfort, a mindless bliss. 'And you wouldn't have got TB.'

'It was in the family,' she said, rueful.

'Your mother didn't get it. Nor your brother.'

'Only Dad,' she said, 'and me.'

'Nobody's ever had it in our family. If Merton hadn't died when he did he'd have disowned me.'

'The shock might have killed him,' she said.

He laughed. 'We'll never know. But he brought up eight kids, though they hated his guts. Not that it bothered him.'

'He must have had a struggle.'

'I expect so.'

'It's never been owt else, has it?' she said, 'for our sort.'

He knew everything she was going to say before it came out, felt his blood draining away. He wanted to be on his own. 'Fit for the trail?'

She took his arm as they got up. 'If you are, love.'

They walked down to the bus stop holding hands.

Chapter TWENTY-TWO

Looking in every window for a photo-frame, he stopped to shelter in the doorway of a secondhand bookshop. Buildings lived longer than people, hadn't altered for as long as he could remember. Only he had changed, grown older.

The rain loosed itself on to dull slates and into the gutters of Mansfield Road. A bell sounded as he went inside, rows of shelves filling the dim room. Fumes from a paraffin heater came through the half open glass-panelled door to a back cubby-hole, unblinking eyes beneath bushy brows making sure he didn't nick anything.

He picked up *Poems in Prose*, and the simian-looking proprietor with thick grey hair put out a hand for his money: 'Not a bad choice, Turgenev. I was going to keep it, but my house is falling down from too many books. When the neighbours complain, I tell 'em it's subsidence from Cinderhill pit.'

'You like Turgenev?' Brian was surprised.

His pale blue eyes glared. 'Listen, when the world's on the eve, and fathers and sons are about to go up in smoke, and you look forward to a bit of first love in a nest of gentlefolk, who wouldn't?'

Brian rattled back, 'Who can tell? When the idiot's possessed in the house of the dead the punishment must fit the crime.'

The man had only half his teeth, and needed a shave. 'Don't let the Russians grind you down, whether you're a raw youth or a lemon-toff. Come inside and have some coffee. Push kith and kin to get in. What's your name, by the way?'

He told him.

'Just out of the army, eh?'

'What makes you think that?'

'The way you're standing.'

'Air force.'

'Same thing. Sugar?'

'Two.'

'You'll have one, and like it. Most of it went at breakfast. We're lucky to have coffee, these days. Come to think of it, we're lucky to have anything. Sit on that box. What are you doing with yourself?'

'Doing?'

'Work. Profession. Trade. Occupation. Something to keep you out of the mischief thereof.'

He was a wordy bastard. 'Nothing.'

He stirred the coffee with a bit of stick. 'Private income, eh? I've yet to meet someone gainfully employed in this town. God knows how it's run. I only seem to get members of the idle middle classes in here, and you're no exception. If the rest of the world came in I might make a bob or two.' The coffee was bitter bottled stuff, and tasted of heater fuel. 'My name's Tom Boak. You didn't ask, when I asked yours, which says a lot about you.'

'Such as what?'

'You're supercilious, not to say self-centred, and you want to be a writer, eh?'

He admitted it, not liking himself for answering questions too easily. 'How did you know?'

'You don't buy Turgenev to mull over in the bog, and that's a fact. Have you written your first novel?'

'I'm trying.'

'Take your time, that's the main thing. I've been writing a play for twenty years called *Destiny's Cat*. It's in the bag, but I can't leave it alone. I never know when it's finished. You'd better not stay too long, or I'll read you some. But come to my house on Saturday night. A few of us talk about the only thing in the world that matters – literature – meaning Joyce and

Hemingway and E. M. Forster, to *maim* but a few. We call ourselves the Cinderhill Group. I started it up four years ago after my wife died – God bless her. Had to do something to keep myself going.'

'I'm sorry.'

'Well, it worked.' He reached a shelf without getting up from his battered cane chair. 'Read this, and you'll never look back.'

Brian saw a photo of the author on the back – with a beard, and born at Eastwood. 'How much?'

'Two bob to you. As soon as you stop writing like him you might get somewhere.' Brian's back was to the door, and he heard the bell go. 'My God, another customer,' Tom said. 'My heart can't stand two in one day. It must be the rain.'

A heap of books slid on to the lino as he stood up to greet a tall abstracted woman holding an empty shopping basket and an umbrella. 'Can I pay for these?'

Tom took them from her. 'Everybody seems mad on Lawrence today.'

Brian noted the heavy lids to her eyes. Lizard lids, he said to himself, though they weren't so obvious when a smile put life into her face and showed the bow-like shape of her lips. She opened her New Look coat in the dense air, a brown frock buttoned down the middle and fastened by a belt. Her hair was held back by a ribbon, showing a large amount of pale forehead – as he had observed on seeing her in the foyer of the Continental Cinema. Her remark that she loved Lawrence's works suggested that he'd have to read them, even if only to find out something about her.

'I've just sold him *The Rainbow*.' Tom nodded. 'Maybe he'll let you have it when he's finished.'

'Take it now, if you like.'

'I've read it.'

'Call it three bob.' Tom winked. 'One of 'em's a first edition, or the first edition I've seen.' He offered her coffee. 'This chap writes novels, the next D. H. Lawrence, if he's not careful . . .'

She put the florin change into her purse. 'I must go shopping.'

Tom stood. 'I'd better introduce you.'

'I'm Anne Jones.'

He held her hand too long, though she didn't resist. 'What's your novel about?'

'Malaya. I was stationed there a couple of years.'

'That's more than he told me,' Tom said. 'He's secretive, so I have high hopes.'

She said how interesting that he had been in Malaya.

'Fighting the Communists,' Tom waffled on. 'England's white hope. He was killing so many they had to send him home. I was in Russia after the last war, shooting at Bolsheviks in Batum. I didn't like it, though.'

'I should hope not,' she said.

'I tell a lie. They shot at us – right out of it. And we were glad to go. I'm a writer as well, but nothing so topical as Malaya. What do *you* do?'

'Survive, I suppose,' she said. 'Not very interesting.'

'I'm in the air force,' Brian said, 'but on my way out. Then I'll have a pension – a private income that wouldn't keep a fly.'

'Nor hurt one.' She spoke an attractive, well-enunciated English. 'I've never seen such a young pensioner. Do you have a beard in your pocket?'

Tom got moody because the conversation was passing him by. 'Maybe he stopped a bullet.'

She put on her gloves. 'I must go, though.'

The bell tinkled as she went out.

Tom offered more coffee, shook the bottle's treacly guts into the saucepan. 'Did you see those eyes?'

'Whitey-grey?'

'Missed nothing. The sort that sees through metal when she's roused. If I wasn't over fifty I'd go for her.'

'I'd go for her if I was ninety – except I'm too busy.'

Tom rubbed his back now and again, as if stricken with lumbago. 'So you're being invalided out?'

He didn't care who knew. 'A touch of TB.'

'You can't go wrong, can you?' He pulled down another book. 'Read that. It ain't translated from Russian. Nor is it all wind and piss, like a lot of D. H. Lawrence.'

He flipped through *The Way of All Flesh*. Another Nottinghamshire man. Born at Langar, it said on the back.

'I'll give it to you, on the understanding that you'll read it more than once in your life.'

He could have stayed talking till the shop shut, but Tom implied that he had something to do, though the place was so filthy that Brian could not imagine what it was.

They played draughts at the living room table.

'My sputum's negative,' she said. 'The doctor told me this afternoon.'

He had caught her on the cusp of the body's decision whether or not to succumb – and backed a winner. 'I knew it would be.'

She made a move. 'I've got to take it easy, though.'

She was out of the valley of the shadow, which was all that mattered. 'It won't be hard.'

'Mam's ever so pleased. Nobody wants a woman with TB, she told me. But I said it worn't my fault I'd got it. There was nothing I could do about it. I didn't like having it, did I?'

Her eyes shone with anger at any possible injustice. He slipped a white piece in, and got her to king it. 'You're recovering. You must be stronger than you think.'

'I don't know about that.' She scanned the board for a move that would box him in – hex, hoax or harry him. Rashness lost him some pieces. 'People die,' she said, 'no matter how strong they are. Two women passed away when I was in the sanatorium. I'll never forget it.'

His mobility foxed her, and she lost a king. 'They'd left it too late.'

'P'raps I'll be able to go out to work soon.'

'What's the hurry?'

'I'll have company, won't I? I worked at the sweet factory when I was fifteen. I'd got a bit better, and the doctor said I could. After a few days an ambulance came for me, one afternoon in November. I couldn't breathe. I lost a lot o' blood.'

He hadn't heard about her working, and in wondering if it was true, he lost a piece. 'They shouldn't have let you go.'

'I wanted to.' She hemmed him in, but he released himself by surrendering another. 'I used to play draughts with our Ben.'

'He must have been good.'

She smacked his wrist. 'Hey, yo', it was me as was good.'

Falling into her trap, he could only shuffle forever and get nowhere, so he pushed one piece into such a position that when she took it he couldn't move without being wiped out.

'It'd be nice to earn some money. I'd just feel better.' She set the pieces back on their squares, and attacked up the left flank. He also launched from the left, no head-on collision. 'But you seem worried about me.'

He smiled. 'Not likely. In a while you'll be going out every night.' She didn't believe it. Nor did she want him to remind her of the possibility that he might feel it to be neither his duty nor his inclination – let alone love – to go out with her. She couldn't fathom him. Her expression said that something was wrong, though whether with him or herself she did not know.

He wouldn't know she wasn't pregnant till her period didn't start, but it was no use worrying unless he knew for sure. Their photograph looked down, as if she couldn't be anything else. He held her hands over the draught board. She wanted a pledge such as: I'll do all I can to get a divorce, then we'll be married. In a silent minute he lived through such a future, but honour told him not to speak.

He was fed up with hints that if he felt all was not well with her – and maybe only he was aware of it at the moment – then he ought to do something about it. He knew what it must be, and what he should say, but he would dive headfirst off Castle Rock rather than speak the words which would send him down that avenue of eternally blossomed trees.

In the junk shop he had seen a neat oval frame for half-a-crown, stuck between a barometer and a set of wobbly fireirons. Now he was imprisoned in the photograph, set on the living room sideboard for everyone to see, wed in all but spoken words – and she had to be satisfied with that.

He won the game.

'A penny for your thoughts,' she said.

'One game to you, and one to me.' He hated being asked. His thoughts were his own, such as they were. He drew his hand away. 'Why don't we go on a picnic by the Trent?'

She had read his thoughts with an accuracy he found intolerable. If he stayed she would limit him into nothingness. He couldn't wait to get back to Nora, even if they only met as if by accident on the Downs.

'Your head's thick with thoughts. I could cut 'em with a knife.'

He stood, any alteration of scenery welcome, as if he had spent all his life with her. 'Let's go to our house for an hour.'

She held his arm in the street, and Mrs Bull stared them into the yard. Her tight lips didn't respond to his good evening. 'Old slit-mouth,' he said.

Lillian tutted. 'She don't want us to know she ain't got her teeth in.'

'All she does is gossip.'

'I feel sorry for her. She's got nowt else to do.'

Pleased to see them, Seaton cleared the supper pots off the table, turned the wireless down and drew up chairs.

'I wish you made as much fuss of me,' Vera joked, going into the scullery to mash some fresh tea.

'I allus do, you know I do.' His good mood lasted till Lydia knocked and walked in. He disliked Vera's sisters, maybe because they were all taller, or because they were Merton's children, and he had never liked him, either. She wasn't asked to take her coat off, though Vera made sure she got a cup of tea. 'I've just been to see a gel in the street who works in our department,' Lydia said. 'She broke her leg, and can't get to work. Me and the other women had a collection for her, and it came to over ten quid, so it'll see her right for a bit.'

Hard work at the tobacco factory, packing and stacking from the age of thirteen, she was an overlooker, and hadn't married after her boyfriend died. As a kid Brian pictured her with hundreds of other women sitting at benches rolling fag after fag with the sort of little rubber machine Merton used on Sunday to turn out his weekly smokes.

Seaton's mood changed when she gave him a packet out of her Players allowance. He even asked if she'd like something to eat, but she turned to Brian and then to Lillian:

'So this is your lady-love? I hope you'll be happy with him, duck.' She stroked Lillian's hand. 'You'll have to watch him, though. He's a bit of a lad, our Brian is. Look, he's blushin'! He don't need to, in front o' me. When he used to come and

251

stay at his grandma's as a lad he got so black one day running round the Cherry Orchard we thought we'd give him a bath. It was summer, so we filled the tub in the yard, and me and Em'ler had to chase this little black lad till we got hold of him and pulled his clothes off. We scrubbed him all over and he was a little white pig by the time we'd finished!'

Lillian laughed, which brought her closer, though he wouldn't hold her hand with others looking on. People from the past were in a frame, small figures far away, and he couldn't see himself clearly, only Lydia, Em'ler, and his dead grandparents.

'Them times'll never come back.' Lydia's regret was mixed with gratitude that the years had moved on. 'Not now your grandma's dead. I'll never get over what a rotten old swine Merton was, though. Nobody could have been worse than him.'

Brian recalled how Merton had Nimrodded him from the earliest age – he didn't know why. 'Nimrod!' he had shouted in his sergeant-major's voice for the first time, and Brian looked up, knowing he meant him, so that hearing him universally maligned distorted all memory.

'Our George came in at half past one in the morning,' Lydia said, 'and couldn't light the oil lamp for fear Merton would hear. God knows what he'd bin up to, but he was so hungry he went down the steps into the pantry to get a scoop of jam before going to bed. Mother kept a special jar only a third full to trap flies and bees, and in the dark our George gets a wooden spoon and stuffs half the pot into his gob – he was so clambed to death. When he was halfway up the stairs with his shoes in his hand he realises what he's eating. Maybe a bumblebee still tickled his throat. He goes crackers trying to get it out of his system, and wakes Merton up, as well as mother. So we all get up, and there's George in the kitchen trying to spit the muck out. In the end he runs in the yard and does it by the coalhouse door. Merton never laughed so much in his life – the old bogger. But we had some times in our family, didn't we, Vera?'

Lillian leaned across to Brian and kissed him.

He handed her down from the bus, wanting her to enjoy the day because next week he'd be gone, couldn't say when he'd be back. At the riverbank near Stoke Bardolph a couple of fishermen looked intently at their floats. 'When was the first time you went out into the country?'

He held her hand, and tried to remember. 'On a bus from school when I was five. We lived in some old back-to-backs near Albion Street, and I'd never seen grass. A lane went off the main road and there was a field at the junction. I kept running across it, from hedge to hedge. After a while the teacher made us run races, but it didn't spoil my enjoyment. Tables were put out, and we had tea and sandwiches.'

From the raised path going towards Burton Joyce they saw a gull reconnoitring the ripples of the curving river. 'My father took us to Matlock,' she said, 'and we went up the Heights of Abraham. Later we had tea at a café. Another time we went to the Sherwood Foresters memorial at Crich. Dad had bin in that regiment, and he wanted to see it. I'd like to live in the country, though, in a cottage, with a garden I could sit in.'

'Maybe you will, one day.'

'One day!'

'It's not much to want.'

'Where would you like to live?'

'I'd like to live in France, or Italy.'

'Why do you want to go to them places?'

'I don't know. I just do.'

There was bitterness in her laugh. 'You must know.'

He resented having to give coherent reasons. 'Ever since I knew that other countries existed, I've wanted to get out. I'd like to go to Malaya, but I can't get a job that would take me back there.'

They paused in their walk, and she rubbed her face against his shoulder. Off the path he lay his raincoat down. 'Your throne. You look even more like a queen today.'

'I wish I felt like one.'

'You are one. Look at the river. It'll do whatever you tell it.'

A throaty cock sounded from a farm. 'Will it turn backwards?'

'You're a queen,' he smiled, 'not God.'

'Oh well, that's that, then.'

'You're in a funny mood.'

'I can't help it.'

'Better in a funny mood than no mood at all, I suppose.'

'I don't know about that.'

He kissed her. 'If anybody asked what I wanted most in the world I'd say it was to be sitting by the river with you, and watching the ducks go by.'

'I'm a different person to what I was a month ago,' she said, 'and you'll be going away next week.'

'There's nothing I can do about it.'

'I don't suppose there is. But you'll come back, won't you?'

'In a week or two. I'll write, as soon as I know.' It would be easier in a letter, though he had no idea what he would say.

'Will you wear your uniform when you leave?'

If he turned up in such a rig Nora might wonder if he had only one suit. 'Why?'

'I'd like to come to the station with you.'

'It's a long way. Won't you be tired?'

She was scornful. 'I'm here, aren't I? I want to see you off properly.'

Like an everloving engaged couple. 'If you want to.'

'I want to very much.'

He didn't want her to see him off. You had no thoughts of your own when you were with somebody else. 'I'd be glad if you would. And if you do feel tired I'll give you the money for a taxi back.' She got very little on National Health.

But she balked at such concern. 'I can pay for my own.'

'Suit yourself.'

'You're in a funny mood, as well,' she said.

The sun made him drowsy, easy-going. He had chosen a good day. A lacewing jumped off his shoe. There was a haze on the river, as if someone under the water had lit a stove.

'I wonder what it's like here at night,' she said.

'Why's that?'

'It's so perfect now.'

'I'm glad you think so,' he teased.

She looked at him, as if he knew nothing, and was incapable of thinking anything. 'It must be so pitch black you can't see a hand before you. I'll bet the water's icy, even after a day like today. I can just 'ear the owls hooting, and see things going through the grass.'

He stroked her arm, not wanting her to be so far away. 'I'll read you some poems. I brought a book.'

She put on a meagrim face at his assuming that such a novelty would make up for everything – whatever it was – but he lay at her feet and read some verses from 'Maud', then 'Mariana of the Moated Grange', and 'Ulysses', not even stopping when an angler went by.

'Did you like that?'

She clapped. 'Read me some more. I'll never forget, you reading poems to me.' He told her the story of Odysseus, and about the Trojan War, gleanings from Homer and the Classical Dictionary.

'Hungry now?'

She lay beside him, and the rich smell of the grass seemed to grow sweeter.

'For food, I mean.'

'My period started last night.'

There was no better day. He took out the flask, potted meat sandwiches, cakes and apples. 'The food of the Gods. How are you feeling, then?'

'My back ached this morning, but it's gone now.'

Since that first night he had taken precautions, hoping it would be all right, but now it was, and he was free. He smiled at her appetite.

'Must be the fresh air. I'm not pregnant, that's one thing.'

'You've put on weight, though.'

'It's not surprising. Now read me some more. I don't want the day to end.'

Neither did he.

Changing buses in the middle of town, Bert was the last person he wanted to see, but he accepted his invitation to have a drink, because Lillian said she would like one. 'It'll be nice to sit down.'

'He's my cousin.' Bert walked on the other side of her. 'And we're more like brothers, but he never comes to see me.'

'I've been busy,' Brian told him.

'I can see you 'ave. Courting is what I call it, eh, duck?' He nudged Lillian. 'That'd mek anyone busy, especially with a nice woman like you.'

They found a table in the Peach Tree. 'I work too much to go courting,' Bert said. 'Not that I'd find anybody as 'ud 'ave me – for more than a night or two.'

Brian could only laugh, while hoping that the floor would give way under him. Lillian asked where he worked.

'Nowhere as yo'd think much of,' Bert said. 'I'm not clever like our Brian, who went and got TB. He'll never have to wok again.'

'I'm not a cripple,' Brian said.

'I never said yer was. What I do for ten quid a week is sweat blood on that bleeding lorry, but all yo've got to do is spit a bit o' blood in yer 'anky now and again and they'll send you a pension book forever.'

Lillian laughed more openly than she had done all day.

'She appreciates me,' Bert said, 'don't you, duck? If I had somebody like yo' I'd get married and settle down. All I want is a nice young woman to think summat of me, and I'd be at that church in a flash.'

'I'll bet you would.'

He patted her wrist, and she pulled her arm away, fastening her coat. 'You can stop that.'

'I'm not like our Brian. He's a dark bogger, he is. You can never tell what he'll do.'

'Belt up,' Brian said, though observing that whether she liked Bert or not there was a familiarity between them that he could never attain with her.

Lillian excused herself, to go to the toilet.

'Serious, is it?'

'No.'

Bert nudged him. 'She's a bag o' bones. You want to get a woman with some meat on her.'

'She's a marvellous person,' Brian said. 'And don't you forget it.' He'd never been closer to giving him a blow in the chops.

'So is it serious?'

He got down to the basic lingo. 'Shut yer fucking rattle.'

'I thought so. I'd go for her, though, even though she is too thin. Feed her up a bit. Put a kid in her.'

He stood politely so that she could sit down. Brian got more drinks. 'Let me know if your sister gets divorced.'

'I ain't got a sister, sharp shit!'

He couldn't, or wouldn't, take his stare from her, but he was only doing it to make Brian jealous, or to make Lillian feel wanted, or because that's how he behaved in front of any woman, or because Bert was Bert, in which case it was futile to feel offended.

She found him lively and amusing, she admitted as the bus rounded Canning Circus on the way home. 'He's a bit rough, though, that's all.'

'He always was. Comes from a rough family, but he's a good pal to me. We had marvellous times when we were kids.'

She held his hand. 'When you was sitting with him I felt you didn't get on very well.'

'We're used to one another. We don't show much affection.'

'Still,' she said, 'I can see what it is you like about him.'

Chapter

❧ TWENTY-THREE

'I shan't be calling in tonight,' he told her. 'I've got to see a man who owns a bookshop.'

She thought it was a joke. 'That's a new 'un.'

'I mean it. Somebody I met last week.'

'Can't you see him in the day?'

Only two evenings remained before he left for Berkshire, and he was robbing her of one. 'He wants me to take back some books I borrowed.'

She stood at the kitchen table, rolling out dough for jam tarts, having promised him a treat, and a promise was a promise, but now he wouldn't be here for her to keep it. 'That's all right, then.'

'I'll call in in the morning.' He didn't see why such a small matter should be so threatening, since he had been with her every night for as long as he could remember.

'You can if you like.'

It seemed unjust. Last night they'd heard Tchaikovsky and Vaughan Williams at the Albert Hall, a concert that made them lovers forever, inseparable. She had been shy of going: the audience would listen in peculiar and embarrassing attitudes. She'd feel out of place. But he had booked seats. It's like a theatre. You'll see. I'll get a programme, and you can read about what they're going to play. Just doll yourself up again, and everybody will look at you and think how lucky I am.

'I've never been in the Albert Hall.'

'I've only been a couple of times myself.'

'Do they play "God Save the King"?'

'I'm afraid so.'

She felt for his hand during *Romeo and Juliet* and he noticed her tears. He returned the pressure, though not too hard. Passions ran deep, and her soul was too delicate for him to deal with, wondering what would become of her.

'You know I want to see you every minute I can,' he said. 'I'll see you tomorrow.'

'I want you to,' she answered. 'You know that.'

But he didn't, particularly, and wouldn't have bothered if he hadn't been leaving in a few days. He ought to want to. He should be killed on the spot, almost wished for it to end the pain. 'It's just that I can't come tonight. It means no more than that.'

She used the lid of a tin to cut circles of paste. 'I'm sorry. I don't know what I'm thinking about. I'll stay in and read. I'm halfway through *Anna* – how do you say it?'

'*Karenina*.' Russian names weren't strange to him since the war. 'Do you like it?'

'Some of it's beyond me, but I like all that about Anna and . . .'

'Vronsky.'

'I'm wondering how it's going to end.'

'I won't tell you.'

'No, don't.'

He hesitated at Tom Boak's semi-detached set back from the road. Not knowing what to expect, he never expected anything. He only hoped. Wanting, but not knowing what he wanted, he was consumed by hope, open to all impressions, fuelled by the voracious desire of someone to whom every breath was hopeful expectation, a state of optimism which, because it was normal and neutral, might be considered happiness, except that he thought as little as possible in case equilibrium would be upset, and he was prevented from seeing every scene in the world as a scintillating novelty. Only what he read had much influence, which was why he mostly tackled the great and the classical.

Modern writers were more mystifying at the moment, and if he read them it was only to see what was being done.

The house was half concealed by elderberry and privet, a strand of bramble snaking on to the pavement. He was about to walk away, but rain worked through his mackintosh, so he went to the door and knocked.

A woman asked him into a fusty-smelling hall. She had thin lips, and glasses on her bony face, a little pointed nose emphasised by fair hair drawn tight over her head and clipped into a bun. A purple brooch set off the blouse buttoned to her throat.

'I've come to see Tom.'

She spread his coat over the banister to dry. 'Who else? My name's Wendy, in case you're interested.'

Maybe Tom had remarried. 'Are you Mrs Boak?'

'Christ, no.' Her bloodless face managed a smile. 'I'm a civil servant, a penpusher, who likes books and music, so I come to this den of cultural iniquity now and again.'

People were flaked out in various postures, listening to piano music from a gramophone pick-up. Tom pointed to an armchair so deep that, once down, Brian wondered how he'd ever get up. He faced the curtained bay window, and clockwise took in each person with glances that he hoped would be unnoticed.

Tom Boak put on the light, the last notes dying. 'Good old Scriabin. But you know my views about music: Bach was the last great composer.'

Jim Bailey felt for a cigarette. 'Which one? There were about forty, if I remember.' He was a lanky bald-headed man, a navy-blue beret balanced on his knee as if it were an alternative skull. His artistic sketches were thought a lot of locally, Tom said, introducing Brian, but he was trying to get them shown in London. At which Jim made a face that would have had Tom boiling in hell.

'I'd say the best composer was Gershwin.' Ted Gedling was a fair-haired young man who smoked untreated tea in a short black pipe, which may have accounted for his vacant expression, Tom quipped, and the time it took him to get in on the argument. He worked in a travel agent's, and thought John Dos

Passos the greatest novelist of all time. He imitated his style, and plagiarised his plots – insofar as it was possible – but the stories lacked either relevance or reality, Tom went on, because they were set in Nottingham or thereabouts. He was flaked out next to Anne Jones, and Brian couldn't decide whether they were holding hands or not.

Wendy mentioned that Mozart was a great composer, and Tom moved as if to get up and slam her, then fell back smiling to show he might actually be fond of her. Her expression suggested that an unspecifiable struggle early on in life had made her guarded and mean, but that she was quite able to deal with an overbearing old bastard like him. Hard to know what to make of it, but Brian thought he had better weigh up every person new to him, otherwise he'd be dead, and wouldn't know why he was here.

'Let me finish by introducing this new *aficionado* of the arts.' Tom continued to bawl out such daft comments that only Anne Jones bothered to shake hands. Ted Gedling got up, and Brian took his place next to her. 'I called at the shop,' she said, 'hoping to see you. Tom told me all about you, though.'

It couldn't have been much, unless the bloody gossip had made up some rigmarole, though Brian didn't mind, since she seemed to have found it interesting. The only other person – so quiet as to be hard to notice, and he felt that she liked it that way – was Grace Rutland, a dark and stylish woman of middle age whose poems he had seen in the magazine bought in Berkshire so long ago. What she was doing in this place he couldn't imagine, but was pulled from his speculations on Tom asking how his novel was progressing.

'I start tomorrow, and won't know till I've finished' – which staggered him for a moment.

'What style do you write in?' Ted Gedling demanded.

'Style?'

'Stream of consciousness, first person singular, or what?'

'Stream of piss,' Jim Bailey called, 'or first person jugular. Neither's the way to write.' Nobody could decide which was, and after they'd argued for an hour Anne turned and asked Brian if he had read anything by James Joyce.

'Oh yes,' Jim chipped in, 'that superfluous writer known in

the trade as a pint of pickled peppers – though he did stop O. Henry James Joyce Cary dead in his tracks!'

Brian felt ignorant but, like a jackdaw, hoisted a few items into his maw for future consideration. 'Not yet. Maybe I'll try him.'

'What *does* inspire you?'

It seemed a false way of putting it, since you only needed to be inspired by yourself. But he reeled off about half the catalogue from the back of an Everyman Library volume. She believed him, though he could see Grace Rutland's eyebrows hit the heaviside layer. He had, however, read more than she thought.

'You'll ruin his native talent,' Tom said, 'though I don't suppose he'll find that till he's finished imitating all the rubbish.'

'I'll lend you my copy of *Ulysses*,' Anne said, as if there were only three in the world. She also mentioned a novel by Arthur Fairbone called *Love in the Snow*, which title Ted Gedling screwed up his already screwed up face at, and said it was a bigger bag of shit than *Women in Love*, which put him in the pigsty as far as Grace Rutland – or anyone else – was concerned. Brian couldn't credit how he had stumbled into such a clan of backbiting loonies, and supposed that none of them could understand it either. Certainly, it was hard to imagine Lillian feeling easy, not to mention Nora. Tom called for a couple of women to rustle up coffee and food, and Wendy looked to Anne, who said *she* wasn't going into the kitchen just to give the men a thrill. 'We aren't living in the Middle Ages.'

Grace Rutland waited to be served because she was, after all, a published poet, but Brian volunteered. 'I'll give you a hand.'

'Our coffee will curl their hair,' Anne said, 'and give them boxers' noses.' She stood by the sink. 'I can't think why Grace doesn't like me. Must be our argument about the *Epithalamion*.'

The kettle was as black as a cannonball that had lain three weeks at Borodino, though the water seemed clean enough. He lit the gas, recalling that he had read the *Epithalamion* when in love with Rachel. 'Who can argue about that?'

She stroked her cheek. 'Or was it Chaucer? It must have been. You can't argue about Spenser, but Chaucer's wide open.'

'Sounds like I've got to read him.' Wendy spread slices of

bread, and patterned the biscuits on a plate with an expression close to happiness for someone who was Tom's lady-love. Brian emptied half a tin of Lyons into the pot, followed it with boiling water, then topped the lid with a tea cosy.

'You make it like an expert,' Anne said. He'd never done it before, had merely thrown in a lot, on the assumption that the more you use the better it will be. Her stare put him under a magnifying glass. 'Tom said you had tuberculosis.'

He wanted to deny such a defining word, tell her to mind her own business. Tom Boak deserved a kick in the balls. She assumed him to be a worse case than he was, but there was no word for it that he liked. Tuberculosis assumed you were ill, while consumption meant you were dead, and TB sounded too respectable to signify anything at all. Perhaps phthisis was the best word. 'A very poetic disease,' she went on. 'All great artists have it.'

He thought she should be smacked down. 'A lot of 'em died young of it, as well.'

'Everything costs something.' Laughter showed her lovely white teeth. He'd had a side tooth yanked out on the troopship because of an abscess, and they weren't so spotless anymore. She looked at him closely: 'Do you spit blood?'

'I haven't for a day or two.'

She took a bottle of milk from the shelf and drained it into a saucepan. 'I was looking forward to seeing you cough into your handkerchief.'

'Like Chopin?'

'Or Lawrence.'

'It's not so easy.'

'Try.'

'Bollocks.'

'I knew you'd say that.'

Wendy flinched in the background.

He noticed Anne's wedding ring. 'Is your husband a doctor?'

'A dentist. But don't spoil my evening. He works so hard he can only sleep by the end of the day, unless he goes to the Conservative Club.' She ran a finger down the draining board. 'Everything's filthy in this kitchen.'

'When I mention it,' Wendy poured scalding milk into a

jug as if Tom cringed at the bottom, 'he just tells me to get on with it. But I work late every night.'

Back in the salon he registered the names of Hemingway, Faulkner and Upton Sinclair. Anne commented on Tolstoy, mentioned Sartre and Camus, one thought flowing into another, while Grace Rutland hogged the poetry department. Jim Bailey talked about D'Annunzio and Gaudier-Brzeska, Tom conducting them like an orchestra, as if every new name jacked up the score of a monthly competition. Lawrence's story of *St Mawr* came up, and Brian remarked that his blacksmith grandfather would have known how to deal with the bloody horse. He hadn't read the story, but when Ted Gedling took a copy from the shelf and treated them to a few pages Brian reminded them of Raskolnikov's similar nightmare after he had been sent to Siberia for the murder of the old pawnbroker and her sister.

'Lawrence had read Dostoevsky,' Grace Rutland said, 'and must have been influenced by him. How right you are to point out the comparison.'

Ted Gedling muttered something about the twelve basic plots. 'I suppose all great writers poach off each other.'

Brian was grateful for Grace's approval. Maybe she thought his remarks were the narrow outlet of a full reservoir, and that he wasn't as empty as she supposed – or as he knew himself to be.

Tom stood when Ted packed another bolt of dark substance into his pipe. 'These meetings get more and more rewarding, my dear friends, especially when we have new blood among us, but the evening's closed, because for one thing it's half past ten, and for another Edward Gedling Esquire has gone as long as he is capable without another fill of his noxious opium pipe – or whatever crap it is. The whole house becomes uninhabitable if I let him smoke too much of it.'

Maybe it was some of the stuff Kirkby had brought back from Malaya and unleashed on the streets of Nottingham. Anne leaned close. 'Walk me to the bus stop.'

He wanted to be alone, but waited at the gate. The pavements were wet, plates of light around each lamp post. 'Will you be here next week?' she said.

'I'll be back with the air force.' He fell in beside her. 'Unless I go absent without leave.'

She took his arm. 'That would be fun, if you did it for me.'

Such daft enthusiasm was foreign to him. He'd do it for nobody. 'I'll be back in a month.'

'What will you do then?'

'Nothing.'

'It's so funny that you've got a pension.'

He asked where she was brought up.

'London. I came here with my husband a couple of years ago.'

He didn't know why he told her that he was married. 'But I don't live with my wife anymore.'

'How did you manage that?'

'I just left.'

'I wish I could.'

'Aren't you happy?' he wanted to know.

'Who's happy?'

'Some people are.'

'Are you?'

'I don't think about it anymore.'

'You don't need to, I suppose.'

'I've got more important things to think about. It's a matter of first things first.'

'That's one way of putting it.'

He was glad to reach the bus stop.

'Let's walk to the next one.'

'If you like.'

'You must let me see your stuff.'

He didn't fancy showing anybody, though he was flattered to be asked. 'Do *you* write?'

'I paint sometimes. In a studio at the top of the house. It passes the time.'

'Did you train for it?'

She laughed. 'No. I just experiment. Are your poems about tuberculosis?'

'You've got that on the brain.'

She put her head so close that he felt her warmth, and a ticklish brush of hair. 'It's romantic.'

Why deny it? She was barmy. He didn't like her, and he had

265

missed his last bus, but he said: 'You were going to lend me that novel.'

'*Ulysses?*' She told him about Joyce's book. 'All the great English writers are Irish.'

They argued for a while, as if putting forward the most talented members of a football team. 'Still,' she said, 'you must read James Joyce – though you won't be here next week.'

'Send it to me in Berkshire. I'll let you know what I think when I get back.'

'You can write and tell me. Then I'll know you got it.' They were at the top of Mansfield Road. 'You'd better leave me here.'

He wrote his address by the street lamp. 'I'm thinking of leaving my husband,' she said. 'I can't take anymore.'

Silent, he didn't move. What could *he* do about it? She was his height. Her coat smelled of rain, but her cheeks were dry and warm, hair springy at his lips, his fingers around the secret part of her neck under the collar of her dress. He pressed his lips so hard he felt her teeth, wanted to say something, no meaning to such kisses, away from the lamp, by a wall. She didn't speak, and he couldn't understand how they'd come to be kissing, because he was without passion, wanting only to get free of her. Maybe she sensed it, because she suddenly murmured goodnight, and he walked quickly away.

Ma Bull and a couple of neighbours were at the yard-end, and Vera walked behind Seaton, who carried Brian's case. Mrs Robin, expecting her son back from Scouts' Camp, stood diffidently aside, disliking everyone in the yard. At election times she put a Liberal poster in their window to tell people that no one voted Labour in that house, or to inform them that they bothered to vote at all when the rest of the yard was too feckless to care. A coalman ambled on to the street with his empty sack, and waited to see if owt was up. Likewise a window cleaner. Mrs Verney was joined by Liza Atkin down from the bookies. 'Yer'd think it was a bleddy funeral,' Seaton said, as if blaming Mrs Bull for drawing the crowd.

Brian helped Lillian into the taxi. She wore her best for the big event. Spruced and polished, trousers pressed and cap at the correct angle, his civvies lay on top in the case so that he could change before getting to London.

She held his hand as they passed Robinson's Mill, where his mother had worked at the age of thirteen. He kissed her, tasting lipstick to be wiped off later. He had calculated when to arrange for the taxi to come, so that she would not stand too long at the station. There might not be a seat on the platform.

'Maybe the train'll be late, anyway,' she said.

'They often are. Nothing runs on time.'

'It's a miracle they run at all. I can't understand why they aren't crashing all the time, like bumping into each other in a crowd.'

She stood, pale and quiet beside him, looking across to the opposite platform, her lips set as if the waiting was unbearable, which it certainly was to him. But she held his hand, got closer to the edge, till he asked her to move back in case a non-stopping train caught her. She seemed tired. 'Do you want to go home?'

'I came to see you off,' she said, 'and I will.'

Was he trying to get rid of her? He put an arm around her shoulders. 'I'm glad you've come with me.'

'Are you?'

He wasn't. Being seen off by her must surely mean the end of something. 'I've told you. What more can I say?'

She turned away. He felt no struggle. He was two people, both of them himself. To say what she wanted to hear would have been a lie, and he wouldn't lie to make her happy. He had left it too late. If he told her, she would know he was lying only to make her happy. She knew the truth. Yet he knew it was in his power to undo that truth, to send her home happy – or full of anguish and uncertainty at the notion that his words were false. She couldn't be happier than that. But if he said the words she so wanted to hear they would no longer be lies, which was why he wouldn't speak. He wanted to cast off the shirt of Nessus that he had pulled over himself. The sky spat on the lines, wafting smoke through the station canyon. He would feel better when far away, but until he got there he was empty. The spot they stood on was tormented to the middle of the earth.

'Are you going to write to me?'

He was relieved to hear her voice. 'Every day.'

'I believe you.'

Ancestral iron strengthened him in not speaking. He wanted to, but what was good for him must in the long run be even better for her. He would not be deflected. Yet he wanted her to say 'Don't go. I love you. Keep on loving me. Marry me when you can. Live with me.' Such words would harden him even more, as she well knew, just as trapped in the silent dialogue, her expression telling him only to go. He knew too much, and his silence forced her also into knowing too much, so they were both mute.

The engine steamed in, a signal to embrace, her lips firm on his. There was a delectable and eternal smell to her make-up. He wouldn't go. He would stay, marry her as soon as he could, both of them happy forever. She was his fate, his only love. 'I'll be back soon. I'll write to you. Take care of yourself. Keep on eating plenty.'

She was dry-eyed. 'Have a safe journey.'

People pushed their way in. Climbing the steps with his case, his cap fell. She picked it up, and smiled. 'A present from me!'

'Thanks, love.'

He found a seat, and pulled a window open. She couldn't reach his hand before the train moved.

Wires rose and fell, messages of love and death humming along them. Posts flicked across his vision like the arm on a radar screen. He lived out his destruction as if watching it on the pictures. He should wait for a locomotive from the opposite direction and throw himself out, mangled unto death.

The train went along a curve, bringing a smell of mellow and fruitful fields, such air inducing him to sit down and read.

Chapter
❧ TWENTY-FOUR

'Nice to see you,' Nora said, everyone listening, all of them looking. 'Did you have a good leave?'

'Yes, Sister – a wonderful time.' No one could know.

Good to wallow in the healthy mire of mutually supporting subterfuge. She played it well. 'I suppose you got your refills all right?'

So did he, dodged a wheelchair, searched out his old bedspace, the same smell of ether and floor polish. 'If we'd known you were coming we'd have got the traffic lights going,' the orderly said.

He held from looking. She'd gone into the office. He craved to hold her, loved her because he yearned for everything about her that was unknown.

The shout: 'Seaton's here! Does he look the same? Is his backbone a string of conkers?' Joe from Liverpool said he wouldn't know where to put it. 'You can tell he's a virgin by that little pink spot in the middle of his left hand!'

Brian littered a dozen condom packets over his counterpane, postage stamps for letters to paradise – that had accumulated in his mackintosh pocket. An electric flash of insanity impelled him to action. 'Three for half-a-dollar, and I didn't blow 'em up like balloons, either.'

Joe's face took some colour. Good job he had TB or he'd

have had a heart attack. The others laughed at his embarrassment. 'Get the bloody things off my bed,' he said.

The airgunner paused at his occupational cure-all, file held like a miniature sword. 'The sister's coming, you bloody fools.'

Heart banging at his stupidity, he trawled them together, but she slotted charts into a bed near the door and went out. 'You should have left 'em,' Frank laughed. 'You might have set her on.'

She came back, ever busy, carrying flowers from the centre table as if their whiff of decay bothered her. Sun lit every angle in the long room. 'Who are you looking for?' Joe cried. 'Can't you believe you're back?'

He took off his mackintosh. In Rawson's place a man with a long nervous face was reading a Penguin book, feet twitching under the blankets. As if inviting the monotony to a competition he reached for a piss bottle, took the cloth off, and put it between the sheets.

Brian passed Frank a cigarette. 'Has Harry gone?'

A window was open, the match flame like a moth coming out of its chrysalis. 'He went, last week.'

'Where did they send him?'

Frank scratched his nose. 'Home – not wanted on voyage. The final resting place. He woke me up one morning, but there was nothing anyone could do. Screens around the bed. Oxygen. Everything came up. It looked like a slaughterhouse.'

The long-faced man put the bottle back on the floor. 'Very cheerful. I only got here yesterday.'

'If your name's on it,' Joe said, 'you don't even have time to send a postcard. All them bleeding little corpuscles!'

A rain squall dimmed the ward, and he closed the two nearest windows. 'He was all right when I left.'

Frank stretched his legs under the clothes. 'He got worse. All in about a week. They moved him to a sideward, in the end.' He went back to *Titbits*. Rawson was old news, but Brian had slept in the next bed for months, lived by him, thought him set slowly back to health. A trick had been played, by whom, by what, he couldn't say. Rawson's spirit shed his life like a tree a leaf it can't hold on to. Death was stronger, waiting for him to relax his fingernails.

Ditch the mumbo-jumbo. Rawson caught it, had gone for a burton, nothing to be done, the way of all flesh. But he felt anguish at being more than halfway fit, at the same time craving to join those already in the dark, as he had after Baker was killed in the jungle.

The squeak of shoes, and Nora held a tray. 'Thought you might like some tea and biscuits, Seaton. Keep you going until supper.'

The impersonal glance brought her close, hard not to kiss her into life – get life back into himself. She stepped away, as if also tempted, or knowing that he was, sensing danger. 'I heard about Rawson,' he said.

'It was such a shame. But we did our best, let me tell you.' She spoke as if he had mentioned a parcel that had gone missing, and he wondered whether it was part of her act, or a normal pose she couldn't hide. 'He was poorly, but I did think we'd pull him round.'

He took the tray, a few volts as he touched her fingertips. 'It's a surprise.'

'A nasty shock, I know. But get your tea. You look as if you lost weight during your leave.'

Glad to hear it. 'I borrowed a bike, and cycled a lot.'

She pursed her lips in disapproval, a perfect role. 'Don't overdo it when you leave us for good.' She had a way of turning from a person as abruptly as if he had been swallowed by the earth and she didn't want to know how or why. He had to recall her letters to know that she couldn't have forgotten what they said they'd signified for each other.

'She's taken a bit of a shine to you,' Frank said.

'I was born lucky.'

'I wish she'd do the same to me. I'd love to get it up her. I'd use my best furlined zip-fastening french letters. None of your tenpenny ones for her.'

He wanted to scare the bile out of him. Go and ask Joe to give you a wank, you foul gett. But it was button-lips, coming and going, because he too must seem no more than one of the old gang hankering after the untouchable ward sister with the flaxen hair and comfortable bosom. He walked quickly, purposefully up and down, then stopped and sat by his bed.

A slight smile, eyes bright and blue. 'A hospital isn't the only place you can be cured,' she said when she came again after tea. 'But don't exert yourself. Physically, I mean.' He wondered how long the play could go on. Act two, scene one, and without warning the fire curtain would smother them. 'You look better already. But get into bed. Have a good rest before tomorrow.'

'Yes, Sister.'

'Not so much "Yes, Sister", either,' she said. 'Go and change in the end room, and put your clothes in the locker.'

She walked away. Fuck you, his lips said.

'You must have been a bad boy,' Joe crowed. 'She doesn't like you anymore.'

'They're all the same,' he said. 'Fickle.'

He ambled, defeated, to hang his uniform in the sideward, don institutional garb, pull on bedsocks, step into slippers, fasten a dressing gown around him and get back to being a patient.

Arranging his shirts in the locker, the door behind him, he waited, and when the latch clicked it was Nora going off duty, weather shoes on, a costume hiding all but her face, hair taken back under the grey headdress, short cape over her shoulders. 'I couldn't bear not seeing you for a moment.'

She made no move, an anxious smile till he touched her face. 'I don't exist without you,' he said. 'You know that.'

'We'll arrange something, darling.'

Both hands at her hips, he kissed her cold, pliant mouth. She touched him. 'Your letters helped me to bear it. I couldn't sleep at night, for wanting you.'

She was asking him. He was exhausted, would faint in her arms, was at last with someone who belonged to him absolutely.

He lit a cigarette when there was no more sound to her footsteps, didn't want to read, or talk, or write letters, only to cut himself off in sleep. He followed the trolley in to help give out the suppers.

The small and wiry night sister flashed him such baleful dislike that he thought she must know. Secrets galvanise the brain, pictures on the screen before his eyes. Lillian, going home from the station, was taken by a bout of coughing, choking in agony, scores of people walking by, her tormented face paralysing him. But his pen turned into a dry stick, and when he tried to write her a letter, he scorched in the light of two fires, not knowing which to burn in, or which to flee from.

The supper wagon was pushed away, the evening drink gone down thirty gullets, cards shuffled and dealt, talk breaking after the boredom of the day. Last night he'd been with Lillian. Now he was back in the hospital routine. In the middle of an island, the sea was invisible, but the island was moving, and he was no more aware of where to than of the earth turning on its axis.

Thousands of watts burned behind closed eyelids. At six o'clock he took towel and ablution bag into the bathroom, sleep like a blanket still muffling the ward. The coughing hadn't started, though day pressed at the windows. He put on his uniform of shirt and battledress tunic, and on his way to the lavatory after breakfast heard Nora tearing a strip off an orderly for not returning the food bins to the kitchen soon enough. Coming back, she was at her desk, glasses on to check the laundry lists, ticking one thing and not the other. The orderly passed, a pair of towel-covered bedpans held in front, as if going to fit tin shoes on an elephant.

She turned, pen in hand. 'I'll come and see you as soon as I can.'

If their desire wasn't equal, there was nothing between them, but the confusion of her gaze dissolved his resolution. He put his arms around her, pliant breasts under her clothes.

She took him by the elbow. 'But you'd better go now. I'd be cashiered, and so would you.'

Marked for life – on which issue their views were the same. She touched his wrist. 'It'll be all the more wonderful later.'

The same girl she had rollocked about the breakfast trolley came in with the mail bag. 'You're only just back from leave, Seaton, but I expect your tests'll start in a day or two.' The orderly would say she had seen them holding hands. She hadn't, but it was close. Nora looked through the mail. 'You might as well play postman now you're here, and give it out.'

The book had a scrawl inside the green cover: 'I said I would, so enjoy it. Let me know you've received it. Anne.'

He wondered whether Nora had seen her name and address on the back. People can write to each other, Anne had said, so he sent an acknowledging note, then sat reading till the MO came on his rounds, Nora by his side. 'I'm glad you're looking so well, Seaton. Everything go all right on your leave? Sit down.'

When he got out he would never call anyone sir for the rest of his life.

'I expect you're champing at the bit, so we'll get things going as soon as we can. Make the schedule up, Sister.'

The usual routine. Temperature. Pulse rate. Blood pressure. Sediment. X-rays. Sputum. Weight check.

'We liked having you, Seaton, but if all goes well we'll be seeing the last of you. Any plans?'

He didn't know why he said: 'I'll go to France, or maybe Italy.'

'Live the high life on your pension, eh?' He believed him. 'Not that the Mediterranean has an especially good climate for your type, though I don't suppose it can do you any harm, either.'

Perhaps he still wasn't clear of tubercle bacilli. A year ago he didn't believe he'd got it. Who could say that he was free of it now?

Reading at the long table, he sensed her appearance, confirmed by the peculiar faint squeak of her duty shoes. 'We need more of your blood, Seaton, for your sediment rate. I'll do it in the office – if you can spare me a moment from your thriller.'

Orderlies came and went, and she took a needle from the sterilisation bin. He spread his fingers. 'I walked on the Downs yesterday.'

'Aren't we energetic?'

'The birds'll be migrating soon.'

She rubbed alcohol on the pad of his middle finger. 'I wish I was. Hold still.'

A slight shaking of the hand. When it became steady, she smiled. 'I expect you're used to this.'

'I never get used to anything.' He had little time to speculate on how blunt the needle was. The passion he felt was subtle, as if they hadn't yet slept together. The end of the tube turned red. 'What do you do with it afterwards?'

'We drink it, Seaton. Waste not, want not.'

A patient went by in a wheelchair. 'Take some more, then, Sister.'

She eased the needle out. 'I will when we need to paint the town red. Don't forget your X-ray at two thirty.'

Reading *Ulysses*, he realised that every thought in the mind must be related to one that had gone before. He'd always known, yet had never properly formulated the notion to get advantage from it. When an image manifested itself he worked backwards to connect one event with another, until the progress to his present state of mind became obvious. No thought came out of nothing, not even those meanderings in his notebook, but grew logically from something else. He had previously backtracked only in problems of mechanics or radio theory, but now it became an automatic process, so that the mind would never be idle or empty unless he willed it to be.

Therefore when Lillian came into his mind, it was not by accident, or by her own telepathic jump, but because he brought her there, speculating on how she was, and what she was doing at that moment. She had given him a copy of their photograph, which he had not brought with him, but yesterday, looking through the Tennyson Selection, he re-read *Ulysses*, and remembered her happiness when he had recited it on the riverbank. Today, looking at the title of the novel, her face ricocheted into his vision, and he was more pleased at tracing the connection than at having remembered her.

In the evening Nora said to him in the office: 'You're looking better since you got back from the north. Must be all that walking on the Downs.'

'I go there every day.'

'I wish I could.' A slight shift of her forehead was a signal that she would meet him.

A westerly wind wiped his face, bleak almost purple fields rolling away under low cloud, birds circling as if his bones were after all worth picking. Cap in belt, he walked over the hill, heart soaring at the flash of their manoeuvres, the flexibility of wings.

Wind blew the ashes away when he burned the french letter packets in the circular trench of the burial ground. An Austin car was parked on the lane, and a middle-aged man in plus-fours, and a woman wearing a raincoat, stood at the Saxon fort to look at their map. 'I told you it was here,' she said in a piggy kind of whine, 'and you didn't believe me.'

The man grunted, a lower register. 'I can't read the map *and* drive the motor – can I?'

They had saved petrol for an outing, but he hoped they would go elsewhere. A rabbit, ears straight and paws lifted, scooted down the slope when he clapped. Nora walked from the direction he was heading in. 'Don't embrace me. People are watching.' The elderly couple stood on the mound of the dead, a few yards apart, unable to make up their tiff. 'Walk on, as if we've passed a few remarks about the weather.'

He joined in the game, inmates of a prison as big as the world. They saw a common airman talking to a nursing sister. But she wore a navy blue civvy coat, so they wouldn't twig, though her white stockings made her plain enough. Trickery gone mad. Why should he care? She had a persecution complex. His old mates at the factory wouldn't believe he indulged in such a pastime, would laugh all over the street at his refusal to cut the Gordian knot no matter what the result. But if you loved a woman you did what she wanted, blind and stupid if you didn't, so he played the moves with enjoyment, necessary till he became a fully certified civilian, when such acting would no longer be called for, though if she then stipulated some new version he would act that out as well – any that she devised until such time as none was called for. Everything in life was a game, anyway.

He looked into the wilderness, no house or castle, the landscape clean. He could be whom he chose. Only with Lillian had he been himself. When all was clear they descended into the circular moat, green walls sheer on either side, to kiss without fear or hindrance.

Time was up: all checks under the bridge, and autumn on its way. The MO wished him well. His troubles were over, the nightmare hardly remembered. His ability to ignore the fact that there would be no more normality was the first victory of his life. Nora waved. 'Look after yourself, Seaton. We don't want to see you again.'

Joe scratched himself. 'What a bitch. Won't even shake hands.'

Brian picked up his case. 'She's busy.'

An orderly stopped him. 'You can't carry that. I'll bring a trolley.' They looked after you to the end, emoluments unto death, sent him on the last descent of the hill and the final trip through town on the back of a covered lorry. The same old steamwhistle screeched from the valley, a bundle of smoke flattening the sun. His head felt like a jack-o'-lantern, well-lit within as he stood on the opposite platform to the London train.

The George Hotel at Stoneminster was in a state of genteel decrepitude. In the room the bed was high with bolsters, counterpanes and pillows, and smelled like that of his grandmother's, still musty from the sweat of travellers who had been robbed by highwaymen. Brown paper lining the drawers reeked of cheap books bought as a kid for a penny each. There were two pisspots under the bed, and pages were missing from a Bible on the dressing table as if someone had used them in an emergency. A verse hanging out of kilter said: 'He asked for water, and she gave him milk . . .'

He banged out the leaded frames to let clean air into the homely room. In civvies he was a plain mister who had come into the mainstreet hotel and asked for a room booked by his wife – which she was in all but a sheet of paper, for he felt more married to her than he ever had to Pauline.

He polished his shoes, washed, and changed his shirt. Even waiting was a pleasure, sitting in an oak chair, her spirit already in the room. Downstairs, he positioned himself in the lounge and, half asleep, wondered who was asking for him at the desk in such a bossy voice.

'I've told the manageress to bring us our tea.' She held his hand under the table and whispered: 'How do you like being out on a dirty weekend?'

He wanted to go upstairs with her.

She laughed. 'Well, *you* would, wouldn't you? What's the room like?'

'Fine.'

'Then don't look so glum, my sweet.'

'I was trying to be serious.'

'Such a newly married couple?'

The room wasn't clean. 'Still,' she said, 'it's just right for what we want.'

'What do we want?'

'Shall I spell it out for you?'

'Just tell me.'

'Fun and games. Orgasms – if you must know.'

It was a room to be remembered. He stayed cool till she could no longer hold herself, then timed the approach that experience had taught him.

'I love the things you say.' She closed the window and drew the curtains. No more speeches, he held her close. She undressed by the bed. 'I like to watch you,' he said.

'A dirty young man!' She took off her blouse. 'Still, better than someone my own age.'

The few years difference didn't matter, but she teased him, reminded him, as if he wasn't aware of it. Mutual passion levelled them to the same age. 'Still,' she said, 'I can't think why you love me.'

He was afraid that if she began doubting his love she would end by doubting her own. 'If I knew I wouldn't know.'

'Don't you ever think about it?'

'I love you, that's all.'

She lay down. 'Then do something about it.'

He didn't care that she was in a strange mood. They slid around each other's bodies, in and out through the steam of love, root and branch carrying them downriver, into the boiling foam. 'We could be miles from anywhere.'

'A boat on the ocean,' he said.

'Then no one would hear us. Especially me. I caught myself out.' She had whinnied like a mare. 'And you're a bull.'

'A bull fucking a mare.'

'Makes me want it again.'

At supper in the dining room: 'Now you can tell me what you really did on your leave.'

'I wrote all about it in my letters.'

'There's not that much paper in the world.'

Lillian had found out, had written to let her know the facts. The balloon would go up, but what went up must come down.

'Do you think I had time to do more than what I told you about?'

She touched his hand. 'I love you because you're so straight with me.'

The silence was more his. Hers would have been full of love, but his silence was intolerable and had to be filled.

They had coffee in the bar. A man set out a row of four briar pipes, cleaning each in turn with a penknife and a white fluffy ramrod. He was about forty, with dark combed-back hair, wearing a suit with a waistcoat and watch chain. He sipped a tankard of beer, a local solicitor, Brian said to her, who went through the same procedure every evening. He took out a tobacco pouch, drew a large ashtray towards him, and filled the first pipe. When he lit the tobacco he puffed as if he had waited all day for the pleasure, wafting the smoke affectionately, not really wanting it to vanish, as if he would send out a hand and put it in his pocket.

'Something's upsetting you.'

She was trespassing. When they were alone in their room they discarded whatever both found necessary to forget. If she had reasons for loving him he could find more for loving her, which made the union equal, a notion which filled him with the anguish that was inseparable from love. 'We go our different ways in the morning,' he said. 'I should keep a stiff upper lip, I suppose.'

'I rely on you not to be that sort. There are enough of those about.' She leaned close. 'But there's only one of you. And only one of me, come to that. In a month I'll wangle more leave, so if you can tear yourself away from that dreadful Nottingham we can be together at Queen's Bay. I gave you the key to the door, so go on your own, if you like. You can write in peace. There's plenty of tinned food in the cupboard, and you have my permission to use it.'

Even while on his first pipe the solicitor was rearranging the others, deciding which to smoke next. He tapped and poked and fondled, pausing to draw more nectar from his tankard. A happy man, though maybe his brother had been killed in the war, and his wife had left him. On the other hand he had plenty of work, and his daughter called once a week.

'I wonder what you'd spin about me if I was sitting there.'

'Lurid yarns,' he said.

'I'm sure.'

'I may go to Queen's Bay. There's nothing for me in Nottingham anymore.'

'Was there ever?'

'I was brought up there. But I've always wanted to get away.'

'Why does everyone make such a fuss about leaving the place they were brought up in?'

The man got another pint, lit his second pipe. Grandfather Merton rolled a hundred fags a week, and had his quart of ale on Sunday. Order was the spice of life. 'I loved my grandparents more than my own parents.'

'Children often do. My grandfather wasn't very lovable. When we went on a visit we had even more Bible than we got at home. I don't think my grandmother liked him, either. I loved her, so perhaps that's why I've never wanted to be married. I suppose I'll go on like that.'

He hoped for her, and feared for himself. 'I live from day to day. Hard to do much else.'

'You do seem taken up with writing, though.' He thought she only half liked the idea. Admit nothing in case it didn't happen. 'I'm not sure yet.'

'We wouldn't be human if we weren't taken up with something, would we?'

'There's nothing else I can do.' Wondering what would become of them spun his thoughts into a maelstrom. 'I only know I love you. You're the reason I like being alive.'

She gripped his arm. 'We have more in common than you think. Let's go upstairs before I faint. But first I must ask the manageress to wake us at six. If I'm not on duty before nine I'll get shot. You can sleep off your excesses if you like.'

The solicitor, or whatever he was, emptied the dregs of his tankard on to the dottle in the ashtray as decisively as if all his past life was there; stood up as if in fact he had been four years in the army; and tugged a crease out of his waistcoat as if in the future he would do something that would startle the world. Then he walked into the street.

They were going upstairs. 'I've paid the bill,' she said. 'Came to four quid.'

He was enraged at her highhandedness. 'I was going to do that.'

'It's my pleasure as much as yours. Just think of the difference in our pay.'

He didn't want to, had enough cash to settle their reckoning.

She caught him up as he put the key in the door. 'Don't mope.'

'I never mope,' he swung around.

Her gaze wavered. 'All right. Pay the next one. I won't mind. I'm a modern woman. We'll stay at the Ritz. You'll be washing cups and saucers for the rest of your life.'

In the room she embraced him. 'I love you dearly. I know I should have talked to you about it first. Sorry.'

The nightgown slipped down to her pale blue stockings. 'Gets cold in these places.'

He wondered how many of them she had known. 'Where did the stockings come from?'

'My grandmother's trunk. Funny how long things keep.' Her body was cool, as if she had bathed in a stream and dried herself. 'Don't put your pyjamas on,' she said, 'or I'll think you're still at the hospital. We'll get warm in bed.'

His grandmother must have worn similar stockings before she married, though Merton, the domineering old blacksmith who even as a young man must have been old, hadn't allowed it afterwards. Nor did he imagine Merton would have counted down from a hundred to hold himself back and give more pleasure – the least he could do to prove his love, though what kind of love could it be that must be proved? On the other hand, was there any sort of love which didn't need proving? Perhaps the only value of such thoughts was their effect in holding him back, in which case any words were a form of love for her, if not actual proof, and as if by way of acknowledgement she guided his fingers to her mouth and took them into the warmth.

Impossible to read anyone's mind, detect secret thoughts breaking like bubbles out of the murk. You only knew for a certainty what people thought when they spoke, and unless they were in anguish you could not know what they felt, because who would speak except out of love or anguish? Even in anguish you must not speak, and what could be said in love soon reached its limits. There were many different reasons for anguish, but only one for being in love.

Her eyes closed, face in repose, breasts slack across her chest. The weight on his arms was inflexible, until they bent so that he could kiss her. Where she was, he did not know. They weren't in the same country, he not with her if she was wondering where she was, because he could never know and neither could she – if she was at all concerned, which he hoped she was not. Knowing nothing about her made him want to be so far in her that they were one being.

Yet so as to know why he loved her he wanted to know why she loved him – as if her reasons would provide more information about himself than about her. But he had to glean what he could from whatever she chose to give away. Maybe she wanted to know the secrets of herself from what he said about her, though she knew well enough who she was, and while her self-knowledge might make her the stronger of the two, it also made her more vulnerable, because he certainly knew who he was, especially when he didn't try to find out. He relaxed the strain on his elbows and let himself pour into her.

'We'd better get some sleep, or the wind will blow us away in the morning.'

'Over the Downs, I expect.'

'To a worse place than that,' she said, 'if I'm not mistaken.'

He stroked her under the sheets.

'No more hanky-panky, my sweet. Set me off again, and I'll be so bleary-eyed they'll rag me unmercifully in the mess. Let's just drop off like innocent babes.'

He moulded himself against her. 'Like brother and sister?'

'Sounds exciting.' She turned for a kiss, and he pressed her under him until she relented, and he thrust uncaring, empty and without thought, the four-stroke cycle pistoning on and on until he was satisfied. Then he put out the light.

Chapter

❦ TWENTY-FIVE

'You're full of malice,' she reminded him.

'Do you think so?' Perhaps she was right. He was learning fast. You learn quicker when people insult you than if they say they love you.

'Yes, I bleddy do.'

'Thanks for the news.'

'It ain't news to me, I'll tell you that.'

Five minutes seemed to go by.

'Why do you say I'm full of malice?'

'I should have known from the beginning. I suppose I did. I felt it, anyway. But I didn't say owt.'

They sat in a pub downtown.

'If you'd said it, I'd have known where I stood.'

'I wasn't sure. It only crossed my mind.'

'Lots of things cross *my* mind.'

She was scornful. 'I can just imagine. But you never tell 'em, do you? Sly, and full of malice – that's what you are.'

Perhaps he was. He knocked back his whisky, went to get more, and a gin-and-It for her. She was near to crying. 'You didn't even give me a proper address when you went to Berkshire. You could easy have done it. It wouldn't have hurt you.'

He was sorry, and touched her hand. 'I knew I wouldn't be gone for long.'

She pulled away. 'Five weeks nearly.'

He had asked her out to tell her that he didn't want to see her anymore. 'You don't call that malice?' she said.

'I wanted to tell you how things were.'

'You think I didn't know what was coming?' She was bitter, and self-taunting. 'I knew it from the beginning, but hoped it wasn't true. Nobody's got that much rottenness in them, I told myself.'

Not having anything bad to say about her did not make him feel any better under her corroding accusations. She looked fit, the colour in her cheeks not from rouge. He knew nothing about her. Only what she told him, and what he could see. He knew more about Nora because there was so much to know – so much he didn't know and might never know.

'Why don't you look at me? You never look at me.'

'I don't do anything else.'

'Allus at other people. If you don't look at me you can never know owt about me.'

He knew everything about her, right to the bottom of the barrel. But maybe that was the same as knowing nothing. He couldn't tell himself what it was that he knew about her. There was too much. He didn't know where to start.

'I loved you,' she said. 'You know I did.'

'I'm sorry.'

'I still love you.'

He nodded. He loved her, but was aware of how crude he could be under his veneer of adaptation to that world which only seemed better because he knew so little about it – though he didn't doubt that he was part of it.

'I loved no one before you,' she said. 'I thought we were going to be together for always. I took it for granted. Wasn't that daft?'

He only wanted to get away from her. 'I'm sure it wasn't.'

She laughed, as if talking to someone else, tapped his arm playfully, her old self again. 'I dreamed last night that we had a wedding, but the funny thing was I woke up with tears on my face. We was coming out of the church, and people was chucking confetti over us.'

Entrenched silence was the only response, sandbags behind

– and mud in front that you waded through without flinching. 'Some dreams are good. And some are bad.'

She was morose again. 'If I knew the difference, why was I crying when I woke up? It was a happy dream, worn't it?'

'You would think so.'

Another five minutes went by. Maybe the drink would cheer her up. Inability to say anything might indicate a lack of honesty and wit. But the deliberate holding back could be a weapon. He didn't intend it to be, he had nothing to say. She drummed the table with her thin fingers. 'I was happier while the dream was on than I'd ever been in my life. I'll never forget it.'

'That's marvellous.'

'So why did I wake up crying?'

'Who can say?'

'That's what I'd like to know.'

'You knew, that's why.'

'Knew what?'

'You knew it in your sleep. Dreams can never be real. I've had dreams, and I was glad they weren't real. I've woken up happy because it was only a dream.'

'I suppose that's how it is,' she said.

'I reckon so.'

She trembled.

'Are you cold?'

'I don't know. I might be warm. I'm not sure. I think I'm all over the place. I don't know where I am.'

'You'll be all right.'

'Will I?' It was a plea.

'I'll guarantee it.'

'It's all right for yo'.'

It wasn't, but it was no use telling her, because she couldn't be expected to believe him. It would turn out to be more all right for her than it would ever be for him, but she wouldn't believe that either. Nor could he, but he had to think something to avoid his destruction.

'Do you love somebody else?'

Her question was meaningless, because he had never loved her.

'Do *you*?' he retorted.

She laughed, the same arid tone. 'I can't be in love with anybody else, can I?'

He supposed not. Time slipped by in silence, and he hoped an earthquake would swallow them, or at least him. 'There are plenty more men in the world.'

'I could kill you.' She assumed that he knew what he was saying. 'It's malice, that's all I can say. Nowt but malice.'

'Say that word once more, and I'll smack you in the chops.'

'I don't care what you do. You've done too much already for me to care.'

He seemed genuinely surprised. 'Have I?'

'You know you have. You're not that daft, I do know that much.'

'Thanks.'

'It's no thanks to me.'

'I was hoping it might be.'

'If I'm not right about that I might as well hang myself. I hate the sight of you.' They stared at each other. 'No, I don't.' She reached for him, and they kissed, in the middle of the noisy pub. They could bicker for an eternity, to the end of their lives, and then there would be no reason getting on at him for wanting to leave her. 'Aren't we daft?' she smiled. 'Everybody's looking at us.'

He held her hand. 'They must think we're a right couple of lovebirds.'

'I suppose they do.'

'I'm sorry.'

'You don't need to be. It's nobody's fault.'

'I'm still sorry, though.'

'If only we kept our traps shut. That'd be best, wouldn't it, duck?'

He nodded. There were things best not said, lest you be accused of malice. She would find a bloke who was loving and loyal, worth twenty of him, and get married, have kids in a nice house, and live happily ever after. That was what she deserved. She looked into his eyes. 'I know you've packed me in, but will you come to the house now and again?'

She might as well have pole-axed him, but he pressed her hand, and recalled a framed print in his grandmother's parlour

286

of an adoring youth and his sweetheart, a couplet underneath which said: 'If you love me as I love you, nothing will ever part us two.'

'Of course I'll see you again.'

'I shouldn't have asked.'

'Why not?'

'I'm ashamed.'

'A man might ask as much.'

'I want to die,' she said.

'What the hell for?'

'You wouldn't know, would you?'

He was afraid. 'Yes, I would.'

'How do you know?'

'I would, that's all.'

'Are you sure?'

The hot sting of her untouched gin slashed into his face.

In the open air by the pub door he was afraid to bang into walls or people. The pain burned his lungs. He coughed and sweated and cursed. He would pulverise her. But there were two entrances, and she'd gone out through the other, having had the last word, right enough, which made him feel better because he supposed it was just. Less blind than he thought, he swabbed the sting away, ducts overflowing on to his jacket.

He walked between shops and offices, closed, shuttered – dead to the world. The whisky he had drunk in the pub mushed his brain. His mother had scrubbed at an estate agent's twice a week and took him with her when he was four. He observed everything from a corner, and one morning a clerk gave him a penny, a large copper coin he looked at for days before knowing what to do with. Who was that person, and where was he now? People you once knew were dead, or had become too old for you to know who they were if you passed them on the street. Soon everyone would be dead, and so would he, and in the meantime Lillian had faded into the evening, and maybe she was right in saying that he didn't look at her when they were together. But on his own he saw no one else: she was on the bus, knees drawn up, peering at her image in the window, as he had often seen her doing.

In Parliament Street he walked into a café for a cup of coffee and a cheese cob. Students, dressed much like him, and barely younger, joshed each other. A dark-haired youth pushed a pastry into the face of his blond friend, and when the bald proprietor told them to clear out Brian was surprised that they obeyed. Scorning their behaviour, he wished he could share in whatever they were given to learn. But he was on his own, under the guidance of an interior gyro compass which pointed in a direction right for him and nobody else.

He sat by the fireplace after breakfast.

'You look all dressed up and nowhere to go,' Vera said.

Which was exactly how he felt.

'Why don't you go out somewhere?'

'I intend to.'

'Go up and see Lillian.'

Arthur, glue-eyed at the *News of the World*, leered. 'She's chucked 'im. She's got somebody else.'

'And who might that be?' Brian said.

Arthur laughed. 'The vicar, I suppose.'

He went upstairs for his jacket. Nora's door key was a reminder that he need never feel like a refugee. But he was idle, lackadaisical, short-tempered, only happy when in his room writing about Merton's family over and over again, the same anecdotes until it seemed he had invented them.

Without reason to leave, or cause to go, he typed a copy of each letter sent to Nora, as a journal for himself. Every few days a cheerful response came back, but absence dimmed her just sufficiently to make his desire more tormenting.

Downstairs, he said to Arthur: 'Come on, let's go out.'

'I'm just reading about this man, caught in bed with his mam.'

Vera snatched the paper away. 'That stuff'll turn your brain.'

'Teacher says I ain't got one.'

'Tell him he's a bleddy fool, then.'

'Teachers are numbskulls these days,' Seaton pronounced from the fireplace.

Brian was at the door. 'Are you coming, or aren't you?'

On the bus Arthur asked: 'Where are we going?'

'Misk Hill.'

'What for?'

'A walk. It'll do us good.'

They sat on the top deck.

'My feet'll sweat,' Arthur said.

'I'll buy some ice-cream to cool 'em down.'

Arthur squeezed his hand. 'Good owd Brian!'

In Hucknall Market he looked at the map. 'See that church?'

Arthur glanced. 'You shouldn't point at a church.'

'Why not?'

'Grandma towd me not to. She said it was wrong. Don't know why.'

'Maybe it is. But you know what's inside?'

He gave a horse-laugh. 'God?'

'Byron's heart's buried there.'

'Who's he?'

'A great poet.'

He bought ice-cream from a barrow. Arthur threw the paper down, licking before it could melt. They walked along a street of small houses towards the outskirts. 'Is the heart still beating?'

'I shouldn't think so.'

'Who ripped it out of his body?'

'A surgeon, I guess.'

'Was he still alive?'

Brian laughed. 'He died in Greece.'

'Did he fall in?'

'In?'

'You said 'e pegged out in grease.'

'Greece is a country.'

Arthur looked at him slyly. 'Must be slippy.'

Brian wanted to go to Argos and Sparta. Thermopylae and Thebes, from one landscape of ruins to another.

'Boris would have ripped it out while he was alive.'

'Boris?'

'Karloff.' Arthur prodded him and laughed, falling into step. 'I saw it in a film. He'd have ripped it out, and pushed the body over a cliff. Then he'd have got hanged.'

'You've seen too many pictures.'

'I love 'em. I could go every day, 'xcept I don't get enough money. I can get into X-pictures now. I tell the bloke on the door I'm sixteen, and he believes me because I'm tall.'

'What about school? Don't you like learning?'

He guffawed. 'I hate school. Soon I'll be able to get a job and earn some money.' He remarked on the tidy gardens of new houses and neat bungalows. 'If I'd got one I'd grow things, like grandad. We do gardening one afternoon a week at school, and I like that. They show us how to plant things. I'd like to live in one of them houses. If I earn a lot of money I'll save up and get one.'

A large black farm dog strained at its chain by a barn door. Arthur took a penknife from his pocket.

Brian shouted above the barking, 'What's that for?'

He opened the blade. 'If it comes for me, I'll kick its fangs down its throat.'

'It won't touch you. It can't get loose.'

Brian's airforce boots didn't convince him. Arthur ran into a wood, and came out sharpening a stick. 'The next fucking dog as yaps at me gets this in its ribs.'

'You're a case,' Brian said.

Arthur waved it about. 'If I'd got some cord I'd mek a bow and arrers. Then I'd pin it to the ground. I hate dogs barking at me.'

'You sound like grandad.'

'That owd bastard.'

'I thought you liked him.'

'He towd me off for pulling up his taters.'

'You wouldn't like anyone who pulled up your potatoes, would you?'

'I was only six. I wanted to see what was underneath.'

At Misk Farm they climbed a stile, and a dog's milder protest didn't reach the button of Arthur's wrath. 'Yo' bin up 'ere before?'

'I used to bike it after work.'

A dead branch cracked through the trees. 'Who showed yer where it was?'

'I found it on the map. The top's over five hundred feet above sea level.'

'Will I be able to breathe?' He ran on to the plateau of a large field, arms in front like pistons, fair hair bristling, coming to rest at a gate with black and white cows beyond.

Suburbs started three miles away, houses and factories under mountainous cloud. Faint haze emphasised a rich squalor of memorable dreams, his past in the semicircle from north to south already eroded by recent travels, and the X-ray that severed him from those people who lived between his favourite perch and the chosen river.

'It's smashin' up 'ere.' Arthur hurled a stick. 'I'll come up on my own now I know where it is. When I start wok, I'll gerra bike.'

A shunting train was pinpointed by feathers of smoke. Brian held him tight. 'Don't ever leave it. It's your hill.'

'Eh, fuck off!' Arthur broke away. 'Are yo' trying to fuck me, or summat?'

Brian laughed. 'Come on, loony, let's get down. Maybe I'll buy you another choc-ice.'

'I like you when you tek me out and buy me things,' Arthur said. 'I'll buy yo' summat when I'm earning twenty pounds a week.'

'Don't call me Chuck.' His fingers tightened at the pint jar. 'I was christened Charlie, and a bonny baby I was. The church stank rotten when they dipped me. And it worn't in Jordan water either, though it should a bin. I expect I was terrified in my swaddling clothes, because who wouldn't be at that age? Or any age, come to that. I've allus thought it should be agen the law to christen anybody before twenty-one. A vote, a name, and a rifle, that's what I'd call the perfect society. Russia ain't like that. Still, nowhere is, is it?'

'We've got to keep hoping,' Brian said.

'I know, but I was fed up with people threatening to set the dog on me. All I know is I left school at fourteen to work in a factory, and though I'm not complaining, because somebody's got to do it, I don't like being told it's good for me. You know what it's like. I'd get out tomorrow if I could. Anybody would, with any sense. All them middle class boggers want us to work in factories so's they don't have to do it. You can't blame 'em, but that's why all the Party members from the bourgeoisie go on about the noble working class, and what a hero Stakhanov was for tripling production in a single shift. I'll bet his mates wanted to murder him for showing them up as slackers.

'So when Comrade Gerald got up at the meeting in his tweed coat and red tie to yap about the dignity of labour and the revolutionary power of the masses the other day I got mad – and let him have it. Phil Greenwood and Henry Priestly tried to stop me shouting, but I had to tell 'em what was what, and I was the only one on the platform who knew. The people in the audience laughed, but Paul Sandby and Tom Butler dragged me out, the vicious boggers thumping me as they went. My wife ain't said a dicky-bird to me since, and Percy won't speak to me, either. I could cry, though, I could. I could cry like a baby, because I don't think I wanted to say what I said, even though I'd been thinking it a long time.'

'Maybe you should have argued it out instead of bottling it up.'

'I expect I should,' he said earnestly. 'But I'm a freeborn bleddy Englishman, Brian, Sherwood to the backbone, and I couldn't face them boggers trying to prove white is black, and me having to swallow it.' He paused and smiled. 'Anyway, you've listened like a pal. I've been waiting to talk to somebody, and when you walked through that door I knew my luck was in.'

'I couldn't get a word in edgeways. We'll have a whisky, and a couple of cigars on it.'

Charlie wagged a finger. 'In the Party you drink beer or tea, and smoke Woodbines. Owt like shorts and cigars at any time except at Christmas, and it's a clear case o' backsliding. I feel terrible being out on my own, but I still look after them hosiery machines at work. I might 'ate the bosses, but I do my bleddy stint, mate.' He sat back, smoking and sipping. 'You mek me feel like a toff.' A shade of gloom fell over his face. 'I'll have to find summat else, though. I still believe in the Rights of Man.'

'Everyone needs to belong,' Brian said. But he'd done with belonging. Don't join two pieces of string, Seaton always said, the only advice he agreed with. Belonging was for others.

'There's an anarchist mob in town,' Charlie said. 'They don't believe in any bloody government whatsoever.'

'Sounds sensible.'

Charlie gave a lantern-jawed all-hallows know-everything Nottingham laugh. 'You're more working class than I am, for all your posh talk.'

'It's a good job you've puffed my last cigar, or I'd get offended. Otherwise, thanks for the compliment.'

Charlie winked. 'I'll hang on in here for a while. A woman from work's coming in in half an hour, and I might have a nobble on. She's ever so nice.'

There was a saloon bar and several snugs, and getting out along the crowded corridor was one step at a time in case he splashed somebody's pint or stepped on their toes. Inside a small room, against a wall by the half-open door, Lillian and Bert were holding hands, faces close, drinks and empty glasses between.

Even on the street he passed nothing without a quick photographic appraisal, faces stored in the vaults for later use. He wanted to break in, tell her not to listen, to run, to save herself. But she was a grown woman and knew what she was doing. Bert might be good for her, and she for him. His oldest blood-brother cousin had stolen his sweetheart, had at one swoop robbed him of two people he loved. A likelier story was that they had met in town by accident and were having a casual drink. Impressions that came to him when he was alone were more vivid for being shared with no one else.

Chapter
❧ TWENTY-SIX

Kids ran wild in the terrace, squealing as if the Turks had got among them with the bayonet.

His room was a refuge until he could go back to Nora – who understood him as much as he wanted to be understood by anybody. More than that would be an obstacle to his tolerance of himself and others. He listened to music, pulled away only when his mother called that food was ready, or when Fred came up to get something from his cupboard, brought back to real life as sharply as when, on nightwatch in the paddi field, a squeak of morse shot him to alertness from a satisfying snatch of sleep.

'Fuck off!' Arthur called. 'Leave me alone' – kicked the front door for refuge because four youths were punching into him.

The squeak of the window, and Brian called for them to stop. 'There are four of you to only one of him.'

'Bollocks!'

The biggest landed a bang at Arthur's head, who lammed back with his fist, shirt ripped and nose streaking blood. By the time Brian would get through the parlour they'd be safely away, and knew it, so he climbed on to the windowsill, let himself hang by his hands, and dropped the last ten feet. He pulled the two biggest aside, smacked their heads together, and lashed out at the others, till all four went clobbering down the street.

Arthur stared. 'You jumped from the bedroom winder!'

As if it was the Empire State Building. But he had scraped his knees, wouldn't rub the pain. 'They'd have pummelled you to bits.'

'No, they wouldn't. I was winning.' His head looked like a battered tomato. 'Yo' stay down 'ere, and I'll go up to the bedroom. I wain't tell Mam and Dad if you show me how to do it.'

Brian pushed him along the terrace. 'Let's have you inside, and wipe the blood off your snout.' Arthur trawled a jersey sleeve across his nose, the rawboned stalwart who would carry his own weight for any distance that fate or an army put on him. 'You'll break your legs, unless you fall in a special way. We learned it in the air force.'

'No, you didn't. You're limpin' a bit. I'm not blind.'

'We'll go in the woods and find a tree,' Brian promised. 'Then I'll teach you how to land properly.'

'All right.' But he couldn't help blurting out as soon as they got in the house that Brian had hurled himself from the bedroom window to stop some youths bashing him up.

On the way to the bus stop he saw Bert crossing the cobbled street as if he owned it, and went towards him with open arms. 'What are you doing down this way? I was hoping I'd bump into you, though. We can go to the White Horse for a drink.'

'They aren't open yet.' Bert marked the line of the paving with a foot, as if about to play hopscotch.

He took his arm, to turn him around. 'We can go for a walk till they are. Talk about old times. Or come on home. We can have a bite to eat. I haven't seen you for ages.'

Bert stepped away, mouth set. 'Well, I suppose you've got to know, sooner or later.'

He knew, right enough. 'What's that, then?'

'I've got a date.'

'Ditch her, and come with me.'

'I can't.'

'Dates are ten a penny. You've often said so.'

'It's with Lillian.'

He bit his tongue into silence, eyes half closed. 'What do you mean?'

'We're courting. She towd me she'd packed you in, so I saw nowt wrong in it.'

Brian stood, as if to get a clearer look. 'I can't think of anything better.'

'Shake on it?'

'Sure.'

Bert wasn't convinced. 'She's a smashin' gel. A real treat.'

'As long as you look after her.'

'You mean like yo' did?'

They'd talked about him. What had she told him? He was pricked with guilt. 'Better than that.'

'I can't think why you packed her in. A marvellous woman.'

'Neither can I.'

'Well, you did,' he said slyly.

People packed each other in all the time. 'Remember me to her.'

'What do you tek me for?' They shook hands again. 'I'm taking her to Yates's.'

'Good for you.'

'Got somebody else?'

'No.'

'I've never known anybody as crafty as yo',' Bert said with a wink. 'Except me.'

'Brothers in arms.'

He hoped they would be happy. 'For ever and ever.'

The city library, a fine specimen of Co-op Gothic, stayed open late on Saturday, and he skimmed through books about Malaya so as to make his account more convincing. Wallace's *Malay Archipelago* filled half a notebook.

People sat at tables like clerks in an enormous office. When a man spoke to a woman a hissing came from all sides as if he had fallen into a snake pit. He got up for an atlas, and on a map of the world traced his slow boat to the Orient, unable to believe he had been there. He didn't know where he was, and in order to get back to reality walked out into the freezing drizzle, and stopped at the nearest beer-off on Mansfield Road to buy two quarts of ale. The bus for Cinderhill was almost empty, and he read a few pages of his typescript on the way to Tom Boak's.

'He's still in the bath,' Wendy said, 'and I've got to go up and scrub the bookshop grime off his back.' Her hair was cut short, the parting neater, her grey eyes suggesting a livelier mood than usual. 'Go into the salon, and talk to Grace. I'll be down in a bit. He hasn't got a very big back.'

Grace wore a pencil skirt and cashmere sweater, pearls strung across her small bosom, shapely legs stretched out from the leather pouffe. Having paid six bob for *Noises of the Oak* he couldn't think of anything else to say except: 'I liked your poems. Are you going to read some tonight?'

'I might try a couple of new ones.' She wrinkled her nose at the shouting and laughter from upstairs. 'What about you?'

'I'll give them a story. Do you think it will be a full house?'

'Full enough. Anne Jones is back, so I hear.'

'Maybe she'll liven the place up a bit.'

Grace frowned. 'She's very opinionated.'

'Don't you like her?'

'That would be flattery.'

He liked everyone he liked to be liked by everyone else, and wondered what Grace said about him when he wasn't there. Tom came in, hair swept back and shirt open to the waist, damp curls on his chest smelling of carbolic – his usual spruce appearance. He unscrewed the top from a quart of ale.

'Mighty generous,' he said to Brian. 'We'll drink it before the others come.'

'I'll wait for coffee,' Grace said.

'Novel finished?' Tom asked him.

'I'm writing short pieces.'

'Stories?'

He mentioned reading Maupassant and Flaubert, and Tom opened his arms in despair. 'Get stuck into Defoe and Fielding. Dip your lily-white hands into the living language. Drink style. Bathe your effete sensibility in the robust vernacular. Leave the foreigners – bless 'em – till later, if you want to be an English writer.'

'Trying to preach me a sermon?' Brian stood up. 'I wouldn't read anything at all if I didn't bloody enjoy it.'

Tom lit a Woodbine. 'You ex-servicemen always get so excitable. I wish I could read Carlyle and Macaulay all over again. In Russia I had Ruskin in my tunic pocket. *Open Sesame* I think it was called, but it kept a head on my shoulders.' He sent Wendy into the kitchen to make the evening's sandwiches, and when Brian offered to help, said he should talk rather than waste his time. No one had much to say, however, so he put on a Schubert sonata. 'I don't suppose it'll animate us, but it's lovely stuff, all the same.'

Ted Gedling came in, wearing a black sombrero and an undertaker's cloak. He was followed by Jim Bailey who hugged a portfolio of engravings as if it was full of plans to organise the world into the perfect republic ruled by him.

'It's a reading night,' Tom said when they were settled. 'Anything, as long as it's in English.'

Ted revealed the colours of Notts Forest under his cloak. 'What are *you* reading?'

'I'm the chairman.'

Grace took a sheet of paper from her handbag. 'This is from a book I'm putting together.'

'Jim can start,' Tom said, 'being the eldest. We'll work down the evolutionary scale till we come to the young apes, meaning Ted and Brian.'

Jim pulled his beret from under the cat, and covered his baldness. 'I'll read a few pages from *The Horse's Mouth*. You all know about Gully Jimson, but for myself I can't have enough of him. Joyce Cary is the best writer of this century, though the snotty critics don't think so. Delights too many people, I suppose. Anyway, here goes.'

Grace recited a love poem out of her intensely private life, so precisely metred and internally rhymed that the matter seemed very personal indeed. Her husband managed a shop in town, and because nobody knew of any scandal it was assumed that their discretion was of an impenetrably high standard.

Ted Gedling read *Killer from the Coalmine*, a story in dialogue which, Tom winked, reminded him of D. H. Hemingway, or was it Ernest Lawrence? Certainly it wasn't easy to tell why two men waylaid the butty going home on Friday night and beat him half to death, though Ted explained it was because of some dark deed in his past.

Wendy led in someone Brian hadn't seen before, and Tom

stood up for a slim man of about fifty, in a grey suit and spats, who leaned a silver-handled cane against the bookcase, where it rested till the cat knocked it over. He had regular but worn features, icy blue eyes in deep sockets, wavy grey hair and a clipped moustache. Tom asked where he had been for the last three months.

'Laid up. Dyspepsia, mainly. I finished my book, though. The thirty-ninth.'

Ivor Raskell wrote mystery novels, Tom said, and not only got them published, but made a living. They were privileged to have him with them, if only for an hour − as if that was all anybody would be able to stand.

'Every book earns a hundred pounds,' Ivor said, 'and I'm supposed to live on it. Luckily I get translated into Swedish. I also write articles and short stories.' He talked as if they had come only to hear him, and Tom's expression said that was how it should be, though Ted glazed his features to show what he thought of such success.

'I enjoy your books,' Grace said. 'You keep me guessing to the end, and I like that.'

Anne Jones came in, a shadow by the door balancing a tin of biscuits on her head. 'They're good enough to be in Penguin Books,' she said, sitting next to Brian. 'Glad to see you back in the world of the living. I thought you'd had a haemorrhage.'

Tom took the wrapping from the biscuits and sent Wendy into the kitchen to set them on a dish. 'But leave a few for the shop.' His tone was neutral enough to be impolite. 'You're just in time to hear more readings.'

'I hurried all the way from the bus to hear the poems.'

Grace stopped shuffling her papers. 'I wonder whether you'll think it worth the effort?' She glowered, then looked down and exercised her throat. Brian needed all his attention and wit to understand her poems, but felt she had worked hard to make them subtle and profound, and leave a trace of reality. Anne liked them, but Grace took her remarks as meaning something else, and Brian found it difficult to imagine what form Grace's loss of temper could take in the Boak salon, where an edgy peace was always more interesting than open conflict.

'Brian can start the prose ball rolling.'

His hand shook, which Ivor Raskell understood. 'I wouldn't read any of my hacksaw stuff for a pension. Anyway, it takes guts, and being a writer I don't have any. All a writer needs is patience, persistence, hard work, and luck. And perhaps a little talent – but not all that much.'

Ted Gedling burned another hole in the pact of non-belligerence. 'Do you mind if I write that down?'

'I don't mind if you choke on it,' Ivor responded, pleasantly enough.

'We must let the young keep their illusions' – Jim Bailey opened his portfolio – 'otherwise they'll have nothing to lose when they get older.'

Ted scribbled that, as well. 'What an evening!'

'I'm partial to a bit of flattery.' Jim showed sepia-looking engravings of a lithe nude woman whose face was hidden by a band of hair. Anne held one out, and looked at Grace, who seemed too engrossed to notice. 'We could produce a magazine between us,' Tom said, 'with all this talent. But now it's time for reading.'

Brian unfolded his papers. An old blacksmith was walking into town to buy a dog. The last one was so ill-treated it had strayed on to the railway line and been killed. Merton was dressed in his best suit, boots, bow tie, watch chain, flower in his buttonhole, and flat cap. Tall, a glare in his good eye, everyone got out of his way. The events took place about ten years ago, but he was old-fashioned even then. He lived what he read, became the person he told about, wasn't altogether glad to be back in the Boak house, though he obviously couldn't stay inside what he had written, and must get used to accepting no place at all as his permanent dwelling.

'Not bad,' Ivor said. 'In fact I enjoyed it. You always hear something interesting at Tom's. You certainly brought the old chap to life for me, though it's got too much D. H. Lawrence. You'll have to get rid of that bloody nuisance, for a start.'

'I found it a bit Rupert Brookish,' Ted Gedling muttered, 'especially where you go on about the sky.'

Anne asked him to show her the typescript. 'There's a place where the narrative needs expanding. I'll mark it with a pencil.'

'Would such a person,' Grace wondered, 'actually buy a dog? Wouldn't a friend or neighbour give him one?'

If they liked it, he was glad. If they didn't, it wasn't important. There was more where that came from, though he wondered how long it would take to get to it.

'Another thing,' Ivor said, 'is that if you start sending your stuff to magazines, make sure it's neatly typed, and double spaced on good quarto paper with twenty-five lines to a page. It makes a difference, let me tell you.'

He gave more practical advice, and Brian thanked him for taking so much trouble. After Ted's piece, exhaustion sucked him into a private chamber of the mind, and he felt his hand enclosed by another, till he was drawn back to the room, the lights dimmed for a Beethoven piano sonata. When he opened his eyes, the hand relaxed, the music finished, so that he wondered if he hadn't dreamed, though if he hadn't he didn't suppose she could have meant anything by it.

Life was too short. He wanted to write a novel. He was nearly twenty-three, and might be dead before he was thirty – a vast number of years away! Nine years ago he had left school and started work, and five years later he had gone to Malaya, at that time an unimaginable event in the future. So he changed his mind. Life was so long it seemed as if he was living forever, in which case it wouldn't matter when he died.

Coffee was brought in. 'For the road,' Tom said. 'It's only fit for mixing concrete anyway when Wendy brews it.'

Anne stood up. 'If you said that about me I'd pour it over your head – scalding.'

'I wouldn't say it about you, would I?'

She waved at Wendy. 'You might – once.'

'Men!' Wendy said.

Ted lovingly picked out a bit of dried horse turd and some old sock scrapings from an Oxo tin, and paused in stuffing his pipe when Jim Bailey said that Dos Passos hadn't written anything good since *USA*. 'Some say he's a traitor to the working class, with the latest stuff.'

'He's seen sense,' Tom said, 'which may be fatal.'

'Great novelists can do what they like,' Ivor said ruefully. Curtains drawn, the air was thick, too much being said, on one hand too trivial, on the other a sentence ambiguous enough to last a month. Brian's chest was fastened by a band of iron, a cough bringing a mouthful of salty phlegm from the depths. He decided to leave. 'I think I've got a poem coming on. Or a trilogy.'

'See you next week,' Tom said. 'We can't do without you.'

Life was too short. The place and the company also made him feel that life wasn't worth living, so he would see no one, get out of Nottingham, go back and gaze at the green waves while waiting for Nora at Queen's Bay – where he would write a novel.

Unable to sleep, he sat at his desk. Arthur grumbled, curled up like a cannonball. He looked through the typescript which he had read at Tom's, and found Anne's pencil scrawl: 'Meet me at the Shalimar on Monday about eleven, or else!'

When he woke, his lungs ached. That was the day he needed a refill, already so late that any delay could be dangerous. The lung was a paperbag working overtime, wearing thin and ready to burst if not pushed into quiescence by another thunderbolt of air.

She would be waiting. Or he might go, and she wouldn't be there. Anything could stop her being where she said she would be, for she was more unsure of her life than he was of his. One week she was with her husband, the next in London with relations. She was flexibility itself, attached yet free, as if neither family nor husband liked her and she didn't have the patience or resources to care.

The same coat was draped on the back of her chair, *The Listener* folded under her handbag. It was worth putting off his refill, to get one of the Cinderhill Group away from Tom Boak's house. 'I read your message.'

A sceptical twitch. 'I didn't think you'd come.'

He tried to look amused. 'I'm here, aren't I?'

She sipped her coffee. 'More fool you.'

Pride held back his sarcasm, an effective tactic to keep quiet. It worked. A smile showed her shapely lips. 'Are you glad you came, then?'

He wondered what he was doing, since he knew nothing

about her and wasn't much interested. 'Why did you ask me to?'

'I think your writing's good.' His laughter cracked through the café. 'And you've got TB.' A reason for silence, and anger with himself for having told people. 'I want to catch it off you.'

'You're crackers,' he said. 'If I was contagious I'd be on the buses all day, giving it to as many people as I could – not just you.'

'What a clever idea. Put it in a story.'

She stood, tall and somewhat gawky, with grey-brown eyes, short brunette hair, and a rather pronounced chin. 'My turn to get the coffee.' In the queue she took money out of a leather purse, and when she came back with the tray he noticed a wrinkle in her stocking.

'So you decided to come back to Nottingham!'

Her expression of panic and loss turned into a smile on sitting down. 'I'm the same person wherever I am.'

'I'm not sure whether I would be.'

'You're not me, are you?'

She treated herself too harshly – unless she was putting it on, and he couldn't be sure – inner scorn ready to overwhelm her and anyone close. She tapped a rhythm with her spoon, then spoke as if what she said was a continuation of what was in her mind. 'I haven't made him happy. My husband, I mean. He'll be glad to get rid of me.'

He offered a cigarette. She didn't smoke. 'Why should you make him happy?'

'Shouldn't I?'

'Has he made *you* happy?'

Her answer was too quick. 'Who could? Why should I expect anybody to make me happy if I can't do it myself?'

'I don't believe in happiness.'

Her features relaxed. 'It must simplify things no end.'

'If you expect to be happy you torment yourself so much that you never can be.' Being in the hospital had taught him something.

'I wish I'd heard that a long time ago.'

He leaned back, ash dropping from his cigarette. 'You wouldn't have believed it. You had to wait and hear it from me.' He wanted to go, but hoped she would break off first. 'I'll be leaving town in a few days. Somebody lets me use a cottage, where I can write.'

'I'd like to live on my own,' she said.

'Why don't you?'

'You can't just vanish.'

'Why not?'

'My husband wouldn't let me.'

'You're over twenty-one.'

'He hangs on to me.'

He laughed. 'You mean he keeps you, and gives you spending money? Why don't you get a job?'

'I suppose I should. I went to Exeter to read Law because my father wanted me to be educated, but I left in the second year. He didn't want me to, but I couldn't go on. I met a chap, and married him. If I was at home and leaned back in my chair like that my husband would tell me to stop in case I broke the legs.'

'Can't he afford to buy a new one?'

Laughter made her a different person. 'He'd remind me of all the work that went into it. It's not a matter of money, he'd say.'

He coughed, a handkerchief at his mouth. She leaned forward. 'Any blood?'

He showed her. 'Sorry.'

'Try harder.'

'No good. I'm cured.' He regretted not having gone for his refill, and resisted telling her in case she had an orgasm on the spot. She stood abruptly, as if realising he wasn't saying all that came into his mind – or as if he had served her purpose for that day at least. She asked, fastening her coat as they went out: 'When you go back to your cottage, will you come and say goodbye? If I'm still here, I mean.'

They walked by the theatre. What the hell did she mean? 'I hope you are.'

'Do you?'

He might as well say yes.

'You can give me a kiss.'

They stood at the edge of the pavement, people hurrying by. 'It's no good,' he said. 'I'm not contagious.'

'You've been coughing all morning.'

Maybe he was, at the moment. 'I was only trying to impress you.'

'You *are* funny!' she said, walking quickly away.

❧ TWENTY-SEVEN

He stacked wood outside the kitchen door, and brought the saw in so that it wouldn't rust. The sea gave up its bounty, days pulling endlessly along. He worked to get the place clean and livable, and eradicate the smell of damp, as thorough as if the CO's inspection was due in the morning. Windowframes looked glassless: Nora would appreciate a neat billet.

The inside finished, he worked in his shirtsleeves, clipping brambles from around doors and windows. He burned rubbish on the beach where dog roses grew out of the shingle, standing to leeward to avoid smoke. A letter from Nora proved that he lived there.

A Nottingham newspaper had published a story and taken another, both set in Malaya, and paid him three guineas. A magazine paid half a guinea for a poem about sunrise over the jungle. He opened the newspaper a dozen times a day to see his name in print.

Every morning, with a full fountain pen and a stack of paper before him, he wrote about Dick Spoak (instead of Boak) and those who went to his house, but he varied their relationships. Anne Jones fought with her husband, and Grace Rutland visited her boyfriend at his cottage in the country. In the story he made out that the person who was himself was in love with Anne, who in the end went away with Jim Bailey. As for Dick Spoak, the stove in the bookshop overturned while he was making love to Wendy, and they perished in the flames. Ted Gedling became a best-selling novelist.

Each morning he shaved, polished his shoes, washed socks and underwear, or opened his service 'housewife' to put a button on shirt or waistcoat. He cooked breakfast, managed on a sandwich for lunch, and made a quick meal in the evening, unwilling to stand more than half an hour at the stove.

There was little at the village shop beyond the rations, except bread and vegetables. The man behind the counter still carried a handlebar moustache from his time in the air force as an armourer, so the old lingo united them, and with a wink he passed Brian a tin of Spam and half a pound of bacon at little above the ration price.

After lunch he turned up the wooded lane and ascended the cliff to watch ships labouring through the equinoctial gales like logs of wood. Cut off from himself, he was more interested in the characters in his novel than his own life, so didn't envy the ships their journeys anymore.

He fell asleep on the sofa, and woke exhausted in the morning. Out of dreams that were too deep to get at him came the nightmare of Lillian and Bert and Nora endlessly asserting their views with venomous conviction, he unable to match their anger because any he might have was buried too deep either to be put into words or belittled by argument. One of the three was victorious, but he always woke before he could see what they would do. Shamed by his terror, he ran away, not wanting to know.

He traipsed about the house when he couldn't write – neither jot a tittle nor tittle a jot. People and places dissolved, and words were air instead of plasticine. The sea rested from its gales, the white flower of undulating spume tops striking the shingle like a cavalry regiment which had been given the wrong orders. His impeccably attired Death walked along the beach, but he whistled an SOS and passed undisturbed. Tormented by thoughts of the future, he decided that he didn't want to know whether or not he was to have one. He sat by the window at dusk, rubbed a hand through his hair to make sure the skull was still in place, then drew the curtains and went into the kitchen to quell ordinary hunger.

∽❦∽

A letter from Chuck Varley which he read at breakfast said: 'Dear Brian, your mother gave me your address. I just want to say I saw your story in the *Weekly Mirror*. I liked it, but you've got to forget your antics in Malaya and tell stories about working people. You know all about them, and that's the only material you ought to use. It's pure gold. I know that's what they used to say in the Party, but I'm talking about real people who don't know about any Party. I'll bet you're frothing at the chops by now, but I did like your yarn, only don't forget what I say. You've got a responsibility, so don't stay away from Nottingham too long. Everything's here for you, and I know you won't let us down. Your old pal, Charlie.'

He used the letter to make the fire, wanting to put factory, family and the town out of his mind as soon as possible and forever. Then he regretted not keeping it for Nora to see.

In Dover he looked up publishers' addresses in the library, inscribed the names on slips of paper, and shook them in a vase to choose. Rain drove against the window, beads of water gathering on the inside of the sill. He enclosed a letter with the parcel, keeping it unsealed so as to put in stamps for its possible return.

He stood in a queue and, weighed and paid, the novel bumped into a canvas sack. Books were written and published, so why not one from him? Smoking an after-lunch cigarette, he mused that he could only act if he thought he had nothing to lose, or didn't care whether or not he lost.

From the public call box he got beyond the snotty-sounding WAAF at the switchboard. But the line was bad. Bloody bomb damage, he supposed. 'Darling! How are you?'

He told her about sending his manuscript.

'Wouldn't it be wizard if you became famous?'

What could he say?

'Are you coping?' she asked.

He felt flat, unresponsive, far away, hoped she couldn't tell. When out of contact he was in love. 'Yes, sweetheart.'

'I can't wait to see you. Only four days. I've been so browned off lately, I can't tell you how good it is to hear your voice. I'm happy you're at the cottage. Now I can think of both with love.

I really miss you.' They would see what they could do about spending more time together.

He agreed, thinking nothing could be done. He would set fire to the house, and wonder how far out to sea the flames would be seen. Ashes and black stumps in the drizzle would be all that remained of his love. Fire sooner or later burns itself out – to be written into a poem which would itself be burned. 'I love you, but I've no more change. My last shilling's gone.'

'Goodbye, then, my dearest.'

Desolation overwhelmed him, knowing he loved her, that she stood between him and death. 'Goodbye, darling.'

He only knew who he was when with other people – unless he was writing, and he only knew who other people were when he was writing about them. But the people he wrote about were not the people he knew, and the people he knew were rarely the people he wrote about. Often, the people he wrote about were like himself, though not exactly him; he only glimmered traits or facets, and immediately forgot they might have any connection with him.

He was rarely able to transfer what was in his head on to the page without it seeming altered or distorted, or flat like thin ice with no water underneath, which melted in the sun before even his own face could be seen in it. He struggled to make scenes read the same when written about on paper as when he listened to them in his head before writing them down. But between one stage and the next something happened. Words and phrases which came to him as the instruments of transfer were too ordinary, and when fitted together did not reflect the feeling of his original inspiration. Sometimes, however, the effect was the same, clarity in the head translated in shining exactitude on to the paper, and sounding the same to the head when read back aloud. He used such a section as a kind of tuning fork, a standard to bring the rest of the story up to the same level. Confidence and enthusiasm led him to believe that he succeeded more times than not.

At Dover she kept her coat on in the café. 'I have a surprise for you. A present for both of us really – all wrapped up in pink ribbon.'

She's pregnant, he thought. 'Don't keep me in suspense, my love.'

'I wangled fourteen days, instead of seven.' Leaning close, she poured their tea. 'You needn't turn pale.'

'Did I?'

'Deathly pale. Expected me to say I was pregnant, eh?'

'I wondered.'

'That would let the cat out of the bag, wouldn't it?'

He had a vision of wading a mosquito-infested valley in the middle of Borneo, eluding the single-engined float plane.

'I give myself a good washing out every time.'

'And it works?'

She patted her stomach. 'Never fear.'

'I don't.'

'But you do look pale. You haven't been taking care. "He's lost weight," I said to myself when I got off the train. And you're coughing. We'll have to put a stop to that.'

She ate quickly, her first food since morning. 'You'd better finish that cake.' There was a queue on the pavement. 'I hate people waiting to jump into my shoes. Let's go, or we'll miss the bus.'

He noticed a darkening under her eyes. 'Every night, I'm done for,' she said, 'and can't sleep. That's why the MO took pity on me and gave me fourteen days.' Unpacking, she refolded each article for the drawer, an unnecessary neatness, he thought. On the ward her work cut her off, and she seemed so remote that he wanted to know her more than he had wanted to know anyone.

He would never succeed, so he loved her intensely, if he loved her at all, when she was absent. He didn't know the real Nora, and never would, did not know if he cared whether or not he would ever know her. Maybe there was no real Nora. The real Nora was the empty Nora who stood before him, the impregnable Nora. He didn't believe it. If he did, it would be him who was empty. You could never know anyone unless you turned into them, and then you wouldn't know them any better than they were able to know themselves – or than you were able to know yourself. Whenever he thought such things he was not himself. He wouldn't know her until he wrote about her, but at the moment he could only write about people he didn't know.

She straightened the clothes. The sight of her body dissolved all thought. He had made the bed after breakfast, as a good airman should, but she folded the blankets again and dropped the sheets on the floor for the washtub as if he had slept between them too long which, he thought, he probably had.

'Let me help.'

'I'd rather you didn't.'

He sat on the bed. 'I was too engrossed in my writing to do it properly.'

'Far more important.'

He held her, but it wasn't the time for kisses, the barometer being too low, weather due for a change, wind veering, moon waxing. Either the moment hadn't come, or it had gone.

'We'll dress for dinner,' she said. 'It's so long since we were together.'

'Too long.'

She drew away. 'Let's not brood on it' – took his arm, facing the mirror.

'Made for each other.'

She frowned. 'Father used to say that, and Mother hated it. Still, we do look good, don't we?'

Downstairs, she said: 'Get on with your writing, or whatever it is. Leave the rest to me. I was planning our evening on the train.'

Changed into his suit, he sat at the desk, revising a story, the clatter of pots sounding from the kitchen. He twisted half a dozen pages into the grate.

'You make wonderful fires. Mine usually go out.'

He took a bottle of wine from a cupboard by the fender. 'This is better than the stuff we used to drink in Malaya.'

'I suppose that place meant a lot to you.'

She seemed not to like the fact. 'My best friend was killed there.' She shivered, still in a thin frock.

He lay more wood on. 'You'll soon get warm. Baker, the star wireless operator on the station.' He sounded like the whisky-swilling planter he had never known. Then he caught

311

himself about to say something which he knew he should have grown out of. But he couldn't resist. 'I was by his side when a bandit got him.'

'Don't let it depress you.' She kissed his hand. 'I know what it is to lose someone.'

Not the same, he thought.

Leaves rippled in the forest, bullets ricocheting from the trunks of iron trees, voices buried except for words which he could not remember – and a crack in the undergrowth that scrubbed Baker forever. 'So I met you,' he said, 'to make sure there was enough wood for the fire. The only proof I didn't stop a communist bullet is that I'm here in this cottage by the seashore.'

A slight pressure would snap the stems of the thistle-shaped glasses. He had survived another kind of bullet. 'We had a dozen once,' she said. 'Open the wine, and I'll go up and change.'

She was not in tune, no reason why she should be, but no one ever was with anyone, a happy situation otherwise you couldn't speculate on what they were thinking.

She wore a low cut white satin gown, beads around her neck. 'I said I would put on a dress, though it took some getting into. Do me up, darling.'

Hard to say for how long the jungle would leave him alone. He remembered a full length portrait of Queen Alexandra on a cigarette card. 'You look beautiful.'

'They knew how to get themselves up in those days. None of your New Look for them.'

He fastened the line of pearl buttons dividing left and right, and kissed her pale neck, from where the warm hair was taken vertically up. She loved wearing her uniform, he knew, everyone needing a disguise from the world. 'When my sister Sarah comes we often dress up, out of the old trunk under the eaves. We do look a pair, I can tell you.'

To embrace her in such regal rig would distort the illusion of the courtier, who was here only to pour her wine – in the hope of getting her drunk. The shine of her expression told him she needed relaxing after her labours, and the slow journey on British Railways, therefore he must get her to respond to his passion. She was firm-mouthed against all relaxation, a state nevertheless interesting because he would try to break it. Being the victim of her moods, she had so few that he could use them to his advantage.

The ox-tail soup came out of a tin. 'But we live like that, these days.'

'Delicious.'

'On tuppence a week before the war you could have a cook and a bottlewasher.'

'Not the same today.'

'Are you glad?'

'Things change,' he said. 'There's nothing you can do about it.'

'Sensible. You're looking better already.' Her lips trembled. 'I feel peculiar tonight.'

'Better than starting off feeling normal. Then you would finish the evening all mixed up, and that wouldn't do.'

'I love you,' she said, 'because you really think about me.' His system was too mechanical, and he was often surprised at getting the right response. Treatment at the hospital was on similar principles, and she had known cause and effect to succeed countless times – as it had with him. She believed in it.

'You're right,' she said, when he shared his thoughts, but could tell by her glance that she was uncertain, as if hoping there might be a way beyond such ready reckoning. He also hoped there was, but couldn't yet see how.

She came in with the blue Dalton platter as if she were a duchess serving a farm bailiff, reminding him of what his Aunt Ada must have looked like, waiting at table as a tall young woman. Fried Spam, boiled potatoes and cabbage: 'A camper's meal, but it's the best I can do. I'll get some meat tomorrow.'

He poured more wine. 'What a banquet!'

They touched glasses. 'I'll always love you,' he said, 'but I want to know everything about you. Then I'll never leave you.'

She laughed. 'Otherwise you might?'

His guard was down, when every utterance must be rehearsed. 'Never.'

'I sometimes think you're a villain.'

'I try not to be. Tell me about your other boyfriends.'

'Only one, before I met you. I've led a dreary and blameless life.'

'What was he like?'

It was too painful, or she didn't trust him. But she did. 'He was good-looking, tall and dark, with beautiful wavy hair. I'm afraid I fell rather heavily for him. But our love was unrequited. Do you know what I mean?'

He might, if she would explain.

'He was fond of other men. Well, we were together once or twice, but it never came to much. He said he would marry me when the war was over. Wanted a family and children. I might have settled for that.'

Hanky-panky of that sort had gone on at Kota Libis, but he had been sleeping with Mimi, and wouldn't have been interested, anyway. As for the others, they were only lads, except for one of the sergeants, of whom it was said that you'd better not drop the soap in the shower when he was passing by.

'Now there's nothing between us you don't know about,' she said. 'It happened five years ago, after all. But he wasn't like you. You're a man who can love me. That must have been why I chose you.'

'I'm privileged that you did.' Only delicate advances would do. By allowing himself to be chosen, he had chosen her, which she didn't know yet. He preferred it that way.

She made coffee. He smoked a cigar. When the wine was finished they sat by the fire, her body close. She was a complicated watch with countless small pieces, measuring time till some accident shattered it – impossible not to love her. He had come full circle, bone idle and safe, which was how life must be for all he had to do – an as yet indefinable yearning, scoffed at because it seemed out of character with someone who had only believed in action.

To say nothing was death. Her skirt trailed before the fire. She was held in by her gown, encased in her skin. She was weeping, and since it was clearly not because of him, but out of grief for her lost boyfriend, for herself, maybe for all the world, or simply a mawkish poppy day from which he was excluded, there was no point in asking why. He knelt to kiss

314

her. 'Don't be unhappy. I'm sorry about it all.' His voice failed, as if he too had been in love with the bastard who had scarred her for life.

Embers winked in the fireplace, like a German city after a raid. 'Help me,' she said.

'I'll do anything for you.'

'I must go to bed.'

Upstairs he undressed her. She put an arm around him. 'Why did you make me so drunk?'

'You're just done-in after such a long day.'

'Are you ashamed of me?'

He smiled. 'No.'

'I would be.'

'You're not me.'

'I'm not, am I, darling? Just as well, I suppose.'

He'd never seen her so helpless. 'Go to sleep.'

'I can't be without you.'

'I love you.' He walked down the stairs.

At half past ten no window was lit along the lane. Trees swayed and rattled. He wanted to walk to the main road, get the first train out of Dover, buy a ticket to Nottingham. He would run up the station steps, dive into a taxi and go to Lillian's. Something was wrong, but he couldn't think what – as if she was dying after a haemorrhage. A stupid idea. She would spit in his eye. He threw down his cigarette. A policeman stood at a fork in the lane. 'Where are you going?'

'For a walk.'

'Do you live at Queen's Bay?'

'Yes.'

'Do you have any means of identity?'

A passport in an inside pocket.

'Thank you very much, sir. That's all right. We have to check now and again, around here.'

Walking back via the undercliff, someone zigzagged across the beach, headed towards the footpath leading to the cliff top. There were two men. Let the copper catch them if he could. Maybe they were smuggling butter and brandy from France, and if so – good luck to them.

⁂

Nora was asleep.

A tin drum was banging him into battle as he lit the stove to make coffee. The rattle of cups and saucers woke her as he walked upstairs. He picked her vest and bloomers from the floor. She was robust, fit for life, renewed, arms towards him. 'I slept as I've never slept before.'

He was agonised, exhausted.

'And you, my sweet?'

'Never felt better.'

He threw cold water over his body, boiled a kettle to shave. A canyon in the grey ash of last night's fire was filled with crumpled poems and stories, reducing the weight of luggage in case he fled. He smiled, would never do it, could not control moving pictures that played in his brain. He lay dry sticks over the paper, a wigwam that flared up and warmed the room. He put on his tie and jersey, sat down to read, a sharp northwester harrowing his senses but keeping him alert.

She called him. He loved his name on her lips, as he loved hers on his, left off setting the breakfast table and went to do what, considering who she was, and after what she had told him the night before, was no more than his duty. She wanted him, she said, and he got into bed, and all too quickly felt the roots being burned out of him, backbone melting into liquid fire. That was how she liked it, a flush, she said, cleaning her out.

Wet leaves lay in patches between decaying rosebay, tall thistles bordering the worn fields. They held hands, shoes muddy, sky reflected in larger pools of water, air tasting of salt. 'Walks like this will soon cure you. By the time you're thirty even the refills will be over.'

'How far is it to Studwink Farm?'

She pulled the map from her handbag. The wind turned it into a crumpled kite, and she clapped when he stopped it falling into the mud. 'You're quick. You'll live forever.'

Such optimism was the greatest care she could give. But he didn't need it, counted the kilometre squares. 'About ten miles there and back.'

'It's my favourite walk.' Up and down the straight bridlepath, they crossed a road and entered the farm area. 'I know the people who run it. Their daughter got into nursing, thanks to me.'

A herd of light brown cows had been waiting for them for the last half mile. Two black cats ran from a seat near the back door. The farmer was about fifty, had short grey hair, and deep lines on his face, grim features that turned to a smile at seeing Nora. He wore a flat cap, and a grey shirt without a collar, open at the neck, and looked at his hands before lifting one to be shaken, calling into the house to say who it was.

She indicated Brian. 'I'm showing him the countryside.'

His wife was a tall woman wearing a flowered pinafore. 'How's Alice getting on in Canterbury?' Nora asked.

'She loves it.'

Brian wondered what Alice was like, how good-looking she was, wanted to meet her, did meet her, fell in love, walked the fields, the finest summer in living memory, made love, was with her, had it from her – fucked her, life one long shooting in of spunk. The country air made him want to fuck everyone in sight.

'You'd hardly know her,' Farmer Jim said. 'She's a different girl now.'

'We've got something for you. We know how it is, with all this rationing.' His wife came back with a chicken wrapped in greaseproof paper, six eggs, a piece of bacon and a few sticks of rhubarb.

Nora said no, but the farmer's wife said she should. Jim said she must, and so she did, was handed the goods in a carrierbag. 'You have to keep it hidden, with all these inspectors snooping about.'

'I'd hang 'em from the trees,' Brian joked, giving them a laugh.

'They're such good people,' Nora said on the way back. 'I call now and again, and usually come home laden like a thief in the night.'

She was respected wherever she went, and in a few years Farmer Jim's daughter would have the same status as Nora because Nora had helped her. In the air force he had had status. He no longer had any, was left with the advantage of a paid

317

idleness which enabled him to observe the world instead of being part of it, to see himself and the world as clearly as if looking through a magnifying glass. With neither qualities nor qualifications, neither art nor skill that anybody wanted, except perhaps an ability to write stories, he channelled his driving force into ambition unspecified. Luck he expected because it needed neither money nor education. Blind faith he had, born out of beneficial ignorance which would slowly dissolve. Work was easy because he tackled it obsessively rather than by intelligent effort. He had the curiosity to read everything and to know everything, without questioning whether or not it was within his capacity to know anything at all.

Envying such people as Nora and the farmer, he would not at the same time try to gain a similar place in the world. The idea of a job was difficult to accept. To work in an office among other people would be a come-down. He knew now that he wasn't made for it, never had been.

If he hoped to gain money one day from his ambivalent function in life it was only because the pension was too small for the travelling he craved. With pay accumulated in the hospital, and six weeks' severance money, he had thirty pounds in the bank. The few guineas earned so far seemed a miracle, but one which he hoped would recur and on a grander scale.

Nora was not impressed at the sight of his printed story, or enthusiastic about a fee which was barely two days' pay for her. She sat before the fire, glasses on, flipping the pages of his novel too quickly for him to believe she was reading with care. 'They're the people you told me about in your letters.'

'They're the only ones I know, though some of them I made up.'

The papers rested on her lap. 'I thought writers told stories about exciting people.'

'Maybe that'll come later.' He wanted to throw the stuff on the fire, except that it would reveal how deeply he felt.

'Who's this Rebecca Smith the hero seems set on?'

It didn't happen till near the end, and then she went off with Jim Bailey. 'A made-up character.'

'She must be.' The pages rustled on to her lap. 'You certainly didn't mention anyone like that in your letters.'

'That's because I didn't meet anyone like her.'

'The husband's a lawyer.'

'He had to be something.'

'She seems the only invention, so far.'

'You might find one or two more.'

'It's intriguing to see how your mind works.' She stood. 'I'll finish it later.'

Her unfounded suspicions stimulated him, but if he embraced her it was only because it seemed the best way to conceal his embarrassment. 'You're thoroughly untrustworthy,' she said, 'but I love you, all the same.'

He wondered how long this more than perfect life could last, till the morning she woke him with a cup of coffee and a letter from his mother.

'Dear Brian, I'm writing this so I can be the first to tell you. Lillian has cut her throat, but they try to say it was an accident. Her mam found her. She had been going out with that Bert, and people heard she was going to have a baby. I can't write anymore. But I thought you would like to know. They bury her tomorrow.'

Chapter

❧ TWENTY-EIGHT

She would think he was sleeping, always telling him to lie in, it's good for you, you need all the rest you can get.

Going downstairs, he held the saucer with both hands to stop the cup leaping before him. She was alert in the morning, bright talk winding her up for the day, as if night had been a desert and she needed renewing. Dawn for him was bleak. On even the best mornings he wondered why he had come back to life. No day could be richer than dreams, no life more perfect than sleep – till he was properly awake.

The table was laid for breakfast. He went towards the sink, brisk. She sat, reading the *Daily Express*. He washed his face. She leaned over for a kiss. 'You're pale this morning. Bad dreams again?'

'Too much sleep always brings on that tubercular look.' He eased her from the chair and kissed her, to make the day seem normal. 'I was dreaming about you. We were in paradise. Dante could never have imagined it. Then you went away, and I woke up desolate.'

Her laugh of disbelief saved him. 'I don't think paradise would be quite my cup of tea.'

'Nor mine – if it was real.'

She held him. 'What a shame I must be off tomorrow.'

'It's an awful thought.'

'And you don't look well. I worry about you. You should take more care.'

'I can look after myself.'

'Of course. But even so.'

The last thing he would do was look after himself in any way that mattered, in which case woe betide anyone who got in his way to do it for him. She poured his tea. 'I must stay in this morning and clean the place, leave it like a new pin for you.'

There was a fried egg on his plate.

'At least you have a good appetite,' she said.

'We both have.' Become unreal, appear abstracted – as if before writing something or other. A stone inside was battering him to pieces. I'm writing a story, he might tell her. For you. Yes, my love, she would say, I know. Keep at it. Practice makes perfect. You'll succeed, I know you will. You've got what it takes. I love you for it.

Speech is the enemy of reflection, he would put in his note-book. He wanted the peace to write, to be himself, though bombs tore into his interior landscape, till he could be a whole person, cobble a smile from the fragments, convince her that nothing had happened, practise on her at being himself.

She laughed. 'If ever I'm off my food, send for the under-taker.'

He didn't want to be out of her sight.

'Any news in your letter?'

'It's from my mother.' He had rehearsed the reply. 'All well, but I must write to her.'

'It's always better to let them know.' She had steamed the letter open, knew what was in it, was playing with him. 'You're right,' he said, an easy smile.

To crawl back upstairs would betray him. He could cough as much as he liked, but to show that he was depressed would widen the gap till they were invisible to each other.

'Look after yourself when I go.'

'I will.'

'Promise?'

'I certainly do.' He was incapable of going out, but what was impossible must become an impulse.

She passed the marmalade. 'I heard you coughing.'

'The usual morning bout.'

'I can't bear to hear it.'

'It's nothing serious.'

'I'm beginning to think the sea air is bad for you.'

'I like being on the coast. I can see the sky.'

'People often love what's bad for them.'

He was unable to control his laugh, and she looked wide-eyed, as if he had turned into a different person.

'I know that too,' he said.

'My sister went to the Pyrenees last year, and told me how wonderful it is. I'll sell this place, and find a cottage in the mountains.' She leaned close. 'I'd give up my job.'

Her spirit flooded his defences. You couldn't take such money abroad these days. It was a dream. 'Sounds nice.'

'I would do anything for you.'

Leave me alone. The breadknife was inches away. He was someone else. If he killed her he would be hanged. To kill himself would be a shorter route. He dug his spoon into the marmalade, spread it like cement over a brick. 'As a matter of fact, I feel rather well.'

She was glad, didn't want to seem silly, touched his arm lovingly. 'You must go for a walk. Take the fieldglasses. The air's so clear you might see France. You'd like that, I know.'

Wood was scattered along the shingle. He threw it back. Take it all. Everything had a rhythm. He loved nothing except a well-ordered world, the inexorability which people worshipped and called God.

Nora said they must talk about their future. She might sell the cottage and get a place near the hospital. She didn't know what to do anymore than he did. 'I can buy a car out of my savings,' she said on their way to the cinema in Dover. They held hands through the film. She had many plans, was unnaturally bright on that final day, unreal, as if frantically searching, unable to find him.

Beyond the golf course he walked over tufted grass to the cliff edge, thinking that after death you blacked out, coaldust forever, softened into oblivion, so neutral you never considered it. Lillian was in him, wouldn't leave him, saying she would have lived if he had said he loved her, only that, those few words that wouldn't harm a fly, and if he had said it he might have been right, but he had bitten the truth between his teeth like a musket ball, and kept silent, so wanted to slide over the cliff because for the rest of his life he would love no one but Lillian. Ships were stuck on the seascape like flies on a board. He tore up his mother's letter, gulls chasing the bits as if they were bread.

Worn out and sick, a bout of the flu. When Nora had been gone a week he walked along the beach, forcing his back straight so as not to be taken for an invalid by anyone spying through bungalow curtains. Nora had done enough. He would rent a cottage in Berkshire for ten bob a week. No electric light, he would use an oil lamp. Water would come from a stream. He would forage for wood, cook in the fireplace, cut himself off, unless she wanted to see him. Plans were as common as stars.

Lillian's anguish gnawed. He hated himself for having met her as much as he had loathed himself for being blighted with TB. Whistling a mindless tune, he pulled at the roots to get himself on hands and knees to the cliff. He was afraid to go to Nottingham and pass those places where they had been. Low cloud fled inland to leave a clear sky. The knife at Lillian's throat, he wondered at her strength to push it in, eyes open, lips silent at the blood. The sound of his scream forced him away.

Houses in the next village stood between the trees. Food on the table. A dog almost pulled the fence down to reach him. He was sent off. I'll call the police! A gull disputed territory with a crow on the shingle. Into the wind, close to the cliff, he wanted wings, to glide over waves, sink underwater, struggle till he grew warm.

Strengthened by the rhythm of his walk, images harassed him with metallic vividness, Lillian's face a doll's head streaked with paint, as if whoever made her had run away when she was half finished.

Bedclothes high, he couldn't stop shivering. The letter under his pillow cried like a child which must be smothered. Scattered in the air, swallowed by the birds, it had come back. Nightmares gave off firmer words than dreams. Torment him for the rest of his life, but pity and grief was a sham, a laugh which racked him, eyes wet but heart dry. The clickstop of recollection was beyond control. Did you speak, my love? said Nora. But Nora had gone. He was silent. Despair got the better of Lillian. Bert had abandoned her, though you couldn't blame Bert, being who he was. Bert had taken on where he left off. Baker had been killed in Malaya, and they had carried him down through the jungle to be buried. Lillian had cut her throat.

Floating in the sea, he ached with cold, the wind blowing ice and fire in one breath, a boat on the rise and fall. Gripping the bedrail, he called her name in silence, her name locked in him like a barbed wheel, teeth pressing his lips to enforce silence. He shouted, in silence, for him to be silent, laughing in silence so that he should stay silent forever, or until he could write about her, which he thought would never be, the only memory being his silence.

His pyjamas clung with sweat, as if he had been grabbing on piecework to make up his factory stint. He couldn't get out of bed, and be what his body would be, held the rail. He let go. Bury it, bite the slag, chew the swarf, swallow the nightmare's bile.

He couldn't fall, stood at the window, sunlight over the sea. When cool air dried him he pulled his shirt over his head. A condensation trail from some aircraft now invisible crossed the blue sky and cut it exactly in two – above, heaven as far as you could go; below, the earth on which his feet were planted. The division was absolute and he did not know which half he wanted, or whether he would be able to get it if he did know.

Duty called, Nora said, and abandoned him to his torment with that thoughtlessness on which – as he well knew – the world spun. No wonder we won the war, but the war's been over almost as long as it was on. Duty was not part of him, and if he had told her about Lillian, duty would have called her even more sharply. He had acted in a manner unbecoming a human being by keeping something from her. Condemnation was a luxury he denied her. If he had fallen on to her compassion, of which he believed she had some, there would have been rage and tears perhaps, loathing and recrimination, but she would have felt rich in the bounty of her forgiveness – you're only

324

flesh and blood, we're only human, what else could I expect? – and brought them newborn out of the storm, Lillian consumed in the stoke-hole of their passion. There might have been real love in place of the infatuation they no longer knew what to do with. But he sheered off such ultimate trust, as if he wouldn't recognise it anyway.

The jungle was with him, his comfort and strength. No matter what accent he spoke in, what he read or wrote, a life of rectitude was not for him. He composed a letter. Our love is too good to continue, too virtuously stable. We must separate to keep it perfect. If not now, when? If it is now, 'tis not to be. If it is not to be it will be now. If it be not now yet it will come. The readiness is what we need. At the risk of making her feel worse he would say that she was faultless, and because no one can be without faults she would be a victim of his inability to find any.

My Dear Nora, I love you more than I have ever loved anyone. More than I can ever love anyone. You saved my life. Your head was the last vital stepping stone across the swamp.

He threw the letter with its stamped envelope into the fire. Even so, he would never know what dry ground meant. If Nora hadn't existed he would still have relinquished Lillian, and if Lillian had never known him, she would still have killed herself. He walked around the room, speaking his letter, till he didn't know which woman he was talking to, unable to do anything except talk to himself.

He sat at the desk, felt that Nora was in the next room. I'll support you for as long as you need me, she said. With such a person he had no troubles. Write for me, she asked him. You know I shall look after you. But all he wanted was not to want, and for nobody to want him.

Studs of rain fell on the shingle. With each minute he was less able to move. They had nothing to say. Dear Nora, perhaps I shouldn't tell you, but it has to be like this because I can write more easily than I can talk. I'm leaving you. Sorry about this. Hope all goes well. You're not my sort, and I'm not your sort. Somebody has to say it first. Not that I know what my sort is, but at least if I'm free from somebody who is not my sort I have a better chance of finding out.

Who can discern errors? Clear us from hidden faults, to where there is no speech and no words, and neither voice is heard to the end of the world. He heaped the grate with stories, poems, old letters, school reports rescued from the Mullinders' wardrobe, even the diary kept in the jungle. Flame touched the corner of a sheet like the tongue of a cat which thinks its milk might have been poisoned. He bet on its success, watched it turn hungry and slide from page to page till he had to move from the heat. Too late to put it out, the ash made a chevron he couldn't look at.

His suitcase was packed, typewriter on the table. A letter waited to be posted telling her how he was (as if he knew), asking how she was (as if she would tell him), cataloguing his walks (by now he'd done them so often they bored him), what poems he was writing and the stories he was mulling over (classified information to all but himself), the antics of the birds (he no longer noticed them), a visit to a pub in Deal (which he had not made) where he had met a couple at the bar and discussed books and writers. The man was an officer on the ferry, his wife a schoolteacher, and they invited him to their bungalow (lies like everything else).

On the morning of leaving a letter came:

'Dear Brian, I don't know for sure how it happened, because you didn't see fit to tell me, but I must be honest, and tell *you* that I don't want to see you again. Something was wrong at the cottage, but I didn't say anything while I was there in case I was mistaken. I felt it was better to let things go than have an unpleasant row, which I couldn't stand.

'Something was very wrong indeed. You shouted a name in your sleep. Not that I cared. It could have been the name of an aunt, for all I know, or from a story you're writing, I dare say. But in those last days there was a strange attitude I couldn't put my finger on. Something had happened to you, which I felt very strongly, and you didn't tell me about it. Not telling me about it was worse than telling me a lie, and to me telling a lie is the worst thing one person can do to another.

'I've waited a few days before writing, though it's final because I know my mind. I'm more upset than when I made

326

the decision, but I know it's for the best. I could never come to terms with your way of looking at things.

'Will you please push the key through the letterbox when you leave? Yours truly, Nora.'

Chapter

❧ TWENTY-NINE

At Beeston Lock the broad Trent shouldered over the drop, and spread between waterlogged meadows. Anglers stood in waders where the current was placid, floats twitching in midstream. Beyond the river the grove of Clifton was concealed among trees.

He had put his case and typewriter into the left luggage and come here by bus, unable to go straight home, wanting a walk, to get whatever was left of him sufficiently into one piece so as to face the reality of a world without Lillian. He walked by bay rose and bulrushes towards Trentside Farm, nondescript marshland plated with rubbish tips. Two youths pedalled their bikes across a surviving field, arms horizontal like circus performers. A low sky threatened rain, and gnats bothered him. The old places were trampled by surveyors marking out lines for drains and foundations, pylons appearing where he hadn't noticed them before. Fields would be covered by avenues and crescents, drives and closes. The Nook and the Cherry Orchard had gone in an orgy of spoliation, new estates building on open country beyond Wollaton Park, the Hemlock Stone surrounded and a suburb planned for Clifton to make Henry Kirk White turn in his dusty grave.

There was no world without Lillian, no matter what was covered, she couldn't be eradicated, he was on his own from now on, a dubious box of tricks on two legs that he had to keep moving even if only to discover what the box of tricks had in store. So the backbone was everything, the Merton blacksmith-grit to sustain him, if any was left out of what had come to him in the first place.

He felt as if he had just arrived from the troopship. The rest was folly. Walking down the street, three ragged-arsed children fought on the steps of the house where Lillian didn't live anymore.

'Mrs Verney wouldn't even come back after the funeral,' his mother said. 'Ben and one of his mates cleared the house, and the landlord got another family in next day.'

'I wish I hadn't gone away.'

'Well, yer did, didn't yer?' She folded her arms over her chest. 'What a shame she went out with that Bert. The police had a word with him, but there was nowt they could do. She should have stuck with you, and not gone off with him. I don't suppose she knew when she was lucky – like a lot of people.'

'Where's Bert now?'

'Nobody knows. Nobody wants to know, either. It's bleddy good riddance, I say, though I expect he'll be back soon enough.'

Seaton was at work, the others out or at school. A mongrel yapped in the yard. 'I feel terrible about it.'

'We all do. But it worn't your fault. You can't stop anybody doing a thing like that. So get this cup o' tea, and let's have a fag. That bogger took the whole packet to wok this morning.'

He gave her one.

'How long are you here for this time?'

He shrugged. 'I don't know.'

'Well, yer've got yer bed upstairs. You can allus stay 'ere when you like.'

'Thank you.'

'You're my own son, aren't you?'

'No doubt about that.'

'There bleddy ain't.' She puffed at the Senior Service. 'You allus smoke good fags, anyway. They're twice as thick as Woodbines.'

'Coffin nails.'

She laughed, inhaling happily. 'They're bleddy good coffin nails, though. I do like a fag, you know that.'

'It helps.'

'I'll say it does. Do you want a bit o' cake?'

'Have you got any?'

'I can nip across the road.'

'I'm not hungry.'

'You've got thinner.'

'No more than I ever was.'

'I suppose not. Was it nice in Kent?'

'Yes. Right on the sea.'

She passed the racing page of the paper across the table. 'Pick us a winner.'

'You always lose, you know that.'

'I won ten to one last time you picked me one. Me and yer dad 'ad a good night out on that.'

He looked down the list. 'What about Carrier Wave?'

'Yer think so?'

No idea why he chose it. 'Back it.'

She snatched the paper for a look. 'I'll risk a couple o' bob.' She tore a page from the back of a writing pad, kept in the cupboard with insurance policies and the family birth certificates. 'Shall yer be going back to Kent, then?'

'No.'

She laughed. 'Has she chucked yer?'

'Out on my neck.'

'Serves yer right, I expect.'

'You can say that again.'

'Our George never stuck with anybody long, either. It's on'y the women as does that, bleddy fools that we are.'

There was a picture on the wall, of a woman holding a child on her knee, both entranced at a robin on a bough, his father's favourite, lovingly framed. On the chimney piece was an ornamental shelf, with a row of diamond-shaped mirrors Brian remembered his father making before the war. His memory went backwards, like a vision seen the wrong way through a telescope, and Seaton was being taken away by the police for non-payment of food debts, Brian as a four-year-old sitting on the linoed floor of the room they lived in. His mother raked grey ash so as to see the glow of the coal behind the bars. 'It's still 'ard to get this bleddy stuff.'

'Isn't there plenty down the pit?'

'Not for us. They on'y let you have a quarter at a time. Arthur got me some the other day, come staggerin' up the yard with half a hundredweight on his shoulders, laughing his head off.' She took a letter from behind the clock. 'This came for you.'

The usual king's head on a twopenny-ha'penny stamp, torn across on opening. 'There are two places I spend my time. One is in the reference section of the library, and the other is in the Shalimar (remember?) drinking coffee. You can find me in one or the other. Have you stopped spitting blood? I'm dying to know!'

Mrs Bull's diamond-tipped stare as he went out of the yard and up the street reminded him, in case he needed it, that he was looked on as Lillian's murderer. 'He started her off, didn't he? That bogger got her out of bed, didn't he? He was the first to tek her out, worn't he? If it 'adn't bin for him she'd have been here today, wouldn't she? And look at the way he walks up the street, cock o' the walk, as if he owns the bleddy place. It's terrible what some rotters get away with.'

Lights in town were on by three o'clock. He looked around the tables in a bookshop and bought a secondhand guide to Southern France. The smell of print never changed, nor did a coal fire in the basement that, too reminiscent of times long gone, drove him back on to Wheeler Gate.

From a booth he phoned Edgeworth to ask how business was. He imagined the secretary beckoning at the workshop door, and Edgeworth the old gaffer wipe his hands on a mound of cotton waste, thump the off-button of his lathe, and step into the office where they kept the phone.

'Coming to ask for a job?' It was a worthwhile laugh. 'I didn't think so. What? You might go to France for a few months? I went once, and damned near didn't get back. Still, I expect you'll be all right. Look, my son's home for a while, so why don't you come to a little supper on Saturday? Me and the wife will be glad to see you before you go off on your travels. I'll get the secretary to send a note telling you how to get there. About half past six. Must get back to the machine. A rush order came in yesterday, export-special.'

The air turned his shoe leather into cardboard, got at his body through the paper of his mackintosh. People hurried for buses, heading for the comfort of their toast and tea. The cold at Queen's Bay came off the sea with three thousand miles of mild gulf behind it, but here the dampness was corrosive and hungry, robbing him of all sense except that of survival.

She sat reading at a table, and didn't notice him, so he turned to walk out. Then he changed his mind and placed himself opposite, setting her bag of books on the floor.

'Stranger,' she said. 'Talk to me. Tell me where you've been.'

He came back with coffee, only wanting to look through his guidebook. 'I was in Kent, doing some writing.'

'On your own?'

To tell her the truth would mean a confession, impossible for him. 'Some of the time. I was working on a novel.'

'Do you think it will be published?'

'I hope something might, one day.' He told her about the stories and poems already printed.

'Are you going to write anything else?' Her questions prompted him to ask what she was doing with her life. She crumpled the covering of her cake. 'Oh, I wish I knew. My husband wants to see the back of me, but won't let me go. When I'm with him he only wants to kick me out, and when I go he does all he can to get me back. And if I stay with friends they get fed up with me after a day or two. I'd like to go to a place where nobody can get at me. I seem to have a bad influence on everybody.'

'Not on me.' He wouldn't allow it. One battlefield was enough.

'I'd like to visit the Castle,' she said, at no response in his set features. 'I've been in Nottingham two years and haven't been there yet.' She wanted an offer to take her. In the grounds they sat on a bench near Albert Ball's statue. Lillian was coming down the ramp from the museum, holding his arm. They had been happy, but happiness was in the past, because you never felt it at the time. A veil of frost squeaked as her shoes stepped over the grass.

She taunted him when he came back with more coffee. 'You're not even coughing.'

He had read in Dostoevsky that if you wanted to bring on a more convincing aspect of consumption – and a realistic cough – all you had to do was swallow raw tobacco mixed with brandy.

'Why don't you try it?' she said. 'If you coughed all the time we wouldn't have to speak.'

'Can't you find a better pastime?'

She got her own back. 'Call it getting to know you.'

'Do you think we ever can?'

Her wanness didn't crush him. 'Life's lobotomised me,' she smiled.

'Me too,' he said. 'Aren't we lucky?'

'I sometimes think I was lobotomised before I was born.'

He'd only suffer for new words, new concepts grown out of somebody else's experience. He told her he intended to put as much distance as he could between himself and England. 'If I were free,' she said, 'I'd visit all the museums – the Prado, the Louvre, the Hermitage.'

Now they had something neutral to talk about. 'One day we might meet on the Champs-Elysées. Or the Nevsky Prospekt,' he told her.

She was different when she laughed, and he wondered who else she was friendly with, how she passed the days, unable to fix her much beyond their meetings at Tom Boak's. What was her husband like? She never really said. Was he tall or short, dark or fair? Did he wear glasses or not, was he bald or not? Poor bloke, whoever he was, someone he would rather think about than meet, no wish to tangle with anyone connected with her.

'I must go home, but walk me some of the way.'

Iron filings and gritty sulphur palled over the city, every breath scraping his lungs. She took his hand in her excitement: 'Are you all right?'

'I shall be.' The coughing forced him to rest. He must flee, or die. At the top of the hill the mist lifted to reveal glimmering upper storeys of the houses. She took off her gloves to say goodbye. 'I'm sorry what I said about you spitting blood.' He held her hand, as if touching a more intimate part of her. He neither liked nor disliked her. She seemed to be two people who, if they got to know each other, might become a single person. He didn't want to see her again.

All problems were insoluble unless he assumed he was leaving. He took wireless manuals, some guidebooks and novels off the shelf and put them in a kitbag, which he dumped on the floor of Tom Boak's shop. 'I'm clearing my room out.'

'Sit down, then, and get the weight off your lungs.'

Noxious coffee brewed on the patterned oil stove. 'As long as I don't have to drink any of that.'

'A little beef tea is what you want, by the look of you.' He shook the books out as if they were bricks. 'Dead set on leaving, then?'

He sat, a nod and a grunt.

'I won't say I didn't expect it. But you're a better man than I am, Gunga Din. Anne was asking for you yesterday. I hope you're not contemplating anything serious with her.'

Never let anyone see you were angry. 'Oh no, it's Grace Rutland I'm after. I'd give my right lung for a go at her.' Cut all wires, watch the ends smoke and flash, but don't get close enough to burn your fingers.

'Anne's too competitive,' Tom said. 'She'd eat you up.'

'Are you trying to get me off with her?'

'It's just that she wouldn't be much good to you. Or to anybody else, come to that. And I think a lot of you.'

Nobody liked her, but he wouldn't ask why, because he had nothing to learn from Tom. In fact the only thing he had ever learned in Nottingham was where True North was – so that he could go south.

Tom arranged the books into a pile. 'A fiver?'

More than he'd expected. 'Maybe I'll have that coffee after all.'

'Where will you head for?'

'I'm still having fun with the map. Somewhere between Marseilles and Italy, I suppose.'

He buttoned his stained cardigan against the kind of cold hard to notice because it was so heavy with the reek of paraffin. 'The Labour Government don't like rats leaving the sinking ship.'

Brian laughed. 'When I step off, it'll lift a bit higher out of the water.'

'What about the fifty quid travel allowance?'

'I'll be lucky if I have that much. But if I have, nobody'll stop me getting it out. I wasn't four years in the air force for nothing.'

A boy came in and asked did they have any comics. Tom said only me, and chased him out. 'You don't seem in a good mood today.'

'You're asking too many questions.'

'Well, you aren't going abroad with your mates in the army, are you? You can stand a lot then, even bullets. But once you're down among the palm trees, the casinos, and the dark-eyed maidens, without a penny or a crust of bread, you might hanker for home.'

He resisted telling him to get stuffed. 'Everything you say has already gone through my head.'

'In one side and out the other, I suppose. Anyway, come to our gathering on Saturday and give us an opportunity to shed goodbye tears.' He put a certain smile on his lips: 'Me and Wendy's decided to get married, though I don't expect you'll be here to see it. I might be twenty years older than her, but she's very good at scrubbing backs. It's what every secondhand bookseller needs.'

Lights from the bridge sheened on that magic band of water separating north from south, city from country, oak from olive, mildew from hot pines and baking rock.

Beyond the river, but still clustered to the city, were bigger houses than those of the Meadows, space at the front, and longish gardens at the back. Further out were villages, towns, other cities, and then London – a stepping stone for going south, only to be tackled when he was good and ready. But if he never got there he wouldn't care, as long as it did not stop him going south, beyond England, nearer the girth of the sphere.

At Cropgrave he orientated himself by the church, and easily found The Laurels, a hundred-year-old red-bricked house almost smothered in ivy. He pulled a crease from his waistcoat and straightened the Windsor knot of his tie, feeling well turned out in pinstriped demob suit, sharp trousers and glinting shoes

335

as he walked between Edgeworth's large old Austin in the drive and a fancy sports car parked as far from it as possible – as if the Austin would eat it given half the chance.

Mrs Edgeworth answered the bell. 'I'm glad you were able to come.' There were plants in the hall, and an umbrella stand, and he took in a framed picture of a Spitfire presented to Edgeworth, he supposed, by Rolls-Royce for keeping them going with engine parts all through the war. He was sure she'd arranged the old-fashioned furniture in the lounge, whose large bay windows would look on to a garden when the curtains were open. 'This is our son Richard.'

Brian shook hands with a slim dark-haired man of about twenty with a hawklike nose, dressed in jacket and flannels, shirt open at the neck with a bit of coloured rag for decoration. 'What will you have?'

'Whisky.' He hoped they had some.

'Water?'

They must have that. 'Neat.'

'Gin for me. Here's to you.'

Mrs Edgeworth looked pained because he hadn't given her the chance of offering the booze. Or maybe she thought Richard wasn't friendly enough. 'I'll tell Ted you're here.'

'So you used to work at the old man's dark satanic mill?'

'Before I joined up.'

'More fool you.'

Richard's hands were delicate and lily-white, and though Brian hadn't done any labouring for a few years, his had been bigger than most youths' met in the air force or hospital. Perhaps Richard was still smarting from the handshake. 'You've got to work somewhere.'

'Blimey! Who told you that?'

He sat down. 'What do *you* do?'

'Nothing – if I can. Why should I, when the old man's rolling in spondulicks? He was a war profiteer, and he's always telling me to pull my socks up. I've practically worn them out making the attempt.'

Brian wondered where he'd lost all sign of a local accent. He seemed immature, wandering around in a different world. If his old man and all his trappings vanished, what would he do?

Edgeworth wore a smart navy double-breasted suit, the first time Brian had seen him in anything but blue dungarees. 'Richard's made you welcome. He can do that, at least.'

'I'll pour one for you, if you like, Dad' – his tone implying that if he did it might contain a few grains of poison. Edgeworth noticed it – he was no fool – but took a chance. 'Two fingers of gin. If I have more, the ulcer bites me to hell and back.' He turned to Brian. 'You look fitter than any of us, whatever you've got.'

Brian enjoyed the large piece of meat at dinner, and told them so. 'We have connections,' Mrs Edgeworth said, as if no one had praised her cooking before. 'Ted does something or other on one of his machines for a farmer, and we're too friendly to charge him for it, so the farmer lets us have a joint now and again.'

'That's what this government's dragged us down to,' Edgeworth said, 'the barter system. We'll be living in the Stone Age next, if Attlee doesn't get turfed out.'

Amusement at his wrath might have united the family, except that he went on about it too often. As it was, Richard laughed as if he would go crackers if he didn't, and Brian wouldn't fancy being within a hundred miles of Edgeworth if the ship did begin to sink, since the scramble for life would make the *Titanic* look like a happy boating party on the Trent. 'We manage all right,' Edgeworth went on, 'though God knows when we'll really get back on our feet. Still, it's taken a Labour Government to make us use our initiative. The war didn't do it half so well.'

Hard to talk when there was so much to eat. The bickering between Edgeworth and his son went on until Brian realised he had been invited to tell them what he was going to do now that he had left the air force. After he had described his life – in general terms – at Queen's Bay, Edgeworth said: 'We enjoyed your stories, didn't we, Mabel? Now I know why we've been taking that dull old rag all these years.'

Mabel suggested they should get a house there when they retired, but Edgeworth said he fancied Devon, though thought they ought to get Richard off their hands first.

'All I want is an income.' Richard crushed the hot end of a

cigarette into his half-eaten steak. 'I don't think that's too much to ask.'

'Income?' Edgeworth in his rage could only go to the fire and throw on half a hundredweight of coal from the brass-handled scuttle. 'You'll end up in the dole queue, though there aren't any, at the moment. Everybody takes prosperity for granted, and I keep things going to the limit, but it's hard work, let me tell you. When I came back from the Great War' – he took an extra deep pull on his cigar, and blew the smoke towards Richard, as if it was the smokescreen through which he would attack – 'I'd got no heart in me. I thought I'd never walk straight and upright again. And I didn't. That'd 'ave led straight to the dole queue. Instead, I grubbed around till I found an old shed and put a secondhand machine in it, I turned out a few candle-sticks and ornamental faglighters, and things everybody thought nobody needed. Took me ten years till I got another bloke to come in with me, and that was during the Slump. When everybody was fighting to stop going under I was inching my way up. Not too fast, but fast enough. You ask yer mother what it was like. By the Second War I had twenty blokes under me, bloody good blokes, what's more, but then most of 'em got called up so I pulled in the young lads and the women, bless 'em. No, I won't say it's bin a struggle. It was more of a challenge, all the skill I could muster, mixed with the miser in me. I only counted every penny when I had to, though not anymore. But I started with bugger-all, so I know how easy it can be lost if you don't watch it.'

'It won't be my fault if it is,' Richard said in such a voice that Brian felt sorry for him.

'No, but it'd help if you'd give me a hand at the factory. I'm up to here with things at the moment.' He had a piece of boiled fish instead of steak, but you would think he had eaten human flesh by the way he turned crimson when railing at his son, after the mild and sentimental account of his humble beginnings. Mabel passed water and a pill, and poured wine for Brian.

In the lounge he smoked one of Edgeworth's best Jamaican cigars, the house an oasis in the desert of austerity. *Swan Lake* played on the radiogram, while they sipped their coffee. 'So what are your plans?' Edgeworth asked. 'You've heard enough from me.'

Brian stood in front of the fire, a thumb in the top right pocket of his waistcoat. He only had plans when people reminded him of an idea he had thrown off in conversation and, as if holding him to what he had said, impelled him towards action, not knowing that such intentions had been smouldering all his life. 'I'm going to find a cottage or a room in the south of France for a few months, so that I can write a novel. All I want is the peace to work.'

'You've got ambition,' Edgeworth smiled. 'I'll say that for you.'

Brian realised his ludicrous posture, and sat down. 'I'll be able to draw my pension there, and I hope to make something by doing articles to tide me over.' He had written to the editor of the same local weekly asking if there would be a place for pieces about his travels. 'Send them, by all means,' he had heard, 'and if we publish you'll get the same rate as before.'

'I'm sure you'll succeed,' Mabel said. 'As for you, Richard, when are you going to settle down and do some work? I really think it's time you stopped disappointing us.'

Brian was amused at her sudden resumption of the attack, but wished both of them had waited till he was out of the house before using him as an example of ambition and industry. He looked forward to half past nine, when he would be able to leave.

'You're always at me.' Richard's lips trembled. 'You don't give me a chance.'

'We kept you out of the army' – Edgeworth now spoke less sharply than his wife – 'hoping you'd get down to something.'

Brian thought it might have improved him if he had done a military stint like everybody else, sensed that Richard wished he had in fact served, and didn't altogether thank his old man for having kept him out only so that he could be taunted with it forever. Brian knew his own luck in having parents who didn't care whether he got on or not, and who thought that as long as he stayed alive there was nothing to worry about.

Edgeworth walked him to the bus stop. 'A bit of night air will do me good. I hoped Richard would have offered to drive

you back to town in his motorised pram, but it seems not.'
They stood under a light by the church. 'I wish you luck, but
let's hear from you. Putting pen to paper shouldn't be too much
for a chap in your line. If you stay long enough we might even
motor down and see you. We haven't had a holiday for years.
But I do wish our Richard would get stuck into something.'
He kicked a stone into the gutter with irritation. 'I'm boggered
if I know what the hell to do with him.'

The big man with the factory was whittling on about his
worthless son, and Brian didn't know whether he wanted an
opinion, but said: 'He seems right enough. I'm sure he'll come
round soon. Maybe he's only waiting for a chance to show
what he can do. You should try to leave him alone for a bit,
and when he's found his way he'll take to something. I'll bet
you won't be able to stop him then.'

'Do you think so?'

'You ought to tell him that he can't come into your factory
– not even over your dead body. Then he might want to.'

Edgeworth grasped his arm and looked into his face. 'By
God, you may be right. We're just too close to him to think of
things like that.'

And too old, Brian surmised. Edgeworth handed him an
envelope as he got on the bus. 'Here's something to help you
on your way.'

Nothing was visible beyond the lighted greenhouse which
floated him back to town, yet everything he saw through the
glass reminded him of Lillian, as if it was daylighᵗ outside. And
when there was no reflection her face stayed as if a picture had
been painted there, fixed for always, on any bus or train he
would ever travel on.

He called at the travel agent's to ask about boat fares and train
times, copying the data into a notebook. He bought a grammar
to improve his French.

'You've only just come back from Malaya,' his father said.
'Ain't this place good enough for yer?'

'That's not the point.'

'He's got itchy feet.' Vera understood his urge. 'Like me, a
lot of the time.'

340

'When I get itchy feet,' Seaton quipped, 'I stamp my boots down and kill the fleas. Nottingham's allus bin good enough for me.'

'There's no point arguing,' Brian said.

Just home from the factory, Seaton still wore his overalls, a band of oil stain around his middle, the sud smell reeking in the kitchen. His cheeks were fleshy and pale, spotted with blackheads. Only his hands were washed. 'No bogger ever took any notice o' me. Still, you might be glad of us some day.'

Brian had stopped listening to that sort of advice since going to work, and before then he hadn't taken much notice, either. He picked up a card from the shelf. 'What's this?'

'It's to vote with,' Vera said. 'I've got one as well.'

'You can chuck it on the fire,' Seaton told him.

'You can't expect to influence things if you don't vote,' Brian said.

Seaton's laugh seemed unnecessarily bitter. 'It never made any difference as far as I can see.'

'It's only a local election,' Vera said.

Brian wasn't yet on the electoral list. 'Where's the polling station?'

Vera pointed. 'Up at the school.'

He put on his jacket.

'You'll get summonsed,' she laughed.

'It says Harold Seaton, doesn't it?' And because it didn't describe him as short, stocky, black-haired (but nearly bald), too daft to worry and too dispirited to bother, he knew there was no risk of being recognised.

He walked out of the yard and up the street. Wreaths and crosses made to order, a notice said in a window, and he wondered for whom. No difference would come of his vote either, clandestine or not. In any case he didn't mean to linger in this familiar labyrinth of streets angled neatly one from the other, so couldn't care less what happened to them. They were eternal, never to disappear, part of him for as long as he breathed. He would vote for whatever meaning they might have, for the Jerusalem they might one day represent, with their state of order and permanence.

He walked into the redbricked, steepled school where, having been taught to read and write, he had received the key to any door whose lock he cared to pick. Tellers had little to do, but he had seen posters and knew who the candidates were. A man at a table asked his name.

'Seaton, Harold.'

In no way like him, now or ever, he was taken from the list, and in the booth made his mark for what he supposed would be the first and last time.

Between Jim Bailey and Ted Gedling, she was fixed by the music, eyes unseeing, able to analyse every nuance a second before it came. No longer deadened by what tormented her, her face had found a state free of oppression. Ted Gedling swivelled his eyes at all angles without moving his head, while Grace stared before her as if the music distorted her world rather than soothed. The way into her consciousness, and therefore her affections, could only be by a fragile door, and Ted Gedling, swaying back and forth, and beating time with a finger, glanced at her as if to put his foot through it wouldn't be worth the trouble. Wendy looked crossly at Tom as if he had threatened to break off their engagement for not scrubbing his back soundly enough, then nodded Brian towards a chair. Heavy curtains and the closed door held in the smell of tobacco and coffee, and mulled thought for the music to cut through. The muffled noise of a car expanded, and nobody knew when it diminished. Tom sorted records to decide on the next gramophone treat.

Anne's lack of awareness at brushing the hair from her forehead made him want to know her, but it would take all his life because she was guarded by so much barbed wire that he couldn't be bothered to find a way through. Tom's house would be there when they were dead, and such music always played. There was no time, he didn't care where he was, where he lived, but felt the music ordering his emotions. Ted Gedling released Anne's hand, and went out for a go at his Benzedrine.

Brian sat by her, and Ted couldn't care less that his place had gone, flopping on to the carpet as if made of rubber, gazing at the ceiling. 'Don't give him any coffee,' Jim said. 'Just pour it over him. He won't notice.'

Ted sat up and smiled. 'That might be better than having to

342

boil custard over the gas, and breathing it up till you're dizzy. I'm always game for a new sensation.'

Tom put on some Tchaikovsky. 'Bucket shop on the loose,' Brian whispered, and Anne's laughter made the others wonder what he had said about them. She ignored a glance from Grace, and pressed his hand, as if the romantic bombast was getting through to her. 'You were the only one who was with me while the music was on,' she said.

Tom looked up at Brian: 'So this is the last time you'll be with us?'

It will be, whether I leave or not, he was going to say, at a twitch in Anne's hand. She must know the shape of every man's hand in the room, he thought. 'Go to Venice,' Jim Bailey said. 'I went on a sketching trip before the war.'

'In Spain,' Ted Gedling warned, 'a pal of mine struck a match on a poster of Franco, and the flics didn't let him go for a week.' He lay back and said no more, as if whatever he had sucked up in the lavatory had done its work.

Aimless talk. He had no place here. He had stories to tell, needed time to write them, because life was too short to be washed over by meaningless chatter about writers and writing, when all he needed was to read, and remember, and use his imagination in order to fabricate tales, beat them into shape like a blacksmith hammering a bar of steel into a shoe on which a horse could travel to the moon and back. Lillian had left a continent of emptiness inside him, and he had to fill it with people of his own creation, if he was to go on living.

Sadness at parting made the parting more certain. No one else would wound him or leave scars. He walked on sheet metal, nothing underneath and no possibility of falling through. He could not be more empty, or more illuminated within.

A woman on her doorstep asked if he could spare a fag. Her wiry grey hair had long ago seen its last perm. Despairing eyes, and a skin with as many lines as iron filings around the north and south ends of a magnet, made a vision under the light. She knew where to stand, whether she lived there or not, the tragic face of all the women he had known. But she grinned when he opened his cigarette case, and he held a match while she lit up.

'That'll be me one day,' Anne said.

'Don't be bloody silly.'

'Oh well, I can't help thinking things like that.'

He'd had enough of her. She smiled as if satisfied that she had made him think so. They walked into the street where she lived. 'I don't want to go home yet.'

'Why don't you leave? Get a job, and a room somewhere?'

'My life won't change.'

'You can't tell till you do it.' Her misery was make-believe, without reason, couldn't be real unless she had no food, shelter, clothes, money – and she had all of them. That was Seaton talking, or his grandfather. He should have known better than to think so.

'The man I was living with before I got married went off with somebody else. Then I got married myself, because I was bored, and didn't want to stay at home. I wanted to change my life. Anything would do. I still want to change it. My husband's older than me, so it's like being married to my father.'

He was tormented by her. 'How old are you?'

'Twenty-two. What's that got to do with it?'

He didn't know, nothing to say, nothing more to ask. He was tired of walking, of listening to a tale of misery which he could well invent. She could go on forever, never get tired. 'My husband's gone to London. He'll be away till tomorrow, so come in with me.'

'Are you sure?' Maybe she was testing him, and he didn't know whether he was expected to pass by accepting or turning down her invitation. He would never tolerate being tested by anyone.

'Don't, then, if you don't want to.' The house was one of a terrace, steps leading up between railings. She opened the door with a Yale key from her purse, and he followed her to a kitchen at the back. 'Do you have a charwoman to help with a place like this?'

The house was spotless, without soul, like a hospital. She made coffee. 'Whenever I get one, they don't like me, and leave. Let's drink it in the guest room.'

He followed her up the straight stairway. The place was big enough for a boarding house. He was tense, ready to fight or run, wouldn't know which till something happened, as if an ambush had been set. He didn't trust her. The odour of tobacco, spices, plant soil and stale gas seemed unconnected, as if she had chosen the house to burgle, tried a key for luck, and been able to get in.

A double bed was made up ready. 'My room, when I want to sleep apart. Let's undress.'

She spread her blouse, showing a flimsy pink brassiere, laid her skirt on a chair, and drew off her knickers. She leaned over to pull back the bedclothes, a mole on her left shoulder. Then she turned, small breasts, slim waist and hips. He lay his trousers over the rail. But he couldn't make love. She didn't want to, either, retreated from passionate contact now that it threatened as from a damaging fire when he made a move. He was glad, though he couldn't think why, but it was the first time he hadn't cared to, and wondered why it should be like that with her. He stroked her breasts. 'There's another man's smell.'

'The bed hasn't been used for months, except by me.'

He thought a door banged.

'It's the wind,' she said.

There was no wind. He didn't want to get into a fight, kill or be killed.

'He goes to London whenever he can. He has a mistress. I know, because I found the letters. I didn't even burn them. He caught me reading them. It was cat and dog for weeks.'

'The only way to survive is not to care.'

'How naïve. It's not possible.'

'No?'

'Don't you worry about anything?'

'Only my writing. I did have a son, but he's gone. For good. Not that I was ever sure he was mine. Everything's gone – except myself, and even that I have to watch.'

She sat in the middle of the bed. 'I've cared about you ever since we first met.'

He made a gargoyle face. 'Excuse me while I die.'

'You see?' She laughed. 'At least you have a sense of humour!'

He was sorry for her, regretted coming into the house, wanted to dress quickly and get out. 'Shall I cough myself to death?'

She kissed him. 'Please.'

'I do it every morning, to bring myself to life.'

On his way from the toilet he opened a door into a large room. An elaborate dressing table was covered with cosmetics – which he thought she didn't use. A double bed with high pillows had a fancy lace coverlet. A man's pipes rested on a bookcase, a cap sat on a chair, and a blazer showed from a half-open wardrobe, a flowery dressing gown on the back of the door.

She was gentle, no violence in her, strangely untouched, almost untouchable, as if her mind had been blasted. He had no wish to find out anything about her.

'I'm beginning to feel sexy now,' she said. 'I couldn't do it before. Must have been psychological.'

He went to her, too late to wonder why, no protection for either of them, the world open on all sides, he with a stranger and she with a stranger, both strangers and always to remain so, yet neither uneasy nor out of place with one another. If he felt love it was only for her unthinking action in asking him into the house, as if what happened meant even less for her than it did for him.

'You have too much life,' she said. 'I want some of it.'

'Take what you like. There's plenty more where that came from.' He cradled her, stroking her back, smoothing her neck with care and affection, till she seemed to be asleep. Both knew what they wanted, and that neither could give it to them. 'What if I asked you not to go away to France,' she said, 'or wherever it is?'

He felt a danger that pulled him irresistibly into wakefulness. 'I'd go anyway.'

Her response did not surprise him. 'I thought so. But why don't we go together?'

He didn't answer.

'Oh well,' she said, 'I'll have to find someone else.'

Chapter

❧ THIRTY

His mac was patched, moisture getting to his marrow though his heart was dry. He did not know what drove him on, up and out of smoky Bulwell, away from bus smells and market aromas to the air of the cemetery in which most of the dead from that part of the city were buried. He would never be, but he was drawn to it like the north-pointing needle of a compass, he didn't know why, didn't want particularly to go up there, but didn't care enough about it not to go, nor care enough to worry what it was that pulled him on, and so let himself be drawn with a drifting inexorability. Now and again he stopped, not exhausted, but he needed breath, so turned and looked back over Top Valley where there was still a farm between him and the city. He looked with dull eyes, uninspired, turned and walked on because all that was interesting to him was in front, in the cemetery whose gates he now saw. As if to reward him, the drizzle stopped when he got there but he hardly noticed – not even when a slant of pale sun draped suddenly along a line of wall and over a beech tree growing just inside.

He walked the avenues, the names on the stones a vocabulary of biography, homely names that had surrounded him all through life like spring saplings, words shouted and mentioned and called and often whispered – names as well known as his own, better than his own, sliding by his quickly-registering eyes as he walked at a set pace along the gravel, looking but never pausing, knowing why he had come but prepared to spend as little time as possible among the thousands of gravestones and bare mounds.

He gave himself half an hour, as if his ambition or any desires that he wanted from life were set for achievement to the beat of a clock that would always be part of him. But he did not control time absolutely, or even at all, because at the end of the bespoke half hour he still hadn't come across her grave, so gave himself another five minutes, then a further ten, and walked the deathways for almost an hour till he saw a new stone in the distance and even without knowing the name realised from his heartbeats that that was the one he had come for. There could be no mistake because, much to the shock of an old woman crooning to a sheaf of daffodils in her arms as she hovered over a grave, he cried out and hurried on as if electricity was being fed into his heels.

Finding it, he grew calm, and wondered why he had come, wasted his time, what the hell in all his sentimentality he was doing here. But he knew. It was to say goodbye. You could not go away without saying goodbye. There was no one else to say goodbye to. He did not need to say goodbye to anyone else because they would be alive when he came back. If they weren't, it would not be necessary to say goodbye. But with Lillian he had to say goodbye whether he came back or not because he would never be able to say goodbye again, since it would never again apply. She was the only person, in any case, that he had to say goodbye to – the rest was immaterial, of no importance whatsoever.

He had come into the world alone and would go out of it alone, alone from now on and forever to be alone and alone and alone no matter who he knew or wherever he went. So it was more than any part of his future life was worth not to come up to this bleak plateau of a cemetery and say goodbye to the only person with whom he had not felt alone and with whom he would have gone on not feeling alone if she had continued living even if he hadn't lived with her. He carried no flowers, nothing in his hands or arms, nothing, only his breath going out like steam and melting into nothingness on the empty air. He did not even hear his own goodbye, and neither did she, and he did not know who did hear it, but it was the only goodbye uttered in his life spoken with what heart was left to him. He watched himself, as he lit a cigarette and smiled at his stupidity in coming all this way on a whim, watched himself spreadeagled on the mound of her grave as if in basic infantry training, dropping to sight and fire his rifle at an oncoming enemy, taking cover and with sufficient skill and instinct, loading, aiming and pulling the trigger on whoever might be advancing to destroy him – spreadeagled however in a grief he hoped never again to be a victim of – watched himself, this tawdry and tearful spectacle that he was imagining only for the delectation of a heart which he believed in but which at the same time he did not want to be controlled by. He walked away, ashamed that someone might have seen the image he had scorched there.

'You've packed that case twenty times,' Arthur said.
'No doubt I'll pack it another twenty, especially with you looking on.'
'When are you going?'
He couldn't make everything fit, large though it was.
'Soon.'
'You allus say that.'
'The day after tomorrow.'
'Whereabouts will you go?'
'To France.'
'Can I come?'
'What for?'
'I want to fuck a Frenchwoman.'
'You're too young to fuck anybody.'
'I fucked Betty Ashdown last night. I'm nearly fifteen, don't forget.'
'You'd better be careful.'
'Why?'
'You might get somebody pregnant.'
'I'm not daft. I used a spunk-bag.'
He laughed. 'Where do you buy 'em, at your age?'
'I got it out of your cupboard.'
The laugh was strangled. 'Are there any left?'
'Only two.'

'You can have those. But when I've gone you'll have to buy your own. I'm buggered if I'm going to keep you in french letters.'

'What are you going to do with your uniform?'

'It'll stay on the back of the door, in case I get called up again.'

'You've got TB,' Arthur said.

'I'll be cured in a year or two.'

Arthur was as tall as he was, and hadn't done growing. 'Would yer let 'em send for you?'

'If there was a war, I expect I would.'

'I'll never go in the army.'

'You will, when the time comes.' He fitted in his Bible, the Tennyson, a Shakespeare and a few Penguin books.

'It'll be heavy,' Arthur said.

'I'll manage.'

'Let me come to France, and I'll carry it.'

'I can't afford to.'

'I'll go on my own, when I've got some money.'

'I'm sure you will.'

He repacked the case, laying books on the bottom so as not to crush his clothes.

'I'll miss yer, our Brian.'

'I'll miss *you*. But I've got to go.'

'You don't have to do owt yer don't want to do.'

'I know, but I've got to do this.'

'When are you coming back?'

'In about six months.'

Arthur got off the bed. 'More like six years, I reckon.'

'It might be.'

'You'll be cured in that 'ot country.'

'It's not so hot.'

'Will yer be famous?'

'How do I know?'

'You know bogger-all,' Arthur cried.

'I've got a lot to do before I'm any good. It might be ten years before I get anything published.'

'Do you want me to carry your case to the station?'

On the balustrade of Wollaton Hall the muzzles of six cannon were set in his direction. Artillerymen rammed in gun cotton,

350

powder and balls. In damp silence came the order to fire, the crackle of tapers followed by thunder and flame. He walked through smoke unscathed, amazed to be alive.

Getting out of the country was like planning Operation Overlord. Phase One: St Pancras Station, London. Phase Two: Overnight at Bed and Breakfast. Phase Three: Boat Train for Dover. Phase Four: Paris, Rhone Valley, Alpes Maritimes.

Tickets were in his pocket, as well as travellers' cheques issued by Edgeworth's bank, where he had also opened an account into which his pension could be paid, and from where it could be transferred to France. He filled in forms for permission to do this, and with more than a hundred pounds he would be cushioned as long as he stood the test of living cheaply in an unfamiliar place. As an ex-serviceman the nearest British consul would meet any medical expenses to do with his illness. Let the lung come up and take its chance, he said. I can't be bothered with refills anymore. That's barmy, he responded. I've no intention of dying.

An escarpment of windows glistened from the great Elizabethan mansion, Lord Willoughby's pride before he died a pauper from the expense, and in the afternoon light Grace Rutland came down the steps. She had been peering into the Natural History exhibits to check some specimen that would root an elaborate image into common knowledge for one of her poems. A long olive-green coat with large buttons shielded her fragile frame from the dankness, a trailing scarf and Tyrolean-style hat hiding her dark hair. You would know her for a poet anywhere, he said, and brought a smile at his compliment. 'We thought you'd gone. Or so Anne Jones led us to believe – though she's not with us anymore. Did you know?'

They walked down the hill, Grace evading the odd deer turd while looking straight ahead.

'How do you mean?'

Her outright laughter was a rare sound. 'She's gone to live on a remote Scottish island with Ted Gedling. Seems they decided they were in love – or whatever it is – and almost the next morning they were gone. Strange that they waited such a long time, but you never know when lightning will strike.'

He hoped he sounded disinterested, but Grace was no fool, which made it hard, though he wondered if she wasn't concocting a bit of gossip. She had never liked either of them, and her malice cut like a scalpel. 'Her husband – rather a nice quiet person, by the way – came to Tom's last soirée, to see what anybody could tell him. He was very upset. I think she'd given him a hard time. But nobody knew anything, though a few days later Wendy received a letter, posted from Glasgow on their way through.'

'I suppose it had to happen,' he said, 'with someone.'

She took off her glove to shake his hand. 'Send me a copy of your first published book.'

You'll be dead by then, he was about to say. 'God knows when that'll be.' He escorted her to the car park.

'Your modesty is a cover for your overweening conceit,' she said. 'Too much pride, that's your trouble. Much like me, I suppose.'

She dropped her keys, and he snapped down to pick them from the mud. 'You mean I'm stiffnecked?' he smiled.

'Positively biblical.'

From her he took it as praise, and said goodbye. If he was stiffnecked it was the way he was born more than the way he liked it. If you weren't stiffnecked you couldn't be yourself, and everybody became stiffnecked as soon as they met someone they disagreed with. If you weren't stiffnecked enough to hold your own you wouldn't know what you thought, and if you didn't know what you thought – which he didn't much of the time, anyway – you might as well hang yourself.

'I'll be going to work soon,' Arthur said when they were at the station, 'so if ever you get short of money over there, just let me know.'

The large ex-Malayan suitcase was to one side, his typewriter on the other. A letter from the publisher that morning said they regretted not making an offer for his manuscript, because it wasn't suitable for their firm. He hadn't expected it to be, the rejection a sure sign that he had to be on his way. 'I wouldn't take your hard-earned cash.'

'Well, you can.' Trains steamed to other platforms. 'I love railway engines.'

'Why's that?'

'They're big and black. They go fast, and they take you to places.'

Brian gave him half-a-crown. 'Here's something for ice-cream.'

'Won't you need it yourself?' He fastened his jacket against the raw air. Carrying the case had made him sweat, now he shivered with cold. His face was thin, as if he was hungry, and a button swung from his jacket. His overcoat had worn out long ago. Brian hadn't noticed him till now. 'Take it. I'm flush at the moment.'

Arthur looked at him. 'Are you going away with a woman?'

'What makes you think that?'

'I would be – if I was yo'.'

'Well I'm not. I'm going by myself.'

'You'll be lonely, wain't yer?'

'I expect so.'

'You'll soon have a woman, I bet.' He hauled the case into the compartment and found his brother a seat. 'Write me a letter, our Brian.'

'I will. Don't get into too many fights. And don't get any women pregnant.'

'Don't worry about that. I'm not daft.'

'If you do, I'll be back to sort you out.'

Arthur bit his lip, showing anguish.

'Got your platform ticket?'

He nodded.

Brian pulled the window down to answer his farewell.

The forecourt of St Pancras was scruffy and crowded, and could do with a CO's inspection to get it in order. He felt nothing, wasn't even a percentage of himself. Smoke chafed, the familiar smell as when a cold swamps the senses with nostalgia. He recalled Lillian's grave, even while standing, went back to it as if actually there, searching the vast cemetery under a ceiling of peppery rain that hit his cheeks like hail from a shotgun. IN AGONY SHE LIVED AND IN AGONY SHE DIED. REMEMBERED BY BROTHER BEN AND EVER MOURNING MOTHER. The inscription took the iron out of his soul. She was the fuel in the rocket propelling him away, too much pain to stay in the same land, though the further he got the bigger part of him she would become, until the passing of time destroyed her. A wound becomes a scar only to prove that what put it there will never leave you alone.

He didn't believe it would happen, felt no responsibility for himself, at certain moments didn't want to go, couldn't believe in the power of his own irresistible purpose. He was committed to going to a country he didn't know, of whose language he could mimic a few words and phrases, and without a place to live when he got there. He was on a conveyor belt without the sense to erase the bravado which had inched him into such a scheme. In a story by Maupassant, a man who was to fight a duel shot himself because he couldn't face it. Yet it would be worse than suicide to avoid your fate, even if you could, which you can't.

Not knowing why, he couldn't make himself leave the station and walk across the road into London. Feet stuck, standing to look at people moving to and fro from trains – happy families going through, men, women and children on the run for visits or holidays – as if they were the cement of his fascination, of his sudden lassitude. He was afraid, the journey's end too far away, was impelled to go back. It had all been a joke. I just wanted a day in London. A few days, no more. Sweat and terror stumped him. He laughed to himself, luggage at his feet; impossible to move.

Climbing the high slide in the recreation ground as an infant, shoes clattering on the iron steps that echoed with your eagerness to get up, and then sitting for a moment at the top with a glance at flowerbeds and bowling green, houses and buses beyond, before being pushed by others coming up behind – or letting yourself be pushed, though you couldn't get off any other way – the feeling was one of blind fear before conquering, overcoming the kind of panic which forms part of the mathematical curvature of action.

Up out of the steps of the Tube came half a dozen men with their bags, ex-army packs, cheap suitcases, one with a parcel tied with string under his arm, pushing each other and laughing as if they had gone a few over in their lunchtime booze. He was fascinated by such vitality and companionship, which he had once been part of, here today and gone forever, a continent he had broken away from as if in some cataclysmic storm, doomed to become an island of himself. As they strung out, and rushed around the corner towards the ticket office, he spotted his cousin Bert who, his quick eyes never failing to fix on anything that might be good or bad for him, looked back.

Brian was surprised he had recognised him so quickly, because Bert had grown a moustache, a thick-falling fair mouse of a tash hiding the upper line of his mouth, that gave him the demented expression of a short-arsed warrant officer who terrorised recruits, a wide enough bush that emphasised the fiery glint of eternal deprivation in his blue eyes that Brian would have known anywhere.

The rattle of trolleys, steam whistles, unintelligible train announcements mixed with the shouting of porters, rushed him into one with his consciousness. Bert stared, alone because the pack had run on, his eyes large with anxiety and curiosity, a shaving cut on his chin, hand lifted to greet him as he patted each pocket of his jacket for the stub of a cigarette.

Brian knew the gesture, and offered him a whole one.

'What yo' doin' 'ere?' Bert said, an unfriendly tone.

'Passing through.' Brian had no questions, no handshake, though none was offered. 'And you?'

'I'm with this lot. We go from town to town working on building sites. Contract labour, it's called. We contract ourselves, and don't pay owt to the guv'ment.' He smiled. 'Thanks for the fag. I'm skint till I get a sub tomorrer. We're off to Leicester now. Got a six-week job up there.' His trousers were patched, but his jacket belonged to a good suit. 'We earn real money. The only trouble is, I spend it. Just the life for me, though.'

Brian was cold towards him, yet curious. 'Don't you go back to Nottingham, these days?'

He settled for the old wide grin, but his cheeks were hollow, as if he had been living rough, existing on pies and booze. 'I expect I'll risk it, one day.' The others were yelling for him to get a move on. 'Well, I'll see yer when I see yer. Keep yer end up.'

He ran, swaying with his kitbag, and Brian walked out of the station. The past was hard to forget, was a stone in the shoe, but if it wasn't there he wouldn't know that he was walking. He avoided a horsedrawn van and a bus to get across the main road, struggled down the street with his luggage till he found a bed-and-breakfast place.

The room would be twelve-and-six a night, and he signed the book, undid his mackintosh, a button for each floor. Locking the door behind him, he took off his coat, then pushed himself up and down on the bed which felt rickety enough to crumble under his weight.

He looked into the square, with its bare trees, and houses dolled up for a few more decades. Spring would be here any minute, leaves flourishing. Good to be on the run, alone, without limits. He sat by the window, opened it for air as he smoked, birds still singing in the trees.

From being afraid of nothing he had become wary of everything, yet he was exalted on realising that all his actions so far had been rooted in an alien timidity. He hadn't been born that way. Circumstances had made him so. The jungle he had been brought up in had instilled nothing but fear, which had shaped all his decisions. The Malayan forest had been congenial. The jungle was natural, but uncomfortable, and he no longer wanted to live in one, would slough off the disadvantages like a snake its skin, fight to achieve a clearer consciousness (already half attained in inspired moments) which must eventually become all of him.

Nor would he any longer waste his spirit trying to break beyond the radius of his basic self, but would move to wherever it was impelled to take him. Nothing could pull him from the illuminated tableland he walked on, the horizon a circle and not a distant line in front. Anguish and vacillation gave him the ability to love only those who loved him, because his love of writing meant that whoever loved him would have to do so in spite of its unshakable domination, a torment which he could not share.

❧

356

At Dover he went into the saloon for a six-shilling lunch, served by waiters, which made him feel like a traveller. The forlorn moan of the ship's whistle for departure caused him to smile, easing his emptiness. Back on deck, the sea calm and the air frosty, the coast of France was a line of putty-like cliffs through the mist, England out of sight, the wood of the rails sticky with salt. Be a good soldier, and never look back, he remembered his father saying, turning his eyes from the direction of Queen's Bay.

People on the train from Calais stacked their skis on the luggage racks, such veteran travellers that he did not have to wonder how they managed a long trip on a fifty pound travel allowance. If he was a government snooper he would open their skis with a tin-opener and find the five pound notes. He leaned against the window, keeping to himself, a born deserter on the move.

In Paris a porter wheeled his luggage to the bus, and he knew how much to pay because a tariff was indicated on the wall. Remembering maps from old guidebooks, he ticked off the boulevards as the bus trundled through to the Gare de Lyon, fabulous goods displayed in lighted shops.

He asked about the train to Nice, easily understanding what he was told. No supper on board, he bought an apple and a bottle of water from a trolley on the platform, sorry it wasn't a better meal for his first night in France. But he didn't care. Every rattle and shake took him south. He opened his airforce jack-knife and cut the apple in half, swigged back the water. A middle-aged French couple looked on. The woman had short thick reddish hair, a face swollen and pale, hazel eyes and a tired smile. Her husband had a distant look, as if they hadn't done the journey for twenty years, and in between something had happened which had taken youth and happiness with it – as it must for everyone – though neither seemed unhappy, only exhausted.

He managed to tell the woman that he had come to live in France. He was a writer, he said, pointing to his typewriter on the rack above, laughing inwardly at making gestures he had picked up from films. He felt drunk, wasn't, realised he was happy, the train swaying in darkness through the land of battlefields heard about since childhood, the country of Hugo and Flaubert, whose language he would learn.

He smoked a cigarette in the corridor, blackness beyond the line of windows, couldn't sleep, didn't want to, though he hadn't rested for weeks. He sat on his suitcase because he had given his seat to a woman, retreating deeper into himself, an old man and a young man in the same physical system, not knowing where he was, but elated and calm, his spirit flowing with the train, without thought, beyond love, displaced – dozing into sleep as if on a troop train.

Light outside, dawn, and a man dressed in a brown uniform and a peaked hat laced with scrambled egg like a general's put the blinds up and said breakfast was ready in the restaurant car.

He spelled out station names east of Marseilles. The waiter brought coffee and brioches, toast and jam. He spread the butter, no rationing anymore. The Frenchwoman told him that artists who wanted to live cheaply should go to Argentat-sur-Mer, which he found on his map and read about in the guide-book. 'You'll rent a chalet in the hills, or a shepherd's hut for a few francs. Artists don't need much to live on. Vegetables are cheap, and so is bread and fish.'

The sky was blue, empty – implacable. Through palm branches the sea was as clear as the sky, Corsican peaks beyond the horizon. They passed red-roofed villas, fields of carnations, mimosa groves, plantations of lemon and orange trees. Even inland, mountains gave off perfumed air. Alone in his compartment, he felt as if he had never had the sun on his face before.

Having lived so long, he felt young and inexperienced, fresh to life, eyes opening at last. He had done what he had longed to do. Done what, he couldn't explain, except that he had yet to do it. But fear had gone, leaving no trace, though reality was bound to bring it back. Living from day to day, he would no doubt stay where he was while his existence was so precarious, which was how it should be, so that it might never happen that he would wake up and find himself back in England, unless he got a book published. He stood by the door with his luggage. He was speaking to himself, and wondered whether he would ever do anything else, when the train stopped, and it was time to open the door and get out.